PRAISE FOR

The Guncle

"A formerly famous gay sitcom star is suddenly tasked with raising his niece and nephew in this sweet, saucy novel." —*Vogue*

"In his heartwarming, humorous new novel, Steven Rowley shows readers the true meaning of family, reminding us that everyone—even parents—is only human." —*Travel & Leisure*

"The author of *Lily and the Octopus* and *The Editor* delivers arguably his funniest and most poignant novel yet." —*E! News*

"[A] moving, feel-good summer escape." —*Newsweek*

"Deeply entertaining." —*Real Simple*

"A laugh-out-loud heart-warmer." —*Oprah Daily*

"[A] brilliant tale of loss and love." —*Good Morning America*

"[A] funny and heartwarming beach read." —CNN

"[A] feel-good story, perfect for summer." —*AARP*

"Rowley hits the sweet spot between hilarity and heart in this endearing charmer." —*The Christian Science Monitor*

"Often hilarious, sometimes devastating, and genuinely touching." —*New York Daily News*

"Chronicles grief in a way that offers a lot of comfort to the reader, and while at various points is a definite tearjerker, it often unlocks the humor and joy that can still be found after those we loved are gone. . . . Wistful, warm, and very funny." —Fodor's Travel

"As hysterically funny as it is profound, *The Guncle* is the perfect summer read for anyone who's looking for a good time with amazing characters without forfeiting deep and meaningful discussions that will feel like a balm to the soul for anyone who's ever lost someone."
—*The Nerd Daily*

"Cue some family growing pains and humorous antics, and you get this heartwarming novel you'll devour in a flash." —*theSkimm*

"A big-hearted, laugh-out-loud-funny kind of book that's sure to stay with you long after you turn the final page." —*PopSugar*

"Rowley uses the juxtaposition of lifestyles and situations for an enormous comic harvest without once forgetting the sorrow and tragedy that have resulted in the situation. The characterizations are rich and wonderful, and Rowley writes with a tenderness, affection and empathy about life, sorrow and family that's the stuff of pure heart."
—*The Day* (CT)

"Hilarious and heartwarming . . . Auntie Mame-like laughs, lessons and hijinks ensue as Patrick—a once-famous gay sitcom star—deals with a midlife crisis while launching a second act." —*Boston Spirit*

"A sweet story of family, with plenty of laughs and even a few tears."
—*Parkersburg News and Sentinel*

"Equal amounts of heartache and witty bon mots." —*Palm Springs Life*

"Influenced by comic dialogue that would make Neil Simon jealous, the novel's serious undercurrent of loss gives way, in the end, to a warmth that will make readers smile. . . . A funny, gentle tale of family and friends, and a salve for the wounds they often cause." —*Library Journal*

"Patrick is a memorable character, and it's genuinely thrilling to read screenwriter-turned-novelist Rowley's take on the mechanics of stardom. . . . There's true insight here into the psychology of gay men, Hollywood, and parenting. A novel with some real depth beneath all its witty froth." —*Kirkus Reviews*

"Heartwarming, hilarious . . . Rowley finds humor and poignancy in the snappy narrative. . . . Readers will find this delightful and illuminating." —*Publishers Weekly*

"Rowley's sensitive and witty exploration of grief and healing soothes with a delectable lightness and cunning charm." —*Booklist*

"Never going too dark, *The Guncle* is a sweet family story that offers an unexpected yet inevitable ending." —*BookPage*

"This hilarious and heartfelt story will make you laugh, cry, and want to be a better person." —*BookRiot*

"One of the hottest beach reads of the year." —*SheReads*

"Warm and funny . . . [Rowley] continues bringing the hits with this feel-good read that still has depth and meaning." —*Scary Mommy*

"Beach read alert." —*PureWow*

"A warm and deeply funny novel . . . With the humor and heart we've come to expect from bestselling author Steven Rowley, *The Guncle* is a moving tribute to the power of love, patience, and family in even the most trying of times." —*Frolic*

"*The Guncle* is a love letter to the gay uncles (guncles) and their love for their nieces and nephews and will keep the reader entertained from beginning to end. . . . Rowley brilliantly taps into the loss of a loved one and the grieving that comes after." —*Instinct Magazine*

"*The Guncle* is a story that deftly balances humor with deep sentimentality. Perfectly folded into the lines of Rowley's narrative is some of the wittiest banter mixed in with some of life's most philosophical lessons. . . . Rowley creates a wholesome narrative that digs deep beyond the surface, past the drollery, pulling at heartstrings and keeping the reader hooked with his tactful intuition for a beautifully balanced dramedy." —*Paperback Paris*

"The Palm Springs-set tale promises plenty of kaftans as well as family drama." —*NewNowNext*

"A heartwarming story . . . Quirky and fun . . . Light and sassy and warm—like an Aperol spritz atop a pink flamingo floatie. The perfect book for the upcoming summer season." —KMUW

"[A] heartwarming story." —WBUR

"A heartwarming and delightful story of love, loss, and the bonds of family." —*BookBub*

"Steven Rowley has triumphed again with his new novel *The Guncle*, an exuberant but tender story about life, death, family, and love. Rowley's protagonist is a modern-day Auntie Mame with every bit of that unflappable flapper's sharp wit and fabulous wisdom. This book is a dazzling banquet of laughter and insight; with it Rowley has proven himself to be one of the great comic novelists of our time."

—Camille Perri, author of *The Assistants* and *When Katie Met Cassidy*

"Patrick, the hero of Steven Rowley's effervescent, utterly charming, and affecting novel, is the dearest friend you haven't met yet. You'll root for his two adorable charges as they navigate a terrible loss, and for Patrick's own heart to make a long-overdue comeback. A cleverly subversive story about what makes a family."

—Christopher Castellani, author of *Leading Men*

"*The Guncle* is super funny, charming, and tender. Love, loss, and Palm Springs are the perfect ingredients for a delightful cocktail."

—Gary Janetti, author of *Do You Mind If I Cancel?*

"Patrick is a famous bon vivant, caftan-wearing gay uncle with a fabulous house in Palm Springs. He's an unlikely family member to help his niece and nephew work through their feelings of raw grief after their mother dies, but it turns out he's exactly who the kids need—just as he needs them to help him address his own, less recent loss. Steven Rowley's assured and moving page-turner is studded with laugh-out-loud humor and moments of profound feeling and insight. This book hit every note on my emotional register, and I savored it like an Aperol drunk poolside with friends on a hot, desert day."

—Christina Clancy, author of *The Second Home*

"Delightful, sharp, and very funny, *The Guncle* is the cocktail equivalent of the fourth sip of your martini while you sit poolside at sunset. I loved lingering in this world (and loved reading the dialogue out loud). A novel as much about family and friendship as it is about style and sass, it's a divine mix of *Terms of Endearment* and *The Birdcage*."

—Timothy Schaffert, author of *The Perfume Thief*
and *The Swan Gondola*

PRAISE FOR

Steven Rowley and *The Editor*

"Steven Rowley has hit a home run. What a stunning portrayal of family this is. At equal turns laugh-out-loud funny and searingly poignant, Rowley has created a truly unforgettable story of a son trying to understand his mother. *The Editor* is one of those exceptional stories that is both a joy to read on every page and also deeply profound and significant. It took my breath away."

—Taylor Jenkins Reid, author of *Malibu Rising* and *Daisy Jones and the Six*

"Filled with whimsy and warmth, the *Lily and the Octopus* author's second novel centers on the complex relationship between a fledgling writer and his fabulous editor, the latter of whom becomes a mentor, friend, and maternal figure. Oh, and she happens to be Jacqueline Kennedy Onassis, but that's Mrs. Onassis to you." —*O, The Oprah Magazine*

"A journey of self-discovery . . . Ultimately a story not about celebrity but about family and forgiveness." —*TIME*

"Witty and heartwarming." —*InStyle*

"Sweetly evokes a mature Jacqueline Kennedy Onassis. In 1990s New York, James Smale is an obscure first-time novelist, but his editor is world-famous. In this delicately observed tale the steely Jackie becomes not just the midwife of the angsty gay Smale's manuscript, but of a wider reconciliation." —*Sunday Times* (UK)

"A sweet and charming novel, perfect for fans of Jackie O." —*PopSugar*

"[A] delightful slice of historical fiction."

—*Entertainment Weekly*, "The Must List"

"[A] sharp, funny sophomore novel." —*Town and Country*

"Steven Rowley is the best-selling author of *Lily and the Octopus*, and he's honestly outdone himself with *The Editor*." —*Cosmopolitan*

"[A] funny, poignant novel about a young writer and his fabulous editor, Jacqueline Kennedy Onassis." —*Orange County Register*

"The resonance of Rowley's originality and sensitivity shines on every page. He has written a refreshing, superbly crafted novel of hard-won self-discovery filled with big, well-paced scenes and a pitch-perfect blend of humor and compassion that will charm and fully engage readers. In this refreshing, imaginative novel of self-discovery, a debut author has his work—and his life—edited by the inimitable Jacqueline Kennedy Onassis." —*Shelf Awareness*

"A poignant tale . . . Rowley deliberately mines the sentiment of the mother/son bond, but skillfully saves it from sentimentality; this is a winning dissection of family, forgiveness, and fame."
—*Publishers Weekly* (starred review)

"While diving deep into questions of identity, loyalty, and absolution within the bonds of family, Rowley, author of the beloved *Lily and the Octopus*, soars to satisfying heights in this deeply sensitive depiction of the symbiotic relationships at the heart of every good professional, and personal, partnership." —*Booklist*

"Woven into the turbulent queer community of early '90s New York, *The Editor* touches on mother/son relationships, what it means to be a family, and the tension of unresolved secrets." —*them.*

"Set in a world before emails and internet, when sons called their mothers collect and typewriters were still the tools of the trade, this is an absolutely delightful read." —*Edina Magazine*

"Told with warmth and humor, Steven Rowley's charming second novel tells the story of a mother-son reconciliation, facilitated by a most unlikely fairy godmother. *The Editor* offers a delightful, fictional glimpse of an iconic American family—but it is, at heart, a tribute to every family whose last name isn't Kennedy."

—Chloe Benjamin, author of *The Immortalists*

"*The Editor* is an absolute delight from start to finish. Steven Rowley writes such evocative, compelling characters, and his ability to buck the cliché in favor of true nuanced emotion is a gift. Rowley's portrayal of the unconventional relationship between a charmingly uncertain James Smale and the one and only Mrs. Onassis made me laugh, nod and eventually, cry. I adored this book!"

—Sally Hepworth, author of *The Good Sister* and *The Mother-in-Law*

"The first time Steven Rowley graced us with his presence, he told us an unforgettable story about a dachshund with an octopus on her head. This time, he flawlessly gives life to an American icon. *The Editor* will have you weeping tears of joy when it's not quietly breaking your heart. It's a study of mothers and sons, unlikely friendships, and how we go about collecting the scattered pieces of our pasts. It takes guts, humor, and immense talent to write a book like this. Lucky for us, Rowley has plenty of all three."

—Grant Ginder, author of
Honestly, We Meant Well and *The People We Hate at the Wedding*

"When you've loved an author's debut, there's a little bit of breath holding when you are presented with the second. Well, exhale, because Steven Rowley's *The Editor* is an absolute triumph! By page three, I announced aloud, 'I LOVE THIS BOOK.' And it didn't stop even after I finished it. Rowley is a master of creating characters you fall in love with, and never want to leave. *The Editor* is irresistible."

—Julie Klam, author of *The Almost Legendary Morris Sisters* and *You Had Me at Woof*

"What fun! This droll and wonderfully poignant book gives you full access to one of the most fascinating figures of the twentieth century. A delight."

—Henry Alford, author of *And Then We Danced*

"This funny, warm and thought-provoking novel is the next best thing to having Jackie O. around to make us see how the larger-than-life characters in our own histories—our mothers—are as human, fallible, and as prone to heartbreak as us kids. Keep tissues handy. I had to use a bedsheet."

—Julia Claiborne Johnson, author of *Better Luck Next Time* and *Be Frank With Me*

TITLES BY STEVEN ROWLEY

The Celebrants

The Guncle

The Editor

Lily and the Octopus

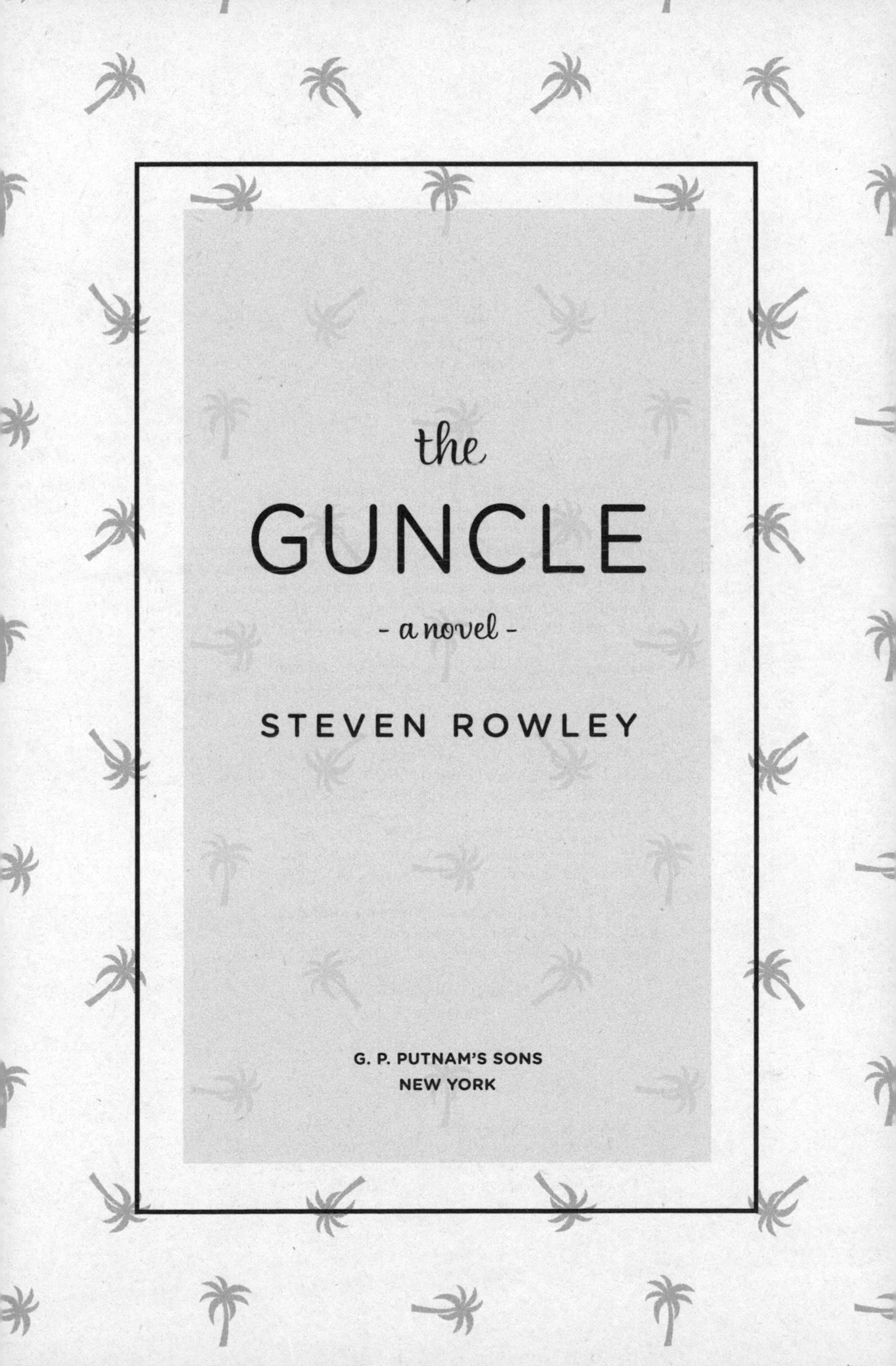

the GUNCLE

- a novel -

STEVEN ROWLEY

G. P. PUTNAM'S SONS
NEW YORK

PUTNAM
— EST. 1838 —

G. P. PUTNAM'S SONS
Publishers Since 1838
An imprint of Penguin Random House LLC
penguinrandomhouse.com

The Library of Congress has catalogued the G. P. Putnam's Sons hardcover edition as follows:

Names: Rowley, Steven, 1971– author.
Title: The guncle: a novel / Steven Rowley.
Description: New York: G. P. Putnam's Sons, [2021] |
Identifiers: LCCN 2020049239 (print) | LCCN 2020049240 (ebook) |
ISBN 9780525542285 (hardcover) | ISBN 9780525542292 (ebook)
Classification: LCC PS3618.O888 G86 2021 (print) |
LCC PS3618.O888 (ebook) | DDC 813/.6—dc23
LC record available at https://lccn.loc.gov/2020049239
LC ebook record available at https://lccn.loc.gov/2020049240

First G. P. Putnam's Sons hardcover edition / May 2021
First G. P. Putnam's Sons trade paperback edition / April 2022
G. P. Putnam's Sons trade paperback ISBN: 9780525542308

Printed in the United States of America
8th Printing

Interior art: Palm tree pattern © Rvector/Shutterstock

BOOK DESIGN BY KRISTIN DEL ROSARIO

For

Evelyn, Harper, Emmett, Elias, and Graham

"Never love anyone who treats you like you're ordinary."

—OSCAR WILDE

"You said, oh girl, it's a cold world when you keep it all to yourself."

—PAT BENATAR, "SHADOWS OF THE NIGHT"

THE GUNCLE

All right, here goes nothing.

Patrick held his phone in landscape mode and waited for the autofocus to find Maisie and Grant. The children looked slight, smushed together as they were, even Maisie, who was already nine. If the camera added ten pounds (and Patrick had spent enough time in front of cameras to know the old cliché to be true), then his was irreparably defective. Maisie brushed her hair out of her face; six weeks with him in Palm Springs and it was already lighter from the desert sun. Grant mindlessly tongued the space where his tooth used to be.

"Sit up," Patrick encouraged, but it wasn't their posture so much as their fragility that made his niece and nephew appear small, both of them a bundle of raw nerves eager to be exposed. He smiled as the camera brought them sharply into view. As an exercise, what was the point of the summer if not helping them come into focus? Patrick hovered his finger over his phone before calmly hitting record. "Tell me something about your mother."

Maisie and Grant turned inward, each willing the other to speak. Patrick had never witnessed such a case of debilitating stage fright in his entire career. The two children negotiated in silence, almost telepathically, the way close siblings sometimes can, and eventually Maisie, the oldest by three years, spoke first. "She was tall."

Patrick looked out from behind his phone. "She was tall? *That's it?* Giraffes are tall. Your mother's a giraffe?"

"NO!" They were both offended by the suggestion.

"Don't yell at *me*," Patrick protested. "It's up to you to lead with something better than her height."

Grant took a swing. "She was strong. One time she lifted the thofa to vacuum under it."

"CUT." Patrick stopped recording. Of course he wanted Grant to think of his mother as strong—Sara's treatment had robbed her of much of the resilience that defined her—and he was even willing to overlook his nephew's lisp, even though they'd been working on it in the quiet of late afternoons, but he wasn't about to let Sara suffer the indignity of sharing space in this video with a Dyson upright. "You kids are *terrible* at telling stories."

Maisie grew agitated. "Well, what do you want us to say?"

"What do *I* . . . Being in a video was your idea!"

Grant kicked his little feet in frustration, stubbing his toes on the coffee table.

"Don't scuff my furniture." Patrick held his phone out to Maisie. "Here. Record me. I'll show you how it's done." Maisie started to protest, but Patrick wouldn't hear of it. "Tsk tsk tsk."

Maisie reluctantly accepted her uncle's phone and held it up to record him.

"Higher," Patrick said.

"What?"

"Higher. Stand up."

Maisie stood.

"Higher!" Patrick leaned forward and coaxed Maisie's arms in the air. "Honestly, it's like you want me to have four chins. Guncle Rule—What number are we on? *Know your angles.* Everyone has a good side. Even children, who should be photographable from all sides but aren't." He sat back in his midcentury leather club chair and motioned for Maisie to hold her camera position. "Never mind, we're getting way off track here. See the red button? That's record."

Maisie was losing patience, and the attitude she displayed when pressed was bubbling to the surface. "Tell me something I don't know."

"Stockard Channing's real name is Susan."

Maisie lowered the camera, annoyed.

"Well, you didn't know that, did you? And now you do." Patrick coaxed Maisie's arms higher to reclaim his angle. "Susan Stockard. Stockard was her last name."

"Who'th Thtockard Channing?" Grant asked, tripping over the mouthful.

"Oh, good lord. Rizzo?" Patrick waited to see if that registered. "In the movie *Grease*?"

Grant shrugged. "We haven't theen it."

"*What?* You've never seen *Grease*? When I was your age I watched it like a hundred times. The way John Travolta swung his hips . . . ?" Blank stares. "It's fine. *Grease 2* has a more progressive message on gender. And frankly, if you want the best of Olivia Newton-John, we should probably start with *Xanadu*."

"Everything you say is nonsense words," Maisie protested.

"Look, just because you find these to be erudite conversations, I'm simply stating facts. Now, do you want me to show you how to do this, or not? Please. Hit record."

Maisie did as she was told, if only to speed things along. "Tell us about our mom."

Patrick closed his eyes and conjured an image of Sara. When he opened them, he looked squarely into the camera's lens. "Our friendship began in darkness. Your mom asked if I wanted to see the view from the roof of our college dorm and I did. We took the elevator to the ninth floor and then inched up a final, musty stairwell, the fire door slamming shut behind us. Your mom led. She was inclined to do that. I followed, huddled tightly to her as if we were a duo of teen detectives about to uncover some ghastly twist in our case. We were sweating, I remember that, even though it was the second week of October. I must have been bitching about it because your mother called me an 'artful complainer.' Now, that was a euphemism if I ever heard one. You guys know what a euphemism is?" Patrick looked to each of the kids; clearly they did not. "It's a milder, indirect way of saying something that might be otherwise harsh or embarrassing." He studied their expressions to see if it was sinking in. "You're both looking at me like you're a couple olives short of a martini. BOOM. Euphemism for not keeping up."

Grant scrunched his face. "I don't like oliveth."

"It doesn't matter. I'm teaching you two how to tell a story." Patrick pointed at his ear to get them to listen. "So, the door below had locked shut and the one above wouldn't open, and try as we might, there was no going up. Or down. We found ourselves stuck in that stairwell for hours with nothing to do but share skeletons. She asked if I was going to tell her my *biggest* secret, or if I was going to wait and do the whole gay-by-May thing. Your mother had my number, right from the start."

"What's gay by May?" Maisie was lost, but to her credit she held the camera position.

"It's that thing where you wait to come out until sometime in your second semester."

"How do you share a thkeleton?"

"Skeletons are embarrassing facts you want to keep to yourself."

"No they're not, they're a person of boneth!" Grant was clearly ruffled.

"And they're both very scary! You know, storytelling is building a rhythm; these constant interruptions are not helpful. ANYHOW. Turns out the door above us wasn't locked, just stuck, and eventually we found ourselves on the roof, basking in the most extraordinary sunset. I had my camera with me, and I got off a few shots of your mom looking resplendent bathed in pink light. I told her she looked beautiful and she said, 'You'd think differently if you saw me two noses ago.'"

"Mom had *three* nothes?"

"Grant! What did I say about interruptions?" Patrick cleared his throat. "That night on the roof she told me life was going to be easy, I remember that. I promised her the same, but she looked at me as if I were hopelessly naive. She said life was different for girls—harder. But she told me I was talented. That I might even be famous one day. I had that kind of head."

"What kind of head do you have?" Maisie asked.

Sara meant large, but for the sake of the story Patrick said, "The kind with only one nose."

"You *are* famouth!"

"Well, fame is measured on a sliding scale, but your mother was right about a lot of things." Patrick's eyes glazed, thinking how tragically wrong she was about others. "Eventually, campus police came and told us to move along. We'd tripped an alarm, if I recall." Patrick paused; it might have been that joint they were smoking instead. "Our friendship began in darkness," he repeated, remembering the stairwell. "But your mother? She was always my light."

Maisie quietly pressed stop and lowered the phone to her side. There was indeed a right and a wrong way to tell a story, and her expression said she wanted to know everything that happened next.

"That was really good, GUP."

Patrick leaned forward to reclaim his phone. He motioned for them to sit back together. "Now, let's try this again." He imagined himself Mr. DeMille, the children now ready for their close-up. "Tell me something *special* about your mother."

SIX WEEKS EARLIER

ONE

At 8:38 a.m., the temperature was already hovering in the high eighties, on its way north of one hundred—unusual perhaps for May, but not unheard of. The desert sky was cloudless, a vibrant cobalt blue you wouldn't believe was real until you spent enough time underneath it to ensure it wasn't some sort of Hollywood effect. Patrick O'Hara stood curbside in front of the small airport, lost. The mountains surrounding Palm Springs were herculean; they worked overtime to hold back all kinds of weather—clouds, rain, humidity—everything except for wind, which accounted for the majestic windmills that stood like palace guards at the entrance to the Coachella Valley. The palm trees waved gently in the breeze, but did not so much as bend. In this moment, Patrick wished he had even a fraction of their strength.

An old Chevrolet convertible in robin's egg blue eased past him, pausing at the speed bump, the driver taking extra care not to scrape the automobile's low carriage. It hiccuped over the barrier, and then resumed a reasonable speed around the corner away from the terminal, following a line of dignified palm trees toward the airport exit like it was driving into an antiquarian postcard. It's something Patrick loved about Palm Springs, the city's timelessness. The days were long, and so clean with sunlight it was impossible to distinguish one from the next. For four years now he'd been holed up in his midcentury desert estate, the one he'd purchased with his TV money (handsome compensation for costarring in nine humiliating seasons of *The People Upstairs*, plus syndication, plus streaming, plus a surprisingly robust run in France), in the aptly named Movie Colony neighborhood south of Tamarisk Road. It wasn't his intent to cut himself off from the world so completely, but the city invited it. In the old studio days, actors who were under contract were not allowed to travel more than one hundred miles from Los Angeles in case a picture needed them on short notice. Palm Springs sat exactly on that line, one hundred miles as the crow flies; it became an escape—as far away as actors dared go.

When he first relocated, Patrick invited friends to visit, people in the industry mostly—oddballs he'd collected over a decade and a half in Hollywood. Sara once brought the kids for a week and they laughed and splashed in the pool like no time had passed; she made fun of him and his celebrity in the way only old friends could. Then, slowly over time, he stopped reaching out. And people stopped coming. Sara had legitimate reasons, but others just seemed to forget he existed at all. Those who observed his trickling visitors, like JED, the gay throuple who lived in the house behind his, went so far as to call him a recluse. John, Eduardo, and Dwayne would pop their grinning faces over the wall that divided their properties with friendly (but barbed) taunts, like a Snap, Crackle, and Pop who fucked. His housekeeper, Rosa, encouraged him to meet someone. "Mr. Patrick. Why you have this house all alone?" The answer was complicated and he skirted around it, knowing if he moped she would feel sorry for him and make his favorite ceviche. But to Patrick, his situation wasn't that dire. He was simply . . . *done*. For nine years he had given a side of himself to the world, and what he had left he owed no one.

Patrick slung his baseball cap low over his eyes as a man pulled his Lexus into a white zone, hopped out of his idling car, and said goodbye to a friend or business associate with a hearty handshake. Patrick nodded to the friend as he walked past, and was rewarded with a smack from the man's three-racket Wilson tennis bag as he slung it over his shoulder. Patrick was invisible. Anonymity, as it turns out, was easy enough; it had been just long enough since he'd been in the public eye. As for the rest, the trick was not to overdo it. A disguise had to be ordinary. Hat and sunglasses. Navy shirt, not too fitted. (A physique always drew eyes.) Anything more looked like you were *trying* to hide, and that invited attention. Nod hello, look the other way. It almost always did the trick.

Patrick pulled out his phone and texted his brother, Greg. *I'm on my way.*

The calls began just after midnight, but he'd had his phone set to DO NOT DISTURB. He awoke early to thirteen missed calls (never a good number) from his parents and a fourteenth from Greg; no one left a message longer than "*Call me*," and Greg had not left one at all. It was a fight he'd had with his mother years back when she phoned at some ungodly hour to inform him his father was having a stroke; he returned her call in the morning.

"Where were you last night when I needed you?" his mother had asked.

"In bed, where most people are."

"The phone doesn't wake you up?"

"I have it programmed not to ring before seven a.m."

"What if there's an emergency?"

"If there's an emergency, I'll deal with it better on a full night's sleep." The logic seemed infallible to Patrick. And almost as if to prove his point, his father's "stroke" turned out to be a mild case of Bell's palsy.

Last night, however, the calls were warranted. After a valiant two-and-a-half-year battle, Sara had quietly slipped away. A loud roar rumbled then pierced the sky as a plane took off down the runway. Patrick rattled as the sidewalk vibrated, but he was otherwise numb. This wasn't happening. Not a second time. Not after Joe. And this loss of Sara was coupled with guilt. He promised when they'd met that he would never let her go. And then life intervened. She went north and married his brother. He went west and found fame on TV. And slowly, over time, he did.

Let go.

Patrick glanced down at his suitcase, almost surprised to see it there. He had no memory of packing it. Here he was, about to board a plane for the first time in years, something he used to do all the time. Even the network's private plane once or twice when they needed the cast in New York to appear together on *Good Morning America* or, god help him, *The View.* Now he was nervous, his stomach brittle. He told himself it was the occasion as much as the flight, not that it mattered. Patrick adjusted his aviators; he turned and walked inside the airport, letting the sliding glass doors open for him then close, reflecting the mountains behind him.

Baggage claim. Patrick's eyes scanned right past Greg to a cluster of gossiping flight attendants before recognition set in. He was expecting his father to fetch him in Hartford and so was surprised to find his brother on the other side of the glass. Greg looked depleted, thin; even from fifty feet away Patrick could read his distress—the younger brother suddenly older, as if he'd passed through some weird vortex and aged a decade in the however many years it had been since he'd seen him last.

When Greg spotted him, Patrick's carry-on slipped off his shoulder, the strap catching on his elbow, the bag stopping mere inches from the ground; he attempted a feeble wave. They stood there, two brothers, confused, a glass wall between them, like Patrick might bang on the glass and reenact the ending to *The Graduate*. But he didn't. Patrick knew; he'd seen the movie dozens of times. It might feel good in the moment, but the harsh realities of life lay ahead.

Patrick made his way through the sliding doors, past the sign that said NO REENTRY, straight for his younger brother, hugging him tight, holding the back of his head, his fingers buried deep in Greg's hair. "I'm sorry," he whispered. Greg was trembling. He squeezed his brother until Greg fell limp, free of emotion, for a fleeting second at least. *"I'm here."*

They waited for Patrick's checked bag in silence; the parade of black luggage moved at a funereal pace along the conveyor belt, town cars full of mourners in procession. They would be in such a motorcade in a few days' time. Neither brother said much on their way to the parking garage, not when Greg struggled to find the parking ticket at the prepay machine, except to usher those in line behind them to go ahead (he had absentmindedly tucked the ticket in his wallet), nor when he couldn't remember on which level he had parked the car. Patrick stayed calm and even grabbed his brother's hand when he started to turn like an animal, in rapid, panicked circles.

"Shhhh. We'll find it," he whispered.

"THAT'S HOW YOU DO IT!" The voice came from around a concrete pylon, some idiot, breaking their moment. Patrick reflexively waved as if that were the first time anyone was clever enough to shout that at him and not the eleventy millionth. *That's how you do it!* was the catchphrase that made him a breakout character on his ABC sitcom in the back half of season two. He'd delivered it faithfully at least once an episode since, and the studio audience—usually shapeless Midwesterners in oversized clothing who couldn't get into *The Price Is Right*—always went wild; the second banana, for a time at least, eclipsing in popularity the top. "You're *that* guy, right? What happened to you?"

The question reverberated through the parking structure. *The People Upstairs* was the last sitcom that defined the era of network television; a special season three episode aired after the Super Bowl. The cast was on the cover of *People* magazine. Even a Golden Globe, for Patrick. Now people watched television in three-minute increments on their phones, if they watched anything at all. More often than not they preferred to watch themselves, making videos with filters that softened their ruddy complexions, or gave them whiskers and noses like cats.

"Yeah. I'm that guy," Patrick agreed calmly.

"Hey, say it. Say your line."

"Now is not the appropriate time."

"C'mon! Do it," the man urged.

"Okay, that's ENOUGH!" Patrick let go of his rolling suitcase and charged three steps toward the stranger, angry enough to hit him. It was Greg who pulled him back, suddenly aware they were holding hands.

The man shook his head and fished his keys out of his pocket. "Dick."

Patrick quickened their pace in the other direction, ushering Greg along before anyone overheard the altercation. It's not like he knew where the car was parked, but the last thing he needed was to attract a crowd. He kicked open a stairwell door and, once they were safely through, put his hands on his knees while he collected his breath.

A guy in a UConn hoodie came bounding up the steps two at a time like it was an Olympic track-and-field event. Patrick moved to the left to let him pass. He listened as the man ascended two more flights and kept his ears perked until the footsteps faded entirely.

"She, she just . . ." Greg began.

"I know." He wanted the safety of the car before they did this, but if it had to be in the stairwell, then so be it. "Mom told me."

"Three weeks ago she told me she wanted Steely Dan's 'Reelin' in the Years' played at her memorial and I told her to shut up. I couldn't believe the end was this close. But she knew."

Patrick turned slightly so Greg wouldn't see his own pain. "She knew everything." He should have come earlier. He should have been there to say goodbye. But he reasoned she was no longer his and hadn't been in years. Every moment he spent at her side stole a moment from Greg or the kids.

Greg shook his head. Patrick focused on the window in the stairwell; someone had etched their initials with their keys. Beyond, planes were taking off and coming in, lights in formation dotting the evening sky.

"The doctor said that after a—" A car screeched around the corner just outside the door. Greg looked at each raw concrete wall as if noticing this prison for the very first time. "I guess it doesn't matter what the doctor said. I was there with her, but she was gone before the kids could arrive." He retched three times before doubling over, bracing his hands on his knees. Patrick pushed his suitcase back, stepped forward, held his brother by the hood of his sweatshirt, and winced.

"Come here," he said after it was clear there was nothing in Greg's stomach to empty. He helped his brother up half a flight to the next landing, away from this scene and, maybe, hopefully, closer to the car. He dragged his suitcase behind him, disgusted by what he might be dragging it through, knowing already he would burn it and buy new luggage upon his return home.

Greg wiped his mouth with the back of his hand, grabbing the railing to steady himself. "How did you survive this? With Joe?"

Patrick stopped cold, as if caught in a horrible lie. He pinched the bridge of his nose (where he could still feel the scar from the accident that took his boyfriend) and inhaled sharply. *I didn't*, he thought. *Survive*. That was always his first response. But he was here, wasn't he? He was the one still standing in the face of loss anew. He pointed up the rest of the stairs. "Let's look for the car up there."

They walked the aisles of this new level, Patrick having relieved Greg of the key fob and clicking it every few feet to listen for a telltale honk or to spot a set of flashing taillights. They ambled up one aisle and down the next for four or five rows before either of them said another word.

"What are you doing here?" Patrick asked.

"Huh?"

Patrick stopped to look at his brother. Why wasn't he with the kids? "*Greg*."

Greg stopped, turned back to face him, but didn't answer.

"I thought Dad was picking me up."

"I'm a drug addict."

The cross talk was almost comical; Patrick tried hard not to laugh. It was one thing for Greg to employ humor as a coping mechanism for grief, but it was another for Patrick to come off in any way cavalier. So instead he just said, "Is this where you meet your dealer?" He looked up at the nearest post, which said 4E. "Should we pick up some catnip before we go home?"

"It's not a joke." Greg sat himself down on the bumper of a white passenger van, gently, so as not to set off an alarm.

"I'm not laughing," Patrick said. A man in what he thought must be tap shoes walked quickly down the aisle behind them. "I'm confused."

"What's not to understand?"

"Like, heroin?"

"WHAT? *No*. Pills."

"*Pills*. What kind of pills?"

"Vicodin, oxy, fentanyl, tramadol. I think I once took diet pills I found in my assistant's desk drawer."

Patrick was half horrified, half intrigued. "Did they work?"

"Did what work."

"The diet pills."

"You mean, did I get high?"

"No, did you get *thin*." Greg didn't answer and the silence dragged on, but Patrick thought, *Good*. He was angry now on top of everything else, and no longer wanted to be as quick to comfort. In fact, he was now questioning his brother's dry heaves. "How could you let this happen?"

"Half the country is addicted, don't you watch the news?"

No, Patrick did not watch the news. No good ever came from the news. "How long?"

Greg shot his brother a look. That look, the one he picked up in law school and fine-tuned as a junior associate. "Three years, Patrick. It's been almost three years. Since the diagnosis. Since I started gunning for partner. I couldn't do everything. I couldn't . . ." He reached for the words to continue. "Be what everyone needed me to be."

Patrick rested his forehead on the side of the van, absorbing the cool from the metal. Jumping forward three hours in time meant it was pitch-dark, even though he was wide-awake. "Are you high right now?"

Greg glared at him with disgust until Patrick pulled his head away from the van.

"Does Mom know?"

It took Greg a moment to answer. "No one knows. I'm telling you first. Look, can we go somewhere, please? Even . . . I don't know. McDonald's?"

"Why, do you have the munchies?" Patrick responded with snark, even though he couldn't remember the last thing he'd had to eat. Perhaps some sort of snack bar on the plane.

Greg stood and shoved his hands in the pockets of his sweatshirt jacket before looking down at his shoes. "So we can talk." He looked up at Patrick. "I need you to take the kids."

"Okay. Whatever I can do to help." The family would need him to do any number of tasks this week, so he might as well step up to the plate. "Take them where?"

"*Take them*, take them."

"I don't underst—WHAT?" He scanned Greg's eyes for any sign he was kidding. "Oh, hell no."

"Patrick."

"You *are* high. That's absurd. You're being absurd."

"Patrick!"

"On its face it's preposterous. I turned down a chance to present Best Supporting Actress in a Comedy Series at the Emmys two years ago. You want to know why? It was too much of a commitment. No. You're asking the wrong person."

"There's a facility. In Rancho Mirage. Only ten miles or so from your house. There's usually a waiting list, but I called this morning and they made a space for me. Extenuating circumstances, and one of the named partners at my firm knows someone on the board."

"So, I'm *not* the first person you told." Patrick didn't know everything about addiction, but he knew enough to start tracking lies.

"I told work. I had to." Greg sighed. "I have to do this *now*."

Patrick thought back to when he smoked, in part to stay TV-thin, and how trying to quit right as his show was being canceled led to several relapses. And how a cigarette sounded so good right now in the face of this news, this new cancellation. "But is now the best time?"

Greg started shaking, determined to close the sale. "The kids are going to need their father, not half the father they've had for the past few years. Now is the *only* time."

Patrick's head buzzed with logistics; the walls of the garage felt like they were closing in, the floor and the ceiling about to pancake. The cars, and they along with them, would be crushed and discarded, junked. "I only brought two pairs of pants."

"I want you to take them back with you to Palm Springs. The only way this is going to work, the only way I'm going to be able to do this, is if I know they're nearby. They're my strength. They're all I—"

"Stop it. Stop it now." Patrick didn't know if he meant Greg's shaking or the preposterousness of the request.

An older couple ambled toward the Cadillac parked across from them, the woman on the man's arm. It took them an agonizingly long time to get in their car.

"For how long?" Patrick knew better than to even entertain the idea with such a question. But it just slipped out.

"Ninety days."

"*NINETY DAYS!*" It echoed through the garage, sounding more like a jail sentence than a favor. He shouldn't paint himself as the real victim here when a man had lost his wife and two children had lost their mother. But he'd lost someone, too. "You're out of your goddamned mind."

Greg burst into tears.

"Oh, god. Okay. Just . . ." He reached out to comfort his brother, but couldn't decide where to place his hands. "You should know I'm an alcoholic." Patrick wasn't, but he was grasping at straws. Maybe he could check into this facility, too.

"Patrick. You're a social drinker."

"I live alone in the desert, how social could it be!" Ninety days sitting in a sharing circle talking about his feelings while sober seemed like hell on earth, but it had to be better than babysitting, and maybe the facility had a chef and masseur. Patrick lifted the key fob in the air and pressed the button furiously, searching for the car, his arm spinning around like a periscope that had just broken the surface. *Goddammit, Joe,* he thought, as he often did in times of great stress. *Why wasn't I the one driving?* But he wasn't. He was buckled in the passenger seat when Joe was T-boned by a fucking teenager out for a joyride. That was just his bad luck.

And then, out of the darkness, a chirp. They both spun around. Finally, the car. They could argue about this later.

TWO

"It's brunch. You don't know brunch?"

"Is it breakfatht?" Grant asked while being strapped in his car seat. He was six and had a pronounced lisp.

"No." Patrick gave the straps a good tug. Secure. Thirty-six hours had passed and the subject of his taking the kids had come up nine more times. He volunteered to treat them both to brunch without other adults just to avoid a tenth. "Fingers on noses," he said before slamming the door. Did he really just utter that out loud? It was something his mother used to say.

"Is it lunch?" Maisie waited for an answer as Patrick crossed around to the passenger side.

"No." He checked the straps on Maisie's booster. Tight, too tight. "How do you kids breathe in these things? Christ." She was nine now and no longer needed the chair, but she was on the smaller side and Greg warned him that she preferred it.

"We just do."

Patrick stared at the kids. Grant had Sara's features, including (impossibly) her third nose; Maisie had her hair and kept it pulled back off her face with some sort of elastic. He closed his niece's door before climbing into the front passenger seat.

"Then what is it?" Grant threw his arms up, exasperated.

"It's both. Breakfast, lunch. Brunch. Get it? Didn't your parents teach you about brunch?" Patrick bit his lip. Their mother wasn't even in the ground and now Greg was about to vanish, too—now was not the time to be critical. But how do you not teach your children about the most important of all meals? He would trade an arm to be able to give Sara a stern talking to right about now—brunch was an early pillar of their friendship. "Sunday brunch?" It was a last-ditch effort to see if it rang any bells.

"It's Thurthday!" Grant screamed.

"Chill out, little man. No one can be that uptight about brunch."

"You're on the wrong side to drive," Maisie pointed out.

Patrick took a deep breath. He didn't drive, not since the accident. For years the studio sent a driver or he'd spend his own money to hire a car. He was paid a ridiculous sum, and it was easy to convince himself it was a necessary expense. Then, with the rise of Uber, he never had to think about it again. "Not in England."

"We're not *in* England, GUP."

"*New* England," Patrick said, as if that explained anything. He shot Greg a text asking if he would drive them. "And why do you keep calling me GUP?"

"I forget. Ask Dad."

Great. Patrick stared at his phone, willing it to buzz with a return text. Already, two minutes alone with these children was two minutes too many. "I just don't drive, okay?"

"You don't know how?" It was clear Grant had never heard of an adult not knowing how to drive and he wasn't about to let it go.

"I know how. I don't like to turn my head because it makes lines in my neck, so I can't use reverse."

"You don't have to, GUP," Maisie said. "The car has a camera." She pointed at the screen on the dash.

GUP. There was that name again. GUP, GUP, GUP. They'd been calling him that all morning. "I know it has a camera, Maisie. But cameras lie."

"No they don't. Cameras can't speak!"

"They find a way."

"How?"

"I don't know. Wait until you turn forty, then all they do is lie." Patrick thought of the recent headshots he'd been strong-armed into sitting for by his agent's new something—*assistant*—and how they'd required an arduous effort from the retoucher.

Greg opened the driver's door and hopped into the seat. "Someone call for a ride?"

"We need you to drop us at the restaurant."

Greg started the engine as he fastened his seat belt, all one fluid motion.

"Why do your children keep calling me GUP?"

"Gay Uncle Pat." Greg's expression said it all. *Duh*.

Patrick was appalled. "Seriously?"

"What," Greg began as he gripped the wheel, "you don't like being gay?"

"I don't like being *Pat*."

"Are you our guncle?" Maisie asked.

Patrick buried his head in his hands. "Make it stop."

"Audra Brackett in my class has two guncles," she continued. "She's my best friend."

"Guncle Pat!" Grant exclaimed.

"*Patrick*. Guncle *Patrick*. We're not doing Pat." Pat was so—*oh, god*—he didn't even know the word. *Heterosexual*. "And I don't like *guncle*, either."

"What's wrong with *guncle*?" Greg asked.

"What's *right* with it? It sounds like *cankle*." Patrick flipped down his visor to catch Maisie's eyes in the mirror. "Calf and ankle," he said before she had a chance to inquire.

Greg threw the car in reverse, looked over his shoulder, and backed out of the driveway.

"You don't have to do that, Dad! There's a camera." For the first time Patrick recognized a little bit of himself—the know-it-all—in his niece.

"Yes, he does. I'm going to teach you some things while I'm here. That's Guncle Rule number one. Okay? If we must? Cameras are your enemy as much as they're your friend. Scratch that. That's Guncle Rule number two. Guncle Rule number one: Brunch is splendid."

◇◇◇◇◇

The restaurant hostess smiled when Patrick entered holding the kids' hands. People tended to do that when he was with them, he noticed. Smile. No one ever frowned with concern that he'd kidnapped two children; not one person's facial expression the equivalent of an Amber Alert. Couldn't they see how unnatural this all was for him?

"Three, please. Or, two and a high chair."

"I'm too old for a high chair!" Grant screamed.

"Jesus." Patrick sighed audibly. "Three, please."

The hostess smiled even wider. "Three it is."

"Are you still serving brunch?"

"Of course! Brunch is our most popular meal."

Patrick shot the kids a look. *See?*

"Follow me."

She led them to a corner booth and left them with menus, which they studied with great interest. "What looks good?" Patrick asked.

"I can't read, stupid," Grant declared, although "stupid" came out more like *thtupid*. He put his menu down and swung his feet back and forth, kicking the table.

"No kicking," Patrick said, but in truth he was relieved at least Grant wasn't screaming.

"Who are you again?" Grant asked. He wasn't entirely sure of Patrick's authority in this situation.

"He's our guncle!"

Patrick looked down his nose at his niece. "Don't make me repeat myself. That word is unpleasant."

"You're unpleasant," Maisie observed.

Patrick sneered like an old black-and-white-movie villain. "You have no idea."

"But who *are* you?" Grant implored.

"I'm your father's brother and I was your mother's friend. Got it? You came to visit me once at my house in California."

"We did?"

"I have a pool," Patrick said, as if that would settle it once and for all. "Now, focus. What looks good?"

"I like bacon," Maisie announced.

"We don't eat bacon."

"Yes we do."

"No we don't."

"Yes we do."

"Bacon is pigs and pigs are our friends. Do you want to eat your friends?"

Without hesitation. "If they taste like bacon."

Patrick set his menu down. "I'm a vegetarian. Lacto-ovo. Well, pescatarian, to be more precise. And maybe you should be, too, while I'm here helping because I can't buy all that stuff from the grocer. You know. *Morally.*"

"What's pethca—?"

"Pescatarian. I occasionally eat fish. Do you like sushi?"

"I like hot dogs." Grant perked up just enough to take the conversation backward.

"What? That's like the worst parts of the pig. Like lips and buttholes and . . . I shudder to even think."

Grant laughed.

"Why do you eat fish but not pigs?" Maisie asked.

"Because fish are dumb and delicious. Now look at your menu."

"Yes, but our oceans are overfished." Patrick felt a shadow fall over the table and he looked up to see who was speaking. An older man with graying temples smiled at him while opening a small pad with his pencil. "So there are environmental concerns at play."

"Don't flush the toilet for three months, don't shower for six months, or don't eat *one* hamburger. I'm from California, where there's always a drought, so I'm more concerned about the environmental effects of factory farm—I'm sorry, who are you?" he asked the man.

"Patrick. It's me."

"Me, the . . . waiter?"

"Me, *Barry*."

"Barry . . . ?" Patrick was pretty certain he didn't know any Barrys.

"From high school."

"Barry from high school." *We're the same fucking age, is that what you're telling me?* "Of course." Patrick said *Of course* even though it was still fuzzy. There was only a handful of people he remembered from high school; in most respects, his life began with Sara. "These are my brother's kids, Maisie and Grant. Guys, BARRY."

"It's really great to see you. I haven't heard anything about you since the show went off the air. What was that, four years ago? How are you?"

"Ummm . . ." Patrick stalled, desperately wanting out of a conversation that really had yet to begin.

"You should do another show. You were very good."

"Thank you. That had never occurred to me." Patrick soaked his reply in so much sarcasm it might as well have been a teenager experimenting with cologne.

"Although I thought that last one was a waste of your talents. Remember when we did *Brigadoon* in high school? You were so good!"

Shut up, shut up, shut up.

"So, what brings you back to Connecticut?"

"Our mom was sick," Maisie said, coming to her uncle's rescue. "She died." She and Grant looked at the ground. Patrick winced, surprised to hear a years-long battle summarized so succinctly, then covered his shock with a grimace. He put one arm around each of them and joined them in looking down. They were mourning, you see. Something best done in private.

"Oh," Barry said, his ability to get chummy shut off at the valve. "I'm very sorry." He awkwardly tapped his pencil on his pad as Patrick luxuriated in the silence. "Get you started on some drinks?"

"Kids?"

"Bacon!" Grant perked up, a little too quickly.

Make it believable, Patrick thought, recognizing their grief as a shield against small talk. *Keep the work focused*. "C'mon. Drinks, he's asking. Juice or milk?"

"Juice!"

"Grant?"

"Goose."

"Two juices. Do you have apple? And one mimosa, light on the OJ."

"Our orange juice is freshly squeezed."

"Either way. A whisper of juice. I'm serious. You can really just wave an orange over the glass and that's probably still too much juice." Patrick stared at Barry's golf pencil, willing it to move. "You're not writing this down."

"Two apple juices and one glass of champagne. I'll give you some time with the menu." As abruptly as he had appeared, Barry retreated.

Patrick drummed his fingers on the table. "So, guys. There's something we need to discuss." He looked down at his place setting and aligned the silverware as if he were some footman on *Downton Abbey*. "I thought we could eat brunch, the three of us, and have a little chin-wag." He looked up to nothing but blank expressions. "That means *talk*. Your father, he's very sad with your mom, well, you know. We all are. He's asked me to—while he takes a little time for himself—take care of you."

"WHAT?" Grant hollered.

"Don't worry. I said no. I wanted you to hear that from me. I believe in treating kids like people."

"You said *no*?" Maisie offered an expression that was difficult to read.

"It's nothing personal. It's just. You know. The whole kid thing is not my bag."

"For how long?" Grant wondered.

"Not forever, by any means, or even very long, but for long enough that you would have to come stay at my place in Palm Springs." He wondered if they found this entire proposition as ludicrous as he did, but how could they really? They couldn't possibly remember his house with its pristine midcentury décor, white terrazzo floors—his Golden Globe, for heaven's sake. It was a fine bachelor pad, but no place for children. "Can you imagine? He wanted you to come after Maisie finished school."

"College?" Maisie asked.

"Are you *in* college?" Patrick looked to the skies for strength; there was a wad of gum stuck to a ceiling tile. "No, third grade. You're done next week."

"Where's Daddy going?" Grant was very concerned, justifiably so. Patrick bit his lip; how do you explain to a six-year-old who just lost his mother the difference between temporarily and forever?

"A special place that helps daddies who are sad."

"Will he see Mommy?"

Patrick's heart sank. He thought of the website he had viewed, the one he'd pored over with their sister, Clara, once Greg had confided in her, too. It had photos of beige rooms with small windows, each with its own pitiful Black & Decker coffee maker. "No. The place is not that special."

"Why do you live in Palm Spwings?" It surprised Patrick that all this pushback was coming from Grant and not from Maisie, who quietly studied her menu. "Why do you live tho far away?"

"It's not *that* far away. It's not like I live in Botswana. C'mon. You've been there. Remember? You came with your mom." He realized the trip was now three years ago; Maisie was probably Grant's age and Grant was not even three.

"Dad said it's far because you can't fly direct."

Patrick looked at Maisie with disbelief. "You can from New York!" He sighed. "Look, we're getting off track here, but if you must know, I'm young in Palm Springs. Okay? This is the sad truth for gay men. Forty is ancient in Los Angeles, middle-aged in San Francisco, but young in Palm Springs. That's why I live there."

"You're forty-three!" Maisie bellowed.

"Who are you, the DMV? Lower your voice."

"That's almost fifty!" Grant's eyes grew big.

Patrick took the jab, then closed his eyes and bit his lower lip; the observation was just shy of a hate crime. *Do not punch a child, do not punch a child.* "Can we please focus?"

"Why can't you stay with us here?"

He put down his menu to retake the reins of this conversation. "Well, here has certain advantages. I'm *thin* here. But Connecticut only gets like eleven days of sun a year and I'm solar-powered. I need the sun or else I'll . . ." Patrick had just enough sense to stop himself before he said *die*.

"Or else you'll what?"

He answered in slow motion. "Slow down . . . like a . . . windup . . . toy . . . until . . . I . . . *stop*. But again, we're not the right match. No one would swipe right on the three of us."

"How long will Daddy be gone?"

Patrick tried to recall the details Greg had peppered on his request. "I don't know. Ninety days? Something like that."

"That's three hundred weeks!" Grant exclaimed. Patrick couldn't tell if it was excitement or exasperation.

"We need to check your math on that one, buddy. But it's not your fault. You're the product of a failing public education system. And I share the sentiment. Which is why we have to find you someone appropriate."

As if that were his cue, Barry appeared carrying a tray of drinks.

"Here we are, two apple juices, one champagne. Have you had a chance to look at the menu?"

Patrick had a fleeting thought: *Could Barry babysit for three hundred weeks?* No. Barry was a stranger. He knew enough to know that would not do. He turned back to the kids. "What sounds good? Pancakes? Waffles? Lobster thermidor?"

The kids stared back at him blankly. This news about their dad had left them reeling.

"C'mon. That's the great thing about brunch. You can have almost anything. Pick your poison." *Now* they were at a loss for words. "How about French toast, then? Two orders of toast in the French style with fruits mélangés."

"And bacon," Maisie pleaded.

"Fine. And bacon." Bacon was not a hill to die on today. "And I'll have poached eggs with a side of fruit and also some low-fat cottage cheese if you have it, but no meat because I don't want to hurt any pigs or cows or birds." He looked up and snorted at his niece and nephew, who warmed to his porcine impersonation.

"Very good, gentlemen. And madam." Barry still didn't write any of this down; Patrick was beginning to wonder why he bothered with the pad if it was only a prop. Surely he could make better use of his hands—perhaps hold a tin can for donations so he could afford to dye his hair. They sat quietly as Barry sauntered to the kitchen, each looking around to study other diners presumably living better, more carefree lives.

"Do you guys know anyone you could stay with? Friends who have parents and a guest room?" Maybe the problems held the solution. "C'mon, who are your friends? Who comes over to play?"

"No one." Maisie shrugged.

"No one? What about, what's her name you mentioned?" Patrick snapped his fingers three times. "Audrey Bennett."

"Audra Brackett."

"Yes. Audra Brackett. She sounds nice. What about her?"

Maisie shrugged again as she stacked some little jams. "Our house is too sad."

"Oof." It was a stab right to the heart. Patrick scrambled not to dwell. "So, anything big planned for the summer?" He cringed. Clearly whatever plans they may have had had gone right out the window.

"I was supposed to take swim lessons," Grant said wistfully; even he could sense that was no longer happening.

Patrick looked at the next table for help, three women enjoying mimosas, at least fifty percent orange juice (*suckers*), and individually designed omelets with any combination of thirty ingredients. They ate without constant interruptions and exclamations and Patrick was envious, as if he were already mourning a former life. Should he consider this, taking them in? One of the women made eye contact, recognition, or an attempt, perhaps, at pity. *No. It was out of the question.*

"We'll find you someone. Your grandparents, maybe," Patrick said. "I'll even pay for your swim lessons." Grant seemed to find this agreeable; crisis averted. "Is that really what someone told you? Your house was too sad?" Patrick's heart was still breaking.

"*You* have a pool." Maisie brightened. It was all coming back to her. "You could teach Grant to swim in Palm Springs. Could I have my own room?"

"SHARE!" Grant screamed. Patrick observed he had taken to sleeping in his sister's room, and had, apparently, since Sara was checked into hospice.

"No, I want my own!"

"You're not coming to Palm Springs. We already decided. It's better for you that way. You'll see." Grant flipped his place mat over to look for kid activities, but it wasn't that kind of establishment. "Your father and I shared a room, you know, for a time. We had bunk beds. I had the top bunk. I felt bad for him as I grew and that top bed started to sag. I swear, by the time your aunt Clara left for college and I moved into her room, he couldn't so much as roll over without scraping his nose on my undercarriage. He got his revenge when he discovered a certain teenage pastime and I had to fall asleep with the bed swaying like we were adrift on a gay cruise in monsoon season, if you know what I mean. Anyhow, cheers." He picked up his champagne and clinked glasses with Maisie and Grant, who it seemed enjoyed a good cheers.

"Cheers!" Maisie added.

"Poop!" Grant said, and they both laughed. Patrick wanted to drop his head to the table with a deafening thud, but it would only draw attention to Grant's "joke."

"Can we eat brunch in Palm Springs?" Maisie asked.

Maisie was plotting something out and Patrick didn't like it. "You're not coming to Palm Springs."

"Yeah, but could we? If we were."

"Oh, god, yes. We *only* eat brunch in Palm Springs. Brunch and lupper."

"What's lupper?"

"You don't know lupper, either?" Patrick sighed for effect. "Well, if brunch is a combination of breakfast and lunch, what do you suppose lupper is?"

Maisie got there first. "Lunch and supper!"

"Exactly. It's a mid- to late-afternoon meal, which is good for digestion. If you eat too late you get heavy unless you're European. They have dinner at an ungodly hour and never gain so much as an ounce, but they're evolved and they walk everywhere and smoke cigarettes, which helps, so—you know." Patrick put his napkin in his lap and made a production out of it so the kids would follow suit. "All my meals are portmanteaus."

"You talk funny," Grant said.

"Me talk funny?" This time Patrick did an impression of a chimp, scratching his head with one hand and under his armpit with the other. "I suppose I speak with a certain élan. But that's not a bad thing."

"Why don't you talk like everyone else?" Maisie leaned forward and put her lips on her apple juice without lifting the glass from the table.

"'Be yourself; everyone else is already taken.' Oscar Wilde." Patrick looked at his nephew also gnawing on the edge of his drinking glass. "Don't do that."

Grant shrugged without sitting back in his seat. "I'm being mythelf."

"You know, it's one thing if you throw my own words back in my face, but do not throw Oscar Wilde's. Now sit up like human beings or at least use a straw." Patrick picked up one of the paper-wrapped drinking straws Barry had left for them, tore off one end, and blew a puff of air through the straw so that the wrapper hit Maisie square between the eyes. Grant erupted in laughter. "So what do you think?"

"About what?" Grant managed as he tried to control his giggles.

"About brunch!" Patrick said. "It's growing on you, isn't it?"

"I can only eat thoft foods."

"Why?"

"Loothe tooth."

"WHAT?"

Maisie translated. "His tooth is loose."

"What sort of Dr. Seuss nightmare is this?" Patrick muttered under his breath. "So?"

"What if it falls out?"

"I do not like a loose tooth, I do not like one in this booth. I do not like a tooth at brunch, I do not like foods that crunch."

"Be therious!" Grant implored. "What if my tooth falls out?"

"Then we'll just shove it back in." He took a long sip of his champagne, ignoring Grant's stunned expression. He let the bubbles evenly coat his tongue before letting them slide down his throat. Maybe they weren't so hard to manage, the kids. "Perhaps you can come visit. You know. For a few days. You could even invite Audra what's-her-face."

"Brackett."

"That's right." If they brought a friend, they might even amuse themselves.

"Actually, we can't," Maisie replied.

"You can't?" Patrick was surprised. Relieved, somewhat. But surprised. "You have other commitments?"

"No."

"Then why not?"

Maisie looked down at her plate. "I don't want to leave Mom."

Patrick placed his silverware on his plate, the knife carefully between the tines of his fork. He recognized their grief, how untethered they were from the life they had known. He reached out and pulled the kids close to him, until he had one nestled under each arm. It was his job now to give them something, anything, to hold on to. "Let me tell you something. You can't ever leave your mother, just as she can never really leave you."

Maisie looked up at him, pleading for more.

Patrick inhaled, hoping the oxygen would give him the stamina to continue. Sara was very much there, in Maisie's expressions, or Grant's stoicism. He'd never had any interest in children himself but suddenly recognized some small appeal; Sara had found a way to live beyond death. "She's half of you and you're half of her." He looked at them both, hoping this made sense, hoping that it would sink in. He saw Sara's eyes staring back at him. "So . . . yeah. Just like brunch. Half breakfast. Half lunch." He smiled; they seemed to like this. "We're going to figure this out." Patrick kissed the top of each child's head before pushing them off of him and back toward their own place settings with a sudden nagging that they were in danger of becoming too attached. *There has to be another way.* "Now," he began, picking up his fork and knife to resume eating. "Who here has heard of a snappetizer?"

Both kids stared at him blankly.

"Are you being serious?" he asked. "Boy. You're lucky I got here when I did."

THREE

Patrick could feel his sister approaching before she emerged from behind two enormous parked cars, boatlike sedans they used to give away on *The Hollywood Squares* that seemed no longer to exist in California. His blood chilled ten degrees. He stood his ground in the parking lot between the church and the cemetery as Clara marched toward him with the sense of purpose she'd exuded since childhood—rigorous posture, heavy steps that fell just shy of stomping, always a little bit pained—and with an almost masculine energy that Patrick, in his adolescence, had been jealous of. Her clothing was a pastiche of Style sections in midlist women's magazines (publications perhaps better suited to cookie recipes than fashion), and the sunglasses she wore on top of her head had taken root somewhere in her scalp.

"It was a nice service," she said when she arrived at his side.

Nice. Patrick looked at the sky; the nimbus clouds were gray but not threatening. "Rain held off." He didn't know how to behave at these things any more than she did.

"It's fun to see you back in Connecticut. I thought maybe you were done with us."

"Planes fly west, you know." It was an old argument. When Patrick moved to Los Angeles he flew home regularly for years, every six months or so until he stopped. It was the show, it was his schedule. Everyone assumed fame had changed him. And, to some extent, it had. It gave him the confidence to call out hypocrisy where he saw it. He came home, no one came to see him. After a while he began to wonder: What was the point?

"You're off the hook, by the way. I talked to Darren. We agreed he and I should take the children for the summer."

Patrick's whole body loosened, like he'd just walked out of ninety minutes of Reiki. *Oh, thank god.*

"They should stay in Connecticut to be closer to their friends," she continued.

"Like Audra Brackett. And whomever Grant pals around with."

"Who?"

Patrick blew right past her question. "It was farcical," he offered. "The very idea."

"I mean, can you imagine?" Clara laughed, and she never laughed. Patrick always thought he would welcome it, the sound of his sister's laughter; instead, he was immediately put off. "It was good of you to come." She placed her hand on his forearm and gave it a condescending squeeze.

Patrick had delivered the eulogy. He'd written two on the plane; he gave the version he knew others wanted to hear. About Sara the wife, Sara the mother, Sara the very definition of family. The other was for the Sara he knew. Sara the loyal, Sara the thrill seeker, Sara the irreverent, Sara the brother-fucker. It would have amused him, sharing old stories. The time he took her to the Ramrod, a Boston leather bar, and people mistook her for a drag queen. The time they were arrested for sneaking into the Granary Burying Ground after dark to make rubbings of the gravestones. The time she screamed obscenities in the face of religious protesters the first time they attended Pride. He came close to pulling the second eulogy out of his jacket pocket. But in the end it was for his Sara, not theirs, so he left it in his breast pocket, where it sat directly over his heart.

"Still. Greg asked *me* to take the kids. Not you."

Clara pulled her hand away. "Greg was probably high at the time."

"We don't have to do this."

"Do what?"

"It's not a requirement, is all I'm saying."

"A requirement of what?"

"Our being related. A lot of people just love their family."

"*I* love my family."

"Okay."

"I do!"

Patrick fluttered his lips. "You don't *like* us very much."

"You two don't make it easy." Clara, the oldest, had always viewed Patrick and Greg as twin nuisances, equal bothers to an otherwise orderly existence.

Patrick shrugged and looked out over the cemetery.

"Anyhow, I have the next few months off. I was going to teach summer school, but my friend Anita is going on maternity leave in the fall, so she was more than happy to take on additional classes before then."

He was only half listening. "Who?"

"Anita. My friend Anita."

Patrick surveyed the crowd; it seemed they didn't know what to do. No one wanted to leave, but everyone looked pained to stay. "Greg has a point, wanting the kids near him."

Clara didn't like the look in his eye; he was piecing together a puzzle. "Would you stop? You don't even want to do this. Let's not kid ourselves. I'm giving you an out."

Patrick didn't know what he found more irksome, the fact that she knew he would want a way out, or that under any other circumstance he would take it. He patted himself down; the second eulogy in his pocket crinkled, like Sara asking him a favor.

"Patrick."

"*Clara.*" Patrick locked eyes with his sister. "The kids mentioned they didn't have many friends. That their house had become too sad. Is that true?"

"You know other kids. They're afraid of anyone who is going through something . . . *different*. It will sort itself out."

"What about your kids?"

"What about my kids?"

"Don't they spend time together?" Patrick asked. He hadn't really grown up around cousins, but shouldn't they be forced to be friends?

"They're teenagers."

An image was emerging of Maisie and Grant as loners, just like him. Perhaps he couldn't be a guardian to these kids, but, cousins be damned, as their uncle he *could* be a friend. "Wait, did you say Darren agreed you could take the kids? Or you *should*."

"What difference does that make?"

"It makes a difference to me." Patrick felt himself growing redder. People whispered and glanced in his direction.

"Calm yourself. Your voice is doing that squeaky thing. Remember when you first learned to answer the telephone and people would call you ma'am?"

Patrick nodded at some asshole who was staring at him. "Don't change the subject."

Clara continued. "You have this vision, Patrick, of playing some role. Of stepping in like you're some glamorous Uncle Mame." She chuckled. "Uncle Ma'am."

"Have you discussed that with Darren, too?"

"You're not Rosalind Russell. And it's not what these children need."

"Then why do I look so natural with a long cigarette holder?" He held his hand up to mime just such a thing.

"You don't look natural, you look like you're going to skin someone's dog."

Patrick used to like having a sister. It gave him permission to indulge in the activities he longed to do—color, weave, make paper bag puppets, play dress-up. They could play together, under the umbrella of her interests. When his father suggested he go outside, Patrick could rightfully say Clara was his playmate, she was older—she set the agenda. But she eventually moved on, wanted to do other things. As a teenager she liked reading and, it seemed, just about nothing else. She read a book by Alice Walker about female genital mutilation in Africa and refused to speak to a member of the opposite sex for a month. She read Simone de Beauvoir and fumed about the patriarchy to any male in earshot—even if he were four years her junior. Patrick thought his coming out would restore their relationship; if the problem was straight white male privilege, he no longer identified with the trifecta and now had his own history of oppression. Yet somehow she took his lack of attraction to women as yet another affront to the sex.

"They just lost their mother, Patrick."

The kids lost their mother, Greg lost his wife. Why didn't anyone acknowledge *his* loss? Or remember that he knew Sara first? If it wasn't for him bringing her into their lives, he would be the only one of them at this goddamn service.

Patrick jumped up and down like a swimmer before entering the pool, like a boxer about to enter the ring. His heart raced with dread and adrenaline. "Yeah, I'm going to do it."

"Do what?"

"Take the kids."

"Patrick!" Clara put her hands on his shoulders to hold him to the ground. "Look at me. This isn't a joke. We're not deciding on who gets a lamp. They're children, I'm a mother. I can give them what they need."

Patrick glowered. Darren had two teens from a previous marriage who spent just about all of their time with their actual mother, a conspiracy theorist who jarred her own jams.

"A stepmother is a mother!"

"I'm not arguing that, those kids should be with you all the time."

"Thank you."

"At least then they'd be vaccinated."

"Stop it."

"Remember your wedding? I was bit by mosquitoes but convinced I had mumps."

Clara pursed her lips. "Maisie and Grant have needs, Patrick. Emotional needs. They don't even understand what has happened to them yet."

"Of course they do, they've been living with this possibility for years. What they need is some fun. What they need is a change of scenery. What they *need* is to laugh and be silly and be kids."

"And as the world's oldest child—"

Patrick stopped her. "What they *don't* need is someone trying to take their mother's place."

"I'm not trying to . . . Is that what you think?"

At that moment, Maisie and Grant ran full-speed between them, the younger chasing the older and failing miserably at catching her.

"Watch for cars!" Clara hollered instinctually as they ran away.

Patrick looked down over the top of his sunglasses.

"Oh, give me a break. That's not mothering them, that's just plain being responsible."

"If you say so."

"They are being strong right now because they're surrounded by everyone they know and love and because there's been something for them to do every hour of the day. But people are going to go back home, and they will stop being the center of attention and there will come a time, in a few days or a few weeks or a month, when the reality of their situation hits them and they're going to look to you for meaning. And then what?"

"I can give them all the attention they need, thank you very much."

"Wait until they find out they'll be competing for your attention with you."

Patrick took a few steps away as this new plan solidified in his mind. He could tell them about their mother. Not the mother they knew, but the woman he remembered. Under a cluster of nearby maple trees, his parents were engaged in conversation with Sara's, the four of them huddled in a tight mass. Other family milled about, friends hugged, whispering secrets. Everyone sharing memories of a different Sara no doubt, but he knew the *real* one. And now so could her kids. He turned back to his sister. "Clara, I've got this." He removed his sunglasses entirely to show her he meant business.

"Please. You're terrified."

Patrick shook his head.

"You're not fooling me. You're not *that* good of an actor."

Greg emerged from the crowd, slumped, like he was experiencing a heavier gravitational pull. Patrick put his arm around his brother's shoulders as Clara looked away. The problem with three is that it's always two against one.

"I'm going to do it. What you asked."

"You're kidding," Greg replied. His eyes brightened for the first time in days.

Patrick locked eyes with Clara. "I'm not."

"You're both morons," she said.

"It's my decision, Clara," Greg told her. "I know what I'm doing." And then, to Patrick, "Beautiful speech. Thank you. I couldn't . . . I couldn't have done it."

"Remember what telemarketers called Patrick when he would answer the phone?" Clara asked, softening.

"Ma'am?" Greg asked.

Clara confirmed. "Uncle Ma'am," she said, repeating the joke to herself.

The kids ran by on a third loop and this time Patrick nabbed them. He got down on one knee and sat Grant on his leg.

"You're Uncle Toilet," Grant charged.

Patrick looked up at his sister, doing his best to mask any regret. He knew this was an audition, a callback for network execs—the last hurdle before landing the role.

"Let me tell you something. Both of you." He ushered Maisie in, too. "As a professional who has studied comedy. Bathroom humor is cheap. Okay? Guncle Rule number three. Is it an easy laugh? *Yes*. But it's lazy. It's not the laugh you want. But, I think you'll find if you work harder, dig a little deeper, find the joke that lies beneath the obvious one, that's when your comedy will really shine. Understand?"

They both nodded.

"Okay." Patrick slid Grant off his knee and stood up, resting his hand on his nephew's shoulder. He was loath to employ his own catchphrase, but this situation called for a special exception. "And that's . . . *how you do it*." He winked at Clara, knowing it would drive her a particular kind of insane.

And then Grant had to spoil his triumph by yelling, "You're Uncle Sewer!" before running off to find his grandparents.

Greg laughed heartily, which caused those standing nearby to turn. "Well, you told him to dig deeper."

Patrick buried his face in his hands and grumbled. "Commedia dell'farte." Grant may have won this battle, but Patrick was determined to win the war.

The clouds above darkened in a way they didn't in Palm Springs. A thunderstorm was imminent. Clara motioned toward the car and signaled her husband that it was time to go. She had no desire to lose an argument with her brothers *and* get drenched.

FOUR

"Ith that an island?"

Patrick peered across both Maisie and Grant to look out the airplane window at what lay thirty thousand feet below them. "That's a cloud."

"It lookth like an island." It didn't matter the cards he was dealt, Grant apparently always doubled down.

Patrick turned to Maisie, whose legs dangled below her seat in a way that made it look like she'd grown three inches since takeoff. "There's only one state that's an island, do you know what that is?" Maisie raised her hand. "And don't say Rhode Island, because they just threw that in there to fuck with you." Maisie dropped her hand back in her lap.

"You said a thwear." Grant's eyes looked wide as Frisbees.

"Okay, this is going to be a really long summer if we're going to track every time that I say a swear."

The goodbyes had been awful. Greg did his best to explain his situation without burdening them, but the children were, in the moment, inconsolable. They had just said goodbye to their mother and they were being, what—*sent to live with a stranger*? Even to Patrick it seemed needlessly cruel. Greg cried, the children sobbed, and Patrick did his best to remain stoic. Deep down he didn't think this was any better an idea than they did, but someone had to appear certain; someone had to be captaining this ship. More tears were shed at the airport. Patrick pulled his cap down so far over his eyes, he had to look up to see past the brim. Maisie and Grant each had two checked bags; he never knew children came with so much *stuff*. They ate quietly at the airport Papa Gino's, but none of them had much of an appetite for cardboard pizza or, really, for anything else.

"Can we watch YouTube?"

"What? No. There's no Wi-Fi on this plane."

"Why not?"

"One of the advantages of being on an airplane is that we're disconnected from everything going on beneath us. We're in a metal tube in the sky. It's a time to reflect, read a book maybe, to be with ourselves." Patrick was lying about the Wi-Fi and wasn't sure why. His insistence, perhaps, that there was more to appreciate about planes than staring blankly at a screen, doing something you could readily do on the ground. He carried a torch for air travel from the 1960s, before he was born, when flying seemed glamorous and stewardesses looked like Dusty Springfield or Petula Clark, served chateaubriand off of a cart, and came by every so often to light your cigarette. But since Grant and Maisie weren't old enough to enjoy an in-flight martini, was this really necessary? Shouldn't he loosen the reins, or would that set a bad precedent—would he lose all sense of authority before this experiment began? "You guys packed a few books, right?"

"Does your car at least have a DVD player?" Maisie asked.

"I'm Uber only."

"What does that mean?"

"I told you I don't drive. I have a Tesla, but I keep it in the garage."

Maisie furrowed her brow. It was hard to know where to tear at her uncle's logic when he spouted so many unfamiliar words. "What's a Tesla?"

"It's like a spaceship."

Grant turned his head at lightning speed.

"Not an actual spaceship, but it might as well be, as I don't know how to use it. It's just a fancy car."

"Why do you have a fanthy car if you don't drive?"

Patrick closed his eyes. He wasn't going to make it ninety hours, let alone days. "It was a gift."

"Someone *gave* you a car?" Maisie was incredulous.

It was the studio. They gave them to the main cast when they signed a contract extension for two final seasons. "That happens sometimes when you're famous."

"You're famouth?"

Patrick peered into the aisle to make sure no one was listening. "I used to be."

Grant kicked his feet lazily, hitting the seat in front of him. Patrick reached over to stop him. "We should have taken Mommy'th car. Mommy'th car has a DVD player."

Patrick wished he could go back in time, maybe to one of the nights he and Sara drank 40s in the lounge on their dormitory floor, when they were doing something nonsensical that amused them, like trying to pronounce the word *noodle* in as many accents as possible, to tell Sara that one day she'd be driving a minivan with a television inside. "Well, I don't really leave the house much and I have a TV at home."

"Does it get YouTube?" Grant hollered.

Patrick shushed him. "Inside voices."

"We're outside. The thky is outside."

"The what? The *sky*?" Patrick resolved then and there to spend time with Grant working on his lisp. "The sky is outside, the plane is inside. I'll toss you out the window if you want to know the difference."

"He means is it a smart TV." Maisie stepped in to de-escalate.

"What is there to watch on YouTube, anyhow?" Patrick didn't understand the obsession.

"Kid vlogs."

"What on earth is a kid vlog? You know what? Don't answer that. My TV has TV."

"We don't like regular TV."

Patrick mimed a dagger going into his heart. "You realize I was on TV." What was wrong with kids today? Not liking *television*. Television was everything when he was young, it's why he wanted to be on it. The most mind-blowing day in his life was the day he discovered other children could see Mister Rogers, too. "Hawaii, by the way, was the answer to my question. Hawaii is the only state that's an island."

"Oh," Maisie said.

Oh. He was about to ask if they wanted to go; they could stay at the Four Seasons in Wailea and sit in reserved deck chairs and order virgin piña coladas. But they didn't like TV and they weren't impressed with Hawaii. What did it take to amuse them? "Fun fact about your uncle Patrick. When I was your age I thought Alaska was also an island because they always stuck it with Hawaii in the bottom corner of maps." He thought he could win them over with this; how stupid to think a state that was mostly tundra and ice was an island in the South Pacific. It landed with a thud. "Maybe when you're ten that will be funnier."

Conversation ground to a halt. They'd only been in the air three hours and he'd already run through his best material. Patrick found it difficult to refrain from sharing with them other facts about when he was their age—like that cars and planes didn't have televisions or Wi-Fi, or seat belts, probably—but he knew instinctually that saying things like that made him square. *I'm moderately famous, for god's sake. I can't possibly be this dull.*

"Can I have a fudgesicle?" Grant looked up at him longingly.

"Jesus Christ. You can't pronounce the word *sky*, but *fudgesicle* you nail?" He tickled his nephew so that his observation aped a joke. "When we get to Palm Springs I'll buy you a whole box of fudgesicles."

"Can I sit on the aisle?" Maisie asked.

"No."

"Why not?"

"Because it's been like thirteen years since I even flew in steerage and the aisle seat is the only thing keeping me sane."

Greg had purchased tickets for them in coach so they could sit three to a row. Patrick wanted to upgrade, but his brother begged him not to. It was important, Greg felt, for them to sit together.

"But what if I'm *recognized*?" Patrick tried to emphasize the full horror of that happening. "Can't *you* fly with them while I sit in first class?"

A stern look from Greg as he packed his own suitcase ended the conversation. His flight was the following day so he could focus on seeing his children off. Everything was set. There was no backing out now.

Bing-bong. The chime alerted them to fasten their seat belts.

"What's Alaska again?" Maisie asked. Finally, some traction.

"What's a *map*?" Grant asked more succinctly, with just enough disinterest to close the subject for good.

"Look, all right? Your flying with me is good. It sets a precedent. Instills a love for travel. I blocked three people from my high school class on Facebook for being grandparents before we were forty. *Three people!* Why would they do that to me? And that's your future if you never leave your hometown. So, California here we come."

"What's Fathebook?"

"*Exactly.* Facebook is done. Over. The social media platform for Nana and Papa." Grant was more hip than he knew.

"You could be our *grandparent*?" Maisie was stunned.

"Not your grandparent, *a* grandparent, and NO! *No.* No, I could not. That's the wrong takeaway from what I just said." Patrick cringed. He'd already lied once on the plane and should probably leave it at that. "Well, I suppose *biologically*. But that's not the point."

"You're too young!" Finally, Grant's outside voice was warranted; he sounded as offended by the idea as his uncle.

"Thank you. *See?* Grant gets it." He gave the kid a high-five.

They hit a pocket of turbulence, sending the kids rising an inch from their seats. Patrick reached over and tightened each of their lap belts.

"Ladies and gentlemen, the captain has turned on the fasten seat belts sign. Please remain in your seat."

"You okay?" He placed his hand on Maisie's arm to calm her. She felt clammy, so he plowed forward to distract them. "You know the secret to staying young? *Money*. Guncle Rule number four. Not so you can carve up your face, mind you; don't do that. But if you have money, you're not stressed. Stress is what ages you. And winter and not getting out of your hometown. You guys really should be writing these down."

Patrick glanced over again to see if they were laughing. When he looked back, he caught a glimpse of his reflection in the screen mounted on the back of the seat in front of him. The crow's feet around his eyes. Those lines on either side of his mouth. He thought it might be time to touch up his Botox, consider some of the Restylane or Juvéderm his Eastern European cosmetologist, a woman whose face didn't allow her to laugh and who went by a name like Bianca, suggested might fill in his scar. Or maybe it would be easier to do more than just stop answering his agent's calls. Maybe he should retire from television officially. Then his face could look however he pleased.

"What state are we over now?" Maisie asked when the plane found a smoother path.

Patrick loosened his seat belt to peer out the window again; all the Western states had the same topography, ropy mountain ranges that snaked like macramé, and bland 1970s color. "I'm not really sure. I think we passed most of the square ones. New Mexico?" He settled back in his seat and tightened his belt before he could get in trouble. "Have you ever been to New Mexico? The whole state is one giant flea market for turquoise jewelry. I went years ago on some sort of men's retreat and was chased to the Arizona state line by a diner hostess named Luna with a thick mop of red hair and an angry toe for daring to ask what a Kokopelli was and why they all seemed to have scoliosis. I mean, do you guys know?"

Silence.

"Okay, well, we won't call that a hard-and-fast Guncle Rule, but don't go to New Mexico if you can avoid it." *How long is this flight? Shouldn't they be starting their descent?* It was the stupid headwinds. Flying west always took an hour longer. Patrick drummed his fingers on the armrest. He reached up to open the air vent above him and pulled his shirt away from his body so he could feel the air wash down his chest. "Anyone know any good jokes?"

Nothing.

He fiddled with his own screen to see about ordering some snacks.

"You said there was no Wi-Fi."

"Maisie, I'm looking at snacks. You don't need Wi-Fi for that. Would you like a snack? How about these veggie crisps?"

Out of nowhere, Grant screamed. The kind of deep, anguished, shrieking that wins Viola Davis Oscars, and then Maisie started in, too, more frightened by her brother than from any pain of her own. Patrick's heart wrenched.

"Okay, guys, guys, we don't have to eat veggie crisps. They're not really vegetables, just bullshit potato chips. But we can literally eat anything else." He tried to swivel the screen so they could see, but it only tilted up and down.

Grant's inconsolable screaming continued unabated, much of it straight out of a horror film. That it was so out of the blue made it as terrifying as it was physically painful to the eardrums; Patrick had no idea a child could make such a primal sound.

"Are you hurt? WHAT IS HAPPENING?" He looked over his shoulder several times for help but only to be met with angry passengers staring back at him, so he pulled his ball cap down farther over his eyes as sheer panic took hold.

"MY TOOF!" Grant covered his mouth in horror.

"Okay! Okay! Calm down." Not knowing what to do, he unbuckled all three of their seat belts, grabbed Grant's hand, and pulled him into the aisle. He took two steps toward the restroom with the boy in tow before realizing he forgot Maisie; he reached back until he found her hand, too. Patrick ran them toward the bathroom at the rear of the plane, ignoring the flight attendant near the exit rows calling after them.

"Sir! Sir! The fasten seat belt sign . . ."

He folded open the bathroom door with such force he was surprised he didn't shear it clean off its rails. He stood Grant on the closed toilet lid and yanked Maisie inside, closing the door behind them. It was tight; Maisie was pressed against his leg. He hugged Grant close and said, "What about your tooth?" and kept repeating it until Grant's wailing slowed to a whimper. He ran his hands through Grant's hair and pulled his face in for closer inspection.

"It fell out!"

"Oh, well. Teeth do that. Don't tell me this is your first." He squeezed Grant's mouth open and his lips puckered like a fish. Sure enough, a bottom tooth was missing—Patrick hoped it was a baby one. There was a little blood, but not much. "Maisie, grab a paper towel. And run it under some water."

Maisie did as she was told and Patrick made note of it. *Stays calm in emergencies*. Grant, however, continued to cry.

"Do you know why kids even have baby teeth? I've always wondered that. Why don't they just grow like the rest of your body? It's not like your childhood nose falls off when you're ready to grow a bigger one. Can you imagine if Grant's arm just fell off because his adult one was coming in?"

Grant stopped sobbing long enough to exclaim, "My arm's going to fall off?"

"And your ears. Hopefully not both at the same time or you won't be able to hear."

Grant screamed.

"WHAT WHAT WHAT? It's a joke. I'm just talking out loud. I was wondering because we're born with all of our teeth, baby and adult. Did you know that? A child's jaw holds twice as many teeth as it needs to. It's like how Maisie was born with all of her eggs inside of her."

"I have eggs inside me?" Maisie's eyes bulged.

"Yes," Patrick said. "Dozens of them. Like a chicken. You'll probably grow feathers. And a beak."

Maisie frowned, clearly not fond of this. "You're not supposed to talk to kids that way."

"I'm not?"

"No! You're supposed to comfort us. Don't you know that?"

"Okay, jeez." Patrick took the paper towel and placed the wet part along Grant's gums. Grant instinctively reached up to hold it in place. "Why all the tears, kiddo? You have to tell GUP. I don't understand."

"I . . . CAN'T . . . FIND IT!" He cried so hard he gurgled between words, and tears fell off of his nose. He tried desperately to fill his chest with air, but couldn't, and wheezed like a trauma patient whose lungs had collapsed.

So? Patrick's mind roared, or maybe it was the jet engines. They jostled back and forth in the lavatory, the three of them, protected by the confined space—wedged together, none of them had any room to fall. He wondered momentarily how he and Joe had ever joined the Mile High Club; he couldn't so much as turn around now. *Maybe planes used to be bigger?* The three of them stood there, until both kids quieted, until they were comforted by the rocking motion and the ambient hum. The lighting, however, was terrible. He gave Maisie a look, asking for help, then leaned against the sink so he could see both their faces.

"If he can't find his tooth, the tooth fairy won't come."

Patrick was almost relieved. This was a relatively easy one. "Says who?"

"Says everyone."

"That's nonsense."

Grant's tears slowed; he wiped his eyes with the back of his free hand. "How do you know?"

"Did I ever tell you that when your dad and I were kids we had an old beagle named Phillip? His teeth would fall out all the time. We'd find them just laying on the floor by the wood stove, where he liked to sleep. Your dad and I thought we could make some extra cash by putting Phillip's teeth under our pillows. We made a big production out of it, boasted about our new moneymaking scheme. You know what happened?"

Grant hesitated, and then asked, "What?"

"We each woke up with a Milk-Bone in our bed." Patrick elbowed Maisie. *See?* He could be comforting. "My point is, the tooth fairy knows everything. Okay? She doesn't miss a trick. When we go back to our row, I'm going to find your tooth. But even if I can't, she's definitely going to know that you lost one. Okay? I'll make sure of it."

"I want . . . *Mommy*."

And there it was. The tough one. Only a few hours in. Patrick wasn't going to get off with anything as easy as the tooth fairy. "I know, kid." And then he added, "We're going to get through this."

"How do you know?" Maisie was genuinely asking, each word syncopated like discordant jazz. "How do you know we're going to get through?"

Patrick thought long and hard about how he could make them understand, settling on a quote he had selected for his high school yearbook, one that became eerily prophetic. "'It's not the tragedies that kill us; it's the messes.' Dorothy Parker." As soon as this passed his lips he knew it was the wrong fit. Not because they wouldn't understand it or know who Dorothy Parker was—although they wouldn't and didn't—but rather because, what was this if not a mess? Sara's death was a tragedy, sure. But Greg's addiction was a mess, his asking Patrick to step in was a mess, his thinking Patrick would know how to handle a situation like this was a huge mess of epic proportions. So, he went straight for the truth. "I know what it's like to want someone back, too."

Grant, in a moment of reversion, removed the paper towel from his mouth and sucked on his thumb. His face was tear-streaked and somehow even his hair was wet.

"What if something happens to *you*?"

A pounding on the door startled them all and Patrick immediately banged three times back. "It's not going to, Maisie."

"How do you know?" Her voice had never sounded smaller or more frail.

"Sir?" It was the flight attendant. "Sir, open up!" She was clearly not there to ask if they wanted chateaubriand.

"In a minute!" he yelled angrily.

"GUP?" It was Grant now, needing an answer to his sister's question.

"Because I do." And then he added, "Because I'm not famous enough to die young." *How's that for the unvarnished truth?* "Here. Splash some water on your face. You'll feel better."

More pounding on the door.

"IN A GODDAMN MINUTE!" He looked Grant in the eye; he was still standing on the toilet. "Yeah, I thwore, tho what." He winked and Grant smiled.

He helped them wash their faces and dry their tears. Slowly he opened the door and ushered Maisie out before helping Grant jump down from his perch. Patrick looked at the frustrated flight attendant, who clearly did not earn enough to have to deal with the likes of them. She did not look like Dusty Springfield, she did not look like Petula Clark. She looked, in short, annoyed. "Sorry. Tooth emergency. We're headed back to our seats." Together, like a family of ducks, they waddled back to their row, Patrick's blood pressure slowly returning to normal.

"Here," Patrick said when they were situated in their seats. "Let's look at my phone." He pulled his credit card out of his wallet.

"But the Wi-Fi . . ."

"They fixed it. Didn't you hear? There was an announcement when we were in the bathroom." He mussed Grant's hair and smiled as he handed over his phone. "Why don't you show me what's so great about YouTube. Just don't . . . Guncle Rule number five: If a gay man hands you his phone, look only at what he's showing you. If it's a photo, don't swipe. And for god's sake, don't open any unfamiliar apps."

FIVE

The scream pierced the darkness and Patrick sat bolt upright. *Jesus Christ. Again?!* He had just drifted off to sleep in his own bed—*finally*—and was going to have to reason with these monsters that it was possible, preferable even, to grieve without causing one's own ears, or (more to the point) someone else's, to bleed. He jumped out of bed and ran smack into his bedroom door, forgetting he was still wearing his skin-rejuvenating, silk charmeuse weighted sleep mask. His own scream was deeper, annoyed, and mercifully brief.

He pushed the mask up his forehead. It took a few seconds for his eyes to adjust and confirm that, yes, after two weeks he was finally back in his own room. Yes, the air had just kicked on. Yes, the door was where it was supposed to be. No, this was not the dreadful hotel by his brother's house. No, the noise was not drunken gamblers stumbling off the bus after a day at Mohegan Sun. He stepped out in the hall to find the source of the ruckus. Thankfully he'd had the foresight to sleep in gym shorts instead of his preference for, well, *less*. "Maisie? Maisie is that you?"

It wasn't Maisie, but Grant, shaking in the hall outside the guest bath.

"What is it? Your mom? Your dad? Another tooth? What happened?" Patrick crouched down to put his arm around his nephew's shoulders. He followed the boy's gaze into the bathroom. "Do you need to use the potty again?" They had been through this once before bed. Grant said he usually had help "wiping" and Patrick stood back aghast; it was something Patrick didn't even do for himself since he installed two eleven-thousand-dollar Japanese toilets (sorry, *washlets*) he'd read about in *Consumer Reports*.

"The toilet . . . *moved*."

"What do you mean it moved?" He didn't have the clearest view from his vantage point, but it seemed to be exactly in the place that it should be.

"The lid." Grant finally mustered the courage to look at his uncle. "There's a ghost."

Up until now, their first night had mostly been a success. The kids were enamored with the house ("You have a hot tub?!") and made themselves more or less at home. There was some awkwardness with their bedtime routine. Maisie thankfully showered herself, but Grant insisted on a bath, while bemoaning the lack of bath toys (the pool noodles Patrick had were too large for the tub), and there was a small meltdown about their uncle's baking soda toothpaste being too paste-y. (He argued that children's toothpastes with their bright colors and bold flavors probably *caused* cavities, but relented, saying he would buy one specifically labeled for kids.) Maisie and Grant agreed to share a guest room, at least to start, and Patrick laid in the king-sized bed with them, improvising an elaborate story about a roadrunner and a jackrabbit named Meep and Moop and their adventures in the desert. The kids complained about the metal sculpture that hung over the bed; it was too angular and Grant feigned a fear of rectangles. Neither of them knew their sleep numbers, laying waste to the guest mattress's smartest feature, but eventually, exhausted from the day, they all nodded off. At some point before midnight Patrick awoke and extracted himself, even though he was surprised to find sharing was not horrifically unpleasant.

"Oh, no, no, no, Grant. It does that. The toilet. When you get close to it, the lid rises automatically. That's what it does. It's called a feature. You pay extra for those."

"But there was a light inside." Grant leaned in to whisper in his uncle's ear. "*Glowing.*" He was clinging to his conviction that there was some otherworldly presence at play.

"A night-light. Isn't that great? So if you have to use the bathroom in the night, you don't have to blind yourself with the overhead light."

"It'th not from another dimenthion?"

Dimension? Where do they learn these things? "No. Well, *yes*. But only Japan." Patrick ran his fingers through the boy's hair. "Where's your sister? I suppose she's awake, too?"

Maisie's face appeared around the door, like she was one of the von Trapp children in a thunderstorm. Patrick bit his lip. God help him if he had to do a verse of "My Favorite Things."

"Come here. I want to show you everything that my new washlet can do."

Maisie crept forward in her cat pajamas. "What's a washlet?"

"Well, it's like a toilet. But better."

"How do you know it's better?"

"Because it's Japanese and it cost more than my first car. Look, watch what it does." Patrick stood up and approached the washlet. When he got close enough to trigger the sensor, the lid softly rose.

Maisie said, "Whoa," while Grant still looked on with skepticism.

"And that's not all. Check this out." Patrick opened the drawer to the high-gloss floating sink cabinet and produced a remote control. The toilet lid lowered itself.

"Is that for the toilet?" Maisie asked.

"No, it's for the *washlet*."

"What's the difference?"

"Well, if I have to explain it to you!" Patrick threw his arms up, exasperated. "First, there's the sleek, porcelain design. Have you ever seen anything like it?"

"It looks like you keep dinosaur eggs inside," Grant observed. And it strangely made sense.

"Yeah. Isn't it great? It has ionized water, a UV light, music speakers, a heated seat, the aforementioned night-light to guide your way in the dark, and a twelve-setting wash and dry feature with"—he waved the remote in his hand to end with a flourish—"remote control. *Ta-daa!*" Maybe he could rewrite the song with his own favorite things. He sang to himself: *Ionized water in remote-sensored washlets.*

"It does laundry?" Maisie was confused.

"What? No. That's disgusting."

"But you said washer and dryer."

"Wash and dry *feature*," Patrick corrected.

"What does it wash and dry?"

"YOU! Isn't that fantastic?"

"I don't understand."

"What's not to understand?" He handed Maisie the remote so that she could see it and Grant nuzzled into her side to get a good look himself. The remote was covered in illustrated buttons; some, including one with an aggressive swirl that looked like a symbol the Weather Channel might employ for a Category 5 hurricane, Patrick hadn't yet dare try. "Well, truth be told, I don't understand *all* of it. That button right there looks needlessly hostile, and I think I read in the manual that this other one is for 'front cleaning,' and I don't think that applies to boys. But you can give it a whirl and report back."

"I have to pee."

Patrick looked down at his nephew, who was holding his crotch. Of course. This whole midnight powwow was precipitated by something.

"Step right up, boy!" he said, summoning his best carnival barker, a sort of Pee Pee Barnum.

"Will you wait right here?" All this explanation and the boy was still scared. Patrick vowed to show him the issue of *Consumer Reports* so Grant could become more acquainted.

"Of course."

Grant stepped into the bathroom, freezing in his tracks when the lid rose by itself.

"Go on! That's its way of welcoming you."

Patrick and Maisie turned away to give Grant his privacy.

"I still don't understand how it washes you," she grumbled.

"Oh. It has a retractable cleansing wand. That's what the remote is for. When you're done, you know, it squirts you with clean water and you can select the temperature and the pressure."

"Squirts you . . . *where*?"

Patrick rubbed his temples, but Grant thankfully interrupted. "How do you flush it?"

"I got it, bud!" He leaned down, hovered his finger over the remote control until he found the right button, and said to Maisie, "Press that one," and she did.

"Coooooool!" Grant said, his face over the bowl. "It'th lighting up again!" Patrick guessed he was over his fear of ghosts.

Maisie however was not as easily distracted. She still looked up at her uncle for an answer to her question.

"Where? *You* know. You're going to make me say it? Your *undercarriage*." Patrick felt like he was losing her. "Here, give me that." He reached out and took the remote control and stepped into the bathroom. "Grant. Want to see something else really cool? Put your face over the bowl." Patrick glanced over his shoulder to make sure Maisie was watching.

"What am I looking for?" Grant asked.

"Watch." Patrick pressed one of the buttons and the cleansing wand slowly extended.

"What's that?" he asked.

"What does it look like?"

"It looks like a robot." Grant was transfixed.

"Keep looking." Patrick studied the remote until he found another button to press and the wand spritzed water, squirting Grant in the face.

Grant screamed. And just as Patrick had hoped, Maisie laughed.

"You spwayed me!"

"Here, kid." Patrick tossed Grant a hand towel and it landed right on his face.

"That's tho gross!" He reached up, wiping the towel back and forth across his face.

"It's clean water. It doesn't come from the toilet. It comes from the wall. Just like the sink faucet."

Grant pulled the towel off his head to consider this. His hair stood in a gratifying swoop. Slowly, a smile crept across his face. "Do Maisie! Do Maisie!"

Patrick expected an immediate protest but instead Maisie agreed it was a delightful idea. "Yeah, do me, do me!"

"Suit yourself, stand over the—" He didn't even have to finish; Maisie's head was already in position over the bowl and so he gave the button a good, long push. Maisie screamed as the water hit her right in the kisser and Grant squealed with rapturous delight. He hadn't heard such laughter out of anyone in, he couldn't recall. A long time. Once, when he first held Maisie (she was maybe three months old), she burst out laughing. He didn't even know babies could do that—laugh—and even though he felt awkward holding her with all eyes in the room on him, he couldn't help but feel overwhelmed by this new bit of information.

"Now you! Now you!" Grant screamed, pointing at his uncle.

"Oh, no. There are enough nighttime serums and potions on this face to stock a Bergdorf Goodman beauty counter, so you don't want to get it wet."

"GUP!" Maisie protested, pronouncing his name with, like, seven *u*'s.

"Oh, all right, but just once." He leaned forward only so far before activating the water. He'd done enough in the way of stage combat in college to act like he'd been hit in the face with a geyser, while missing the brunt of the stream. He threw his arm over his face as he retreated, spinning into the towel rack. The kids laughed and laughed and then he, too, broke down in fits of uncontrollable giggles. It was so stupid, but it was a release, a ray of sunshine bursting through the dark cloud they'd been under.

"My turn!" Grant roared, and he stepped forward and bowed over the washlet.

Patrick rolled his eyes. "Guncle Rule number six." Just as Grant turned his neck to look up at his uncle, Patrick let fly with a jet of water, hitting him right in the ear. Grant squealed again, equal parts shock and glee. "Never let your guard down!"

"Me! Me! Me!" Maisie jumped up and down, begging for another go.

"Well, okay, but there is a drought. So let's not go crazy." But as Maisie stood freshly soaked, wiping water out of her eyes, Patrick realized washlet humor was a kind of toilet humor he could get behind.

When Patrick marched the kids back to their bedroom, Grant tugged on his shorts. "Uncle Patrick? The tooth fairy hasn't come yet."

The tooth fairy. Patrick had forgotten. He was now grateful for this middle-of-the-night interruption, imagining the epic morning meltdown that was in store if the tooth fairy failed to make her rounds.

"Aren't you supposed to be asleep for her to come?"

"Yes," Maisie answered before Grant had the chance to.

"Are you asleep now?"

"No," Grant mumbled, admitting defeat.

"Well, then. I suggest you hop to it." Patrick tucked them in before summoning his inner fairy and scouring the house for loot.

SIX

Maisie swiveled on a barstool as Patrick stood across the counter from her, waving a spatula. "What's the matter? You haven't touched your pancakes." The seats were made of seafoam upholstery with a low walnut back floating on top of pneumatic height-adjusting chrome stands, a jackpot find from a local thrift store. Maisie languidly kicked her feet against them as if they were from Ikea and somehow deserved her scuff marks and replied with only a yawn.

It was almost two in the morning when they finally conked out, allowing Patrick to slide the tooth fairy's offerings under Grant's pillow, so he could sympathize with Maisie's exhaustion if not her apparent lack of appetite. It was rare his modern kitchen was used for anything close to food preparation on one of Rosa's days off (unless coffee, protein shakes, or cocktails counted as food); this should be an event. He even, for the first time, used the griddle that sat atop the duel-fuel, JennAir self-venting stove he was forced into purchasing when it became clear a hood would interrupt the flow of the open kitchen.

"You don't eat breakfast? Are you doing intermittent fasting?"

"I don't know what that is," Maisie replied.

"Really? Everyone's doing intermittent fasting it seems. What's the problem, then?"

"Mom made our pancakes look like Mickey Mouse."

Patrick shook his finger. "We're not doing that." *Goddammit, Sara.*

"She came! She came!" Grant tore around the corner holding Patrick's Golden Globe statue. He hopped up on the barstool next to his sister and plunked his prize down on the counter. "What is it?"

Patrick was horrified. "MY GOLDEN GLOBE?!"

"The tooth fairy left it for me."

"Like hell she did!"

After the kids had gone back to bed, Patrick poured himself a nightcap while he waited for them to fall asleep. He remembered struggling with what to leave on the tooth fairy's behalf. He might have even had a second drink, but there was absolutely no way, short of him being roofied, that he put his Golden Globe under Grant's pillow.

"That's mine. It has my name on it. 'Patrick O'Hara, Best Supporting Actor—Series, Miniseries, or Television Film.'"

"Tho?" Grant's eyes were on this prize and he wasn't easing up.

"*So*? Is your name Patrick O'Hara? No, it is not. Have you been in a series, miniseries, or television film? No, you have not. You took that off my shelf and you know it." He pried the statue from his nephew's hands before the boy could get anymore of his sticky fingerprints on it. "If this house catches fire I'm saving this before either of you. You do not touch it. Understand?"

Grant bobbed his head up and down.

"Now, let's go see what the tooth fairy actually left you." He took Grant by the hand and marched him back to his bedroom with Maisie tagging along behind. He pulled something from underneath his nephew's pillow and handed it to him feigning surprise, as if the reward had not come from his personal collection. "It's a *Playbill* from the 2012 Broadway revival of *Porgy and Bess*. SCORE!"

Grant flipped through the program's pages. "Where's the money?"

"It's better than money. It's signed by Audra McDonald."

The kids stood silent, the *who*? heavily implied.

"Six-time Tony winner Audra McDonald?"

"What'th a Tony?"

"Oh my god. You're from Connecticut, so I can understand your not knowing what a Golden Globe is. But a Tony Award? You live right next door to New York!"

Maisie chimed in, a public defender taking on Grant's case. "The tooth fairy is supposed to leave money so that kids can buy toys."

On some level, Patrick knew this, but he didn't keep cash in the house. He had found a few pennies in a junk drawer and some loose change Rosa had collected from his pockets near the washing machine, but knew last night that wouldn't be nearly enough. "It's different in California."

"Why?"

"Because sometimes the tooth fairy runs out of cash after visiting the East Coast kids, and by the time she gets to the West Coast she has to leave prizes. Look, if you're not happy with it, I'll buy it from you. How does fifty dollars sound?"

Maisie's jaw almost hit the floor. "Fifty dollars!"

Patrick was confused. Was that not enough? "Well, how much is fair?"

"I used to get one dollar."

"Fine. One dollar, one dollar!" Patrick yelled on his way back to the kitchen, like a game show contestant when everyone else had overbid.

"No, fifty!" Grant knew a good deal when he heard one.

"Fine, but you have to share it with your sister." The kids hopped back up on their stools and Patrick slid Grant's plate in front of him in exchange for the *Playbill* so they wouldn't get syrup on Porgy.

Grant picked up a fork skeptically. "Mom used to make them like Mickey Mouse."

Patrick rolled his eyes. "So I heard. Look, you don't want to eat ears. Even pancake ones. They're filled with wax and, I don't know . . ." He thought back to what his own father used to say. "Potato bugs." It was day two of this misadventure and he was already resorting to dad jokes.

Grant laughed, and Patrick squeezed some extra syrup on his plate as a reward.

"Further, Disney owns everything. They don't need to own brunch, too."

"Why is this brunch and not breakfast?" Grant asked.

"Because I cooked for you hellions, so it's an occasion."

Maisie lifted the pancake off her plate just enough to peer underneath it. "What do you mean, they own everything?" She seemed very uncertain about her food, even though Patrick was impressed with the pancake's even pecan color. "What do they own?"

"*What do they own?*" Patrick repeated incredulously. "Pixar. Marvel. Lucasfilm, 20th Century Fox, ESPN, the Disney Store, Disney Channel, Disney World, Disneyland, Disney Plus, Disney Cruise Line, Disney on Ice, the El Capitan Theatre, Disney Theatricals, the Netherlands probably, you name it they own it. They used to own me, if you can believe that."

"What are you even talking about?"

"My show was on ABC. Don't you guys read *Variety*?"

"No, we're kids." Maisie finally decided her pancake was safe enough to try, and she sectioned off a small bite.

"What do you read, then?"

"Kid thtuff." Grant's speech impediment seemed exacerbated by maple syrup, as if Mrs. Butterworth herself had stapled his tongue to the roof of his mouth.

"Kid stuff. Hmm. Well, so you know, they had me locked in a pretty airtight contract, turning tricks for the mouse. Which isn't to say my people didn't renegotiate as soon as I had even a modicum of leverage." Patrick rested his hand on the Golden Globe as evidence. "But still."

"Who are your people?"

"Who are my *people*? Well, I got rid of them all. CAA. ICM. WME. SAG. Triple A. Anything with three letters. It's all bullsh—*crap*. Why? Who are your people?"

"We don't have people."

"You don't have people?! Well, you have me. And that's not nothing. Anyhow. Actors are products to the entertainment industry; it's dehumanizing. They chew you up and spit you out. And that sort of thing sticks with a person." Patrick looked out the window in time to see his neighbor Dwayne, the *D* in JED, walking their dog, Lorna. He waved and Dwayne looked up in time to wave back. "We could do pancakes in the shape of something else. Daffy Duck, perhaps. I've always had a favorable opinion of Warner Brothers. I've never done a Warner picture, so that's probably why." Patrick used to enjoy amusing himself by pretending he was an actor under the old studio system, spoon-fed amphetamines to keep him tap-dancing for days; these jokes were probably lost on the kids. Fortunately, the extra syrup had done the trick. Grant swirled his last bite of pancake around his plate in the most elegant pattern, like his fork was Michelle Kwan in Edmonton, 1996.

"Can you do *Paw Patrol*?" Grant asked.

"*Paw Patrol* Pancakes?" Patrick took a long sip of his coffee. "I like the alliteration. What's *Paw Patrol*?"

"They're search and rescue dogs," Maisie explained.

Patrick glanced over at his phone. "Hey, Siri, what's *Paw Patrol*?"

"I found the following results for prawn petrol."

"Oh, for god's sake." Patrick reached for his phone, knocking the wooden spoon resting across the bowl of pancake batter onto the floor. He looked down; it would be easy enough to wipe up off the terrazzo floors.

"Aren't you going to get that?"

"It's fine. Just remind me to clean it up so Rosa doesn't have to."

"Who's Rosa?"

"Oh, you'll love Rosa. She comes on Mondays, Wednesdays, and Fridays. She'll make us a real brunch. Do you like chilaquiles?" The kids didn't know how to answer. Patrick unlocked his phone and typed *Paw Patrol* into Google and scrolled through the results. "Produced in association with TVOntario, which is owned by the government of Canada.

Good one, Grant!" He gave his nephew a high five. "Canada is harmless and the prime minister is a total snack, so we can do *Paw Patrol.* But another time, because we have to move beyond brunch and start planning our day. What are you guys thinking, do you have anything on your calendars?"

"We don't have calendars, either," Maisie said, annoyed.

"No people, no calendars. How do you keep track of your meetings, appointments? Do you have assistants at least?" Patrick threw her a smirk.

"No."

"Well, neither do I. Not anymore. Just Rosa on every other weekday." Since he was mostly pulling their legs, Patrick didn't go into detail about how he preferred it that way. That assistants and agents and publicists often created just as much work as they fielded. (One of his past assistants had reorganized his closet unannounced and sent a shirt that had belonged to Joe to dry cleaning. Patrick had to race across town and beg them to give it back uncleaned; it had long since lost Joe's scent, but that was not the point.) Instead, he picked up his phone and pretended to open his calendar app. "Well, look at that. I have a light day, too. So . . . what should we do? What do you guys do with your friends?"

"What do you do with *your* friends?"

Patrick grew wistful. It had been a long time since he had spent any time with his friends. "We drink rosé and talk about Best Actress Oscar winners. Is that what *you* do?"

"No." Maisie drew her chin into her neck until it all but disappeared.

"Not even with Audra Brackett? It's fun. Like, who is your favorite Best Actress winner?"

"I don't know." Grant shrugged comically, as if he should actually have an opinion.

"Well, that's a bit of a trick question, because there's really only one correct answer and that's Faye Dunaway, 1976."

"That's before we were born," Maisie protested.

"That's before *I* was born, but I still know this stuff!" Patrick paused, doing a quick calculation in his head to see if that was a lie. "I would also accept Isabelle Huppert, 2016, even though they awarded her Oscar to Emma Stone."

Grant rested his head on the counter as if he were terminally bored. "We want to *do* something."

"What do you want to do?"

"I don't know, what is there to do?"

"You guys visited once before. You don't remember what there is to do?"

"I was just a baby!" Grant protested.

"Dinosaurs!" Maisie bounced up and down on her stool with excitement. Patrick had taken them to see the Cabazon dinosaurs featured in the movie *Pee-wee's Big Adventure*. Together they looked at the giant T. rex and brontosaurus sculptures and dug in warm sand for "fossils" (fake bones you could trade in for prizes). The wind had caused the sand to kick up in their faces, but there was a water table where you could "mine" for gold, and it was there Patrick learned how much kids responded to water. Whatever the activity (washlet spritzing, for instance), the wetter the better.

"I was thinking something closer to home. Maybe we could swim in the pool and then this afternoon we could play a game?"

"POOL!" Grant hollered.

"You can each pick a pool float and I'll inflate them while you dip yourselves in sunscreen. I've got a flamingo, a unicorn, a Jeff Koons balloon dog, a slice of pizza. A diamond ring, but that's meant to be ironic."

"Why do you have tho many?"

"For you guys, silly. Also, companies just send me this garbage because I have a pool and a lot of Instagram followers. I even have a lobster your mother gave me one time. A New England thing, I guess. To remind me of my roots. But that's more Maine than Connecticut."

"Can I put my face in the water?" Grant asked.

"If you don't, I'll put it in for you."

"Can we bring the toilet?"

"*What*? No. Why? Pee in the bushes like a normal person."

"To squirt each other with."

"Are you crazy? It's attached to the floor with a wax seal. But we'll get Super Soakers or something later and you can squirt each other to your heart's content. Until then, we'll use the hose."

Grant grinned wide, all teeth (minus one) and gums.

"Just put your plate in the sink."

Grant jumped down from his barstool, collected his plate, and gave his uncle a big hug. "Thanks, GUP."

"It's settled, then," Patrick said, making a mental note of Maisie's nonreaction to it all. "And don't get syrup on me."

"Where's your sister?" Patrick asked as he and Grant stood in their swimsuits, towels flung over their shoulders. Grant had streaks of sunscreen down his arms and across his face as Patrick tried his best to cover him in the lotion Greg had packed in their suitcase. The sunscreen was specifically designed for kids (it had a blue lizard on the bottle), but was total garbage as far as he could tell because it was impossible to rub in—Grant's arms looked as if they'd been painted like fence pickets. And if that weren't awful enough, the kid wore these green goggles tightly around his face, making him look like an albino gecko.

"She doesn't want to thwim."

"What do you mean she doesn't want to swim? She loves swimming. On your last visit, we had to drag her out of the pool just to—*What is wrong with this lotion?*"

"What do you mean?"

"I should not have to touch you this much. It seems inappropriate."

"Why?"

"Nothing. Just . . . nothing." Patrick gave up on the chore and took to rubbing the last bit of lotion off his hands onto his towel. "Maybe we'll just stay inside for the rest of the summer."

Grant looked skeptically at his uncle.

"What?"

"You have a lot of muscles."

"Thank you. One day I'll tell you about gay men and body dysmorphia, but not today."

Grant shrugged. "Can just we go?" He tugged on Patrick's Mr. Turk swimsuit.

"Where'd you get those goggles? Your father packed those, too?"

Grant nodded.

"Just, hold your horses."

"I don't have any horthes."

"Then practice holding your breath."

Grant took a huge gulp of air and clamped his mouth shut. Patrick paused. *He'll know to take a breath before he passes out, right?* He held his face up to his nephew's and could see the boy was clearly breathing out of his nose. *Ridiculous.* He exited and headed toward the room the kids had claimed as theirs.

Maisie was sitting on the edge of the guest bed, looking tiny, meek, staring down at her bare feet, which didn't quite touch the floor. Their suitcases were open, but not unpacked; Patrick said they could wait and see if they still enjoyed sharing a room before they fully settled in.

"What gives?"

She kicked her feet against the edge of the bed, not angry, but clearly frustrated. "I don't want to go swimming."

"Of course you do, put your suit on."

She didn't respond. Didn't even so much as look up. Patrick kept his attention focused on her, but she wasn't going to budge. What was wrong with these kids? He had a swimming pool, for Christ's sake. It's not like Connecticut was littered with them. Wasn't this a big deal? Eventually he threw his hands up and retreated back to the living room to find Grant. "What's her problem?"

"She doesn't like the thwimsuit Daddy packed for her," Grant said.

"What, she wants me to buy her a new one? Is that how this summer is going to go? You guys are going to shake me down for stuff?" Patrick stroked his chin as that sank in. "Because, I've got to hand it to you. As plans go, that's pretty smart and I'm an easy mark."

"It's a thecret."

"*See*-cret," Patrick emphasized. "What's a secret?"

"She doesn't want me to thay."

"Did she tell you snitches get stitches? Because that only applies in prison." He looked down at Grant, who didn't follow. A new tactic was required. "Is she into something else now? Books? Puzzles? The sport Lacrosse? It would help us get outside a lot faster if you told me."

Grant looked up at his uncle and then, after careful consideration, motioned for him to come closer (the promise of swimming trumped his short-lived gig as confidant). Patrick leaned down and Grant whispered the secret in his ear. He furrowed his brow, confused, but only momentarily; what Grant had to say sunk in quickly. When Patrick realized how gracefully Sara had handled the situation, it made him miss her even more. He looked heavenward. "You really were cut out for this; I never was."

"What?" Grant asked, confused.

"Nothing. Got it." He rested his hand on his nephew's head. "Thank you for telling me. Give me two more minutes, bud. Then we're headed out to the pool."

Grant looked down at his arms like he was growing paler by the second and didn't have two minutes to spare.

Patrick rounded the corner to the back bedroom to find Maisie in the same spot. "Follow me." He motioned for her with his hand, and then turned and exited, assuming correctly she would fall in line. They marched back through the living room toward the master suite on the other side of the house, Maisie five steps behind. In his bedroom, Patrick opened his sliding closet doors and pushed a few of his shirts on wooden hangers aside, then waited for Maisie to get a good look. "See these? These are my caftans. This is my morning caftan, this one is my after-sun caftan, this one here is for company, this one is dressy, and this one is the one I sometimes wear after a night swim—right before bed. Do you know what some people would call these?"

Maisie stared at them in awe. They were every color all at once, loud paisleys and tribal designs; some looked like spin art she had once done at school. "Dresses?"

"That's right. Are they? No. Well. *Maybe*. But I don't care. Because they're fun, and they make me feel good, and I like wearing them. When the temperature swells over one hundred, you don't want anything tight touching your skin." Patrick pulled his after-sun caftan off the hanger, a rich midnight blue with a loud yellow and magenta paisley pattern, and pulled it on over his head. "This is the best thing to wear for today, you understand." Patrick affected an old-money New England accent. "Because I don't like women in skirts and the best thing is to wear pantyhose or some pants under a short skirt, I think. Then you have the pants under the skirt and you can pull the stockings up over the pants underneath the skirt. And you can always take off the skirt and use it as a cape. So I think this is the best costume for today."

When he finished, Maisie looked at him like he had two heads.

"That's Little Edie's speech from *Grey Gardens*. You don't know that, either? It's on YouTube, you know. Joe and I used to perform that over and over for each other." Patrick bit his lip, lost in the memory. They would put on the most ridiculous things and march through the house waving small flags.

"Who's Joe?"

Patrick froze. How had he let that name slip so easily? "He was a friend of mine, a long time ago." He moved past it as quickly as he could. "Guncle Rule number seven: In this house we wear what we want, it doesn't matter if it's for boys or girls. Anything goes, anything you want, so long as it doesn't have mean words printed on it and it's not making fun of anyone else. We don't worry about what others think. Deal?"

"Deal," Maisie agreed.

"Now, what would *you* like to wear to swim?"

Maisie touched the caftan's fabric, rubbing it between her fingers. It was soft, rayon or something, not fancy (Patrick's lesson on quality things would wait for another day). It took her a moment to gather the courage to say, "I don't like girls' bathing suits."

"And your mom knew that, so she let you wear shorts and a T-shirt? But your dad wasn't thinking and packed an old swimsuit of yours that you no longer like to wear? I promise you it was just a simple oversight. Go find something to swim in for today, and tomorrow we'll go to the store and get you proper swim attire. That *you* like. A rash guard shirt, with long sleeves maybe, that would help protect you against the sun."

A smile spread across Maisie's face. "I know just the T-shirt."

"Then that is the best costume for today."

Maisie threw her arms around her uncle, gathering the fabric around his waist.

"Okay, well, don't wrinkle it. It's fashion." He took her hand and walked her back to find Grant.

"You're wearing a *dreth*." Even through his goggles he could see that clear as day.

"You want one?" Patrick offered. He was even willing to cut one short for him.

"No." Grant flinched.

Patrick tapped Maisie on the shoulder and gave her a little nudge in the direction of her bedroom. She scampered away to change, leaving Patrick and Grant alone. After a moment of awkward silence, Patrick offered, "This is a caftan, not a dress."

"I'm pretty sure it's a dreth."

"It's a caftan! Do you know who Mrs. Roper is? She's basically my fashion icon."

Grant shook his head.

"From *Three's Company*? Jack? Chrissy? Janet? SUZANNE SOMERS? Let me guess. You don't like television, only YouTube. Jesus, you kids are missing everything."

SEVEN

Patrick didn't have to knock on JED's door; Lorna the Labrador started barking the moment he stepped onto their circular drive. Eduardo, the *E* in their moniker, answered the door wearing some sort of pink wrap that resembled a miniskirt and not much else; it looked downright neon against his beautiful, tanned skin.

"Patrick, mi vecino, my amigo."

Patrick leaned in for a hug, but not too tight; he didn't want to crush the intricate dream catcher necklace Eduardo was sporting.

"How was the trip, you poor thing? Come in, let me make you a drink." He waved Patrick inside, careful not to let Lorna escape. Of the three of them, Eduardo was the most physically fit, and while Patrick was unclear on his age, he suspected by JED's arrangement that he was older than the late-thirties he looked; it seemed, at least to Patrick, that a throuple was not the sort of something you enter when life still felt full of possibility. But honestly, what did he know?

"Is that Patrick?" John emerged from the living room dressed in a more conventional costume, shorts and a tank top with a pineapple design; the two of them side by side would be a lesson for Maisie in wearing what makes you comfortable. "We were planning our burn. You just have to come with us this year."

"Your *what*?"

"Our burn. Burning Man?"

"*Burning Man*." Patrick acted as if it should have been obvious. "As much as I would love to," he added as Lorna planted her face in his crotch. He leaned down to massage her behind the ears. "Scratch that. I would not love to. I'm not cleaning sand out of intimate places well into autumn." His washlet, even with its mystery hurricane button, would be no match for a week in the windy Nevadan desert. "Besides, I came back from my trip with a bit of a surprise."

"Syphilis?" John asked while twisting one end of his handlebar mustache. "Half the people on the playa have *something*. I'm sure it will be gone before then."

Eduardo moved into the kitchen off the hallway to fix Patrick's drink. "I was going to make Patrick a drink; I'll make a round for everyone. Dwayne!"

Patrick continued. "No, not syphilis." *Good lord*. "My niece and nephew, Maisie and Grant."

"Oh, those poor children," John said as Dwayne materialized in the doorway in hospital scrubs, presumably having just come from work (Patrick hoped; nurses presumably shouldn't drink before they start their shift). JED was now fully present and accounted for.

"Those poor children?" Dwayne asked. "Patrick's not *that* awful. I'm sure they'll have a fine time on their visit." He winked in Patrick's direction.

John pressed his forehead against the palm of his hand in frustration. "Their mother just died? The whole reason Patrick went home? We got his mail?" He looked at Patrick apologetically. "We have your mail."

Patrick often wondered how their needs were ever met in this arrangement. Any divisions in a threesome, like with his siblings, were usually two against one. It would be difficult, he imagined, to be in a relationship like this, and also the slightest bit emotionally frail. It was one of the reasons he admired them.

"Why I'm here," Patrick said, and flipped through the stack of his mail on the entry table. He hadn't missed much if the top few envelopes—bills mostly, and a few solicitations for money—were any indication.

"Oh, but stay. Can you stay?" Dwayne asked.

"We're very sorry," John said, placing a hand on Patrick's shoulder.

He couldn't deny the air-conditioning felt good (a few degrees colder than he kept his own house), and while he had his issues with JED, it was already a refreshing change of pace to be around adults. Kids had so many questions. All the time. "For a few minutes."

Eduardo shouted from the kitchen, "I'm making Aperol spritzes!" Patrick heard it in Grant's voice—*spwitzes*—and smiled.

"The kids are with my housekeeper. I left them looking at videos on my iPad. Can you believe it? I have a sixty-five-inch television and they have no interest in watching it."

"They're not size queens like you," John teased.

"Oh, leave them be," Dwayne fussed. "I can't imagine what they're going through. Is your brother here, too?"

"Greg? He's in Rancho Mirage."

"He's not staying with you?"

"Are you ready for this? He's in rehab."

"Rehab!" they chorused. Even Eduardo peered around the corner, his necklace clinking against the hutch. They had a tendency to do this, chime in together. It reminded Patrick of the Bobbsey Twins, books of his parents he read when he was young in which two sets of twins would always exclaim things in unison. He always thought that read remarkably false—that couldn't actually happen with twins, could it?—but now he had a newfound appreciation.

"For what?" John asked.

"Pills. Since Sara's diagnosis. Apparently, it's how he made it through."

"Pills? Come, come," John motioned, beckoning him into the living room. Patrick looked at the décor; there wasn't a knickknack or piece of folk art they didn't love. On the side table was a collection of African carvings in varying sizes of warriors with huge, erect penises, and the house was full of macramé.

Patrick settled in the drab olive-green lounger covered in crushed velvet that he'd silently dubbed the Ike Turner Chair, then kicked off his sandals before resting his feet on an ottoman. "The whole family was shocked. We had no idea."

Eduardo joined them in the living room with a tray of drinks, handing one to Patrick before John and Dwayne reached for the others. "John was an addict once."

"Cocaine," John admitted. "But I don't think it was addiction so much as the seventies."

"We only let him have the occasional drink."

"That's right, only four or five a day. Tops." He winked.

"What was your sister-in-law's name again?" Dwayne asked, taking a seat across from Patrick.

"She was more than my sister-in-law," Patrick said, before realizing he didn't want to share more. "Sara."

Dwayne raised his glass. "To Sara."

"To Sara." In this instance, the unanimous chorus was endearingly authentic; still, Patrick bristled. Once again, more people stepping in to mourn her, when he selfishly wanted her all to himself.

"How wonderful to have the children, though. Not the circumstances, but to have this time with them."

Patrick realized he must have made a sour face when he looked up from his glass and saw JED staring at him from the other three corners of the room.

"You never wanted children?" Eduardo asked.

"No, of course not." Patrick took another sip of his cocktail. "*Did you?*"

"Oh, yes," John said. "Because of my niece, in fact. We were driving one time on the highway. I don't even remember where we were going. But we passed a big truck filled with chickens in wire coops, and white feathers rained down on us like snow. She watched tiny clouds of feathers float around us and then she asked, 'Uncle JoJo?' She called me JoJo. 'Does that hurt the chickens?' *How marvelous*, I thought. We were having this strangely beautiful moment, and she wanted to know if the wind was hurting the chickens."

"I love this story," Dwayne said, as if they sat around and told it every night.

"I just remember thinking, children's souls are so gentle. I wanted to be around that all the time."

Patrick smiled. "This morning Grant asked me what was inside an eel. He had this image of shucking one to see what he would find."

"Well, that's just boys," Eduardo said, and the others agreed.

"I wasn't like that." Patrick chuckled, remembering as a child only caring to know what was inside Julie Andrews that allowed her to hit those high notes. He raised an eyebrow. "You all feel this way?"

John nodded and Dwayne said, "We do."

"Then why not have kids?"

"Oh, sweet Patrick," John chided. "You've been in the desert too long."

"What is that supposed to mean?"

John pursed his lips and his sharp cheekbones became even more pronounced. "It's not exactly a traditional arrangement we have."

"So? This is California."

"It doesn't matter. No one's going to give us a kid. No agency is going to work with us."

"But you would be such good parents!" Patrick pulled a coaster from a stack; he looked at it twice before recognition set in. It featured the X-ray image of a man receiving oral sex. "Maybe after a little baby-proofing."

"That's very sweet of you to say. Still."

"The world is changing, but not that quickly," Dwayne added.

"Well, two of you could adopt formally, and then all three raise the kid."

Eduardo sighed. "Alas, we're like the Musketeers. All for one and one for all."

"Eduardo actually has a child. A son, in Mexico. But he's not allowed to see him." John moved a potted fern away from his chair and into the light.

"You're kidding. That's so unfair!" Patrick didn't know if this was some family or immigration issue and didn't want to pry about anything as personal as Eduardo's citizenship status; they were friends only to a point. And it's not like he was employing Eduardo to get his mail—he had volunteered. On top of that, despite his remarkable successes in life, Patrick knew about as well as anyone that life was unfair; he didn't need it explained to him.

"Them's the breaks." Dwayne shrugged. Eduardo looked at the floor.

"There must be something," Patrick started, then stopped. Who was he to tell JED they hadn't thought this through or exhausted every avenue. These things—adoption, egg donors, surrogacy—were very expensive and he was sensitive to the differences in their financial situations. John had mentioned offhand once that he'd invested well (of the three of them, he was the only one who didn't seem to currently work), but that it took all three of them to afford this house. He gave up and repeated, "Them's the breaks, I guess."

"What *is* inside an eel?" Eduardo asked, begging off the topic.

Dwayne shrugged again and suggested, "More eel?" They laughed.

"Well, now I want unagi," John said, placing his hands on his knees, and they all chuckled again.

"You have no idea the questions I'm fielding. And it's only been two days! Who invented swear words? Why do we have two eyes, but only see one thing? Why don't dogs have eyebrows? What was the last day I was a child? The inanity is endless!"

"I don't know," John said, "it sounds pretty profound. For instance, what was the last day you *were* a child?"

"Oh, heavens. I don't think you ever know. Certainly not at the time."

Dwayne looked up at the ceiling fan and watched it spin. "Wouldn't it be nice to go back, though? To relive that day? One last perfect day of feeling completely safe. Creative. Free."

"What?" Patrick was having none of it. He put his spritz on the coaster. "Who says your last day as a child was carefree?"

"Because if it wasn't you'd already be partially grown up."

"The day before my father died," Eduardo blurted, and everyone fell quiet. Even Patrick, who was reaching for his drink, froze. "Everything changed after that."

John scratched his chin, recalling a memory. "My bicycle was stolen when I was in the sixth grade. It sounds trivial now, but I loved riding that bike. I never rode a bicycle again and I don't know why. Or trusted people the same, for that matter. I don't think I've ridden a bike since."

"I hear you never forget," Patrick offered, referring to John's riding a bike, but perhaps equally about trusting people—a thought that made him shudder.

"That's it," Eduardo said, finally breaking the silence. "We're getting you a bike for your birthday."

Dwayne agreed and John's eyes actually watered, and suddenly it was lovely, watching the three of them. For a loner like himself, Patrick often thought of their relationship as *the* nightmare scenario. Someone always in the kitchen annoyingly standing in front of the spoons, the bar soap in the shower covered in the residue of too many body parts, hands reaching for you from every angle like you were walking through a carnival horror house. But he could see now there was a loveliness to it, too.

"What about you, Patrick?" John asked.

Patrick took a long, slow sip of his drink and savored the biting sweetness. He liked Aperol; he'd read a flavor profile once that described it as approachably bitter (as opposed to say Campari, which was—like himself—inaccessibly acerbic), and it went down easy in the desert heat.

How to answer the question. When *was* the last day he felt like a child? He used to love to sing "On Top of Spaghetti," to the tune of "On

Top of Old Smokey," in its entirety, but couldn't remember the last time he had. Now he couldn't even remember the words. (Someone sneezed on a meatball? That seemed wholly unsanitary.) Should he say that? Or was it when he threw out his last pair of Velcro sneakers, or that other pair with the pockets that made him feel like a kangaroo? Was it the day he first saw Scotty Savoy take a shower after gym? That was an awakening, sure, but the end of his childhood? Perhaps just the end of his innocence—but was that the same thing? In the end he settled on the truth. "I think last week."

To the uninitiated, it would seem like a throwaway answer, a joke, the kind Patrick had long employed to avoid sharing anything real, but JED took it as intended. Specific to Patrick, or not, there was something about being responsible for children that clearly delineated your adulthood from any notion that you were still a child.

"See?" John said. "Profound."

"What about the kids?" Dwayne asked. "Do you think this marks the end of their childhood?"

"No," Patrick said instinctually. This morning he found a blanket on the floor of his bedroom. It wasn't there when he had gone to bed, but there it was at the foot of his bed when he woke up. Someone was sneaking into his room to sleep. To feel safe. That someone was definitely a child. "Not if I have anything to do with it."

They all looked at their drinks, Patrick hoping he hadn't soured their afternoon.

"You know the *New York Times* just published an editorial stating the Aperol spritz was no good?" Dwayne commented.

"I didn't realize Campari was on the *New York Times* editorial board," Patrick stated, and they laughed until the room grew still. He watched some dust floating in a ray of sunlight.

"Top you off?" Eduardo finally asked. "I could make one more round."

"No. No. I should really get back." The kids were probably fine, but he had already shared too much.

EIGHT

The knock on the door wasn't a surprise, it happened from time to time. It was the manner in which Maisie answered that caught Patrick off guard. "What," she said to the UPS deliveryman, like a crotchety old woman in curlers. A week had passed, and despite a continued struggle with the food he served not being—for whatever reason—quite right, they'd settled into a comfortable rhythm of days by the pool and a nightly routine that had Patrick telling stories in bed with them until they passed out from exhaustion and too much sun. Twice he swore he heard them sneak into his room with their blankets and pillows after they thought he was asleep, but if they spent the night, they retreated before dawn. He decided not to make an issue of it. If the kids were getting comfortable in his home, that could only be a good thing.

"Delivery for Jack Curtis."

"There's no one here by that name." Maisie started to shut the door.

Rosa scrambled around the corner from the kitchen, all four foot eleven of her, wiping her hands on a dish towel. "One minute, one minute!" She grabbed the door before Maisie could close it entirely. "You're so fast, little one." Her hands dry, she draped the dish towel over her shoulder. "I can sign."

Patrick appeared from the hall, his morning caftan flowing behind him. (If the kids were going to make themselves at home in his house, he was damn well going to be comfortable, too.) Rosa signed for the delivery and thanked the UPS man. "Here you go, Mr. Patrick. I'm sorry, she answered the door so quickly." She handed him an envelope. "There's three more boxes outside. Big boxes."

"I'll get them. Thank you, Rosa."

"He said Mr. Curtis," Maisie said, confused. "Jack Curtis."

Rosa cupped Maisie's face in her hands, *sweet child*, before returning to the kitchen.

"I'm Jack Curtis." Patrick opened the door and stepped outside. A moment later he dragged the first of three large Amazon boxes into the foyer. It was awkward in size but not heavy.

Maisie looked at her uncle—if he *was* her uncle—completely puzzled.

Patrick stared down at his niece. "What? You don't know my life."

"Who's Jack Curtis?"

"Look, you guys were young when I was last working so I'm not sure how much you know about your uncle. You think of me as a carefree bon vivant, a man of leisure, shall we say, who doesn't have to work, but I can afford to be that way because I was on television. Thus, I have a certain renown. I know that's perhaps hard to understand with your YouTube and your kid vlogs and everyone you know living their lives so openly on the internet, but I'm a private person and I don't want people knowing where I live or what I order online." Patrick stepped over the threshold again to grab the second box.

Maisie was undeterred. She called after him. "Who's Jack Curtis?"

Patrick sighed. "I told you, *I am*. It's a name I use, an alter ego, for making purchases online." He pulled the second box inside. "The house is in a trust, I do other business under my S corp, but sometimes you just need a name to populate online order forms. So, voilà. Jack Curtis." She still didn't seem sold. "You know. Jack Lemmon. Tony Curtis. *Some Like It Hot*?"

"You like it hot? That's why you live in Palm Springs?"

Patrick raised an eyebrow. "Sure. Now keep your voice down," he whispered. "The devices are always listening." He pulled his phone out of his caftan pocket as if to illustrate his point.

Grant materialized by his side. "Whoa. What'th in the boxes, GUP?"

Patrick struggled with the third box, clearing the door just enough to close it behind him. "Bicycles. I bought us three bicycles. I thought we could go for a ride each morning before breakfast. Before it gets too hot."

"Some *like* it hot," Maisie said. Patrick turned his head and smiled into his shoulder, surprised how clever she was.

"Fun. And what'th in the envelope?" Grant leapt in the air to try to snatch it; Patrick raised it out of reach just in time.

"Do I not have any privacy anymore?" He asked, not really wanting an answer. "Jellyfish have one opening that's both their mouth and their butt."

"COOL!" Grant exclaimed and scampered away. Patrick had taken to memorizing a few random facts from an app on his phone each night before bed to use as distraction bombs with the kids. (As an app, it was already more fruitful than Duolingo; last year he was learning Italian until it started teaching him useless words like *pinguino*. When was he ever going to need to say *penguin* in Italy? "*Buonasera*. I'll have the braised *pinguino, per favore*. *Grazie*." No.)

Patrick knew exactly what the padded envelope contained: three books—one for himself on understanding grief in children and a grief workbook for each of the kids. He wasn't ready to just tear it open and start handing out manuals like birthday presents. He was in way over his head and wary of doing more damage than good. This material would require his careful perusal in case it was written by quacks; five-star online reviews were not to be trusted. He would give it his own review tonight with a glass of New Zealand white, after the kids were safely in bed.

Patrick glanced down and was surprised to find Maisie still looking at him. "We good?"

"Did you order helmets?"

"No. Do we need them?"

"Kids do."

"Why?"

"Our heads are squishy."

Patrick palmed the top of Maisie's skull, but found no evidence of this confessed squishiness.

She stood awkwardly, her arms a tangled knot of self-consciousness. "That tickles, Uncle Jack."

Uncle Jack. Guncle Patrick. GUP. Even Patrick was losing track of the names he was required to respond to. He turned to shove the boxes to the side of the foyer, resigned to ordering helmets, when there was another knock at the door. "What is this, Grand Central Station?" Patrick extended his arms until he was nothing but a square of psychedelic fabric with bare feet and a head. Rosa barreled around the corner again, but Patrick held out his hand to stop her, then motioned for his niece to take a second stab at answering the door.

Maisie threw her arms in the air as if she were the only one who ever did anything around the house. Patrick dipped behind the door as it opened, to hide.

"Oh, hello," came a woman's voice, clearly caught off guard. Patrick tried to place it but he couldn't. "I was looking for Patrick O'Hara."

Patrick froze at the mention of his actual name.

Maisie paused, unsure what to say next. "There's no one here by that name."

Patrick was impressed; Maisie was a quick learner. The woman, however, was now thoroughly confused. "This is not Patrick O'Hara's house? Because it's the address we have in the Rolodex. I checked three times before knocking. It's is very warm, by the way. Your door. I think I burned my knuckles."

Maisie remained unfazed. "This is . . ." She poked her head behind the door. "Uncle Patrick, whose house did you say this was?"

Patrick rolled his eyes. "All right, well clearly we don't need today's lesson on the stage whisper, but we might sit through the basics of the *actual* whisper." He stepped out from behind the door. "I'm Patrick O'Hara."

"Oh my god! Yes, you are." The woman, young, maybe thirty, did a little jig. "I'm sorry. It's just . . ." Did she need the restroom? "I loved your show."

"Great. All nine seasons are streaming on Snapchat." He started to close the door. There were a few of these over the years, crazies. Fewer since he left LA. He had no idea what gave them the gall to walk up to a stranger's house to ask for a picture or an autograph, but he had no patience for it.

"Wait, *wait*, wait."

"No need. Whatever you're selling, we're not buying."

The woman wrapped her fingers around the door to prevent Patrick from closing it. He stared at them, annoyed. And also mildly impressed with her manicure.

"No, you misunderstand. I'm Cassie. *OW*. This door really is very hot. Cassie Everest."

Patrick relented, opening the door wide enough for her to thrust her hand forward for him to shake. She was blond like a good Southern California girl, but curvier than you usually see in LA. Her clothes were serious, menswear almost, and she wore sunglasses pushed up on the top of her head like his sister, Clara.

"Cassie Everest? Like the mountain?"

"Could be worse, I suppose. I could be Cassie Kilimanjaro." She laughed at her own joke, but in a way that made it clear she'd told the same joke a thousand times.

"What are you doing here, Cassie Kilimanjaro?" He was suddenly very aware that this nickname for a potential crazy person contained the words *kill a man*. He blocked the door from opening any wider with his foot.

She wiped the sweat from her brow. "I'm sorry, could I come in? It's like a thousand degrees and I just drove two hours to get here."

Patrick stared at her. There was no way he was letting this woman into his house. Certainly not with the kids. Was this some sort of mama bear instinct he'd developed? That was, without question, new.

"Who are you?"

She looked back at him, hurt. "I'm Cassie Everest. I work for Neal."

Patrick recoiled. "Neal." It took him a moment to place the name. "My agent, Neal?"

"The very one."

Patrick was offended that his agent would send someone unannounced to his house, of all places, but at least this woman wasn't a deranged fan (well, wasn't *just* a deranged fan). He gave her one last look. She seemed harmless enough and his front door was indeed directly in the blazing sun, so he ushered her inside. "Kids!"

Grant appeared from his bedroom and lined up beside Maisie.

"This is Mary Matterhorn."

"Cassie Everest."

"Same thing. She and GUP need to have a few words. Why don't you both nap in your room for a bit and then we'll go for a swim."

"We're too old for naps!" Grant bellowed.

"No you're not, I take at least four a day." Patrick stifled a yawn; one sounded pretty good right about now.

"But I'm not tired!"

"Fix yourselves a drink, then. Not too much. Just a light triple." Patrick turned to Cassie. "I'm kidding," he said, but his face remained deadly serious.

"Jellyfish eat out of their butts." Grant flashed one of his trademark grins at Cassie.

"You're missing a tooth," Cassie observed, unfazed. "I read somewhere that squirrels can't burp."

"Is that true, GUP?" Grant looked up at his uncle, his hands clasped, desperately wanting it to be so.

"I don't know, I'm not much of a reader. Go play."

The kids scampered off, and once they were safely out of sight, Patrick motioned for Cassie to follow him through the sunken living room to the kitchen. He opened the refrigerator door, pulled out a cold bottle of Smartwater and handed it to her. "I thought I fired Neal."

Cassie thought for a second. "Ummm, nope."

"I fired someone." Patrick grabbed a second water for himself, twisted the cap, and took a long sip.

"Your publicist. Also your manager, I believe."

"Right."

Rosa was scooping cookie dough in heaping mounds onto a baking sheet. Patrick reached for one and she slapped his hand. "I make these for the children."

"All right, all right." Patrick retreated, surprised.

"I love your hair," Cassie offered. Patrick smoothed his hair before realizing she was talking to Rosa, who had recently dyed her mane an intense shade of violet to hide the encroaching gray. "It's very pretty."

"Gracias."

Patrick turned back to Cassie with a realization. "You're the one who asked me to have new headshots taken! You know I actually had them done? But then I remembered I fired Neal so I never sent them your way."

"Nope. Didn't fire him. Not to our knowledge, anyhow."

"Hmm. Well, I meant to."

Cassie spoke to fill the awkward silence that was certain to follow. "I thought I knew everything about you, but I didn't know you had kids."

"I'm full of surprises." Patrick gathered a few of the breakfast dishes and put them in the sink.

"What does 'GUP' mean? If you don't mind me asking." Cassie raised the bottle of water, offering a weak "Cheers" before taking a sip.

"It stands for Gay Uncle Patrick."

Cassie choked on her water, and some spilled out on her blouse. "You're gay?"

"Cassie. *Tsk, tsk, tsk.*" Patrick shook his head and looked down at his caftan, disappointed. And yet, he had never sat for a coming-out profile—even then it seemed almost passé (he never thought it necessary; he figured everyone knew)—so a cursory internet search might miss that detail.

"Oh, I see now. You're wearing a dress."

"It's not a . . ." Patrick spotted Maisie peeking around the corner. "Yes, fine, I'm wearing a dress. I thought you knew everything about me." He gestured for Maisie to turn right around and head back to her room. "Rosa, would you?"

"No cookies." Rosa waved her finger at Patrick as a reminder before escorting her boss's niece out of the kitchen.

Cassie continued. "About your career, I should have said."

"Huh?" Patrick reached for a spoonful of dough, then thought twice of it, not wanting to incur Rosa's wrath.

"I thought I knew everything about your *career*."

"I'm not gay professionally, Cassie. I maintain my amateur status to compete in the Gay Olympics."

Cassie took stock of the kitchen, fascinated by her surroundings. The gold foiled mirror behind the bar, the quartz countertops with the sparkled flecks, the high-end appliances and chef's stove with six burners, the espresso machine that looked like it should have come with a spokesmodel highlighting its features. It was like being inside a catalog.

"Why are you here, Cassie?"

"Oh! Right. Neal thought it was time you come back to work."

Patrick stopped fussing with the dishes and turned to look at his guest. He narrowed his eyes to really scrutinize her. "That doesn't sound like Neal."

"Sure it does."

"Neal hates me. The only reason he hasn't fired *me* as a client is because I'm essentially retired."

"That's not true." She paused to pick a tactic. "Neal does think you should come back to work, so he can make money. *I* think you should come back to work because your fans miss you."

"Oh, they do, do they?"

"They do! I do. Now is the time. There are so many options available. So much content in search of talent. You could go back to what you were doing. Or enough time has gone by, we could even rebrand you. Go in a completely different direction."

"Like New Coke. Wonderful."

Cassie responded slowly. "That's . . . perhaps not the best example."

Patrick folded and refolded a dish towel a dozen different ways. "What is this about?"

"I'm a huge fan. I think you were underserved by your last show. People want to see what else you can do. A lot of people do, but I'm in a rare position, see, that I can actually do something to facilitate that." Cassie removed the sunglasses from her head and set them on the counter before running her fingers through her hair.

"No. What is this *really* about?" Patrick crossed his arms and leaned against the sink.

He could see Cassie run back over her sales pitch in her head. She'd probably rehearsed it again and again in the car during the two-hour drive from Los Angeles. Patrick had thrown her a curveball and now she was adrift. "Okay. I'm just going to lay all my cards on the table, because I can see you're that kind of guy."

"Well, look at that. You really do know a lot about me." A crash from the bedroom startled them both. "That's it! We're giving away the dog!" he called out.

Cassie looked at him, heartbreak in her eyes.

"We don't have a dog."

She wasn't sure what to believe. "Neal said that if I could get you back to work he would promote me to junior agent."

"And you'd take over my day-to-day? That's his way of pawning me off because I'm a pain in the ass." Something caught Patrick's eye and he looked over Cassie's shoulder and out by the pool. He thought it might be the kids, but it was just the pool guy dragging his skimmer across the water. "Those are my words."

"Nope, they were pretty much his words, too." Cassie smiled. "Except the day-to-day part. He'd keep you on. You're too big a client to hand off to a junior agent."

"Well, then you must truly be a fan."

"Or I must really want that promotion." Cassie smiled again, wider this time, but Patrick didn't return it. That did not mean he was unamused, though. He was warming to this young woman.

"There's nothing we can't discuss," she continued. "What do you want? Do you want to do movies?"

"Oh, sure. A rotten part in a so-so film."

"Well, okay, so *not* movies."

"That's from *A Chorus Line*. Cassie's monologue. Don't you even know who you're named after?"

"Actually, I'm named after my great—"

Patrick didn't let her finish; he hopped up on the counter to sit. "Cassie was complaining about a rotten part in a so-so film. She was a go-go dancer in a movie of the week. But the part got cut, so . . ."

"I never saw *A Chorus Line*."

"Clearly." Patrick felt an unfortunate breeze and pulled his caftan over his knees to cover himself. "What is the training to be a junior agent these days?"

"I have an MBA from Wharton."

"Well, sure." There was no snappy comeback to an MBA from Wharton.

"So you're not saying no to movies."

"I'm not saying yes to movies. I'm not saying yes to anything."

"TV."

"No."

"Limited series."

"No."

"Netflix."

"No."

"Theater?"

"A play? Good lord no."

"No to theater, then. Does that include all live performance?"

"What else is there, the Capades?"

"Well, no. But, say, *Dancing with the Stars*."

"Ew. I'm not wearing a ridiculous costume."

Cassie moved to indicate Patrick's caftan but abruptly curbed the gesture.

"I'll consider a solo show."

"A solo show," she repeated.

"Yes. A one-man show."

"But not a play."

"No. I don't see the point in standing around while other people say their lines when I could have all the lines for myself." Patrick grinned like a hyena.

"You want to have all the lines for yourself."

"Exactly. I think we're starting to feel a connection."

"Would you be willing to write this one-man show? A lot of solo performance is written by the artist."

"Vanessa Redgrave did Joan Didion."

"You want to do Joan Didion?"

"I want to do Vanessa Redgrave. I want to do a one-man show where I play Vanessa Redgrave playing Joan Didion. Other than that, I really think we're done here."

Cassie sighed. Now it was clear. "You're not taking me seriously."

"Oh, was I supposed to?"

Cassie screwed the cap on her bottle of water and picked up her sunglasses from the counter. "It's okay. I'm used to men not taking me seriously."

Patrick slid down from the counter. "Oh, don't do that. Don't you lump me in with the patriarchy—I'm wearing a dress, for Christ's sake. But you show up at my house without so much as a phone call. I don't know you. I don't know what you want."

"It's okay if you don't take me seriously, because I take myself seriously enough for both of us. You might think this is a joke, but I know more about you than you think I do and I drove two hours to have this meeting with you. Has Neal ever done that? I highly doubt he has. I know you were unhappy on television. I know your first love was the theater. I know you're not serious about doing a solo show, because your favorite part of acting is reacting, and that's where you truly shine." Cassie took a deep breath. "I know when you left LA, you didn't go far, because you're not done with your career. You're testing me. That's fine. I will take your test and I will pass it. And I'll go, but this conversation isn't over."

"Tammy Tetons," Patrick said as a smile spread across his lips. "Okay."

"Okay?" Cassie asked hopefully.

"Okay." Patrick repeated, realizing he didn't totally hate her. That seemed . . . *new.* Another crash from the other room. "Don't make me come in there!" He turned to Cassie. "Actually, do you have a job right now? Something out of state that would take me far away from here?"

She struggled for an offer that might do.

"I'm kidding. I have to go. We'll need to continue this some other time."

Cassie opened the calendar app on her iPhone. "Okay, so when would be a better time?"

Patrick raised his arms, making him resemble a kite. "I'm going to need you to figure that out."

"Come back to work, Patrick. Come back to Neal. It's time." She scanned his eyes for any sign this was sinking in. "Promise me you'll at least think about it."

"I'll think about it." But the truth was, at the moment he had bigger things to think about. Like where to buy bicycle helmets.

NINE

If Maisie and Grant were going to insist on keeping the temperature at anything less than one hundred and one, they were going to have to consider a new descriptive word for the hot tub. Patrick didn't force the issue—boiling children while they were entrusted to him seemed unwise. And it was summer, after all; even though the sun had dipped behind the mountains, it was still hovering around ninety degrees (his blood had thinned over the past few years, but it doesn't mean theirs had). Still, it had become a routine. Each evening after lupper they had a post-meal swim and a soak and partook in one of their favorite activities, watching the outdoor solar lights pop on as dusk settled over the yard.

"There's one!" Grant yelled. He splashed the twist right out of his uncle's vodka on the rocks as he raised his arm from the water.

"Easy. Easy."

"It's one of the colored ones!"

"Score," Patrick said with just enough interest to keep Grant from throwing a fit. But the colored ones *were* fun, situated under the citrus trees (tangelo and Mexican lime mostly, a lemon and two pink grapefruit) that lined the back of the property and made interesting shapes and shadows along the white concrete wall that separated his property from JED's.

Patrick looked up for a glimpse of Venus, usually the first light to appear in the gloaming, but quickly abandoned his search. It was getting harder and harder to see without his glasses, which he largely refused to wear on principle ever since his eye doctor suggested it was about time for *progressives*, which, as far as Patrick could tell, was a fancy way for him to avoid saying bifocals. Besides, tonight they were not there just to count the lights and the shimmering stars as they made their appearance in the sky. Patrick had an agenda, developed from the book he'd ordered himself on grief. He took a long sip of his drink for courage. "I was wondering if either of you were missing your mom tonight, because I know I was *missing her*—and I thought we might talk about it." His reading had suggested he find a way to communicate his own grief to light the way forward. And when it came to his own grief, *oh, where to begin*.

Grant sculled across the water, using his cupped hands as oars. Maisie kicked her legs until they broke the surface.

"C'mon. You gotta help me out here. You don't talk to me about this stuff. I'm not sure if you're waiting for me to talk to you. We can't waste the whole summer being polite." Patrick had been wondering of late if Clara hadn't been right. He could clothe them and feed them and keep them alive, amuse them with a playful remark. But was he really what they *needed* in this fraught situation?

Grant propelled himself back to Patrick's side and sat next to him, placing his small hands on his uncle's shoulder. He whispered in Patrick's ear. "You mith Mom?" It was as if the concept took him completely by surprise.

"They were friends, dummy," Maisie said.

"Hey, hey, hey. No one's a dummy."

A bat flew by overhead and Maisie screamed.

"It's just a bat. They're friendly. They eat bugs."

"Bats are for Halloween."

"Well, in the desert they're for summer, too. But they never bother anyone. They just do their thing." Patrick respected them for that and, almost to prove a point, he traced the bat's flight path with his finger across the sky.

"You and Mommy were friends?" Grant asked. He knew the answer of course, but this was also part of what he needed, Patrick reasoned—reassurance. Wanting to hear old stories again and again and again, sifting through them for gleaming new details like a prospector panning for gold.

"We were. Good friends." For a moment he resented them both, perhaps for the clarity of their grief. People understood the horror of losing a mother. They understood who Sara was to them. People didn't know what she meant to Patrick. Or if they had, they had long ago forgotten. "Ironically, better friends before she shacked up with your dad. But that's, you know, just the way of the world. You meet someone and you spend all your time with them and see less and less of your friends. Even if that someone is your friend's brother, you simply can't compete." He still remembered the way Sara protested when he met Joe.

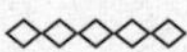

"I never see you anymore."

"You see me. You see me right now!" Patrick exclaimed. It had been a year since they graduated and they were sharing an apartment in New York.

"Lucky me," Sara said. "You must have run out of clean underwear."

Their Chelsea apartment was too small for arguing, which was one thing that made their living together a success. He'd even bitched to Joe on their second date that the closet where he'd kept his clothes was too narrow and he had to bend his wire hangers forty-five degrees. Joe's jealous reply: *You have a closet?* Joe, a native New Yorker, was the wrong audience for his complaint.

"Sara, I gave you the bedroom. I sleep on the couch. You can't get mad if I want to go to Joe's just to sleep in an actual bed."

"So this is about furniture."

"Yes. It's about furniture. *Hard. Wood. Furniture.*"

Sara threw her moccasin at him just because.

"What was that for?"

"Lying to me."

"What lie?" Patrick bent down to pick up the slipper. He ran his finger over the red and turquoise beads sewn across the vamp that made a tiny, glorious bird.

"Oh, please. You're not going there to sleep." She flashed him a devilish grin and ducked just as Patrick threw her moccasin back.

"I am!"

"You don't look the least bit rested."

Patrick glanced in the small mirror by the door. "Don't say that. I have an audition."

"For what?" Sara slipped the moccasin back on her foot.

"A play, a play. What else is there?" Patrick grabbed a script from on top of the TV. It was flipped open to his audition scene. "Run lines with me?"

"No."

"Run lines with me!"

"No."

"Meet him, then."

"Huh?"

"Joe. Come out with us. Meet him. You'll like him."

"I never like anyone you date." And that was true. Sara always thought Patrick sold himself short.

"Joe's different."

"Uh-huh."

"He is!"

"How?"

Patrick took a step closer. He knew they were in danger of becoming codependent. That after five years of friendship he couldn't live without her and she couldn't live without him. If they didn't do something about it soon, it would alter the rest of their lives. "He thinks I'm a pain in the ass, too."

◇◇◇◇◇

Patrick emerged from the memory and looked at Sara's children, alarmed, as if they had teleported into his hot tub from another time. But when? Where? How had almost twenty years disappeared in the blink of an eye? "Your mom and I used to live together. In New York."

"Were you almotht our daddy?"

"What?" Patrick swung around to Grant, nearly spilling his drink himself this time. "No. Of course not." He and Sara had once drunkenly made out in their dorm building lounge, but it ended with both of them reduced to fits of laughter. "This was a long time ago. We had a little apartment in New York, in Chelsea. A one-bedroom, but I slept on the couch. You could do that then, find something rent-controlled in Manhattan and make it work. Nowadays I don't know where we would live. Queens or even New Jersey." Patrick adjusted the tub's jets so he didn't have to talk over them. "Want to hear about it?"

"Yes. Was Mommy pretty?" Maisie asked.

"Oh, very. Fashionable, too. She worked at a magazine. I don't remember which one; not *Vogue*, not *Cosmo* . . . *Marie Claire*. Is that the name of a magazine or was she the first lady of France? No matter, the pay was garbage but she got a lot of free stuff. I went to auditions during the day and waited tables at night in an obscure Greek restaurant, but I was never very good at it. First of all, the consonant clusters are all fucked—*t*'s and *z*'s together? C'mon. And I never really was a people person and that was reflected in my tips, which, fortunately, I pooled with the rest of the staff's to split at the end of the night. They didn't like me much because of that, bringing the pool average down—but it worked out better for me. I don't know. I wasn't cut out for it. One night I accidentally set a woman on fire. Your mom said I came home every night smelling of lamb." Until he met Joe and stopped coming home at all.

"You set a woman on fire?" The look of disbelief on Maisie's face was comical.

"Accidentally."

"Accidentally?"

"Did she burn to a kwisp?" Grant's eyes bulged with excitement.

"There was this dish that was served with an open flame and a woman was wearing too much hairspray, and, well . . . it was the 1990s. No one burned to a crisp. I doused her with house water."

"What's house water?" Maisie asked.

"It's what they made us call tap water." Maisie's expression could best be described as confused. "Yeah, I thought it was bullshit, too." Patrick had done enough performing to know when he was losing his audience; the looks on the kids' faces only underscored what he could already feel. "We laughed so much, all the time. Everything was funny. That's what I remember most about that time. Your mother had the best laugh, that rich cackle that came from the very depths of her soul. We didn't have any money to speak of, but when we would laugh like that, in the middle of New York, when the city would do everything in its immense power to keep you down, we felt rich as kings. I miss that time. It's cliché, I know. But I think it was the happiest time in my life."

Maisie's curiosity was piqued. "Was it the happiest time in Mommy's life?"

"What?" Patrick looked at his niece; this time he could effortlessly read her face. "No. No. Ultimately, we were different people that way."

"When was her happiest time?" It was just like Maisie to worry that she might have been her mother's regret.

"Well, I can think of several," Patrick began. "One, when she was pregnant with you. Although, I don't know why. She was fat and couldn't do anything fun and her ankles were so swollen she couldn't stuff her feet into any fashionable shoes." He splashed a little water Maisie's way and she smiled. "On her wedding day. She looked radiant. You know she and your dad fought over who I would stand up for? Should I be the best man? The maid of honor?"

"That's a girl job."

"Maid of honor? No, it's not. What do we say in this house? Boys can do girl things and girls can do boy things. That's not even a Guncle Rule, there shouldn't even be boy things and girl things to begin with. People should just do what they want."

"What did you choose?"

"Oh. You've seen the pictures. I married them. It was the only way to keep the peace. I was standing up front with both of them; your father had a case of flop sweat, but your mother absolutely sparkled. Not even photos could capture it. She was really happy then. We all were."

"What about me?" Grant asked.

"Oh, she was definitely happy with you. After she had a girl, she most wanted a boy. And along you came."

Grant beamed.

"I remember when I first met you. She was on my case to hold the baby. 'Hold the baby, Patrick. Hold the baby.' Of course, I didn't want to hold you and I told her just as much."

"Why not?" Grant put his hands on his hips and puffed out his chest like Superman.

"Well, babies are dull and you never know when they're going to spit up and I was going through a phase of wearing only Issey Miyake T-shirts and I wasn't about to let you hurl all down the back of one of those."

Grant laughed.

"I didn't care how many more I had in a drawer back home."

"What about you?" Maisie asked. "When were you happiest?"

"Me?" Patrick put his hand over his chest and feigned surprise. "Right now. In this hot tub."

"Really?"

"What? NO! Of course not. Don't be ridiculous. I have a Golden Globe, for Christ's sake. Plus, you make me cap the temperature of this hot tub at ninety-something degrees and neither of you understands sarcasm." He took a long, slow sip of vodka and crunched on an ice cube. Two more solar lights popped on and he pointed. "I told you. I really think it was that time in New York. I didn't know how good I had it. I didn't know it wouldn't last."

There was a long pause in conversation and Grant played with the button that controlled the tub lights. He continued to press it as the water changed from white, to blue, to red, to green, to pink, and then back to white again. Eventually he lost interest and sat down. The bubbles came up to his chin. "Do you believe in heaven?" he asked.

"Do I . . ." Patrick had been steeling himself for a question like this since the funeral, but he hadn't expected it to be presented so bluntly. *Is Mommy in heaven?* That was the tack he was expecting the question to take. Something he could answer with a single word—even if it was not reflective of his belief—and move on. But he wasn't prepared to have to explain his faith, or lack thereof. "That's a tough one. Do *you*?"

Grant shrugged and Maisie looked equally adrift.

"I believe she's not in pain anymore." Patrick squinched his eyes closed long enough not to cry. He pulled Grant onto his lap. He remembered once shooting a two-bit TV movie, the first real thing he'd ever booked, where he was supposed to cry. They had to call "Cut" while he pulled out a menthol stick to rub under his eye, an effective trick of the trade; he wouldn't need such gimmickry now. "I believe she's at peace. And that brings me some comfort when I'm feeling sad. Beyond that, I don't really know."

"I thought grown-ups were supposed to know everything."

Patrick looked across the tub at his niece, where she'd taken a perch on the edge. "Who told you that? A grown-up, no doubt." Maisie wore the board shorts and lycra running shirt they had selected together;

Patrick bought four of each and she practically lived in them, made them her Palm Springs uniform. Her hair was dry with salt from the pool and chemicals from the hot tub and she looked like an effortlessly cool surfer. "We know *some* things. Not everything. Some things, the older you get the less you actually know about them."

"Like what?" Grant asked.

"Like . . . I don't know. *Math*. No one remembers math after high school. At least not the complicated kind." Patrick scratched the scruff on his chin. In the summer he shaved more often than winter, but he'd been lazy the last couple days. He adjusted the jets back to medium. "Why people are so afraid, especially of other people who are different. Hate. I don't understand why there's so much hate in the world, but I guess that ties in with fear. That sort of thing. What do kids not understand?"

Maisie thought about this while cupping her hands around the tub's jets. "I don't understand why people have to die."

Patrick turned off the jets entirely and let the water simmer to a placid calm. "That's an easy one." He turned to Grant to make sure he was listening, too. "Some people are here for a long time, and some people are only here for a short time. And none of us know. That's the beauty of it. We don't have any damned clue how much time we get. So. Guncle Rule number . . . Maisie, what number are we on?"

"Eight."

"See what I mean about forgetting math? Guncle Rule number eight: Live your life to the fullest every single day, because every day is a gift. That's why people die. To teach us the importance of living." Again, Patrick made a face to keep from crying. Not for Sara this time; for himself. He had broken this rule. Over and over again. He reached out for the button that controlled the tub's lights and cycled through the rainbow of colors. For years he'd convinced himself he hadn't, that he was in fact living large. First with the show, and then in the desert—buying a home in a neighborhood with a magical name like Movie Colony, of all things, eschewing work and responsibility altogether. But he wasn't living, he was hiding. From people. From friends. From family. From love. From work. From art. From contributing. From everything that mattered.

"Ow!" Grant exclaimed.

"What?"

"You hit my hand."

Patrick realized he'd swatted Grant's hand away when he tried to take control of the lights. "Sorry, bud. I drifted."

Patrick looked out at the yard as he soothed Grant's hand in his own. The solar lights were now at their brightest and they were surrounded in soft, colorful radiance. Grant chose the pink filter for the hot tub light, completing the effect; they were now floating in a warm, protective womb. The mountains were a faint echo against the last of the evening's light, another, larger barrier protecting them, keeping the worst of the world out. Patrick exhaled, gesturing with his cocktail at the horizons around them. "Life is a very precious gift," he repeated and took a deep breath. "You know what we should do?"

"What," Maisie asked, genuinely curious.

"Throw a party. To make ourselves feel better."

"What kind of party?"

"I don't know. Anyone have a birthday?"

The kids shook their heads. Maisie's was in January, and Grant's, March.

"The kind with people. And lights and champagne and music and fun."

"And kid drinks!" Grant shouted. Patrick had made the mistake the other night of making them Shirley Temples. (*Thirley Templeth.*)

"And kid drinks," Patrick agreed.

It was time for the hiding to stop.

TEN

Patrick sat on his patio in silence, swiveling gently in a chair, lulling himself into some sort of comforting, mindless space. He'd been there a while, lost in his thoughts, before Lorna's bark pierced the darkness, followed by a gentle splash. It was John, on the other side of the wall, diving into his pool for his nightly swim; it always drove Lorna mad and she howled from the pool deck like a lifeguard yelling at swimmers from shore. Patrick smiled and swirled what was left of his ice around inside his otherwise empty glass before setting it on the table. He stood up, tapping one of the lights from the string of Edison bulbs that he'd woven through the pergola. He grabbed one of the other patio chairs, one that didn't swivel, and marched it through the yard.

He secured the chair in the gravel that ran along the back wall of the property, tossed its cushion aside so he wouldn't get it dirty with his bare feet, and stood to peer over the wall. He waved at John when he completed a lap and came up for air.

"Evening!"

John raised his goggles to his forehead and waved back. "Howdy, neighbor." It was a typical John thing to say (*howdy*), so Patrick didn't cringe like he normally might; at this point he was inured. "Sit tight. Let me grab a towel." He leapt out of the pool with a surprising grace and

Patrick was relieved to see he was wearing a Speedo; swimsuits were optional in Palm Springs, never more so than at night. He dried off and wrapped the towel around his waist before joining his friend at the wall.

"How's things?"

"Fine. All I do is put sunscreen on children. Finish with one, start up on the other. Then back to the first to reapply. Ad infinitum. I swear, I should invent some sort of machine. I'd be rich."

"I thought you already were."

Patrick bobbed his head to one side. In truth, he wasn't sure where he stood financially. Not exactly. Money had a way of going out the door fast, never more so than when there was none coming in.

"How are they? The kids."

Patrick leaned on the wall so he wasn't looking down on his neighbor quite so much; he was trying to be more aware of how he positioned himself with others. "Hard to tell. I think they're sneaking into my room at night to sleep."

"They feel safe with you."

Patrick smiled. A memory, a sense memory: the total security of falling asleep as a child with adults talking nearby. "It's weird having them around. Some of my DNA, mixed with Sara's. They're like a shadow of an alternate reality, another life, a heterosexual one, unlived."

"That must be strange."

He pulled at a branch from one of John's lemon trees that hung over the wall. "I tried to engage them in conversation about their mom."

"That's good of you."

"The only way past this is through." He studied John. "How does your mustache stay that way?"

"Huh?" John hopped on one leg to clear water out of his ear.

Patrick mimed curling a mustache at both ends.

"Oh. I have a wax. Seems to hold up in the pool."

"Where is your better two-thirds?"

"They went to the movies to escape the heat. I opted for a swim instead. Nothing really to see in the summer if you're not into superheroes and such, people wearing masks." John took the goggles off his head, his own mask, and played with the elastic strap. "I'm proud of you, Patrick. Talking to the kids. Now, that's heroic."

Patrick agreed, but he wasn't really up for the compliment. "I'm not sure I'm as equipped to handle this as I thought. And I didn't think I was all that equipped to begin with. It's hard to get through to them. I can't get them to relax. Everything I do seems wrong. Not how their mom used to do it."

"They're in shock."

"Still, there was some part of me that assumed they'd be kids. Resilient, you know? They'd grieve, yes. But also fall for my charms and laugh and play in the pool and be . . . *free*." Patrick had even hoped that perhaps he might learn from *them*. That they might know the path out and somehow light the way.

"You could have them talk to someone. A child psychologist, maybe. Someone like that."

Patrick nodded and added a cough. There was a lump in his throat that he wanted desperately to clear. "They want to know about heaven. So, maybe a priest. If only we knew one." He smiled, the thought almost ridiculous.

John wiped his forehead. "I was a minister." The way he tossed it off so casually, solely as information without a hint of boasting, caught Patrick by surprise. He pushed himself back from the wall so hard, he almost fell off his chair. "Don't look so surprised," he added.

"How should I look, then? You're kidding me." Patrick thought back to their conversation the other day. "A coke-addicted, Burning Man–attending, polyamorous clergyman."

John glanced down at his feet, kicking some of the gravel on his own side of the wall until it came to a rest near a succulent. "I know you think we're silly people."

"Oh, come on," Patrick protested, but of course it was the truth. They were a throuple with a collective name.

"It's okay. A lot of people do." John craned his neck to look back at his house wistfully. "It's an unusual arrangement we have. We're the butt of a lot of jokes. We get it. But that doesn't mean we're not serious-minded."

They were silent for a moment. Patrick looked up at the sky, hoping for a shooting star. Instead, the sky was frozen—not even the red lights of a passing plane—although they were enveloped in a warm, gentle breeze.

"What are you doing out here, Patrick?"

"Thought I could use an adult to talk to."

"No," John said. He unwrapped his towel from his waist and placed it gently over his shoulders like a capelet. "What are you doing in the desert?"

Patrick rubbed his eyes until he saw shooting stars on the backs of his eyelids. "I needed a break."

"It's been four years."

"Has it?"

"I think you know that it has."

Patrick bit the inside of his cheek until he thought he tasted blood. "I had a visitor the other day. A young woman. She asked me the same thing, more or less."

"How did you answer?"

"I didn't." Patrick leaned back in on the wall. "I couldn't."

"Because you don't really know." If Patrick wasn't going to answer, then John was going to answer it for him. He had better things to do than stand by a wall in the night listening to the cicadas. Like get back to his swim, for instance.

"I had this agent. Neal. Had, *have*. We were at a party once. The last year of the show. One hundred episodes. One hundred fifty. Something like that. Who even remembers? Everyone was wistful, but restless.

Ready to move on, I think; at least I certainly was. But it was a good run and there was no reason to pretend that it wasn't. Anyhow, Neal was there. I suppose I invited him. Or maybe agents just get invited. There was an enormous cake, I remember that. And somewhere near the end of the night, he grabbed me."

"What do you mean, grabbed you. Grabbed you where?"

"By the taco truck."

"No, I meant . . ."

"I know what you meant." Patrick's chair slipped in the gravel and he jumped on it twice so the legs would dig in. "He grabbed my crotch." Patrick exhaled. "We were both drunk. It wasn't even sexual."

"Of course it was sexual!"

Patrick was surprised by such a traditional definition from someone whose husbands were on a movie date. "He's straight. Married!"

"It's been my experience that doesn't mean a whole lot. You were assaulted, Patrick."

"I suppose. It was also a sign of ownership. He owned me. He got me that show and he had me by the balls. And it just made me think, 'I'm making so much money for this person. WHY?' It wasn't fun anymore. And so I just kind of . . . stopped."

John reached down to pat Lorna, who had snuggled up against his side. "I'm sorry that happened to you."

"It's fine. It didn't really feel like assault. I mean, it was. But I'm not a victim."

John swung his arms around a few times like an Olympic swimmer stretching; he caught his towel just as it slipped off his shoulders. "That's not why you're here, though."

Patrick pretended to give that some thought. He didn't like being so clearly seen. "Do you believe in heaven, Reverend?"

"I do."

"And hell?"

"I suppose. Do you?"

"Hell on earth," Patrick said, and he did a few vertical push-ups off the wall. "There was a guy once. I loved him and he died."

"AIDS?"

"Jesus," Patrick replied, but he supposed that was the difference in their ages. "Drunk driver."

"I'm sorry."

"I don't think I ever healed." Patrick stopped there, and John didn't press. They each avoided the other's eyes.

"Do you miss it?"

"Miss what?"

"Acting."

Patrick thought about it. "I miss *him.*" The insects were loud tonight. The breeze picked up again and swept Patrick's hair.

"Yes, but he's not coming back."

Patrick was almost blown backward off the chair by the brutal truth of that statement. It's the kind of honesty that he would have run from in the past, but in the moment he stood his ground and took it. On the surface, it seemed remarkably selfish; John had two loves, two men in his bed. Patrick had none. But he wasn't going to let his neighbor get the best of him.

"I do miss it. Acting. When I was, I don't know, sixteen, seventeen, I was elected president of my high school drama club. I had put in two years doing supporting roles, but now I was an upperclassman, now was my time to shine. I was to be the lead. And then our director announced we were doing *The Diary of Anne Frank. Sonofabitch!* Right? I was cast as her father. I went around telling everyone, 'Yes, she's the title character, but my character, Otto Frank, is the true lead. He survived. He came back to find Anne's diary. The whole story is framed through his memories. In fact, they should rename it *The Otto Frank Experience.*'"

John smiled. "That sounds like a jazz fusion trio."

"You should know from trios." It was a slight dig, repayment for his comment about Joe, but Patrick was mostly still lost in the memory. "Sixteen-year-old me was a terror."

"*Sixteen-year-old* you?" John was teasing, and this time he smiled. Patrick did, too.

"That's when I knew. I had to act. I had to bring that kind of certitude to every role—no matter how supporting. I haven't thought about that in a while. That monster is still in me. But it's more than that."

"What is?"

"I have to go see my agent, as much as I loathe him. He does have me by the balls. Or, at least the situation does. I'm going to have to work when this summer is done. Help my brother support his kids."

"Didn't you say he was an attorney?"

"Yeah. But I have no idea what kind of medical bills he's facing. The kind of debt they took on during Sara's illness. I don't want him to lose the house. And even if he's okay for now, there's the future to save for. Two college educations. Another ten years? Who knows what it will cost by then. I have to do my part. I owe it to their mother. And that means going to see my agent."

John nodded; he had opened Patrick's eyes—at least a bit. There was no need to say more. "Want me to talk to the kids?"

Patrick thought about it. He wasn't sure John's harsh truths were the right tactic. "Maybe. Can I let you know?"

"Sure. Do you want to come for a swim?"

"I don't have my suit."

John shot him a look. He'd peered over Patrick's wall enough times to know that that never stopped him from swimming.

Patrick glanced back at his own pool. The water rippled in the breeze, glimmering on the surface. "It's all right. I have a pool, too."

"Yeah, but sometimes life is more fun with someone else."

Patrick looked up at the sky again; this time a satellite floated effortlessly across the night. It was no shooting star, but something, in a pinch, upon which to make a wish.

ELEVEN

The halls buzzed and chattered as Patrick marched past cubicle after cubicle, down the agency halls, which seemed dappled with sunlight (but with no obvious windows or skylights, he couldn't tell from where), in search of his agent. He could hear people on their phones actually whisper his name, their hushed tones dripping with juicy excitement, as he walked by yelling, "Neal? Neal!" and wondering out loud where the hell they had moved his office. He didn't judge the cubicle dwellers. They were merely a half step removed from the dreaded (but storied) agency mailroom, and probably only made a few bucks more than minimum wage for the privilege of being barked at or otherwise verbally assaulted by walking nightmares in Hugo Boss suits steeped in delusions of grandeur. They might as well be gossipmongers—they probably didn't even have dental. But had he really been away that long? Were the tabloids right? In four short years he went from network star to Greta Garbo?

Patrick stuck his head in an empty office to see if he recognized anything of his agent's and then spun three times in a circle like a dog might before lying down. "Neal? There's no use hiding from me!"

A young woman approached from her cubicle, her hands clasped in a fashion that seemed inappropriately formal, like an extra in a community theater production of *The Crucible*. "Mr. O'Hara," she said calmly, as if he were a wild animal she had been warned not to startle. "Neal moved offices. He's now at the end of the hall."

"They gave that asshole a corner office?" Patrick should have waited in reception, but he had long been amused by the way Dustin Hoffman's character in *Tootsie* would burst into his beleaguered agent's office unannounced and made it a bucket list item to try. There was no turning back now, so he forged ahead, ducking around the woman, nearly knocking a Rothko off the wall in the process.

Two days earlier Patrick had an eye-opening discussion with his accountant. He laid out his new responsibilities as he saw them and mapped where he wanted to be financially for each of the next sixteen years, when Grant would graduate from college. They talked taxes and property and tuition and bills and insurance and stocks and portfolios and assets and liabilities until Patrick's head swam. He literally swam after their conversation. He dove into the deep end of his pool and thought about never resurfacing. It's not that things were dire; they weren't. They were just considerably more complicated. Patrick the loner would be fine. Patrick the family man had other obligations. When he finally came up for air it was with a fresh list of things to do.

Cassie Everest sat in the very last cubicle and Patrick waved as she looked up, stunned. "Look. I put on pants and everything." He winked at her.

Before she could coherently respond (or really do anything at all), he entered Neal's office, closing the door behind him.

"Patrick." Compared to everyone else who worked in the agency, Neal seemed relatively unfazed. They were roughly the same age, the two of them, though his Armani uniform and demeanor made him seem, if not older, more mature. In twenty or so years in this business he was, at this point, unflappable; he didn't so much as stand up to say hello.

"Neal. Nice office."

"Thank you. Haven't seen you in a while."

"I almost knocked a Rothko off the wall. And is that a . . . *Basquiat*? Do you ever think there's a chance you're taking too much of our money?"

"Sometimes." He scrutinized Patrick. What was this interruption? "Other times I think we don't take enough."

"Charming as ever."

"What gets you out of the desert? Did you finally run out of water? Or perhaps just the face cream you like." Neal adjusted his tie, tightened the knot as if to signify he was only available for business.

"That's homophobic."

"Was it? I'm sorry. I meant it only to sound generally unkind."

"It's a serum, not cream, and you'll be delighted to know I can order it online. Oh, but remember when you used to do nice things for me? That was sweet. You were sweet. Before our marriage turned so toxic."

"I'm still sweet. Just ask my clients who are currently working."

Patrick clutched his heart, even though it was clear he took no offense.

"When's the last time you were even in Los Angeles? Two years? Three? You turn down every invitation I send you."

"What makes you think I'm not here all the time? Because I don't call on you or show up at one of your dumb premieres?" Patrick leaned against the window and studied the view over Century City. People power-strolled the outdoor shopping mall across the way, looking like sped-up figures in an old Charlie Chaplin film.

"Well, I can tell this is going to be productive. If you'll excuse me, I'm supposed to be on a call." Neal picked up the phone for effect.

"You sent Heidi Himalayas to my house."

"Who?"

"The girl. Outside your office." Patrick didn't care for the casual misogyny, but he knew it was the language Neal spoke.

"Cassie? She came to your house?"

"Yes, that's what I said."

"When?"

"I don't know. Last week sometime. Or the week before."

"Is that where she was? I asked her to get me a spoon for my Skyr and she was gone for five hours. I thought she quit."

"Your Skyr?"

"It's Icelandic . . . You're not here to talk about my food, are you? Why don't we cut to the chase?"

Patrick raised his eyebrows while frowning, which was, with the last of his Botox, surprisingly difficult to do. "Well, okay . . . I'm here to tell you I'm back. I don't like you, but I need you." With that out of the way, Patrick took a seat on the leather couch and crossed his legs. He flipped through the covers of the *Hollywood Reporter*, which were fanned across the glass coffee table, before selecting an issue about Hollywood's New Leading Ladies, none of whom he recognized. "Do you have any Fanta?"

"By all means, make yourself at home." Neal leaned back in his Herman Miller Aeron chair and put his hands behind his back. Behind him were more windows and a credenza with a SAG Award.

"Who gave you their SAG Award?"

Neal sighed. "Stephen."

"Really."

"For safekeeping. He's traveling."

"Can I have it?"

"No."

"How's Bethany?"

"You're back after how many years and you want to talk about my wife?"

"Sure. We're friends. How about the kids. They good? You never told me children were so much work."

Neal was confused. "You have children now?"

"Oh, yes. Two. Age nine and six or something like that. Well, they're not really *my* children. They're more like my wards. But still. So much work. The sunscreen, for one. And they need to eat all the time! I'm always fixing them food."

"Don't you eat? Just make more."

"No, I don't eat." Patrick patted his firm abdominals. "Are you crazy? Not since 2002."

Neal stood up, took two steps away from his desk, and then sat back down again. It was like he felt it wise to have the barrier of his desk between him and a possible menace. "Did you steal these children? Do I need to be concerned? Should I get your lawyer on the phone?"

"No, I didn't . . . *What's wrong with you*? They're my niece and nephew. They're staying with me for the summer and are being well looked after."

"Who's with them right now?"

"The gay throuple who lives behind my house."

Neal narrowed his eyes. Perhaps this was some sort of test. "So. You're ready to get back to work?"

"In short."

"I thought your moving to Palm Springs marked your retirement from the business."

"Retirement? Oh, god no. That was the start of my comeback."

Neal picked up a ballpoint pen and clicked it several times. It was surprisingly loud.

"I can't live in Palm Springs and work? Paul Newman lived in Connecticut."

"So now you're Paul Newman."

"In this scenario only. Well, also—we both have piercing blue eyes. Should I do a line of condiments?"

"Get out of my office."

"Salad dressings have been done, but I feel like mayonnaise is poised for a comeback. We could get ahead of the curve on that." Patrick smiled with all his teeth.

"You're wasting my time. Just like you did the last time you called in the middle of the night."

"It wasn't the middle of the night, it was five in the morning. You used to tell me you were up at five in the morning to talk to New York."

"Were you in New York?"

"No."

"Then what were you doing calling me at five in the morning!"

Neal had a point. About ten months after he moved to Palm Springs, Patrick suffered a bout of insomnia. When the sun rose, marking the end of his third sleepless night, he called his agent and said he wanted to go back to work. And then, embarrassed, he never called back to say he was suffering exhaustion-induced hysteria. What he wanted was not to go back to work, but rather to go back to *sleep*. Neal made some calls, which left him with egg on his face when Patrick claimed to have no memory of their discussion. "Look, if you're not into this . . ."

"Did I say I wasn't into this?" Neal clicked the pen a half-dozen more times. "And you're willing to audition?"

"Why do I have to audition?"

"Because you've been away. Because people need to see that you still have it. Because you haven't played the game."

"I don't like playing games."

"Then what *do* you like?" Neal stared at Patrick like he was a petulant child.

"I like tacos. I like parties." Patrick glared to see if his agent would remember the advance he had once made, or if it was all in a drunken stupor.

After a beat, Neal turned red and scoffed. He dropped the pen with a thud. "Okay, well you're playing games right now."

The longer Patrick sat on the couch without a Fanta, the angrier he got. The memory of the taco truck, and Neal's reaction to it, pushed him over the edge. What *was* he doing here? He'd told John he hated earning money for Neal. There had to be a way to earn money and not have this worm leech off of him; now was not the time to be lazy in his thinking. This wasn't about going back to work. It was about moving *forward* to work. "You know what? This was a bad idea. YOU'RE FIRED."

"Oh, I'm fired? You said you wanted to work. How are you going to do that without an agent?"

"I'm getting a new agent."

"Where are you going to go? Across the street? Read your agency agreement. You're not allowed to sign with another agency for six months." Neal picked up a ball of rubber bands and tossed it triumphantly back and forth in his hands.

"Across the street? No. You'd miss me too much. Across the hall." Patrick looked at the ceiling to buy himself a beat. Was he certain about this? *Yes*. Yes he was.

"Across the hall . . ."

"I'm with Annie Alps out there. I'm sure she has my files."

"Cassie Everest."

"Thank god you knew who I meant. I'm running out of mountains." Patrick put his feet up on the coffee table, knowing it would drive his now former agent nuts.

"My assistant."

"Oh, no. She's off your desk. She's an agent now. She has a big new client!"

Neal set the ball down and pressed both of his palms on his desktop like he was bracing himself to stand up. "You don't get to promote people at your whim. You don't work here. Who do you think you are?"

"She said you were promoting her if I agreed to come back. I'm back."

"Back with me!"

"I'm sure it won't be a problem."

Neal was approaching wit's end. "And what if it is?"

They stared at each other in a battle of wills, but the upper hand was Patrick's—it's why he had mentioned Neal's wife. Patrick grinned, pleased with himself. "Then you know what I'll have to say about it."

Neal chewed this over before lifting his arms in the air as if Patrick had him at gunpoint. He let out an annoyed growl.

"That's right. Keep your hands where I can see them."

Neal muttered under his breath; he lowered his arms and made a project of stacking some papers while shuffling some others, waiting for this torture to be over.

"Anyhow, I'll see if Cassie can get me a Fanta. I don't know what it is, I'm just craving a pineapple soda!" Patrick stood and patted himself to make sure he had his phone and his keys. "I'll get out of your hair. I wouldn't want to mess up those sweet plugs." Patrick paused in the doorway. A surprising flash of regret overcame him (*My goodness*, he thought, *people are complex and weird*), but there was no turning back now. "It was good to see you, Neal. Be sure to transfer my files." He waved and, without waiting for a reciprocal goodbye, stepped out in the hall.

He locked eyes with Cassie, who sat stunned in her cubicle—certain she was going to catch a cyclone of shit the second Patrick left.

"Well, it's you and me, kid."

Cassie untangled the headphones from her hair and placed them on her keyboard as Patrick sat on the edge of her desk. "What do you mean?"

"I'm back, but you're my agent. Congratulations. You've got your first client."

"That's . . . not possible."

"I worked it out with Neal. All systems go." The phone on Cassie's desk started ringing and she moved to answer it. Patrick lunged for her headset. "Neal will get it."

"Really?"

"Really."

"You're serious." The phone stopped ringing.

"Deadly." Patrick pulled a pen from a pencil cup and put it in his shirt pocket. "Turns out, you're the one I like."

She stammered a few times before she was able to form words. "I—I—I don't know what to say." A cubicle neighbor of Cassie's prairie-dogged over the partition dividing them to see if she was hearing this all correctly; Patrick met her gaze with a single eye, and she slowly lowered herself out of view.

"Look, I know it's technically outside of your job description, but I'm going to need a few things."

"Sure." Cassie was still too stunned to object.

"I can't remember any of my social media passwords. Can you have them reset? Just look for my name with the blue check marks."

"Of course. Anything." Cassie scrambled for a notepad. "What else can I do?"

"I'm having a party and I could use your help. I need you to invite all my dearest friends. Even the ones I haven't met yet." It was a line from *Mame*, but as soon as Patrick said it out loud he had a newfound appreciation for the wisdom in it. He pulled his new pen from his breast pocket and handed it to her, cueing her to write this down. "*Especially* the ones I haven't met yet. Okay? Use your resources. Shake the fruit tree and see what hits the ground. You'll be there, of course. And invite Neal. He won't come, but what the hell. I'm in a mood." He signaled at her to write. "Maybe it will clear the air."

Cassie scrambled to get it all down. "A party. Dearest friends. Fruit tree. Invite Neal. Okay." Patrick could hear the uncertainty in her voice. Hesitation, perhaps, but not dismissal. Even she had to see the benefits of getting to know him better to do her job with any sort of aplomb. Planning a party, spending more time with him, could only help in the long run. "Anything else?"

"Yes." Patrick ran through the list in his head one more time, the one he'd concocted at the bottom of his pool. There *was* something else. What was it? "Oh yeah. I was thinking of getting the kids a dog for real. Know where I can get something like that?"

Suddenly Patrick had people again.

TWELVE

They sat at Lulu's around a circular four-top that straddled the inside (with its air-conditioning) and the patio (with its misters), the temperature both hot and cold depending on which moment you asked, the kids holding enormous dinner menus that covered their faces. Patrick glanced down at Marlene Dietrich, who, like the good dog she'd proven herself to be from the moment he walked her out of the West Los Angeles animal shelter, sat at the base of his chair, squarely on the patio side.

"There's too many choices," Maisie complained.

"The world is your oyster tonight. There's no need to complain."

"They have oythters?" Grant asked skeptically.

"Look, you asked to come here." Patrick would have preferred any number of other establishments—Copley's, for instance, on Cary Grant's old estate—but Lulu's large, colorful street presence caught the children's eyes. "Just look at the kids' menu. There's like three things. The same three things that are on every kids' menu in every restaurant everywhere in the world. Even I know this, and my experience is limited."

"I don't want to order off the kids' menu," Maisie protested.

"Why not?"

"I'm not a kid!"

Patrick set his own menu down and gripped the table for patience. "Don't be in such a hurry to be older. You're going to spend the rest of your life wishing you were younger."

Maisie glared at him before relenting and picking up the separate menu for kids.

Lulu's reminded Patrick of a cafeteria in a futuristic spaceship, as if people should be lined up at steam tables and carving stations dressed in utilitarian jumpsuits with neat lapels in primary colors after putting in a hard day's work fixing warp drives and flux capacitors. Or rather, it looked like what someone in the late 1960s *thought* the cafeteria in a futuristic spaceship would look like, based perhaps on spending too much time watching *Star Trek* episodes in their stateroom aboard a gay cruise. But it was one of the few places that he knew of that had both a kids' menu and a bar that served a decent martini ("Dry, very dry, just wave the vermouth over the vodka and it's probably still too much vermouth"), which ultimately made it a judicious choice for tonight's lupper.

"Can Marlene be in here?" Maisie asked, always concerned with the rules.

"Why not? She's a service dog."

"No she's not."

"I'm blind." Patrick retrieved the sunglasses that were tucked into the neck of his T-shirt and put them on for effect.

"No you're not."

"Fine. She's an emotional support dog."

"For who?"

"For you. For *me*, if you don't decide on your dinner."

"Why are there olives in your water?"

Patrick was putting out fires left and right. He took a long, slow sip of his martini. "It's not water."

"Can I watch YouTube?" Grant set his menu down, bored.

"No."

"You hate YouTube."

"I don't know YouTube well enough to hate it." But Patrick was certain if he did, that would probably be true.

"Then why not?"

"Because we're having a family meal. And yes, I realize I sound like my father. This is what you've reduced me to in a matter of weeks." Patrick tore off a piece of bread from the basket on the table before remembering he was throwing a party in a week for people he hadn't seen in ages and he didn't want to appear bloated. Panicked, he dropped the bread on Maisie's plate. "Here. This is for you."

Maisie picked up her knife and reached for the butter.

"I got you guys a dog, you can't possibly be bored. Should I take her back?" Marlene sat up as if she understood the threat; to placate her, Patrick dropped another bite of bread at her feet. At the shelter, her scruffy face looked haunted, frozen just so in perfect black and white (black around the eyes with a white snoot and perfect black nose). Patrick lied and told the kids she came with the name Marlene. The shelter was calling her something common like Bella or Sophie; he'd already forgotten. On the drive back from Los Angeles with the sun setting behind them, Marlene, who uttered not one bark, proved to be a true silent star who always found her light.

"No! Don't take her back!" Grant protested.

"Okay, then." Patrick leaned down and scratched the dog on top of her head. "Look, it's not YouTube I have a problem with. It's social media as a whole. And, yes, I know. YouTube is more than social media, but what you watch on there—kid vlogs and whatnot—is. I don't expect you to understand this at your age, but I'm older and I see what it's doing to society, and I don't want to see you fall into the same trap."

"What trap?" Grant started swinging his legs and Marlene jumped back just in time not to get hit. She resettled on calmer turf under Patrick's chair.

"You know. We're hyper-connected, but at the same time desperately lonely. We're overstimulated by bright lights in our face all the time and the promise of more and more content, more and more people to follow, but we're also numb, scrolling and scrolling past images we don't even take the time to recognize, or form a cognizant thought about what they're saying. About us, the creator—not *God*, mind you—the content creator, about life."

"But we're not society. We're just Maisie and Grant." Maisie gave up on trying to butter her bread and dropped her knife with a clang. Patrick took the bread plate from her to help.

"Do you even care about the kids you watch?"

"They do toy reviewth!" Grant exclaimed.

Patrick plowed right over him. "Or do you just watch them because they're there? Because one video rolls into the next in a never-ending parade of I don't even know what. Bullshit, is what it is. It's all bullshit. That's why I used to pay someone else to do my sosh."

"What's sosh?" Maisie looked appalled.

"*Sosh*. Social media? You guys. Come on, now."

"*You're* on YouTube."

"No I'm not, I'm at the dinner table with you."

"No, you're *on* YouTube. Mommy helped us do a thearch." Grant twisted sideways, away from Patrick, before resting his head on the back of his chair.

"Oh, what. Clips from the show? That's copyright infringement. That should be taken down."

"No," Maisie corrected. "A woman was asking you questions."

"Like an interview? My god. Was it that one where I had quinoa in my teeth?" Patrick shuddered and Maisie laughed. It wasn't really funny, though. Patrick still wanted that segment producer fired. That was the problem with the internet. It was the Wild West and nothing could ever be erased.

Grant spun back around to face his uncle. "You could put *us* on YouTube."

"Yeah!" Maisie agreed. It was almost like the two had planned this and were making a rehearsed pitch. If that was the case, Patrick would advise them to work on their subtlety.

"I could order your lupper for you. Spaghetti with extra worms."

"I don't want worms! I want to be on YouTube!"

"No you don't. It's a cult. The cult of self-expression. Everyone wants to put everything out there and the truth is no one cares! No one cares. I'm sorry to say that to you in the face of what you've been through. But no one out there really gives a shit. You know who does care? I do. GUP. So decide what you want to eat, let's order it, and then we can sit here and you can tell me whatever it is you want to tell the masses. And I won't have to go on my phone to see it because I'm sitting right here."

"I don't want to tell *you*!" Grant made two little fists that were ready to strike and yet also adorable.

"Sit still and look who you're talking to. I'm an actor, okay? I understand the need to perform, I really do. But now everybody is performing. That's what vlogging is. Performance. Everyone is performing everything all the time for everyone and there's no *reason* for it. I was at least acting out a story. I went to school to learn how to act, and writers went to school to learn how to write, and directors, even the TV ones, spent years honing their craft, and producers—well, no one really knows what they do, but they seem to work very hard at it. Okay? It has purpose. It has value. People used to want to escape from their lives at the end of the day. Now they want to lie back in bed and watch themselves over and over again and count their likes and comments and shares and followers. Don't you see? They're performer *and* audience. It's just one big masturbatory waste of time!" Patrick pushed a menu in Grant's direction and caught the eye of an older woman eavesdropping. Patrick gave her the thumb's-up; he's got this. "Now, what do you want to eat?"

"No one knowth what you're talking about."

"Let it marinate while you decide on lupper."

"I don't want lupper!" Grant shoved his menu back at Patrick, nearly knocking over a water glass.

Patrick sighed. He'd seen these families at restaurants before, children misbehaving, acting out. Parents ignoring them, looking exhausted, clutching their silverware like pitchforks and tossing back cheap chardonnay like it was the only thing preventing them from stabbing their spawn. He'd judged them then, sometimes harshly. He wanted to do better now.

"I'll have the pizza." Maisie offered a feeble smile; even she felt sorry for him.

Patrick thought back to his years on *The People Upstairs*. Did he know what he was talking about? In the early seasons the cast would gather at someone's house to watch the show the night it aired, first with takeout, later with midlist catering like Maggiano's eggplant parmesan. It was fun, a mini cast party every week for a show with an open-ended run. They were all young, breaking into the business together, and nothing excited them more than being an audience for each other. None of them had ever made money like this, and maybe it wasn't much by Hollywood standards, not at first, but it bought happiness—temporarily, at least. Especially in those early years. For Patrick it was a second chance. A sign he would survive. A reason to believe there would be life after Joe.

And yet, he stopped attending those screenings, and the others eventually did, too. By the fourth season not one of them copped to watching the show and perhaps they themselves were responsible for the series' diminishing ratings. But watching a program you were on had a strange effect; it made Patrick nostalgic for experiences he was still in the middle of living. It pulled him out of it. He was both him, living his life, and some ghostly version of himself, floating above his terrestrial self, watching, judging. He stopped feeling present in his own body. Stopped being able to feel this new joy, and it was eclipsed by sorrow again; perhaps happiness was destined to be temporary regardless, perhaps it never even stood a chance. Now he worried about that happening to the kids.

"Grant? Pizza?"

"I don't want anything!"

Patrick looked back over his shoulder for a way out of this. Three tables over was a party of silver-haired men in tragic Hawaiian shirts celebrating a birthday. At the center of their table was an enormous martini glass containing a mountain of pink cotton candy. He motioned for their waiter as he was passing by. "Excuse me, we're going to start with one of those." He pointed to the cotton candy.

"You're going to *start* with dessert."

"That's right. We can't seem to decide on a main course, so we're going to start with dessert. When you have a moment."

This seemed to get Grant's attention.

"Look, it's not right for me to film you and put you on the internet. That's a decision that your father should be a part of and I don't want to hear any protest out of you. But let's see what you got. Okay? When the cotton candy comes, I want you to do as many goofy things with it as you can think of. I will record you on my phone. Think of this like an audition for YouTube." Patrick sat back in his chair to consider this. Could he use this to their advantage? For better or worse, they were part of a self-documenting generation at ease in front of a camera. Perhaps he could get them to open up by filming them. Get them to talk about their grief in a way that they simply couldn't manage face-to-face. Maybe they needed the camera between them as a barrier, a neutral arbiter who wouldn't judge or ask questions or try to define their feelings or shape the way they expressed them. It would simply record their feelings for posterity. Perhaps it was the perfect therapist. "Deal?"

Grant had his elbows on the table and put his hands under his chin to think about this. If only elbows on the table were Patrick's biggest concern. "Goofy things like what?"

"I don't know, kid. What would you do on your vlog?"

"I don't know."

"Well, that sounds like a rather dull viewing experience. Two kids staring sadly at candy."

"Eat it!" Maisie offered.

"Meh." Patrick shrugged. "I don't think it's fun to sit around and watch other people eat candy when you can't enjoy any yourself."

"But why do we have to be goofy?"

"People love goofy. Goofy bought me my house. There's already a first wave of kids with followers. You're second bananas. Like I was. You gotta ham it up to grab eyeballs."

"Bananas, ham." Maisie scowled.

"Eyeballth," Grant added, grimacing.

The waiter returned with the cotton candy, and when it was placed on the table it towered over all of their heads, a pink Matterhorn made entirely of billowy clouds. "Here you go. I'll give you a few minutes and check back to see if you've decided on dinner." He winked at Patrick. Flirtatiously, conspiratorially, or just in recognition; it wasn't clear.

"Here, let's start with an easy one." Patrick used two hands to pull at a strand of cotton candy until it came loose. He pinched it in the middle and curled the ends, then held it between his upper lip and his nose like a mustache. Except for its pink color, it looked not unlike John's.

Grant instantly perked up. "I want one!"

"Me too!"

"Do you think I'm stopping you?" Patrick pushed the cotton candy to their side of the table so they could tear off the makings for mustaches. He tucked his under his nostrils, and he could feel it melting the littlest bit against his warm skin and the room smelled suddenly sweet, a spun sugar wormhole opening, beckoning, transporting him back to a happier time.

"Look at me!" Grant hollered.

"I am looking at you." Patrick felt like an old-timey railroad baron, his voice affected by the snarl he projected to keep his mustache in place. He nodded to Maisie to make certain she knew he was watching her, too. "Okay, let me get my phone."

Patrick opened his camera and his finger paused without selecting video. "Wait, wait, wait. Let's take a selfie for your dad." He pushed his chair back, careful not to disturb Marlene, and slid around between them. He crouched and put his right arm around Grant and held the phone out in front of them. "Squeeze in!" They were cheek-to-cheek, and for a moment Patrick's heart skipped—for a fraction of a second it actually felt like it stopped beating—and he took in a sharp breath of air. It was so, he didn't know—*saccharine*. And yet deeply genuine, profound; he felt something he hadn't in a long, long time. He closed his eyes.

I love you, he said silently in his head, to himself, to the kids, to Joe, to Sara, to no one. To everyone.

"Uncle Patrick!"

He blinked his eyes open and fumbled with the camera like he was caught, as if everyone in the restaurant had been reading his mind.

He'd never felt more exposed.

"Say bananas!"

"NO!" Grant yelled.

"Say cotton candy, then." This seemed more agreeable.

"COTTON CANDY!"

He snapped the photo, a keeper on the first try. He swung around back to his chair and looked at the picture. It was deceptive, a perfect moment of happiness in the middle of an otherwise tense meal; three sneers employed to hold their pink facial hair in place, when in fact it was the first time in days they were smiling. It was also artful; a column with luminescent tile perfectly captured the light, blotting out the disapproving woman behind them with blues and turquoises and pinks that picked up the color of their mustaches. He looked back in his phone to find his last text chain with Greg, scrolled and scrolled until at last there it was. Their last text, before Sara died, about something inconsequential—a pictorial in *National Geographic* about a climber who free-scaled El Capitan; Greg mentioned planning a future trip with the kids to Yosemite. And then . . . nothing. As if he were silenced along with Sara. Patrick attached the photo and hovered his finger over send. Was Greg even in possession of his phone? And if he was, why hadn't he texted? Why hadn't he checked in to make sure everything was going okay?

"Do a video!" It was Grant. His mustache slipped and he caught it just in time.

Patrick placed his sunglasses on his nephew, then added a pinch of cotton candy on each side where the glasses connected with his ears to make sideburns. Grant laughed and Maisie looked on in amazement. "You look like Martin Van Buren."

"Who's Martin Van Buren?" Maisie asked.

"Who's Rip Van Winkle? Who's Dick Van Patten? No one really knows." He then grabbed the top third of their dessert and placed it like a bun on Maisie's head. "Okay. Now you're ready."

The kids twittered and giggled.

"Do you know what you're going to say?"

"We're going to talk about our favorite desserts."

Grant nodded his enthusiastic agreement; his uncle's glasses slid half an inch down his nose and he tilted his head back to hold them in place, giving the camera a perfect view up his nostrils.

"Well, I'm not one to chase trends, but baking shows are very hot right now. Okay! *Aaaand*. ACTION."

Patrick worked overtime to contain his smile as he hit record.

THIRTEEN

Patrick took one look at Cassie and blurted, "No, no, no, no, no" on repeat, as if a cosmic crisis were bearing down and he had the ability to stop it with the sheer force of his command. "This is a *party*."

The trepidation was apparent on Cassie's face, as she hesitated to even step inside. Patrick could see she thought this was a mistake—the party hadn't even begun and she was clearly panic-stricken that she'd done something wrong. "I'm well a-aware it's a party," she stammered. "I put together the guest list. And hired the bartender. And the valet."

Patrick admired the feeble defense she mounted; in fairness, she had accomplished a lot very quickly. "Well, don't just stand there. Come inside."

The house was immaculate, glimmering white with colorful pillows and ceramics freshly rearranged—glorious vases and sculptures in orange and bronze—including a small metallic-blue Koons. Patrick's Golden Globe sat in its new home, a shelf above where it had previously lived, out of the reach of young hands; it even had its own key light. And yet it was the seven-foot pink-tinsel Christmas tree with shimmering clear lights and glass ornaments that stood as a sort of pièce de résistance that really drew one's eye. Patrick grinned proudly, claiming full ownership, when Cassie finally noticed it.

"Was I supposed to be in charge of decorations?" Cassie asked, worried the Christmas tree was there to cover some further failure on her part, the lack of balloons or streamers or some sort of custom banner. "Or maybe supposed to get ice?"

"No, just the guests and the bartender and the valet, and you did all those things flawlessly." Patrick snapped his fingers three times. "But what are you wearing?"

"A dress." Cassie's shift dress was white, sleeveless—perfect, it seemed, for a desert garden party when it was likely to be over one hundred degrees. She twirled like she was on the red carpet, mistaking the horror in his voice for interest.

"It's white."

"Yes," she agreed nervously.

"Am I keeping you from your wedding?"

"What? Of course not."

"And those shoes?"

"It's a two-hour drive! I can't do that in heels." Cassie's eyes darted as if she knew she were out of her element.

"You look like Louise Fletcher."

Even though her MBA was not an MFA and she lacked a formal education in film, Patrick's remark was perfectly clear: in all white from head to toe, with shoes that were just shy of orthopedic, she resembled not Louise Fletcher but Nurse Ratched. She stared at Patrick. "*You're* wearing white!"

"A white shirt! That's totally different." As if to underscore that difference, Patrick kicked out a leg to display the loud butterfly print of his pants.

"I see." Her expression suggested she didn't really see.

"Well, it's not a disaster. We can certainly fix it."

"We can?"

"NOOOOO! But we can burn this and start over. Maisie!"

Instead of Maisie, Marlene came running from around the corner, her nails failing to find traction on the terrazzo floor. She looked even smaller than her sixteen pounds, navigating the steps of the sunken living room, her splotchy face and tail and button nose standing out most against the white tile. A pink tongue hung limply to one side; any eyes Marlene may have had were lost in the sprouts of dark fur.

"I said Maisie, not Marlene!" Patrick exclaimed, but the dog didn't understand him, and once she found her footing she made her way to his side. "Well, anyhow, Cassie, Marlene, Marlene, Cassie."

"You adopted a dog named Marlene!" Cassie crouched down to envelop the dog's face in her hands.

"No, I adopted a dog named Bella, but Jesus Christ. So she's Marlene now. Maisie!"

This time Grant came screeching around the corner. He was dressed in shorts and a short-sleeve shirt with a dashing bow tie.

Patrick slapped his forehead. "What kind of *Martha Marcy May Marlene* nightmare is this?"

"I can't breathe, GUP." The boy tugged at his tie.

"Breathing is overrated." But Grant started to stomp and Marlene jumped back to protect her front paws, so Patrick undid the kid's bow tie until it hung loose around his neck like Grant was Dean Martin after a particularly intense bender. "Here. That looks way cooler anyhow. Where's your sister?"

"I'm right here." Maisie appeared out of nowhere in an outfit identical to Grant's; she, however, liked her bow tie, looking not unlike how one imagines Diane Keaton looked as a tween. Maisie fell in line next to her uncle, her brother, and the dog.

"Maisie, Grant, you remember Cassie? And where is Marlene's bow tie? Never mind. Maisie, will you take Cassie to my dress closet and find her something decent to wear?"

Cassie started to protest, but was caught off guard. "You have a whole dress closet?"

"It's my caftan closet, technically, but I think you'll find something nice. Maisie, you know what I like." Leaving the decision to Cassie was clearly out of the question.

With a modicum of pity, Maisie reached out for Cassie's hand. "Come. I'll show you."

They took a few steps through the living room toward Patrick's bedroom. "You have a Christmas tree," Cassie exclaimed.

"We found it in GUP's garage."

"It's pink." Cassie thought she would focus on the tree's appearance rather than the fact that it was July.

"I would have preferred blue." Maisie shrugged. *What are you going to do?*

"By the way, who's coming to this party?" Patrick turned around, but Cassie was already gone. "You know what? I'll be surprised." He looked down at his nephew. "Seriously, though. Where is the dog's bow tie?"

Grant looked over each shoulder and then lost interest. "Did you know snails can sleep for three years?"

"Did you know that forty percent of icebergs are penguin piss?"

Grant's jaw dropped. "Is that true?"

"How the hell am I supposed to know?" He mussed Grant's hair to make it look more stylish. "Would you like a martini?"

"I'm six."

"Is that a yes?"

The doorbell curtailed their conversation.

◇◇◇◇◇

By nine o'clock, the party was in full swing. Patrick was both touched and horrified by the number of people who had made the two-hour drive. More than that, who committed to spending the night in Palm Springs; there was no driving back to Los Angeles after an open bar. He should have had Cassie book a group rate at the Parker. Patrick was loath to admit, but she had done a remarkable job with the guest list. All of his friends and a few of his frenemies, but none of his *enemies*, and a smattering of up-and-comers who you would want to be seen at any A-list event. It's like she'd read back issues of *Us Weekly* to see who was in and who was out, or at the very least the list of people he passively followed on gay Twitter.

"Cassie!" Patrick remarked when he finally caught sight of her in his caftan. "Bravo." She looked amazing and knew it, so she beamed and gave him a spin. "And this is quite a crowd!" He was legitimately impressed.

"They're all here for you!" she replied, but her smile was not nearly as radiant as her dress. Patrick raised a stern eyebrow. "*Fine*. And for the Eagles. They're playing tomorrow night at Agua Caliente and I bribed them all with tickets. I can't tell if they're being ironic, but they think Don Henley is cool." She steeled herself for Patrick's wrath; instead he placed his hand gently on her shoulder.

"Well done. And I like that you tell me the truth."

Guests smiled and waved as Patrick weaved through the crowd, many hugged him tight and declared some version of *Where have you been?*, each putting their emphasis on a different word in the question. Patrick smiled back and did his best to remember little inside jokes he had with each of them. He whispered something about a vegan ham to Jeremy Dykstra; they had both been to a disastrous Easter brunch at a well-known publicist's house. He summoned his inner Marlon to yell, "STELLLLA!" at Malina Kuhn, as she had once reenacted in horrific detail her disastrous college production of *A Streetcar Named Desire* in which Blanche DuBois had a lisp (*I have alwayth depended on the kindneth of thtrangers*—he would have to get Grant to say that later). He stopped to place his hand on Max Crosley's arm and said, "Why didn't you tell me?" and when Max said, "What?" Patrick replied, "To bring along my harmonica." He could never pass up the opportunity to quote Eleanor Parker's character from *The Sound of Music* to anyone named Max; in another life Patrick would have made a perfect Baroness.

In truth, it was good to see the house so . . . full. Alive with people. He felt like part of something again, seen. But also strangely like a ghost, invisible. These parties were happening in Los Angeles night after night, week after week, without him. People were happy to see him tonight, sure. They would greet him, then retreat into conversations with themselves, afraid perhaps of becoming trapped in a conversation with the crazy man who *left Hollywood*. He *had* to be mad. Why, after all, would anyone leave LA at the height of their success? What was he doing in Palm Springs? Was he part of a cult? Mentally ill? Addicted to sonic therapies and sound baths? Had he found God in Joshua Tree or was he going to ask them for money, for favors, their souls?

It was off-putting.

But Patrick didn't realize how deep the hole he'd dug for himself in the desert sand had become until he grabbed the hand of Adam Harper; there was instant gravitational pull. He could feel himself, if not quite rescued, buoyed. Like spotting the lights of a distant ocean liner while adrift on a raft at sea, or a diver giving you a hit of oxygen from his tank when yours was running out. It didn't hurt that Patrick wouldn't mind a little mouth-to-mouth from his former costar, but Adam, all six-three of him, was hopelessly, tragically straight. "Come here, you big gorilla."

"Patrick!"

He pulled Adam in for a tight hug and pressed himself maybe a little too close to his old friend's muscular torso. Over Adam's shoulder he spotted Cassie kindly engaging Maisie and Grant as they pointed to each ornament they'd hung on the Christmas tree. It was sweet, he thought, and disorienting: his interest in his niece and nephew outweighing his interest in Adam's torso. He didn't like that one bit and, spooked, he let go of his friend and took a step back. "Prince Adam." It was a nickname Patrick had bestowed for Adam's He-Man physique.

"What has it been," Adam asked. "Years?"

"Something like that." Probably since they walked off of Stage Four on the Disney lot and Patrick never looked back.

"So this is where you went. You're the talk of the town. The disappearing Patrick O'Hara. Or, *were*. People eventually forgot about you." He gave Patrick a slap on the back strong enough to dislodge a hard candy.

"Yeah, well. It's not like any of you are setting the town ablaze." It was perhaps a bad choice of words, given the number of fires Southern California had recently endured. But it gave Patrick some solace, the lack of anything from his castmates approaching success. Adam had starred in a movie as a former tennis pro named Tony who came out of retirement to play a last match against a child prodigy with a mean backhand; the film was laughed out of South by Southwest (how it ever got in was anyone's guess). And that was enviable—a *movie*. The others had short-lived series on some of the lesser streaming services, none of which warranted two seasons.

"You keeping tabs on me, brother?"

"No, but I still have access to IMDbPro. And my agent tells me."

"Your agent."

Patrick lifted his arm and pointed at Cassie as Adam frowned in her direction.

"Great dress. But she brought her kids?"

"They're mine. Kids *and* the dress."

Adam barely had time to react before Daisy Morales and Jennifer Skeen stumbled into Patrick's sight line with wide-eyed curiosity, like they had just stepped off the bus from whatever small town still sent their most attractive ingenues to Hollywood via public transport. "Um, HELLOOOO," Patrick bellowed, and when they turned their heads and saw him, they immediately crouched into two-thirds of the classic *Charlie's Angels* pose. Patrick wasn't keeping track of how many drinks he'd had (he wasn't an amateur, so what was the point?), so was surprised when he opened his mouth and gasped a high-pitched wheeze. Daisy and Jennifer were his other two costars on *The People Upstairs*. Patrick couldn't form words, so instead fell in formation as Kate Jackson until the entire party turned around and applauded, and then they broke, hugged, and screamed.

"I hate you for ever leaving," Jennifer pouted. "LA's just no fun anymore."

"Was it ever fun?" Patrick asked.

"Yes, silly. When we were young and famous!"

Daisy leaned her head on Jennifer's shoulder. "I was on the lot for a meeting the other day and I went by our soundstage and they totally painted over where we signed our names on the back wall! Everything's been undone. It's like we were never even there! Come back."

Patrick wiped a drop of nervous sweat from his forehead. He hadn't had to be so *on* in some time. "Well, gee. You do make it sound enticing."

"Pat-*riiiiick*," they whined, stomping their feet. He studied their faces; they looked both older and younger, copies of their former selves plumped with Botox and fillers (although by a very skilled hand).

"Come, come," he said, eager to move on. "I want to introduce you to my wards."

They spun around and Patrick pointed at Maisie and Grant.

"Oh . . . my . . . god." Jennifer covered her mouth, as if her ovaries had taken control of her speech. Patrick felt something akin to pride. If the kids were anything, they *were* cute—especially in their matching outfits; he could see why they would be the object of maternal desire. "You have a *tree*!"

What? "Not the tree, the children."

"Are they yours?" Daisy grabbed him by the shirt collar and pressed herself against him. "I *begged* you for your sperm and you said no."

"Well, I didn't know you wanted it to make babies."

"What did you think I wanted it for?"

Patrick grasped for an answer. "Decoupage?"

Jennifer laughed. "Ugh. God, I missed you. I missed this. I miss *us*."

Patrick introduced Maisie and Grant to his friends. Maisie did this little curtsy thing that she learned on her own; only Patrick caught the side-eye she flashed when she finished. The girls squealed over their outfits and even Adam was impressed with Grant's loose bow tie.

"I wish I were still that cool," Adam declared.

"*Still*? Were you ever?"

"Fuck you. But don't you just want to give him a scotch, neat?"

"I offered him a martini, but alas." He pulled Grant, suddenly shy, tight to his side and parted his hair to the side.

"How long have you lived with Patrick?" Jennifer asked.

Grant picked at a branch on the Christmas tree. "Since our mother died."

"Oh, my god," Daisy said. "That's hilarious. You're hilarious. Where's the bar?"

She twirled in circles until she spotted the bartender on the patio. Patrick turned to his niece and nephew. "She thought you were kidding. She doesn't really think that's hilarious." He looked up at Cassie standing nearby and made a face. *Oops.*

It didn't work the first time, but Patrick was undeterred. He took the cheese knife and banged on his glass hard enough to shatter even Baccarat crystal, which, since it was part of the bartender's service, this wasn't. "Everyone. If I may . . ." Patrick bit the inside of his cheek. Lame. He was overcome with nerves. Why? It had been a while since he'd had to do any kind of public speaking, but didn't he have a performer's heart? He was looking down at the kid from the new drama on the CW that had tweens aflutter. The nerves came when the kid looked back. Patrick didn't want anyone telling teenagers, but this guy was actually hotter in person in his thick Tom Ford eyewear and sculpted white tee that gave him a perfect James Dean edge. Was it legal to make eyes at him? Sure. Hollywood has employed twenty-somethings to play teenagers all the way back to the dawn of TV. Ron Howard was already balding when he played Richie Cunningham; that one girl from that nineties show was actually the president of SAG when she was editing a high school yearbook on TV. "Everyone?"

He surveyed the crowd. His costars, other actor friends, that burgeoning pop star whom Patrick had told smelled nice. (He misunderstood her reply; when she thanked him and said it was her fragrance, he didn't immediately get that she meant it was *her* fragrance—something bottled and sold with her name on it for girls to buy at malls nationwide.)

Chunky Glasses, Emory something-or-other, wet his lips, put his fingers in his mouth, and whistled so loudly the dog jumped, almost completing a full somersault. Emory winked at Patrick.

Whoa. Does one ever become immune to hot boys winking? "Thank you." He almost said Emory, but what if that wasn't his name? What if it was something else, something trendy and embarrassingly dumb, like Every? "Maisie, Grant, and I wanted to thank you for coming to our little party."

Maisie's little voice pierced the quiet. "And Marlene!"

"Yes, and Marlene." How quickly she'd become part of the family by doing nothing else but resting her chin on his thigh while snoozing. It reminded him of Grant falling asleep in the crook of his shoulder that first night as he told them stories. Suddenly the spotlight felt lonely. He didn't want to be the center of attention without his ragtag crew. It felt wrong, incomplete. "Come up here, kids. For those of you who don't know, it's been a hard year for our family and it's only July." Maisie and Grant made their way to him and flanked their uncle; Patrick reached out and took their little hands. He felt like a political candidate, staging his family for maximum effect. He gave each of their hands a squeeze, how small and fragile and warm they felt in his own. How big and strong he felt in comparison. For a rare moment he liked who he was. He liked who he was with them. Not so much a guardian but a guard, someone to stand between their fragile selves and anything else that dared threaten them. "We decided instead of moping our way through a difficult summer, we needed a party. We needed you. 'Before you can say come and go, and breathe twice; and cry, so, so, each one tripping on his toe, will be here with mop and mowe.' That's from *The Tempest*. I don't know why that comes to mind. Except I'm tripping over myself trying not to break out in a freakish grin." He squeezed the kids' hands again, three or four times, as if he were tapping out the word *happiness* in Morse code. "The three of us have been muddling our way through. Except tonight. Tonight, instead of tripping on our toes, we shall trip the light fantastic." He looked down at a confused Maisie and Grant. "It's an idiom. Anything else I'm missing?"

Grant tugged at one end of his bow tie. "Enjoy our Christmath tree!"

"Yes. A special hat-tip to Jerry Herman, who taught us Guncle Rule number . . . I've lost count: When faced with unimaginable loss, we need a little Christmas."

"Right this very minute!" Emory bellowed. He raised his glass in the air with such infectious enthusiasm, the rest of Patrick's guests followed suit.

"RIGHT THIS VERY MINUTE!"

Patrick looked out over the sea of raised glasses and saw, if only momentarily, the flash of another, happier, life. The Ghost of Christmas Past at work, perhaps, if only it really were Christmas. The spell was broken by the sound of his white lacquer baby grand—an impulse purchase he'd only played once and instead made for an expensive table to display Jonathan Adler knickknacks—and the opening chords of "We Wish You a Merry Christmas." He looked up. It was Cassie. She smiled at him, all teeth and gums, the nervous expression of someone asking permission. Sweet Cassie, who still needed to learn it was always better to ask for forgiveness.

But Patrick gave his consent. And the whole crowd turned and burst into joyous song, looking to each other for a cue. *Are we really doing this? Yes, I think we are.*

And the party raged on like this. Carol after carol, drink after drink. It was the sound of pleasure, of long forgotten joy. Not just for Patrick, or the kids (Maisie settled on the piano bench next to Cassie while Grant sat on top of the piano itself, twirling one end of his bow tie), but for everyone who in the midst of the Hollywood rat race had forgotten to exhale. *Gaiety*, Patrick thought, smiling. And no one seemed to love it more than Emory, who, in the midst of a FA LA LA LA LA, linked his pinkie finger with Patrick's, a gesture so intimate it felt like an entire sex act.

They were on the eighth day of Christmas, maids-a-milking, swans-a-swimming, and whatnot, when the front door opened and Clara thrust her head inside. No one noticed, no one turned, no one made anything of this late entrant who wheeled a carry-on suitcase with a red ribbon tied to its handle (not in a Christmas bow, but to distinguish it from other lookalike luggage) across Patrick's floor, except for gargantuan Adam, who, towering over her, put his meaty arm around Clara just in time to sing, "*Fiiiive gold-en rings!*"

Patrick caught a glimpse of his sister's horrified face out of the corner of his eye and his first thought was *Can you imagine?* and he cackled to himself without missing a lyric. But then he turned and looked more carefully, the words "French hens" flopping off his tongue and plummeting clumsily to the floor like flightless birds. Like, well, *French hens.* He sheepishly waved, the happy buzz of vodka and Christmas draining from his face along with any color his skin's pigment held from a life of year-round exposure to sunshine.

Clara, stunned into silence, looked up at Adam, then across at the hulking hand squeezing her opposite shoulder. She looked around the room, recognizing a few faces from magazines in the supermarket check-out, but not many, then down at Marlene, who was jumping at her feet and sniffing her shoes. She next spotted the pink Christmas tree with its sparkling white lights and colorful ornaments and tried to make sense of it in the context of the general décor of a house in which she had never stepped foot. Eventually her eyes landed on her niece and nephew, Maisie nuzzled into a stranger in a beaded caftan and Grant sitting on top of the piano with his bow tie undone and Patrick's empty vodka glass by his side, looking like Frank Sinatra if he had starred in the movie *Big.* Finally, after all that, her eyes landed on her brother, dressed in butterfly-patterned pants with a curious expression that enraged her, and she re-gained her ability to speak.

"WHAT THE ACTUAL FUCK."

FOURTEEN

"How long was I on that plane?"

The few remaining party guests had broken down into two distinct conversation clusters in the living room; the vibe had irrecoverably dimmed with Clara's arrival. It was nearing one o'clock in the morning and while that's hardly last call in LA, where most of these guests were from, the bartender was only hired for five hours and had already started to break down the bar. As much as Patrick would like to pin this all on his sister, it probably had as much to do with that; this crowd seemed loath to pour their own drinks. Patrick did his best to do a round of goodbyes, thank everyone for coming, but the exodus was mass and he likely missed a few, including Emory, who slipped away into the night.

"I don't know. Five hours? Six? There are headwinds when you're flying west."

"Was it six months?"

"What? No, of course not."

"Then why is it Christmas in Patrickland?"

Grant stepped forward to field this one. "We found hith tree in the garage!"

"Kids, it was already past your bedtime when I took off from New York and so I can't even imagine how tired you are now. Let me use the restroom and then I will help you brush your teeth. Have they even been brushed once since I saw you last?"

Patrick held his tongue. She clearly did not realize what a commodity good teeth were in California. A perfect smile was practically a calling card. He'd rigorously overseen twice-daily teeth brushings for a month now, which, between the two of them—three if you counted Patrick—equaled one hundred and eighty brushings.

"Where is your powder room?"

"*Powder room*. There's no powder in there." Patrick bit his lip. "Unless you count cocaine."

"What?!"

"It's a joke. *Relax*. Just go." Patrick pointed behind him and Clara turned sharply on one foot. He grimaced, and when she closed the bathroom door behind her, Maisie and Grant laughed nervously. They all knew they were in gobs of trouble, but there was at least some safety in numbers.

"Do we have to clean this up, GUP?" Maisie surveyed the living room, which was dotted with half-empty glasses on colorful cocktail napkins and little plates with discarded nibbles that Marlene was dutifully tending to.

"No. Tomorrow's a new day. I asked Rosa to come and we can all clean up together." He took in the chaos around them. "Remind me to pay her double."

"Do we have to take the Christmath tree down?" Grant asked, sadness dripping from the question. The evening had been a high point in their stay and it was sad to think it was over.

Patrick took a knee so that he was eye-to-eye with Grant. "Is it Christmas yet?"

"No. Not until December!"

"Well, I've never heard of anyone taking their tree down before Christmas. Have you?"

Grant grinned broadly. "No."

"Besides. You did such a marvelous job decorating, I should think your dad would like to see it when he joins us. Let's leave it up to show him."

Both kids threw their arms around their uncle and squeezed him tight.

"What on God's green . . ." It was a muffled Clara from behind the bathroom door. "How do you flush this thing?"

Patrick was drained—a kind of exhaustion that you felt in your bones, from the night, from the week, from the month. He exhaled, blowing his hair from his forehead before fishing the washlet's remote from his back pocket, where he'd tucked it earlier for safekeeping (he didn't want guests squirting water all over his *powder room*). He handed the remote to Maisie. "You want the honors?"

A wicked smile formed on Maisie's face. She took the remote with both hands like she was being trusted with the nuclear football, found the button for the bidet feature, clenched her teeth, and pressed hard.

The delay was maybe three seconds. Clara's scream pierced the silence and they could hear her leap up and scramble to safety. Grant laughed first, then Maisie, then Patrick, until they were reduced to a pile of yowling hyenas; it was, in that moment, the funniest thing they'd ever done.

Patrick sat at his patio table picking at the paper on a bottle of spring water. The kids were in bed, together, and Clara had passed out in Patrick's other guest room; the worst of her ire would come tomorrow. Marlene lay at his feet, the patio stones finally cool and offering relief from the warm night air. When he shifted in his chair she raised an eyebrow, then closed her eyes tight, her rhythmic breathing melting into a gentle snore.

Along the back wall, the solar lights were holding their charge; Patrick always wondered if they lasted all night or if they faded at some point in the predawn. He felt guilty for not inviting JED tonight, but he'd never been good at mixing friend groups—especially at parties. Some acquaintances overlapped well enough, but JED was a world apart. Or maybe he was just being a snob. What would his Hollywood friends have to say about a throuple who sometimes wore matching shirts? Fortunately, their house was dark. If they were stewing, they were doing so inconspicuously. If they asked about the party at some future date, Patrick would lie and say he thought they had already left for Burning Man.

An unfamiliar light pierced the darkness above one of the pool lounge chairs, dancing a slow, intricate ballet like a single firefly. It startled him. Patrick squinted until the light sharpened into some sort of focus. It appeared to be the tip of a cigarette. "Hello?" He stood up and walked over to the light, cupping his hands against his brow as if that would help him see. At the edge of the house he stopped to flip on the pool light and the water shimmered a perfect summer blue.

"Great party." It took a second for the voice to register. It was Emory.

"Is that you, Chunky Glasses?" What the hell was he still doing here? Patrick had assumed he was halfway back to LA. He approached his pool slowly, hoping he projected a certain nonchalance.

"In the flesh."

Patrick sat on the edge of the lounge chair next to Emory's, allowing himself a moment to imagine that flesh; he may be a family man now but he was still a man. "I sit here at night sometimes, to look at the stars. After a while your eyes adjust and you can make out the crest of the mountains."

"I was doing just that. Until you blinded me with the pool light." He took a drag on his cigarette before ashing it over the deck.

Patrick had forgotten that people still smoked. "Sorry. I thought for a minute there you might be some sort of bum."

"You get a lot of them out here—*bums*? Scaling your private wall?" His smoky voice rumbled from his throat like an old muscle car bearing down. It added to his James Dean charm.

Patrick laughed. "I thought it sounded less conceited than 'fans.' You shouldn't smoke."

"I don't."

"Neither do I." Patrick reached over, relieved Emory of the cigarette, and placed it to his lips. The paper crackled as he inhaled, or at least he imagined it did; it might have been the little fireworks in his head set off by the idea of his lips being where Emory's had just been seconds ago. "It's nice, the stars. They make me feel unimportant. In a good way. Like my problems don't matter. They're not problems. I'm not anything. Just insignificant bits of star dust."

"Is retirement that stressful?" Emory kicked Patrick's chair playfully and it moved an inch on the concrete, making a lewd scratching sound. "Listen to yourself. Insignificant bits of star dust." He blew air through his lips in playful disgust.

Patrick smiled. "Did I say I was retired?" He handed the cigarette back to his guest. "I thought you left. How is it you're the last one here?"

Emory shrugged. "I love to shut a party down. To be there for the very end. Lots of people say it's polite to leave early. To not overstay your welcome. But I'm amazing. Who would get tired of me? And what greater compliment can you give the host than not wanting his party to be over?"

Patrick thought about this. He had always been a fan of the Irish goodbye; *not* leaving a party had never occurred to him.

"Plus, I have terrible FOMO. After-parties are the best parties. All the interesting things happen at the end of the night, don't you think?"

Patrick hoped the bluish light from the pool masked the reddening of his cheeks as it rippled across his face. "Like what?"

"Like getting to talk to some star dust."

Patrick's heart raced, although it might have been the nicotine. Was this flirting, or a genuine dig at his age and faded celebrity?

"Actually . . ." Emory waved his iPhone so Patrick could see. "Phone's dead. I was hoping you could call me a Lyft." He held himself together for a three-count before bursting into ridiculous laughter, like he'd been baiting Patrick all along.

Patrick laughed, too, if only to be a good sport. He waited for Emory to compose himself, then asked, "Did you have fun tonight?"

Emory removed his glasses and set them on a cocktail table. He rolled his head toward Patrick so that he was looking earnestly his way. Strangely, he looked older without the glasses; there was a fervent zest in his eyes. "Did *you*?"

Patrick watched as Emory stubbed the cigarette out on his pool deck. He'd have to remember to clean that up tomorrow before the kids asked about it. He picked Emory's glasses up off the table and tried them on, then flopped his head back against the chair. It felt intimate. He thought the lenses would be fake, but it turned out they were a weak, but real, prescription. Patrick reached back to recline farther in the lounger. He closed his eyes and felt the weight of the frames push against his face. "I did."

"You sound surprised."

"Mmmmm." His lips tickled as they vibrated.

Emory adjusted his chair until it mimicked his host's and they were equally recumbent. "We talk about you, you know."

"Who's we?"

"Us."

Patrick laughed. He still didn't know what Emory meant. His friends? New Hollywood? The next generation of TV's second bananas? Magazine? "Okay."

"We do!"

Patrick opened one eye and turned his head. "Emory, is it?"

Now Emory laughed. "Yeah." He held out his hand and Patrick took it, but instead of shaking, they just clasped hands.

"Patrick. But I guess you knew that. Since you came to my house and talk about me and whatnot. What kind of name is Emory?"

"Biblical. Old Testament. In Hebrew it means 'happy.'"

"Are you . . . ?" Patrick let go of Emory, the sudden intimacy of holding hands overwhelming.

"Jewish? Want to go skinny-dipping and find out?" Emory winked, a second wink; it was both unbearably corny and undeniably sexy. Patrick laughed, this time genuinely. Oh, to be that confident again.

"Are you *happy*. That's the better question."

"Yeah," Emory said, and then he leaned back in his chair to look up at the stars. "Pretty fucking happy."

Patrick studied the night sky. Except for one of the Dippers, he didn't know the summer constellations as well as the winter ones: Orion and Taurus and Gemini. "Well. You're young," he said, as if Emory's happiness would sort itself out to a general state of malaise. "But you're on TV and that ain't nothing." Marlene appeared out of the darkness, hopped on Patrick's chair, and curled up between his legs.

"Yikes," Emory said.

"Don't like dogs?"

"Just scared me, is all. I thought for a second it was a big rat."

Patrick sat forward and undid Marlene's bow tie; he waved it at Emory to enter it in evidence. *Not a rat*.

"What are you doing out here? If you don't mind me asking."

Talking to a cute boy, Patrick wanted to say. But he knew the question ran deeper than that. "Plotting my next move." He did his best to take in the details of Emory's face without looking directly at him. The thick blond hair that fell in his face when he wasn't leaning back, his bold nose and strong chin—a profile that belonged on currency. He was clean-shaven, a look not exactly favored by most of young Hollywood these days. And yet his face was not baby-smooth; it seemed he could grow a beard in about an hour if he wanted. The makeup department on his show must have to work overtime to make him seem like a teen.

"What is that, like a comeback?" Emory writhed in his chair to find a comfortable position, but the way he did it took on a sexual air.

"Running for president, world domination, EGOT, Tupperware parties. Take your pick."

"Ah. The elusive EGOTT, with two *T*'s."

Patrick rolled his head to look at Emory, and Emory rolled his head to look at Patrick. They locked eyes. *Emmy, Grammy, Oscar, Tony, Tupperware*. Patrick wished he were that ambitious.

"Now you just need someone to enjoy it with." Emory smiled at him.

"Who? You? I'm not calling you a car, so you're moving in?"

"You could do worse."

Patrick thought about it. "I could do better."

Emory laughed it off with a *Nah*.

"I'm just going to focus on surviving the summer. *Then* world domination."

Emory stood up and stretched. His T-shirt rose above the rise of his jeans, exposing a flat, surprisingly hairy stomach. They really must have to shave him between takes. "Swim with me."

"It's like three in the morning."

Emory pulled off his shirt. He was lean, toned, but not intimidatingly ripped. He probably spent all his time doing Bikram yoga instead of lifting weights in a gym. Patrick stared, but didn't leer. He could either join this kid in his pool, something he wouldn't have hesitated to do before he had a houseful of family, or call him a ride. He stood up and pulled off his own shirt in one fluid motion.

"Yikes."

"What?" Patrick asked. This seemed to be his favorite exclamation.

"That was sexy."

Without even thinking about what he was doing, Patrick reached out and undid the top button of Emory's button-fly jeans.

"Wow," Emory said, further impressed. He then looked down at Patrick's pants as if to say, *Your turn*. Instead he observed, "Your pants have butterflies."

Not just my pants, Patrick thought. He turned and took a few steps toward the house, as if he were going inside. Emory stood back, confused. Was this over? Patrick paused for a moment; decision time. A swim would be nice. He was sweaty, after all, from the hard work of hosting (and then the stress of seeing his sister) and the night was still arid and hot. The water would be cleansing ahead of the drubbing he was certain to take from Clara. He was doing a good job; he had been a good uncle. He deserved this. So he turned off the pool light. Darkness. When he turned around, Emory was standing naked, bathed only in moonlight.

Patrick crossed the lawn slowly, kicking off his shoes. He stood face-to-face with Emory before dropping his own pants, and then his underwear, without breaking eye contact. Only then did he deign to glance down.

"So. *Not* Jewish, then."

Emory laughed.

They stood very close without touching, not breaking eye contact. Their breathing slowed and fell into a parallel rhythm, yet Patrick's heart beat faster. What strange and different paths led them to this moment? Emory's involuntary enthusiasm grazed Patrick's thigh. He inhaled sharply, then turned and dove into the deep end the way he had perfected, leaving hardly a ripple. The water was perfect, eighty-three, eighty-four degrees, the way it stayed in July without him ever having to turn on the heater. He swam most of the length of the pool, his arms at his side, his back arched slightly, water whooshing by his ears. He dolphin-kicked twice when he came close to losing steam, until the sounds of the world washed away and he was surrounded only by darkness—a calming, perfect still. He flipped over and opened his eyes, but there was only the night.

He surfaced just in time to hear a second splash behind him.

FIFTEEN

Patrick, Clara, Maisie, and Grant wandered up Palm Canyon Drive sipping milkshakes, looking not unlike the ideal American family from a time when much of downtown Palm Springs was developed. Man, woman, son, daughter, a family outing for ice cream on a blistering summer day. The only thing missing? Matching buttons that declared their like for Ike. But the situation was mixed, at best. All morning they'd griped at one another, their fragile routine upset by an interloper. Clara was helpful in some regards, volunteering herself for mundane tasks: face-washing, breakfast, laying out clothes, brushing Maisie's hair. But everything came with commentary. Patrick's toaster made toast too dark, his coffee was too bitter, the kids used outdoor voices inside. Patrick had his own mental commentary: Clara was too uptight, not helpful with things that *actually* needed doing, forgot to pack her sense of humor; however, he had the good sense to keep his observations to himself. They worked as a family to tackle the house, getting it back in presentable shape, but by early afternoon Rosa had chased them out so she could finish cleaning in peace.

Patrick suggested Great Shakes, a milkshake place whose straws came festooned with a small cake donut. The extra confection was no more than two bites, but Clara opined it seemed opulent when slurping twelve hundred calories of ice cream from a cup (a cup, in Patrick's case, lined with homemade butterscotch). Grant gnawed on the straw of his Oreo milkshake, while Maisie nursed a date shake—a dessert Palm Springs was famous for. Clara ordered something particularly Clara, honey lavender vanilla or some such nonsense (a combination more suited for soap than dessert), and made an increasingly sour face with each sip. She seemed horrified by the whole experience, but found employment for her milkshake by pressing it against her neck in a vain effort to stay cool.

"How do you live like this?"

"It's cleansing, the heat." The kids ran ahead undaunted, fueled by sugar, Grant's little body in particular vibrating pure cookies-and-cream energy. The arrival of family, if anything, made it seem *more* like Christmas, not less, and Patrick insisted no Christmas was complete without gifts. They arrived downtown with a mission: to find presents to open with the roast turkey dinners Patrick planned to have delivered from Billy Reed's.

"Cleansing?"

"Like seasoning a cast-iron pan. It bakes off the hardened layers of grime." Clara didn't look like she was buying it, so Patrick added, "You get used to it."

They paused in the shade under the misters that the business district blasted from the concrete awnings in summer; the fine drizzle they produced made them feel like wilting vegetables in the grocery produce section. Patrick eyed a gaggle of tourists puttering by in an ill-fitting pastiche of pastels. A splotch of Grant's whipped cream sloshed over the side of his cup when he wasn't paying attention and landed with a splat on the ground. He handed his nephew a napkin.

"What are these thtars?"

Patrick glanced down at the Palm Springs Walk of Stars. "With the people's names?" The stars honored celebrities with a connection to the city, whether they were residents or frequent visitors. People from Mary

Pickford to Clark Gable, Elvis to Sinatra. Even presidents, Eisenhower and Ford. "Those are famous people who lived here." Or that was the idea, originally, a sister walk to the Hollywood Walk of Fame. Lately, they seemed to give a star to anyone, news anchors and philanthropists, or just anyone with money to buy one.

"Can we see your star?" Maisie asked.

Patrick paused. "I don't have one."

"But I thought you were famous."

"I am." It was a minor point of contention. A bony whippet trotting by looked up at Patrick as if to say, *Can you believe it?* The dog wore little booties to protect his paws from the hot pavement and Patrick looked back, *Can you believe those?* and the whippet, in fact, could not. "But in order to get one, I'd have to get involved in the community, and you know me. I don't like getting involved."

Clara scoffed, like that was the understatement of the century.

"That's not fair, you should!" Maisie spun around in front of a gift shop selling vintage-looking (but decidedly modernly mass-produced) knickknacks. "Can we look in here, GUP?"

Her outrage was, apparently, short-lived. "Go for it." He ushered Clara into the shade until they could watch the kids through the window, then leaned in to whisper, "Whatever they find in there will be total shit, but act excited anyway."

"You want to know some of the presents I've received from Darren's kids? A tongue scraper. Those bags you use to vacuum-seal sweaters. Paprika, I think, once." Clara wandered toward the opening of the store and fanned some of the air-conditioning her way.

"I'm glad you're here, Clara."

Clara cocked her head, caught off guard.

"This is good. The kids need a motherly presence."

Clara agreed. This was the easiest they'd been on each other all day and it felt agreeable. "It takes a village."

"With a thriving gayborhood," Patrick agreed.

"I'm not sure this ice cream is good for my tummy."

Patrick groaned, upsetting their fragile peace.

"What now?" Clara had risen early, due in part to the time difference, perhaps more from the sun that streamed aggressively through the guest room windows. She was surprised at how long Patrick and the kids slept; she wondered if that was due to their being up far too late for the party or if this was evidence of a new, bohemian schedule. Up all night, down all day. And he was going to further criticize her?

"If I could genocide one group of people it would be adults who say *tummy*."

"What should I say, then? What does it say in Patrick's *Guide to Being Perfect*?"

"*Stomach*. What's wrong with 'stomach'? I'm not seeking perfection, I'm just wanting to have a grown-up conversation with another adult."

Clara shook her head. *No*, nothing's wrong with stomach? Or *no*, I'm not doing that? Even she didn't seem sure. "Welcome to being a parent."

Patrick walked to the corner and tossed the last of his milkshake in the trash. "Look over there." He pointed across the street on his way back. "New Palm Springs. The Rowan, one of our more recent hotels. H&M. Kiehl's. One of those Starbucks that serves wine."

Clara followed his arm to see a beautiful new hotel at the base of the mountains and the pristine facades of fresh construction along the main drag. Even the palm trees looked fresh, upright, a vibrant green, perfectly trimmed. The sidewalk on which they stood was comparatively trapped in time, connecting storefronts that mimicked the look of a small-town Main Street from decades ago.

"This side of the street? Old Palm Springs. I like this side, but I'm afraid it won't be here for long. If it were *actually* Christmas, we would camp out here for the annual Christmas parade. Local marching bands. The fire department. Floats with drag queens. You'd like it."

"Is it this hot at Christmas?"

"No. It's downright cold. Highs in the sixties."

Clara scoffed again; on what planet was sixty *downright cold*? Still, that did sound pleasant—even with wise men in drag.

"You know who's been on my mind a lot lately?" Patrick's hand was wet from the condensation on his cup he'd tossed, so he wiped it on his shorts.

"God, you're chatty."

"Exhaustion. Coupled with sugar."

Clara used her free hand to pull on her blouse and fan some air between the silk and her skin. "No, who?"

"Mom."

"Oh," Clara said. She swiped her milkshake cup in a smooth arc across her forehead, then looked like she wanted to throw it at an older, lumbering man wearing a LOCK HER UP tee. "Why?"

"I have a new appreciation, I guess. It's a lot of work."

"You should have her come out," Clara suggested.

"No." Patrick turned his face upward toward the misters; the water evaporated as quickly as it hit his skin.

"No?"

Patrick closed his eyes. "If they can't have their mother, I don't get mine. Sort of a bargain I made." He stood on his toes and waited until he could feel water bead on his face like dew. "What prompted you to come?"

Clara pretended not to hear. She tucked her napkin into her blouse to wipe under her armpits as she looked into the store after the kids. "I don't know how you live like this."

It was as neat a bookend as this conversation would have.

The house was sparkling by the time they returned, and Rosa had even made sweet coconut and pineapple tamales for their holiday dessert, her own mother's recipe. Patrick thanked her with a handful of cash he'd withdrawn in town and instructions to go home and "spend Christmas with her family"; Clara's eyes rolled so far back in her head Patrick feared they might come all the way around.

By late afternoon Clara had made an about-face on celebrating, but she insisted if they were going to celebrate Christmas, they should do it right. There was no wrapping paper in the house, so they made do with pages they tore from old magazines for the smaller gifts, then cut up several paper shopping bags he had from the Saks outlet in Cabazon for the larger ones. The kids had to use kitchen scissors, but for some unknown reason their uncle had plenty of tape. He let Maisie and Grant draw snowmen with markers they picked up in town and Grant even attempted reindeer, although they looked more like some twisted lab creation—otters on stilts, with horns; Patrick looked forward to putting them out of their misery in the act of zealously opening a gift.

Clara argued for eating their turkey dinners in the formal dining area, a corner of the house Patrick was certain had never been used, and she set his table to look surprisingly festive. The candles he recognized, he'd burned them exactly once during a massage, but the rest of the table setting was a bit of a mystery.

"Where did you get those?" Patrick asked, pointing at both the cloth place mats and decorative runner. It was almost accusatory. Had she brought them with her in some attempt to assert parenting will? Children should eat off of proper place settings, or not eat at all?

"I found them in a drawer under all those shelves."

"*Those* shelves?" Patrick pointed at the shelving unit he had constructed on the far wall in the living room.

"In the drawers. Under that funny paperweight."

"MY GOLDEN GLOBE?"

"Whatever you call it."

"Huh." Perhaps Rosa smuggled them into the house in one of her early attempts to civilize him. Or maybe he'd moved them from a previous house, they could have even been Sara's or Joe's.

Clara taught Maisie about setting a table, including four different ways to fold napkins (in addition to rectangular and triangular, there was something called a cone fold, and a presentation with diagonal pockets in which to tuck a small flower or name card), and Maisie seemed to relish in learning. As much as she eschewed girls' swimsuits, she seemed to have no problem indulging in tasks ripped from a housekeeping primer back when marriage for women was a career. *An enigma, that one*, Patrick thought.

When they were seated, Clara asked if they should say grace.

"No," Patrick said, quickly squashing the idea.

"We can at least say something we're thankful for."

Patrick had plated their take-out turkey dinners, including mashed potatoes and cranberry sauce—the works. He cut his own turkey in small bites for Marlene and placed it in her bowl with a dollop of potatoes, then steamed himself an extra serving of vegetables. They were all more than ready to eat. "It's not Thanksgiving."

"It's not Christmas either. It's not anything!" Clara grabbed on to the table with both hands to calm herself. "Something we're happy for, then. Before we eat this food."

Patrick slammed his fists on the table and the silverware jumped. "Dammit, Clara."

"What? I didn't say before we put this food in our tummies!"

"It's not . . ." Patrick reached for the salt and pepper. He ground pepper over his food like he was a server waiting for someone, anyone, to say *Stop*. "They just lost their mother. You and I lost a sister-in-law. I lost a friend. We've been getting comfortable in our unhappiness, with the fact that life is often unpleasant, and we don't need to pretend otherwise tonight."

Clara removed the napkin from her lap and set it forcefully on the table like she was about to get up. She hovered for a moment a few inches above her chair before deciding, for the sake of the children, to sit back down. "Well, the food looks delicious. We can be grateful for that."

Patrick softened. "Amen." He placed his hand on Clara's forearm, an acknowledgment that he was the one on edge.

"Are dogs supposed to eat turkey?" Maisie asked, peering down at Marlene. If this was of genuine concern or if she sensed the need to change the room's tone, Patrick wasn't sure. But he could have kissed her for dialing the temperature down.

"Are *people* supposed to eat turkey? That's the question."

"YETH!" Grant bellowed with a mouth full of potato mush.

"There are certain people foods that *are* bad for dogs, I think onions for one, and raisins and chocolate. But for the most part, table food is fine. Turkey is fine. But no drumsticks. She could choke on the bones. We can check the list tomorrow if you like."

"Do you think maybe we should check now?"

"No."

"*Patrick*," Clara scolded.

"I think we should eat our food while it's hot." He took a bite of his cauliflower.

Clara cleared her throat to get her brother's attention.

Patrick looked at her, annoyed. "Are *you* choking on a turkey bone?"

"Maisie is asking you if you're sure because she's concerned about potential harm to someone she's become attached to." Clara gestured toward the dog by nodding her head several times to the left.

Patrick's face grew hot, embarrassed that it was Clara who clocked this after the outburst he'd just had. They were actually not a bad team; it was clear why parenting was often done in pairs. "Turkey is definitely fine. Let me tell you a story. When I first moved to Los Angeles I was working as an assistant to this producer guy. Real asshole."

"PATRICK."

"It's fine," Maisie said, twirling her fork in her stuffing. "We're used to it."

"I wanted to quit every day, but, I don't know—I guess I thought he could help me get auditions or something. Anyhow. He used to send me to pick up food for his dog at this gourmet dog food place. All the meals were made with people food but, you know, it was packaged especially for dogs. Low sodium, real ingredients. All that nonsense. But they had turkey. Turkey with whole wheat macaroni. Lima beans. Brussels sprouts. Something like that."

"Gross!" Grant interjected.

"Not for the dogs! Compared to what they're used to eating? This was not for the hoi polloi." Patrick glanced down at Maisie. "*Regular people*. Anyhow, his dog loved it! A few weeks later, this guy's wife gives birth to their first child and before you know it he's asking me to find him a private chef to make gourmet food for the baby. At this point he's on my sh—*naughty* list because he hasn't helped me get one audition. So I'm picking up the dog food one afternoon, thinking, 'Where on earth am I going to find a private baby food chef?' This was, I don't know—before smartphones. Then it dawns on me. Why not just blend up the dog food? Put it in little jars. It's really people food anyway, and without any preservatives or sodium. So, I do it."

"You did not." Clara's jaw was practically on her plate.

"I most certainly did! I drove to the Container Store, which I was already familiar with because a month prior he told me to replace every plastic container in his house with glass because of the PVCs, or the CFCs, or the CDCs, or MTVs, or whatever. So I got these little glass jars, blended up the dog food and, *voilà!* Instant baby food."

"The baby ate dog food?" Maisie's eyes were so wide, they might as well have been propped open with toothpicks and Grant spit out some of his food.

"Dog food, baby food. The kid loved it! So much so, this guy, my boss, he started bragging to all his celebrity friends about this great new baby food chef that I found him. And how they had to hire him, having no idea the whole time it was me! So I bought a couple of those, I forget what they're called—NutriBullets, Vitamixes, whatever they had at the time—and picked up a trunkload of supplies from the pet store, several cases of glass jars, and fired up my blenders. I jacked the price, my profit margin was insane! I swear, for like six months I had every famous baby eating dog food."

Clara had had enough, and leaned over to cut the meat on Grant's plate.

"Did anyone ever find out?" Maisie asked.

"What? No. I started getting auditions on my own and quit that stupid job. Soon after that I booked my show. Guncle Rule number ten: Don't trust any label you don't know. Labels should have a good, recognizable name, like Tom Ford, whether it be his own label or his work for Gucci or Yves Saint Laurent."

Clara added some cranberry to another bite of turkey. "You're filling these kids' heads with nonsense. Don't listen to your uncle."

"Oh, it's not nonsense. It's practical life advice."

"And how many of these . . . Guncle Rules . . . have there been? Ten?" Clara looked around the table for confirmation.

"I think so. Maisie could tell you. She has them written down."

"Well, how about Auntie Rule number one: Labels don't mean anything."

"For people, yes. For consumer goods, god no." Patrick chuckled. "Unless *you* want to eat dog food or buy everything off the rack."

Grant threw his fork down on his plate with a clang. "No!"

"No, what?"

"I don't want to eat dog food."

"Okay, well, finish your people food, then. I tipped the Postmates guy extra because it was Christmas." Patrick winked at Clara because he knew she was dying to scream that it wasn't. She set her silverware down and took a deep breath. "Besides. 'After a good dinner, one can forgive anybody.'" He kicked Clara under the table. "'Even one's own relations.' Oscar Wilde."

Clara was amused in spite of herself and worked hard to stifle a smile.

"Oh, look, here comes Marlene for seconds." The dog circled to Patrick's side of the table and sat wagging her tail. He leaned down to scratch her between the ears. "We should take her for a walk afterward. I think the pavement will finally be cool."

"PRETHENTS!" Grant screamed.

"A walk, *then* presents."

Grant slouched, defeated, but pleasant conversation resumed and everyone cleaned their plate.

Patrick let Marlene choose the route as they weaved their way through his Movie Colony neighborhood; she led them dutifully around the cul-de-sac with the old Tony Curtis estate. There were other Hollywood-star homes in a several block radius—Cary Grant, Gloria Swanson, even Frank Sinatra camped out in the neighborhood for a time when his Twin Palms home became a notorious party house—but Patrick forgot whose was whose, and many homes were hidden from view by high walls and ficus. The streets were wide and empty; they walked straight down the middle of the road and the air was eerily still. Clara stayed behind to do the dishes.

"Is Aunt Clara mad at you?" Maisie asked.

"Who, me? Noooooo."

"Is she mad at *uth*?"

Patrick stopped and put his hand on Grant's head, leaned against him as he lifted one leg off the ground to adjust his Prada slide. "Absolutely not. She loves you guys. Your aunt Clara and I . . . Well, she's my sister, your dad's sister. There's a lot to unpack there. You know how you guys are brother and sister? Sometimes you annoy one another, but you're not mad at each other. Frustrated, maybe. But not mad."

"I'm mad," Grant said.

"Then stomp your feet."

Grant stomped and growled and was instantly agreeable again. Marlene swerved back and forth as they turned onto the main road, hot on the scent of something. It looked like she was navigating an obstacle course set up with invisible traffic cones.

"Can I hold the leash?"

Patrick handed the retractable leash to Maisie. "Don't let her get too far ahead." Patrick closed his eyes for their next ten steps, enjoying the momentary silence.

"I want a turn!" Grant grabbed for the leash.

"Hey, hey. Cool your jets, you'll get a turn." He stepped between the two kids. "Having a brother or a sister. That's something really special. I want you guys to remember that. You *two* to remember that. Aunt Clara wouldn't want me to say 'guys,' as that's the language of the patriarchy." Patrick picked up several stones in the road and skipped one across the asphalt like it was a pond.

"Can we do that?" Grant asked, excited.

"You can't really skip stones on the road. You need a pond."

"We have a pool!"

"*I* have a pool and you're not skipping stones in it."

"Why not?"

"Because they'll sink to the bottom or clog my filter, and guess who has to dive in to get them." He pointed at himself with both thumbs. "But listen to me. The sibling relationship. Brother and sister. That's special. Especially for you. With your mom gone. You need to be there for one another. Hear me? Don't let stupid shit get between you. You'll end up regretting it."

Patrick jumped ahead to grab the leash from Maisie; Marlene was out sniffing something suspicious in the adjacent vacant lot. The last thing Patrick needed was for her to lunge for a dead animal or something equally horrific. He reeled Marlene in and locked the retracting mechanism so Grant could walk her with a shorter lead on his turn.

"Don't make our mistake." Patrick had fresh determination to make things right with Clara. He would lead by example. Be the bigger man.

Person.

Man.

Patrick and the girls sat on the floor around the tree, while Grant settled himself on the couch like a little gentleman, propped up by a navy throw cushion with an embroidered yellow Xanax that was meant to be whimsical—a *pill*-ow, it was called. He'd been meaning to tuck it away since the kids' arrival, given their father's addiction, but he always seemed to forget. Clara noticed, and she was not amused.

"*Really?*" She pointed directly at it.

Patrick waved it off. "Grant, come sit on the floor with the rest of us."

"I want to sit here."

"If I have to sit on the floor, then we all do. Look at your aunt Clara. She can sit Indian-style and she's old as the mountains."

"They don't say Indian-style anymore," Clara corrected.

"What do they say instead?" Patrick wasn't sure who she meant by *they*.

"Criss-cross applesauce," Maisie offered, always ready to help.

"Criss-cross . . . *what*?"

"Applesauce."

"What does that even mean?"

"I don't know."

Patrick scoffed. "I've heard of jelly legs, but applesauce legs? Your legs are just blobs of applesauce and pulpy bits of skin?"

Grant laughed as if it didn't make much sense to him either.

"It's just a fun little rhyme," Clara implored. And then she dropped her voice to a whisper. "Indian-style is racist."

"Sorry. *Native American–style*. It's okay. This is Native American land we're on."

Clara raised her hackles, ready to push back. "What do you mean, Native American land?"

"My property belongs to the Agua Caliente Indians. I own the house, but this is tribal land, and I lease it from them. That's true for a lot of Palm Springs."

Clara was instantly fascinated; the idea of Native Americans retaining land—something they were historically (and horrifically) stripped of—and charging rich white people to use it was of great interest. Maybe this *was* Christmas, and a merry one at that. "How much do you pay?" she asked with delight, as if she secretly hoped it was through the nose.

Patrick didn't answer. "Grant! Hand out some gifts."

Grant scrambled down from the couch and crawled straight for the tree. Patrick had given the kids two twenties each to find gifts for him and Clara at the souvenir store. The kids had been very secretive about their purchases, and Grant passed out their presents with a giggle.

"For me?" Clara asked, feigning surprise in that exact, predictable way adults do when handed a gift. She neatly picked at the corner of the wrapping paper and slid her fingers under the tape.

"C'mon, Aunt Clara!" Maisie implored.

"But you decorated this paper so beautifully. I want to keep that, too." She pulled apart the wrapping to reveal a jigsaw puzzle that said *Greetings from PALM SPRINGS*; each bubble letter in *Palm Springs* contained a different desert landscape.

"For when you get up firtht, you'll have something to work on!"

"One thousand pieces," Clara read from the box. "You must be planning on sleeping awfully late."

Patrick chewed on his lip to keep quiet.

"GUP, do yours next!" Maisie exclaimed.

"It's about time." Patrick locked eyes with Grant and tore his present open, both to destroy (finally) that hideous paper and earn the respect of his nephew. Clara protested, but it was over in a flash. Underneath the wrapping was a small box from Sunnylife; inside were four pineapple-shaped floating drink holders for the pool.

"So you can take your drink with you in the pool!" Maisie's excitement exposed her hand; clearly, this purchase had been her choice.

"Thanks, you two. And there's four, so we can each have a drink when we swim." He enveloped Grant, then Maisie, in big bear hugs before turning his attention to Clara. "Not to worry. They like Shirley Temples for the pool, seven maraschino cherries each."

Clara actually laughed.

"Now you, now you, now you." Patrick pointed to two identical gifts under the tree. "Grant, hand one to your sister and the other is for you. Doesn't matter which, they're both the same. I was going to give you these at the end of the summer, but I guess now seems like as good a time as any."

Grant handed one of the flat boxes to Maisie.

"Ready, set, go!"

The kids had the paper off in a flash, revealing plain white gift boxes. Inside each was a layer of red tissue, and under that was a framed photo of their mother that Patrick had taken on the roof of their dorm building soon after they started college. The photographs caught Sara mid-laugh, her thick, reddish hair cascading effortlessly behind her; back then she would spend up to an hour blowing it straight. Behind them, Boston. It was right before they were caught by campus police, if Patrick recalled correctly. There was a write-up of the incident in the campus police blotter that ran in the student newspaper and, for a second at least, they felt infamous.

"Do you know who that is?"

Maisie grasped her frame with both hands like a student driver grips a steering wheel. "Mom." Her eyes were fixed on the photo. It was from deep in his archives; Patrick was quite sure the kids had never seen it.

"Laugh," Patrick had said as he focused his camera on Sara. The sad truth of "magic hour" was that it was a misnomer; it lasted only a few perfect minutes.

"Why?" she asked.

"Why? Because we just broke onto the roof. We should look like outlaws."

"Jesse James laughed?"

"He laughed in the face of authority!"

Sara sneered at him. "Some outlaws we are. We were stuck in the stairwell for an hour."

"Well, that was my fault," Patrick admitted. "Doorknobs confuse me."

Sara looked at her new friend with awe. "You're so dumb and you're going to be rewarded for it, because dumb men fail upward."

"Would you just laugh?" he implored.

"It's not funny."

Patrick rolled his eyes. "Fake laugh, then. Like I'm fake crying."

Since the light was on her face, Patrick was backlit and she couldn't quite make out the expression on his, especially as it was blocked by the camera. "I hate you."

"You love me."

"I hate you *because* I love you." She laughed for real and Patrick snapped the picture.

"That one's going in a frame."

Patrick studied Maisie as she regarded the photograph. "Your mom was so pretty, wasn't she? She was only ten years older in that photo than you are now."

Grant scrutinized his gift before smiling, then handed it to his aunt for a look. Clara held it up to the table lamp beside her and glanced up at Patrick warmly. Grant nestled under his uncle's arm. Clara mouthed, *Beautiful*. He might have been mistaken, but there was something glistening in her eyes akin to pride.

"Merry Christmas, family."

Guncle Rule number eleven: Make the yuletide gay.

SIXTEEN

Patrick fussed around his living room, picking up stray bits of wrapping paper and ribbon and even a well-hidden cup with the remnants of some cocktail from the party that was—*Good god, could that be possible?*—just the night before. Clara sat with a cup of tea, her legs curled beside her on the couch. The kids crashed hard; they'd been up far too late for the party and having Christmas as a follow-up wasn't exactly resetting the clock—if there was even such a thing as normal anymore. Before bed, Clara spent a good half hour brushing chlorine snarls out of a patient Maisie's hair. She whispered, "Mom used to do that," barely able to muster the words for her aunt. Her eyes were wet, perhaps from discomfort, but it wasn't hard to imagine Maisie herself as a tangle of throbbing memories. Patrick had read to an exhausted Grant, who complained when his uncle skipped a page. "Why do you need me to read this to you if you already have it memorized?" Grant answered by simply making a fist around his uncle's shirt and holding on tight. Patrick decided not to care that it would wrinkle.

"You did a good job, getting them to bed." Clara seemed genuinely impressed.

"We'll see if they stay down." Patrick wiped the sweat from his forehead with the back of his hand. "They've been sneaking into my room at night to sleep at the foot of my bed."

Clara placed her hand over her heart and inhaled sharply.

"How can you drink hot tea?" Patrick asked, indicating her mug. "It's ninety degrees outside."

"It's your air-conditioning. I'm not used to it. I'm cold."

"Would you like me to get you a blanket?" Patrick mindlessly worked to untie a knot from a piece of ribbon.

"There, right there." Clara set her tea down on the coffee table. "Everything out of your mouth is a criticism."

"I offered to get you a blanket. That was me being nice! You're an uninvited guest in my home. I want you to be comfortable."

"That's not you being nice, that's you thinking it ridiculous that I could be cold in the California desert." Clara crossed her arms and rubbed her bare biceps; yoga had been paying off, her arms were the one thing she didn't hate about her body.

"When I have a criticism, you'll know it." Patrick loosened the ribbon just enough to slip a finger through and finally make waste of the knot. "Besides. I'll bet *you* had a choice thought when finding that tea bag. A constant comment, if you will, about my lack of selection."

He'd read her completely. "How do you only have one kind?" she asked.

"Because I'm not a hundred years old."

Clara rubbed her cold feet to bring circulation to her toes. "When did this start?"

"What start?"

"Why are we like this with each other?"

Patrick looked down at the untied ribbon he'd twirled around three fingers. He held them up like "scout's honor." "Look at this. Am I my mother's son? Am I going to reuse this ribbon? Of course not. I'm never going to reuse this ribbon. So, what am I doing?"

Clara smiled. "You know one time I caught her hanging a wet paper towel over the windowsill to dry?"

"You're kidding."

"Swear to god."

To avoid this destiny, Patrick unspooled the ribbon from his fingers and tossed it in the trash. Clara reached for her mug and held it tight in her hands. It said YAAAASSS in bold letters. Patrick regarded it with an expression somewhere between bemusement and horror. "You have it all wrong, you know."

"How so?"

"Greg was the smart one, you were the crusader. I was the trivial one and you treated me accordingly. It's okay. I'm not making a big deal out of it. But that's how it was."

"Well, what do you want? We had different interests. I wanted to change the world, and you were interested in . . ."

"Surviving it."

Clara rubbed her temple. Either the cold air was giving her a headache, or she was suffering jet lag. She took a sip of her tea, which had already cooled. "Where's your microwave?"

"You don't hear me, do you. Every conversation we've ever had, you don't listen. Not really. You look at me. Your mouth stops moving. But the entire time, you're just waiting until it's your turn to talk again."

"I'm not sure you're aware of this, but the problem with the world is not that women don't listen to men." Clara marched her tea into the kitchen and Patrick followed in pursuit.

"You're doing it right now!"

"Am not."

"Are too!" It was amazing to Patrick how quickly siblings could devolve into the language of childhood. "If you were really listening you would have said, 'I'm sorry you feel that way, Patrick. That must feel devastating not to be heard. It was never my intention to contribute to your feeling that way . . .' "

"We're not actors, Patrick. We don't all follow a script." Clara held her breath, failing to stop an impending hiccup. "You want to know what it's like to not be heard? Try being me. Or any of the rest of us when you're around. Or not around! All anyone wants to talk about is Patrick. Do you know what that's like? As soon as anyone finds out we're related, they're no longer interested in me. They're only interested in you."

Patrick opened the microwave drawer that pulled out from under the counter. "I'm sure that's very frustrating. If it's any consolation, I'm sick of hearing about me, too." He hit the button to reheat.

They waited in silence for the microwave to beep. When it did, Clara removed the mug, testing the temperature carefully. "Nothing productive ever comes from litigating the past. It's the past." She headed for the living room.

"Perhaps," Patrick said to himself as he folded and refolded a dish towel before tossing it on the counter with disgust. He really was becoming his mother. He found Clara sitting with a dancer's posture on the nearest arm of his sofa.

"I'm taking the kids back with me," she announced. "To Connecticut."

"What? Where?"

"To Connecticut. You've had your time with them. It's only fair I have my time with them, too."

"I don't understand."

"Look who's not listening now." She took a sip of her tea and it burned her mouth. "This is too hot now." She returned to the kitchen for an ice cube, talking over her shoulder. "I think Greg would agree that's fair. A passing of the baton."

"It's not a relay race." Patrick made a sour face as he heard Clara activate the ice maker in his refrigerator door, imagining tea splashing across stainless steel.

"It's not a marathon, either," she called back.

"We're kind of in the middle of something here. The kids and me." He leaned in the kitchen doorway.

"What's that, Patrick. Throwing parties at all hours of the night?" She set her tea on the counter to let the ice melt.

"Party. *One* party. They had fun!"

Clara sighed wearily. "There's a video of the kids on the internet."

Patrick was confused. Was someone stalking them? A fan perhaps, recording him while they were in public? "What are you talking about?"

"At dinner. You filmed them playing with their food and you put it on the internet. To remind people you exist, to gain sympathy for yourself. I don't know what your scheme is, but I don't like it. I don't like you using those kids."

Patrick was genuinely perplexed. "The cotton candy thing?"

"And that's not even touching on their diet. Candy for dinner? Is that what you're feeding them?"

This was like Whac-A-Mole, new charges sprouting faster than Patrick could swat them away. "Like I'm the first person in history to give a child sugar?" This wasn't making any sense. "Clara. I honestly don't know what you're going on about. I took a video of them. It's on my phone. I can show it to you." Patrick searched the counter for his phone.

"It's not on your phone. It's on YouTube. And god knows where else."

"That's not possible." And then, after he thought about it, "How do you know?"

"I have a Google Alert set up on your name. I'm shocked *you* don't have one."

Patrick frowned. "Why would I have one?"

"So that you know what people are saying about you."

He stifled a laugh at the ridiculousness of the idea. "That sounds like a nightmare." He plopped a few ice cubes into a glass for himself and poured a sip of vodka. "Look, I'm flattered you think I would even know how to post a video to YouTube."

"So what are you saying? You were hacked by China?"

Patrick sloshed the vodka around in his glass. The sound of the ice cubes calmed him.

"And your drinking. Their father's in rehab and you can't not drink for a few months?"

"You drink in front of your kids, I've seen you do it! You think pinot grigio is a food group."

"*Their* father's not in rehab!" Clara traced the edge of Patrick's counter with her finger, stopping just shy of the Post-it with his reset passwords that Cassie had left sitting next to a potted succulent. It wasn't China. He was hacked by Maisie.

"You're not taking them, Clara, and that's final," he said, stomping out of the room. Patrick sank into his sofa, pulling a coaster from the stack on the surfboard coffee table for his drink. It featured an old photo of a woman sporting a beehive hairdo and a caption that read LOVE YOUR HAIR! HOPE YOU WIN!

"Think about what *they* need." Clara leaned against the bookcases on the far wall to keep her distance. She knocked a ceramic bowl to one side with her elbow, then awkwardly returned it to its proper place.

"I *am* thinking about what they need. You know what you told me when Joe died?"

"No, Patrick. I don't know. What did I say?"

"'It's not like you were married.'" Patrick punched the *pill*-ow, scraping his knuckles on the appliqué. "I hate this fucking thing." He stuffed it in the trash bag with the wrapping paper in a huff, tied the bag tight, and headed for the garage through the kitchen.

Patrick discarded the trash in the bins in his garage, then made a chore of restacking the extra lawn chairs until he gathered his cool in the heat. In the corner he found a croquet set and pulled it out to play with the kids. The orange ball came loose and rolled across the cement floor; he caught it just before it rolled under the Tesla, which sat like a lump under a dustcover. Why did he let his sister get to him like this? He'd long ago untethered himself from his family, from everyone. He shouldn't care this much. But it was the continued suggestion that he was nobody, and the nagging feeling that she was right.

When he returned, Clara stood at the counter. They fussed in silence, Patrick sloshing the last of his vodka back and rinsing his glass in the sink. Finally, he couldn't take the silence. "You take them and we're through."

"Through with what? What are we through with, Patrick?"

"God help me, I mean it, Clara. Through. Finished. *Done.*"

"Patrick." Clara gestured to encompass the room. "Look at where you live. You're not part of this family anymore. You're not part of *life* anymore. You're already done. Now it's time for them to come home."

Patrick spun the glass in his dish towel so quickly, not only did it dry but the towel seemed to also.

Clara put her hands in her pockets and studied her toes. "I got a pedicure for this."

"This argument?"

"This trip."

Patrick didn't know what to do with that information. "Someone should give you a medal."

"Oh, god. You're insufferable. I wish I could chalk it up to your own grief over Sara—the sister you never had—but you've always been this way."

"The sister I never—?"

"Please. Let's not pretend otherwise. Our names even rhyme. It's like you recast me with her the moment you met."

Patrick opened his mouth to protest, but couldn't. Following his own advice, he had to at least acknowledge that Clara felt that way, and it didn't require much thought beyond that to understand those feelings were probably valid. So instead he kept his mouth shut.

Clara seemed to respond favorably to his silence. Her tone shifted. "Did I really say that? About Joe? I didn't really say that."

Patrick dried his hands on the dish towel, and fished a clean spoon out of the drawer. "Not when he died. Maybe six months later. It was in the context of . . . It was in the context of something else, some other point you were making. For me to get on with my life. But, yeah. You said it." He pulled open the freezer, took out a pint of expensive-looking ice cream, pried off the lid, and took a bite. "This is awful."

"What is it?"

"Buh-her bwickle." Patrick swallowed. "I sound like Grant. Butter brickle. Maisie picked it out. We tried them all and she only likes old-lady ice cream. Did you see her earlier? She had a date shake."

Clara recoiled. "I thought she said grape."

"No, *date*. Like prunes." Patrick pointed at the freezer. "We probably have some Neapolitan, if you prefer."

"Let me try." Clara opened the drawer for her own spoon and took a bite. "Oh, god."

"Right?"

"You know who would like this?"

He shrugged.

"Greg."

Patrick rubbed his eyes. "Oh my god. Remember when we were kids and all he wanted was rum raisin? Nothing chocolate. No peanut butter. Rum raisin."

"Do you think he thought there was actual rum in it?"

"Always the addict?"

Clara smiled as she set the ice cream down and rinsed her spoon in the sink. "We should bust him out." She meant it as a joke, but as soon as it was out of her mouth it seemed plausible. "We could do it together. It'd be fun."

Patrick had an image of the two of them dressed as cat burglars in the shrubbery, tossing pebbles at Greg's window until they saw a light turn on. "It would be."

"Just for the night. If only to get some better ice cream."

Patrick agreed.

"If I said that to you about Joe, I'm sorry."

"You did say that to me about Joe."

"Would you let me apologize?" Clara blurted before lowering her hackles. "I liked Joe."

Patrick opted for silence again; he reached for the butter brickle before remembering he hated it. He pushed it away from him so hard it tipped over. "I did, too."

Clara looked out the window, but since it was pitch-black she only saw her own tired reflection staring back at her. "I'm almost fifty years old. Can you believe it?" Her voice was pinched, thin, sad.

Patrick covered the ice cream with its lid, pushing until he was certain it was on tight. It was one of those practical tasks you do when you don't know to do anything else. "You think I'm selfish. You think everything's about me. Me, me, me. Always have. But you know what? Self-love for gay people can be an act of survival. You think it made me unserious, while you toiled away in the nonprofit world, or raised money for any number of causes. But when the whole world is designed to point out that you're different, it can be a way to endure."

Clara looked down at the counter and flipped through a stack of Patrick's mail.

"I'm teaching these kids. I have something to offer that others—frankly, *you*—don't." He hoped this would close the door on this ridiculous notion of them leaving with her.

Clara held up a letter. "Who is Jack Curtis?"

Patrick sighed. Once again, she wasn't listening. "I am."

Skeptically she replied, "*You* are."

Patrick smiled and held out his hand in the way he remembered Jean Seberg doing once in a movie. "*Enchanté*."

"See? I don't know who you are. You preach self-love, but I doubt you really know, either." Clara pushed the mail aside as if it were toxic and reached for her purse. She dug through the bag before giving up and emptying the contents on the counter until she found some lip balm. Patrick caught the tickets out of the corner of his eye. He reached out, grabbing them before she could stop him. "Give those back."

"These are airline tickets. *Three* return tickets." Patrick was dumbfounded. "This has nothing to do with parties or my drinking or YouTube. You were planning this all along."

"Patrick. I came prepared. You want to put me on trial? That's the markings of a good parental guardian. Preparation. Frankly, the fact that you weren't prepared for someone else stepping in, the way you've been carrying on? It just goes to show how unqualified you are."

"Oh, god. And you make a show of asking my permission, pretending I had some say!"

"Calm down, Patrick. We can talk about it again in the morning."

Patrick seethed. "We're done talking." He flipped through the airline tickets until he found the one in Clara's name. He handed it back to her while tucking the other two tickets in the pocket of his shorts. "You're not taking the kids. One more word about it, and I'll show you exactly who I am."

He turned off the kitchen light, leaving his sister alone in the dark.

SEVENTEEN

They rose up, the three of them, in the rotating cable car, suspended far above Chino Canyon. The Palm Springs Aerial Tramway on the north edge of town was a tourist destination, a point of interest in the Coachella Valley, taking visitors to the peak of Mount San Jacinto; Mountain Station, their destination, was more than ten thousand feet above the valley floor (at least according to the pamphlet that was imposed upon Patrick when he purchased their ride tickets). It was also thirty degrees cooler—relief they all needed in the wake of Clara's rocky departure. Patrick's insides were jagged like the craggy cliffs, and they were only a few thousand feet into their ascent. Hadn't he just lectured Maisie and Grant on the importance of siblings? Didn't he promise to demonstrate that by example? Instead, Clara snuck in to say goodbye to the kids before he was even up, the creak of the front door and the sound of her cab driving away down his quiet road is what woke him.

"Why did Aunt Clara leave so early?"

"Why?"

"Yeah," Grant added. "Why?"

"Work emergency." Patrick ushered the two of them in front of his perch at the tram window. "Can you see my house?" The cables above them were suspended from towers; they were approaching the third tower of five and they were in the perfect spot in the car's rotation to see the valley floor. The view below was incredible, brown, mountainous, and then endless dusty flats; it was like looking across the arid moonscape of distant, orbiting rock.

"What does she do again?" There was no cell reception here, but Maisie's bullshit detector was pinging.

"I don't know. Something with nonprofits." He leaned down over her shoulder and pointed. "Look at the midpoint of the runway, see how it sits on a diagonal? Now follow that over and to the right. Somewhere in that area."

"But what for nonprofits *specifically*?"

"Raising money. That sort of thing. Nonprofits always need money because they don't have any . . . profits. Why the sudden interest?" Patrick wanted off the topic of Clara before they reached the top. Today was about clearing the air, returning to some semblance of normal, moving on. Mostly, he wanted to settle his guilt.

"That's where your house is?" Grant asked, looking at the dotted horizon.

"YES." *Finally*. Some traction. "That's where you've been living."

The car operator announced they were passing over tower four and advised everyone to hold on for support. Patrick guided Grant's hands to the guardrail; Maisie already had a tight grip.

"Whoa." Grant looked up at his uncle as the cable car swayed back and forth. "It tickles my tummy."

"Mine, too," Maisie added.

Patrick was about to intercede, but in the wake of Clara's departure recognized he needed to work on letting things go. Besides, *tummy* was fine if you were six. "Mine three."

"What are we going to do at the top?"

"Hike!"

"HIKE?!" They complained.

"Oh, come on. You know where PopPop took your father and Aunt

Clara and me? Battlefields. Revolutionary and Civil War battlefields. I take you to see dinosaurs, to the zoo, swimming, on this tram—all of it much more fun. Believe me, you'd rather hike the ridge of these mountains with me than haul ass all over Pennsylvania to see Valley Forge, or Maryland to see Antietam."

"Why?" To Grant it all seemed equally horrible.

"Because of the views! You know what Maryland has? Crabs. You know what Pennsylvania has? The Dutch."

Maisie and Grant shook their heads at one another and they rode the rest of the way to Mountain Station in silence.

"It's cold up here." Maisie kept her arms crossed, partially in protest, partially to keep her body heat contained.

"It's seventy-five degrees!"

"It is?"

"Yes, this is what summer feels like in Connecticut. You've just gotten used to it being a hundred and five." They forged ahead on the easiest trail Patrick had scouted; it was a loop with five scenic overlooks that ran just over a mile. The forest floor was littered with enormous pine cones, the size, almost, of Grant's head. Birds were chirping, chatty but unseen, and the ground was soft with pine needles. It took less than ten minutes in the cable car to get from the Valley Station to their destination, but they were a world apart.

"Look, a lizard!" Grant was beside himself with joy.

"Where, bud?"

"Thunning himthelf on that rock." He pointed to a sunny patch that formed between two trees.

"Good eye."

"Ith it dead?"

"No, just sleeping."

"Are you sure?"

Patrick took Grant's hand. "I'm positive."

Grant ran toward a cluster of trees to study the pine cones that lay beneath them until he was far enough ahead to make Patrick uncomfortable. "Slow down, Grantelope!"

Grant picked up a pine cone and studied it. "Can I keep this?"

"No."

"Why?"

"Bears eat them."

Grant looked skeptical. "Bearth eat pine cones?"

"You know what else they eat?" Patrick picked Grant up in one sweeping motion and threw him over his shoulder. "Grantelopes."

Grant laughed and squirmed. "What's a Grantelope?"

"You are. Like an antelope, but a Grantelope."

"Or a cantaloupe," Maisie observed.

"I'M NOT A CANTALOUPE!" Grant protested more and Patrick set him down on the ground.

A term of endearment, Patrick thought. That was new.

They stopped at the third outlook and sat on a rock that mimicked a bench to sun themselves like lizards. Patrick closed his eyes. It was nice to feel sunshine as comforting warmth and not scorching heat. Although they were ten thousand feet closer to the sun. Shouldn't it be hotter? *Science*, he thought. *Not to be understood*. "Isn't it strange how the higher we get the cooler it is? It's the opposite of what you might think."

Maisie toyed with one of the giant pine cones between her feet. "Not really."

"No?" Patrick opened one eye and looked skeptically in her direction.

"As air rises, the pressure decreases. Lower air pressure means lower temperatures."

Patrick looked at Grant.

"You know this, too?"

"Yeah," he said, but it was clear that he didn't.

"How'd you kids get so smart?"

"School," Maisie said. She gave the pine cone a swift kick and it went sailing over the ledge. "I heard you two fighting."

"Who?" Patrick feigned innocence.

"You and Aunt Clara."

Patrick looked at his fingernails. They were getting long. He remembered accusing Sara once of neglecting her appearance after she had kids, but now he understood—there simply wasn't time. "Families fight sometimes. There's a lot of history."

"Mom and Dad used to fight," Grant offered.

"Oh, yeah?" Patrick's curiosity was piqued, but it wasn't the right time to pry. "Your mother was a fighter."

"Why?"

"Oh, I don't mean it in a bad way. She was spirited. You know. Passionate. That's a good thing. The reason you had her as long as you did. When she was first diagnosed they gave her a year, and she held on for three."

"I didn't like it," Grant said. "When they would fight."

The sky seemed bluer up here, the air cleaner, sharper, as if there was more oxygen in it, not less.

"People who love each other fight. The opposite of love isn't anger. It's indifference. When people *stop* fighting, that's when you should be worried."

Patrick wasn't sure how much he believed that, at least as it applied to Clara. He felt for her, but he wasn't sure how much of a relationship they had to save—and if it was even worth saving. It was truer, he supposed, with Sara. They'd had epic fights. One of their biggest was at the Grand Canyon.

Patrick's decision to move from New York to Los Angeles came quickly; Joe had accepted a job at UCLA and Patrick didn't see the point of waiting a respectable amount of time to follow, especially with pilot season on the horizon. To make this relationship work, he would need a job, too, so he might as well go all in on getting a job on TV. Despite his deep love for Joe, his feelings for Los Angeles were less clear, and moving coasts just to wait tables seemed at best like a lateral move. Joe had gone ahead to scout for apartments while Sara had agreed to accompany Patrick on the cross-country drive.

The trip started well enough. They stopped at Graceland and braved inconceivable crowds; Sara asked a woman in line for a tour if it was always like this. "It's Elvis's birthday today," she had said with a Midwestern twang, kind on the surface but with just enough judgment underneath to express she thought they might be mentally impaired. They took New Orleans by storm and drank Hurricanes at Pat O'Brien's, suffering a hangover for the record books, then went to the School Book Depository in Dallas and eyed the grassy knoll. For six hours they made it their life's work to solve the Kennedy assassination beyond any reasonable doubt, but lost interest as hunger set in and wound up at a BBQ place and then later that night at Billy Bob's, a honky-tonk in Fort Worth. They learned to two-step and line dance and swayed to the music until they were bathed in sweat. They went to Carlsbad and hiked deep underground into a cavern large enough to hold a commercial airplane, and to Roswell to eat Alien Jerky. And then to the Grand Canyon, where they walked to the South Rim only to find the canyon socked in with fog. So they fought. About nothing, about everything.

"Shall we go to Las Vegas?" Patrick asked. He had a vision of himself in LA, a cliché of West Coast living, of going to the gym and drinking green tea and perhaps being a vegetarian. He thought a martini and a bloody prime rib dinner for $4.99 would be the perfect way to bid adieu to his old New York self—even if a classic Vegas martini was half vermouth. Sara, however, was not game for such nonsense and in fact had her eye on Sedona and a massage, perhaps, with hot stones.

"You're already changing."

"What? No I'm not."

"Yes, you are. You're leaving me alone and I already don't know who you've become."

"I'm not leaving you, I'm leaving New York. And we both know you won't be alone." Sara by then was dating Greg, which left Patrick feeling unnerved.

"You said that didn't bother you."

"Of course it bothers me, brother-fucker."

"Don't be vulgar."

Patrick didn't know how he was supposed to be. "You have a replacement me lined up!"

"Well, I'm sorry you'd rather I be a spinster, pining for you from afar."

"Yes, that's what I said. Because there are absolutely no men in New York, so it's either my brother in Connecticut or being an old maid."

Sara walked closer to the rim of the canyon, a ghost barely visible through the fog. It reminded Patrick of their rooftop adventure in college, how nervous it had made him, her standing so close to the edge. How he promised he'd never let her fall. How times had changed. He lifted his hand, curled his forefinger to his thumb, and then pretended to flick her over the edge. She turned just in time to see it.

"Did you just flick me off the edge?"

Patrick did it again. This time he added a sound. "*Pfft.*"

Sara charged over toward him, away from the edge. "What is your problem?"

"What is yours?"

"You chose this move. You don't get to offer opinions any longer on how I live my life!"

"But Greg? *Really?* It's gross. It's like you're trying to have me, my worldview, my upbringing, my DNA, but in a different . . . *sack.*"

Sara was appalled.

"Well, *body* didn't seem to convey my level of disgust."

Sara ran her fingers through Patrick's hair and he flinched. "I'll bet you have the same sack."

"That's disgusting."

"Seriously, though."

"Now *you're* being vulgar. Don't say another word about his sack." Patrick ran away and Sara chased him until they ran in circles like dogs. "Or mine," he added, laughing this time. They both stopped when they realized the fog obscured the canyon's edge.

Sara put her hands on her knees to catch her breath. "All this way and we can't even see it." She carefully approached the edge and looked down, then picked up a pebble and dropped it, watching as it was swallowed by the mist.

"This sucks," Patrick said, but it wasn't clear if he meant the weather or the situation.

"I'm just doing to you what you've been doing to me. Pushing you away to make this breakup easier."

"That's not what I've been—"

"You just flicked me off the edge!"

He instantly saw the connection. It *was* true. He was done with the city, with loneliness, with the claustrophobia of concrete all around him. The endless jackhammering of midtown that made his teeth rattle when he emerged from the subway for work. But he would never be done with her. The thought of Sara not being a presence in his everyday life unsettled him deep in his core. The only way to survive was to disengage. And it was breaking his heart.

But, then.

"Look, look, look." Patrick spun her around and pointed. The fog was lifting rapidly, a thick curtain raised, dissipating into nothingness. And the most incredible thing they had ever stood in front of revealed itself like an enormous, delicious pastry in a thousand flaky layers.

"Oh my god."

They crept closer to the rim, holding on to each other in astonishment. The canyon was the color of every mineral and ore, thousands of years of sediments in rusts and greens and yellows and grays, and there seemed to be no bottom, the mist along the river basin the very last to lift. The world was so much bigger than they were, more mysterious; they were comparatively insignificant to the millions of years of work and splendor that lay before and beneath them.

"Water did all this. Can you believe it?"

The vista continued to sharpen. People ran from the direction of the parking lot, others *ooh*ed and *aah*ed. Patrick and Sara, however, backed slowly away, as if they were in danger of being swallowed—two figures moving slowly backward against the tide of a world spinning forward.

Patrick treated the kids to lunch at the Pines Café at Mountain Station. Grant threw a fit when a bird grabbed someone's french fry from one of the tables on the deck, so they sat inside, securing a spot by the window. They each had a slice of cheese pizza; the kids didn't ask Patrick for pepperoni—they weren't up for the fight—and he ordered the three of them a sad-looking salad to share.

"What should we do?" Maisie asked.

"With our afternoon? I don't know. I thought this would take longer." Patrick took a bite of his pizza, which was doughy and lukewarm, the sauce dry under a heat lamp. As much as he would have preferred actual food—a salad with genuine greens rich in nutrients, or any array of options available to him on regular ground—he was in no hurry to reboard the tram. "We could just hang out here among the trees." Like the air, they were lighter up here, floating above the stressors that waited for them below.

"There's nothing to *do* here," Grant griped.

Patrick glanced up to see a sign announcing Wi-Fi, the magic answer appearing out of the mountaintop's thin air. Without thinking he handed his phone to Maisie. She snatched it from him and, much to Patrick's dismay, already knew his password.

"Hey, did you guys upload our video to YouTube?"

"What?" Maisie feigned innocence.

"The one from dinner. With the cotton candy."

Maisie refused to look up at her uncle, as sure a sign of guilt as there was.

"What did I say about that? About it not being appropriate? Your aunt Clara saw that and blamed me."

They both picked uncomfortably at their pizza; Grant stretched his cheese like it was bubble gum as Patrick pieced together their scam. The passwords were on his counter and he'd been giving them a wider berth with his phone.

"It's okay. I'm not . . . *mad*. I can handle your aunt Clara. It's just. If I make rules, they're to protect you. Okay? You have to respect them." Patrick opened the salad he'd ordered and picked off bits of blue cheese. The lettuce appeared wilted, like their energy; they were all three in need of a boost. "Well, pull it up so I can see how it looks."

Excitedly, Maisie opened the YouTube app and tapped in a few key search words.

"I have the YouTube app?"

"I downloaded it."

Patrick shot her a look, which she absorbed and shot right back. Maisie found the page and handed Patrick his phone to show him. "EIGHTY-THREE THOUSAND VIEWS?"

A family at the next table turned to look. Patrick pulled his ball cap down farther over his eyes.

Maisie took a bite of pizza. "You already had a channel, so we have lots of subscribers!"

"I have. I have lots of subscribers. *We* don't have anything." Patrick let the video unspool on his phone. The kids looked good, happy. Even if it was just a snapshot, a moment.

"Are we famouth?" Grant asked.

"Not even a little bit."

"That's a lot of views," Maisie clarified. "So I'd say a *little* bit." She was developing a bit of an attitude he wasn't fond of, but today he would cut her some slack.

The video ended and Patrick absentmindedly handed Maisie back his phone as if it were hers. "Interesting."

"Can we watch thomething elthe?"

Patrick tried to pierce his lettuce with a plastic fork, but the lettuce wasn't having it. He set his fork down and pushed his tray aside. "Sure."

"Can I choothe?" Grant asked.

"No. I want us to watch something specific. I want to see clips from a show. *Tillamook*."

"Till-a-*muck*?" Maisie struggled to understand.

"Terrible title. Tilla*mook*. Like a cow says."

"It thounds like what a cow makes."

Patrick turned to his nephew. "That's very clever. Let's get some chocolate *moooooook*." He tickled the boy and Grant squirmed and shrieked. "It's a town in Oregon. And also a cheese, I think. And the name of a teen drama on that network I should, because of my advanced age, be too embarrassed to watch."

"Here it is." Maisie handed the phone back to Patrick so she could break off another bite of the pizza crust.

"Is this lupper?" Grant asked, lifting up his pizza as if there might be something more appetizing underneath.

"It's a lack."

"What'th a lack?"

"Lunch-slash-snack. Eat up," Patrick replied.

"Is it really?"

"It's certainly lack*ing*," he said without looking up from his screen because there he was—*Emory*—his face clean-shaven and smooth with makeup. Patrick's heart, while not skipping the proverbial beat, did (against his will) pound a little harder. His finger hovered nervously over the thumbnail. What was the hesitation? Three days ago he'd barely heard of this person. And he'd had, over the years, plenty of these little affairs without giving a single one so much as a second thought. So he pushed play.

And, voilà—magic. Emory, alive on his phone in a glorious close-up, that familiar sparkle in his eye, until the camera pulled back to a two-shot to reveal he was talking to . . . *a girl*.

"Can I see?" Maisie asked. She set her pizza crust down on the paper plate on her tray and leaned across the table to watch; Grant likewise snuggled into Patrick's side. He found them, in this moment, to be an intrusion.

"He wath at the party!" Grant declared.

"Can't slip anything past you." Thank god Emory was wearing more than when Patrick saw him last.

"He's on TV?!" Maisie asked, clearly impressed.

Patrick hit pause and looked at the menu board for strength. It confirmed Patrick's original appraisal: this pizza was the least awful choice. "You do realize I was on TV?"

The kids shrugged and Patrick threw his head to the side, hitting the café window.

"Ith he your boyfriend?"

"What?" Patrick spun around to face Grant. "No. Don't be silly."

"Yeah, Grant," Maisie piled on. "Don't be silly."

Patrick raised his gaze to challenge Maisie. "Why is that silly?"

Maisie said nothing. Instead she spun the pizza crust on her plate, like they were playing Twister. *Right hand on Emory.*

"Is it because he's too young? He's older than he looks. I checked Wikipedia." He didn't inherently trust Wikipedia, but it was right about his own age. Unfortunately.

The crust came to a stop. "Is he *your* age?"

"Maisie." Patrick exhaled, defeated. "No."

"Why do you like boys?" Grant asked sourly, but with slightly more boredom than judgment.

"I don't know, why do you like pizza?"

"Because it tastes good in my mouth."

Patrick wasn't about to go anywhere near that.

"Not everyone thinks that. Some people don't like pizza. To them it does not taste good."

"Why?" Grant asked.

"Why does it taste good to you?"

"I don't know."

"So you just like it, then," Patrick explained.

"Yeah!"

"Sometimes it's hard to articulate why we like something. We just do. We're programmed that way."

"Do you want me to like boys?" Grant asked.

"I don't want you to like anything." Patrick slunk in his chair as a woman walked by dragging two kids of her own. She glanced over at Patrick in solidarity. "Let me rephrase that. I want you to like whatever it is you like."

"I like boys."

"Congratulations."

"As *friends*," Grant clarified.

"Bravo. As you should. Boys can make excellent friends. And if anything changes, you'll know as you get older. Grantelope."

Grant beamed at his uncle. Patrick had a memory from first grade, around the time he was Grant's age. It was the last week of school and a heat wave upended a Connecticut June. Classrooms were sweltering and there was no central air. His teacher told the boys that if they were wearing undershirts, they could unbutton their top shirts or remove them altogether. The kid who sat three desks over from Patrick was named Charlie and, man, there was just something about him. He had a twin sister in the other first-grade class—Heather, perhaps, or Leeza—they were the only set of twins in the school, which gave them a certain mystique, and both of their names sounded like low-cost department store fragrances. Charlie was blond. He was tall for his age and the other kids hung on his every word. His shirt was Western-style, popular back then, and had mother-of-pearl-colored snaps. As Charlie undid his shirt, each snap made a sonic boom in Patrick's ears; he peeled it off and leaned back in his chair in a white Hanes T-shirt, looking like some sort of peewee prototype, a pint-sized Tab Hunter or Marlboro Man. He was effortlessly cool and Patrick knew he would never be that comfortable in his own skin. Not around other kids. As other boys removed their shirts, too, Patrick consciously buttoned his higher, as if removing it would expose him as an impostor. But he looked at Charlie that afternoon with his Steve McQueen swagger and thought, *That's what a man looks like.* He remembered that thought distinctly; both of them were at most all of seven.

"Do you like being gay?" Maisie asked. It caught Patrick by surprise.

"I used to."

"You don't anymore?"

"It used to be cool. Being gay. Counterculture, you know. Rebellious. Now it's all gay marriage, gay adoption. Assimilation. And some of that's good. It's progress. But I liked it more when it was different. Now everyone's in a hurry to be the same." *Look at me*, Patrick thought. *Even I have kids.*

"What's wrong with being the same?"

"Nothing. It's just not for me." He reached for the napkin dispenser and held out a napkin for each kid. "You done?" Maisie nodded, and they all wiped their hands.

Would it be much different, Patrick wondered, if Joe were still here? Did part of his aversion to cultural absorption stem from jealousy? From being alone? He thought of his friendship with JED. They'd found a way to be together and not the same. Why couldn't everyone else? "Never mind me. I'm just cranky today. It's fine. Being normal. Especially for kids your age. As you get older, you will find the freedom to be exactly who you are and eventually no one will care."

He pulled his phone closer so he could focus on Emory. The sexual tension was palpable; Patrick just wasn't sure if it was between Emory and the girl on the screen, or Emory and the man watching YouTube in a mountaintop café.

Grant reached up and touched the scar on Patrick's forehead and held his finger there for longer than Patrick was comfortable with. "You look like Harry Potter."

Patrick took Grant's hand and placed it back by his side. "That's rude."

"Why?"

"Because Harry was a Gryffindor and I'm clearly a Slytherin." He hissed for emphasis.

"I'm going to call you Uncle Scar." *Thcar.*

"Like *Lion King*!" Maisie added.

"No."

"Uncle Thcar!"

"Stop." He turned to Grant to show he meant business. "That's homophobic."

"Why?"

"Because they threw him off a cliff!"

"That was Mufasa!" Maisie crossed her arms, and Grant copied his sister.

"Yeah. Thcar was the lion eaten by hyenas."

"Oh, yeah, I liked him. Misunderstood." Scar wasn't into assimilation, he was simply a power-hungry tyrant. Still, he wanted the attention away from his physical reminder of Joe. "Okay, watch this." Patrick, the magician, pulling a sleight of hand. "I'm going to show you something else."

Maisie leaned in, excited, and Grant crawled under the table and popped up on his uncle's other side with a grin.

Patrick was grateful for the audience. "We're going to watch a few clips of me."

EIGHTEEN

It was Rosa who answered the phone. "Mr. Patrick!" She cupped her hand over the receiver as she waited for her employer.

"Who is it?" Patrick implored as he entered the kitchen, two paper bag puppets, one elephant, one dog, over his hands. It was a craft he used to do with Clara and one he was re-creating this morning with the kids; in terms of activities, he was scraping the bottom of the barrel. While grateful for the interruption, no one ever called the house phone except for telemarketers, and Rosa knew better than to bother him with solicitors.

"*Tu madre*," she answered, looking worried.

Patrick's face soured. His mother? *What does she want?* He tried to clasp the phone with his puppets, but failing, motioned for Rosa to hold the phone up to his ear.

"Don't be mad," his mother's voice echoed through the receiver.

"That all but guarantees I will be." Patrick hastily removed the puppets from his hands, tearing the elephant's trunk in the process. He took the phone from Rosa and stood up to his full height. "Don't be mad about WHAT?"

"Did you get your mail yet today?"

"It's ten in the morning." *What was this about?*

"The important thing to remember is that her heart is in the right place."

Clara. "What did she do?" He glanced at Rosa, who grabbed a dish towel and busied herself.

"We received a notice. I wasn't sure at first why we of all people received it, but apparently you're supposed to notify everyone, and as the children's grandparents we were on the list. It's standard procedure, apparently."

"What. Has. She. Done?" Patrick was being handled by his mother, and he hated being handled. Neal used to do this with news he wouldn't like, parts he missed out on, or if the studio was dragging their heels on a new contract.

"I'm guessing Sara's parents received the same notice."

"Mother!" Patrick could feel his face reddening, his body temperature rising. He wiped his forehead with the back of his free hand, expecting to find sweat that wasn't there. He was about to scream, *Just tell me what's going on*, when he heard a knock coming from the front of the house. "Hold on, someone's at my door." Patrick marched through the living room on his way to the foyer.

His mother desperately tried to keep his attention. "Patrick," she said with a surprising urgency, as if she could will herself through the phone and prevent him from answering the door until she could further explain. He ignored her. The anger rising inside him, the indignation that was fueling his thunderous stride, he was certain would be warranted. He'd have bet everything on it and he whipped open his front door accordingly.

A young Hispanic woman in a white blouse and beige pencil skirt held an envelope. "Mr. O'Hara?" She was maybe five feet tall, harmless enough.

"Sure."

The woman read from the envelope, to make sure she had this right. "Patrick O'Hara."

"That's right." He kept the phone clasped tightly to his ear.

"I suppose this is for you." She handed him the envelope. "Have a good day." Her task complete, she turned sharply and headed back to the car he could see parked in the street.

The envelope was plain, business-sized, white. The front had only his name, scrawled in what may or may not have been his sister's handwriting. It contained multiple pages, folded to fit inside.

"Patrick, are you still there?" His mother. Patrick craned his neck to hold the phone to his shoulder, freeing his hand to empty the envelope of its contents, forms from the California courts. GC-210(P). Patrick scanned the documents. The headline:

PETITION FOR APPOINTMENT OF GUARDIAN OF THE PERSON.

And beneath: *Guardianship of the person of (all children's names): Maisie Lauren O'Hara; Grant Patrick O'Hara.* He'd all but forgotten Grant was named, in part, after him.

"Unbelievable."

"Patrick, I begged you not to be angry."

Patrick took the phone and held it in front of his face like he had forgotten what it was. "I'm going to kill her."

"Threatening violence will not help your cause!"

Patrick hissed at the phone and disconnected the line. He tore through the petition and the supplemental forms until his eye fell across the section he was looking for: *9. The guardianship is necessary or convenient for the reasons given below.*

> *The children are currently in the custody of their uncle, Patrick O'Hara, in Palm Springs, while their father completes treatment at the Coachella Sober Living Facility in nearby Rancho Mirage. Their mother recently passed away. After observing the children in their temporary home, I believe the environment to be unsuitable to their well-being. The house in question is a party home, with*

drinking at all hours, no discipline, no set schedule. It's not amenable to children or the care that they need.

"Party home"? "Necessary or convenient"? Who writes these things? Patrick couldn't stomach any more. He found the signature of the petitioner—Clara—at the bottom of the form. The writing was black, a duplicate. His copy was not stamped, but the originals were no doubt on file with the court, or at least well on their way. The young woman at his door had a busy morning of deliveries: Patrick, the courthouse . . . the Coachella Sober Living Facility.

Greg.

Patrick ran out his front door and headed right for the street. He looked left, then right, desperate to stop the woman, but it was too late. There was no sign of her; perfect stillness marred only by the screaming of the cicadas.

Back in the house, he closed himself in his bedroom. He dialed the Coachella Whatever Whatever Whatever and when someone answered the phone he said he needed to leave an urgent message for his brother, Gregory O'Hara. The message? Three words:

I'm handling it.

Handle it he would.

The Hyatt in Palm Springs was a bland behemoth, spanning an entire city block. It looked as much like a convention center as a hotel, but in a city of high-end guesthouses it provided necessary rooms at a reasonable rate. And it was exactly the kind of recognizable brand that would speak to Clara, who was uncomfortable with the unfamiliar and the frivolous expenditure of money. Patrick sat in the lobby with its slick tile floors and oversized furniture, perched with a clear view of the front entrance. He prayed he wouldn't be recognized, or pegged as some sort of creeper.

How long could he occupy space in the lobby of a family hotel without drawing the attention of security? His white shorts made it look like perhaps he was just coming back from a game of tennis; he wished he'd had the foresight to carry a racket to complete the disguise.

After he'd left word for Greg, he tried Clara next; she refused to answer her phone. He imagined having to stake out all of Palm Springs' hotels, but a quick deduction and a confident call to the Hyatt asking to be connected to Clara Drury was all the detective work that was needed. She didn't answer her room phone, either, but seven rings was confirmation enough for Patrick that she was there. As he fled out the door to his awaiting ride, Rosa was teaching Maisie and Grant the first several verses of "La Cucaracha" on these cheap tambourines Patrick had ordered one lazy afternoon, thinking maybe they had enough talent to start a band. *They didn't.* As much as he was dreading a confrontation with Clara, that it would free his eardrums from certain torture made him feel better about leaving the house. His Uber ride was mercifully silent.

Patrick lifted his thighs one at a time to peel them from the Naugahyde upholstery, his skin like the fruit leather he had relented and purchased at the kids' request for snacking. He scanned through his phone. When he'd exhausted his other apps, he opened YouTube to search for his channel. There were now two videos of the kids; after their mountaintop lunch, he'd led them back outside, much as his own father had marched Patrick across numerous battlefields at the height of his own summer vacations. But instead of citing needless facts, the kind that his father had most certainly made up ("There was a pair of Siamese twins who were devoted Confederates, but only one twin was drafted and no one could figure out what to do!"), Patrick taught Maisie and Grant to juggle the enormous pine cones that lay on the ground. Or tried to—they would invariably land on the kids' heads to squeals of rapturous delight. So much for Maisie's own theory that their skulls were soft. He had posted that video to YouTube himself (under Maisie's tutelage) to spite Clara.

The recommended videos on the app's homepage were foreign to him. One summer of handing his niece and nephew control of his phone and he'd lost his own identity in an algorithm of nonsense. *Almost*. At the bottom of the screen was one suggested video calling just for him—Liza Minnelli singing the title number from *Liza with a "Z,"* her 1972 television special directed by Bob Fosse. Patrick smiled and hummed to himself—he hadn't completely been obliterated. He pressed play and watched as Liza expertly walked the microphone over to the stand. Her white blouse cut as low as her white tuxedo pants were high. She was luminescent, iconic in her *Cabaret* hair and dark eye makeup. Patrick hummed to himself as she spoke to the audience. In his mind he was the one clad in a white tuxedo, wowing a room, leaning into a mic stand and complaining that he had a problem with his name. *People call me "Uncle"—WRONG!*

He glanced up from his phone to see if anyone was watching. The hotel was empty, save for a woman across the lobby who stood with a walker, but she was preoccupied, waiting, he imagined, for a van. No chance he was bothering her. He jumped back into the video in time with the music.

That's Guncle with a "G" not Uncle with a "U," 'cause
Uncle with a "U" goes UUH *not* GUH.
It's "GUN" instead of "UN," "CLE" instead of "CLEE."
It's as simple as can be . . .
GUNCLE.

The sound of heels across the tile floor made him sit at attention, dropping the phone in his lap. Alas, the shoes disqualified their wearer. Clara wore more sensible footwear, suitable for walking, breathable for the heat. Patrick glanced and recognized the hotel's concierge, she'd been back and forth across the lobby a few times now. She smiled at him in passing and Patrick returned his attention to his phone, already playing the next video in sequence: Liza singing "Ring Them Bells." He searched for his own channel and for the video Maisie had surreptitiously posted. It now had two hundred and thirty-eight thousand views. Patrick lowered his sunglasses to make sure he was reading that number correctly. Almost a quarter-million people cared about some random video with Maisie and Grant? Unbelievable. He scrolled through a number of comments.

> Y'all these kids is cyoot.
>
> Hilarious.
>
> Now one with Patrick, please.
>
> I thought this guy was dead?
>
> What did I just watch? This is some white people shit.
>
> I wish Patrick was my uncle!

And several dozen comments that just read: *First*. Whatever that was supposed to mean; these anonymous viewers all thought they were Columbus.

The opinions were endless. He scrolled back through his camera roll, starting to consider what other content he might have. An audience of a quarter million wasn't nothing. If he were to give in and post a third video, what would it be of? Him? The kids? He was so deep in the quandary, he almost missed his sister as she walked through the lobby's sliding doors. Clara looked more confident than she had when she'd first touched down in the desert; she had acquired, at least, the proper wardrobe, and her sunglasses remained squarely on her face as if she were attempting a disguise. Patrick shrank in his chair, forgetting momentarily that his purpose here was to confront. He waited until she was right beside him.

"Ahem."

Clara froze in place. Above them, floors of open corridors; a housekeeper running a vacuum across the top-floor hallway filled the open space with a gentle, distant hum. Whether it served to amplify or defuse the underlying tension, Patrick wasn't sure.

"How did you find me?"

Patrick stood, leaving the backs of his thighs on the tacky chair. He ignored the smart of his legs and motioned for his sister to follow him. "Come."

Clara drew her shoulders back. "I'm not doing this, Patrick. Not without my attorney present."

She has an attorney. He motioned again, this time toward the back door.

"Oh, no," Clara said, as if she'd seen one too many episodes of *Dateline*.

"I'm not kidnapping you, for heaven's sake. You can follow me to a second location."

"I said, not without my attorney."

Patrick stared until Clara blinked, then marched deeper into the lobby toward the pool. He didn't look back; he knew that she would follow, and lag no more than ten steps behind. She wasn't the type to leave things unsaid.

"How *did* you find me?" Clara wanted an answer. They paused at the sliding doors that led outside.

"Like it was difficult. You would never stay anywhere without using points."

Outside, only a few people were swimming. Families mostly, with kids. It was late July now, not exactly peak season. The city was dead. It was the hardest thing to get used to for a New England native, where the summer months counted for everything. Patrick surveyed the pool deck. A young man in a white polo shirt and shorts approached with a drink tray. Patrick removed his hat and sunglasses, then ran his hands through his hair. For once, he wanted to be his most recognizable. "Excuse me," he said, stopping the pool attendant. He had an enviable tan. "I was wondering if we could use one of your cabanas."

The young man looked back in the direction of the shaded tents. "Those are usually reserved for parties of six or more." His face softened as recognition set in. Patrick could always sense the exact moment, the release of adrenaline perhaps, or the nerves kicking in. It was a subtle shift, but not an invisible one. A smile crept across the waiter's face, his teeth sparkling white against his suntan. "But, I don't see why not. Shall I bring you a couple of drink menus?"

"What are those?" Patrick pointed to two frozen drinks on his tray.

"Piña coladas. Doused with a shot of spiced rum."

Patrick smiled. *Party house* be damned. "We'll take two of those."

As they settled in the cabana, Clara wrapped the straps around her bag and set it gently by her side. "Rules don't apply to you, do they?"

"What?" Patrick asked innocently.

"'Those are usually reserved for parties of six or more . . .'"

"Clara, it's the dead of summer. No one's here."

The cabana provided welcome shade and comfortable white furniture that didn't ask for your skin as the price to sit down. Patrick kicked off his shoes and propped an orange pillow behind him; he wanted to appear casual, nonthreatening, to set the tone. His mother's voice, *Don't be angry.* He was doing his best, for the sake of the kids, if nothing else. He had to be what they needed right now.

Guncle with a "G."

"Clara." He realized suddenly he hadn't formulated a plan. "What's going on?"

Clara refused his gaze, focusing instead on the design in the outdoor rug.

"Something's happening. You're in a lot of pain."

Clara frowned. They sat in silence until Patrick couldn't take it anymore. There were other things he had hoped to accomplish with his day.

"Something prompted your visit. You love these kids. But you're not spontaneous."

Clara gritted her teeth, then relented. "Darren and I are getting a divorce."

Patrick leaned back in his chair. "Oh, Clara. I'm so sorry."

"He was having an affair. Multiple affairs, it seems." She looked over at the mountains as if it were no big deal, but the betrayal clearly stung.

"Monogamy is dead," Patrick observed—casually, he thought, but it clearly hit Clara like a slap across the face. He apologized immediately. "Sorry. That was payback for something. This mess."

Clara chewed on her lip and it scared Patrick, the acceptance, the defeat. Clara spent her life raging for everyone, every person maligned by someone else, but she couldn't summon the fight for herself? He sat perfectly still. Only after what seemed like an interminable silence did he inch forward, placing his hand gently on his sister's knee.

"You don't deserve this," he added.

"No. No, I don't."

"We're a fine trio, you, Greg, and me. Law of averages, you'd think there'd be a happily ever after for one of us."

Clara's lips vibrated, and she emitted a sound like a hum.

"And your children, stepchildren. They're Darren's. You're worried about losing them." In an instant, everything was clear—this was transference, pure and simple.

"No," Clara objected sharply. "That's not what's going on." She leaned in to prosecute her case, but the waiter arrived with their drinks, cutting her short. He placed the drinks in front of them, each on a cocktail napkin, then produced a small tray of pool snacks.

"Is there a room number for the charge?"

"There is," Patrick began, producing his credit card before Clara could object. "But this is my treat." He looked at his sister, who kept her intense focus on the ground. "Keep it open."

"Thank you." The waiter smiled and bowed awkwardly, as if he were leaving an audience with the queen of England. Patrick reached for his drink and nudged the other toward Clara.

"Down the hatch," he said, then took a sip and let the slush coat his throat. He pinched the bridge of his nose to combat the inevitable brain freeze, then placed his drink on a side table. "I don't understand. You've been in Palm Springs this whole time?"

Clara nodded.

"Why didn't you say something?"

"You kicked me out."

"No I didn't." *Did he?* The last few days were already a blur. "You skulked away in the middle of the night."

"See? This is part of the problem. Seven a.m. is not the middle of the night!" Clara kicked her legs out in front of her, studying how they looked in her culottes.

"You got some color," Patrick observed.

"My legs look thinner." Clara was impressed with what some sunshine could do.

"Guncle Rule: If you can't tone it, tan it."

Clara frowned.

"That one's a freebie for you." Patrick smiled, delighted to be under her skin. "'Not a suitable environment'? I have to tell you, that one hurt."

Clara sipped her piña colada. She raised an eyebrow—it was surprisingly exactly what she needed. She took another swig of the drink before setting it on the table and pushing it an arm's length away. She was here to set the example, after all.

"And did you think about Greg? Serving him with papers in *recovery*? Risking a setback for him because you and I can't handle ourselves properly?"

Three kids ran by on the pool deck and together they shouted, "Slow down, it's slippery," each equally surprised by the other.

Clara responded, "Greg's mess is Greg's mess." She reached for her drink inadvertently before trying to pass it off as a casual gesture.

"They're not dealing with their grief. Greg thought you could help them. We all wanted to give you the benefit of the doubt." She leaned back in her chair. "For god's sake, there's another video of them on the internet. *Laughing*."

Patrick crept his fingers into the sun and waited to feel a familiar sizzle. He bit his lip to keep from smiling. His posting the video had done exactly what he had hoped: gotten a rise out of his sister. "You'd rather see them cry?"

Clara didn't have the words to explain how they should be, but she knew precisely how they shouldn't.

"They're playing a role, Clara. Inventing versions of themselves to mask who they truly are right now because everyone has told them to be strong. And that's okay. That's part of it. Part of grieving. Part of growing up."

"And who is going to prevent them from getting lost in these roles? From losing a sense of themselves?"

"I am," Patrick said matter-of-factly.

"*You* are."

"What do you think gay people do? Have done for generations? We adopt a safe version of ourselves for the public, for protection, and then as adults we excavate our true selves from the parts we've invented to protect us. It's the most important work of queer lives."

"Patrick, you're an actor. Enough with the psychobabble."

Patrick let it go. He would never make her understand the bravery of the arts. The importance of exploring the human condition, particularly for gay people, who did so with gusto, and with the very tool that they were first rejected for: their large, beautiful hearts.

"Men are impossible. You know that? You, Greg, Darren, Grant one day, probably. The whole lot of you. I swear if I get through this divorce alive I'm going to shack up with a woman." She watched as a father lifted his young daughter out of the shallow end and tossed her a few feet in the air; the girl squealed with delight. Later she might allow herself to think not all men were the devil, but she didn't have time for such naiveté now.

"Is that a coming-out?" Patrick asked, needling her. "Should I call GLAAD? We could issue a press release?"

"Fuck off."

A breeze swept through the cabana and Patrick raised his shirt a few times to feel it against his skin. "I handled it. With Greg, by the way." He glanced down at the sweat forming on his piña colada's plastic cup—no hotel served glass by the pool—and watched as one bead of moisture slalomed through the others. That was him, he thought, finding a way through.

Clara took a handful of pool snacks, these Japanese-looking crackers shellacked with a luminescent glaze. She ate two, then timidly placed the rest on her napkin. They were not at all to her liking.

"You're not going to do this, Clara. You're not dragging Greg out of rehab. You're not dragging Maisie and Grant in front of a judge just because your life is in transition. It's not who you are."

She did not like hearing her motives belittled.

"Contact the court and withdraw your petition. Right now."

"And if I don't?"

Don't be angry. "You want me to threaten you?"

Clara continued to glare.

"Fine. I will have an army of attorneys bury you so deep in a legal avalanche, those kids will be in college before you dig yourself out from under it. I have the resources. You do not." Patrick held his sister's eye until she looked away. When she did, his heart broke for her. "I don't want things to be this way," he said softly.

Clara twisted and squirmed, exhausted. She was done with the heat, done with her family, done with this hotel, done with the fight. Patrick was right about resources, and they both knew he had the resolve and the spite to employ them. It was five more weeks until Maisie and Grant would be home with their father. Back in Connecticut, where she could look in on them more carefully. Away from Patrick's influence. Under hers. Was it worth winning a battle only to lose the war? "Fine."

"Clara, you have such a tremendous heart."

She winced. "But?"

Patrick took a sharp breath. "But nothing. I know you only wanted to help."

Clara sat silently.

Patrick breathed a sigh of relief. He downed the rest of his drink, then ate the slice of pineapple off the rim. "I'm sorry I threatened you. This was bound to get heated, but still. Now come to the house. Let's get your luggage and you'll stay with us for a few more days and get in some good time with the kids."

Clara turned her attention to the little girl in the pool. Her laughter was a trigger, it made Clara envy how simple things used to be.

"Clara?"

"I'll see them in a few weeks."

"You will," Patrick agreed. "But you should also see them now."

Clara's eyes started to water. She could not say goodbye to them a second time. "It's time for me to go home."

A large gust of wind took Patrick's cap; he caught it just before it was lost. He placed it back on his head and held it on tight with both hands. "Remember that story Dad used to tell? About the Siamese twins who were drafted?"

"In the Civil War?" Clara closed her eyes behind her sunglasses, grateful for the change of subject. "Only one was drafted."

"Yeah." Patrick chuckled, the thought of it absurd. "I used to wonder why he made up such ridiculous stories, and now I find myself doing it all the time."

"He didn't make it up."

"It's *true*?" Patrick raised an eyebrow, impressed. *Really.* Which one of his own oddball rules would stick with the kids into adulthood? He looked up at the mountains, framed by the cabana's curtains, hoping he was doing some good. The peaks looked fake in the moment, the way they often did in summer, too crisp, too clear, a facade propped up by two-by-fours in a bit of Hollywood magic. "You'll call your attorneys?" He nudged his sister's bag, and with it presumably her cell phone, closer to her.

"In a minute," she said. She tilted her head toward the sky and let her hair fall down her back. "First I'm going to finish my drink."

Patrick wasn't used to waiting on others, but so be it. *Liquid courage*, he thought. "You'll forgive me if I sit here while you do."

Patrick vowed not to say another word, but he moved over to Clara and sat next to her, placing his arm around her shoulders. She let him, too, without flinching or pulling away. They sat like that in silence, the only sound the occasional splash of pool water followed by a child laughing.

NINETEEN

Patrick ripped off his sleep mask and tossed the covers back in one fluid motion. The room was dark, quiet. Too quiet. His noise machine had stopped . . . *noising*. The air-conditioning was not humming. *What time is it?* He strained to hear the sprinklers on the back lawn; depending on the time of night he could sometimes use their gentle hissing to orient himself. He listened for the kids. Was one of them crying? Calling his name? He leaned forward to look for them, thinking perhaps he'd finally caught them in the act of sneaking in, but they were not there. Only Marlene, who had taken to sleeping on the end of his bed, was curled up in a tight ball. So why was he awake? Was it a dream? He struggled to wrap his mind around his last memory. Was it Joe? He'd been returning recently in Patrick's sleep; two nights ago he was a steward on an airline wearing a uniform with a slick tie clip. He found Patrick in a first-class aisle seat and, crouching down, said, "*There you are. You're supposed to be in 3-D.*"

Then, *BOOM*.

The room lurched, bending Patrick at the waist, first forward, then back against his upholstered headboard like a rag doll with too little stuffing. He was confused, stupefied. Marlene leapt to her feet and let out a surprised howl as she clung with her claws to the duvet. Patrick looked at his bedroom door; it rumbled in the frame. Someone was trying to enter, to do harm, to kill him. The bed pitched forward again, and then up and down, rising an inch in the air before slamming down again on the floor. He grabbed a fistful of covers like they were the reins of a bucking mare. Not someone.

Some*thing*.

Artillery. A ghostly presence. Evil.

Earthquake, Patrick realized once he'd eliminated everything else. And then said it again out loud to confirm. "EARTHQUAKE!" For a split second a warmth washed over him, a certainty that he was going to die. And he was . . . *okay*. Not horrified. Death wasn't welcome, but he was tired of needing to have all the answers, tired of people fighting him—it seemed an acceptable conclusion. Why did this need to go on? He'd lived, he'd loved, he'd done less than some but more than many; he'd be remembered.

Marlene growled, her legs wide, miraculously keeping her footing. It snapped Patrick to attention. He lunged for her, tucking her like a football close to his side as the flat-screen toppled from its stand. The TV landed with a crash.

The kids.

It hit him with a fresh jolt triggered not by the friction of moving tectonic plates but a seismic shift deep inside him. He was no longer responsible for just himself, and it was instantly more than the fresh realization each morning that he needed to get out of bed and make Maisie eggs or pour Grant's cereal or entertain them to distract from their grief.

He was responsible for keeping them alive.

Patrick leapt out of bed. He whipped open his door and ran through the living room to the other side of the house. In the hallway he found Maisie leaning against a wall between the guest rooms, her face twisted with an unforeseen anguish, her features all slightly out of place like she had just sat for a cubist painter. Patrick reached out, grabbed her hand, and yanked her close into his side. The ground kept shaking and he heard crash after crash from the living room that sounded like the entire fireplace crumbling brick by goddamn brick.

"Doorway!" he barked, guiding Maisie into the door frame to her room. Marlene wriggled and squirmed as much as Maisie held him tight.

"Grant's hurt!"

"WHAT?"

The ground belched one last violent lurch and then rattled like a fading echo until everything calmed to a fragile stillness. Patrick looked around, trying to remember everything you were supposed to do in a quake. The gas line? Was that supposed to be checked? Maybe he should shut it off at the source. Fill the tubs with water until the taps stopped running clear? In case they needed the water in the coming days? Get anything out of the fridge they might need imminently in case of an extended power outage? But then Maisie's words came into sharp focus.

"Where's Grant?"

Maisie was crying and clung to her uncle's shorts.

"GRANT!"

He squeezed Maisie's hand and yanked her across the hall to find his nephew in his bed. He wasn't moving. Did he sleep through this? Was that . . . *possible*?

"Grant." Grant didn't move and Maisie burst into terrified tears. Patrick leaned forward to give him a good, well—*shake*. But he stopped just shy of touching his nephew when he saw blood on Grant's face. He let go of Maisie and eased Marlene on the bed to place both hands on the boy's shoulders. A quiet washed over him, the kind that came with adrenaline and a pounding heart. Maisie's crying faded, blending into the dull roar inside his ears; it was like he was submerged in water, his pool perhaps, the rest of the world's sounds drowning in a calming whoosh.

He placed his head to Grant's chest and listened. He felt his heartbeat perhaps more than he heard it and the resulting wave of relief made his eyes sting. He ran his fingers across the boy's forehead to source the bleeding; Patrick hadn't fully realized how much bigger he was than Grant—he could practically palm his head like an NBA player does a basketball. He found the cut along Grant's scalp and applied pressure to keep it from bleeding more. He braced himself with his other hand and allowed himself to breathe. Something on the bed wasn't right. It was hard where the mattress should have been soft. He looked down. The metal sculpture—the one the kids complained about from night one, a midcentury mishmash of gold metal brackets—was now clearly *in* the bed with him. Sure enough, the wall was conspicuously bare.

He heard screaming again, coupled with barking and an orchestra of car alarms up and down the street, as if he'd emerged from the water with an athletic kick to the surface.

"He's okay, Maisie." Information. Information, he thought, would help calm her down. "It was an earthquake. We're fine. Something fell off the wall and hit Grant. It looks scarier than it is." She began to nod and he nodded along with her, helping the knowledge down like he was stroking the throat of a dog trying to get it to swallow a pill. Patrick picked up the phone on the bedside table, an extension he barely remembered he had; nothing. The line was dead. He needed his cell phone. "I need my phone so we can get help. Can you get it? It's on the charger next to my bed."

She stood frozen. She had her instructions but had yet to digest them.

"Maisie!"

She locked in on his eyes. *You can do this.* She backed out of the room without saying a word, as if her uncle's telepathy had worked. Patrick grabbed a bed pillow with his free hand and shook it out of its case. He folded the pillowcase into a bandage as best he could, lifted his hand from Grant's forehead, and slid it underneath before applying pressure again. Grant groaned, but did not open his eyes.

"It's okay, kid. GUP's here. I've got you." What Patrick wanted, though, was someone who had *him*.

Maisie reappeared, thrusting her arm forward with the phone, the charger dangling like a wild, unorthodox tail; she had unplugged the whole thing from the wall. "Good job," he said, relieved to have this lifeline in his hand. He fumbled his password twice before seeing the word EMERGENCY on his phone's lock screen. For the first time in his life he pressed it to dial 911.

It rang. It rang again. It kept ringing.

No answer. *Sonofabitch.*

Each ring screeched in his ear, begging him to do something—*anything*—yet Patrick remained paralyzed by indecision. The lines were down or the operators were overwhelmed—either way, help was not coming. Staying put seemed wrong. Did he know what to do for a concussion? What if it was more than that? Leaving seemed equally unwise. The streets could very well be impassable. What if they encountered live power lines in the street, or coyotes, or sinkholes, or looters? The phone continued to ring. How could emergency services not be prepared for just that: *emergencies*? Patrick knew he had to act. But could Grant have a neck injury? Was it reckless to move him? He would be careful. That was the answer. Together they would find a way through.

"C'mon, Maisie. We're taking the Tesla." He hoped to god it would start. Was it fully charged? Yes, of course. He never took it anywhere. Did it lose charge from nonuse? They were about to find out. Patrick wanted to laugh—there was a certain "*To the Batmobile!*" quality to it all—but he was pretty certain that if he did laugh it would not really be because anything was funny; it would be a release, the kind that quickly dissolved into tears.

"GUP." Maisie covered her mouth with both hands.

"What?"

She whispered. "Your Golden Globe."

Patrick closed his eyes for no more than a second; was she simply reminding him that he once said he would save his Golden Globe before them? Or had she seen something in her run through the living room, the award broken on the living room floor, the globe itself rolling deep under the couch never to be seen again. It didn't matter. Things change. Priorities realign. And right now, everything was crystal clear. "Fuck my Golden Globe."

Grant groaned again as if to voice his concern that perhaps it was his uncle who'd been hit in the head. Maisie gasped. She inched toward the edge of the bed to peer at her brother.

"It will be okay, Maisie." Patrick peeled the pillowcase slowly from Grant's forehead; there was blood, but it didn't appear to be gushing. "Sit with your brother for a moment while I get my stuff."

Maisie took Grant's hand and Patrick melted. As he bolted for the hall, he heard Maisie reassure her brother. "GUP says it will be okay."

The roads were surprisingly clear. Patrick gripped the wheel with both hands in preparation for an aftershock. The spring winds that whipped along 111 were strong enough some nights to push a car into an oncoming lane if the driver was unaware; he'd even heard more than once about a truck jackknifing and tipping over. What could an equally strong force do from below? When he noticed his hands turning white, he loosened his grip. He'd seen too many disaster movies where the roads were splitting and falling into massive sinkholes behind a hero who was trying desperately to escape, and that one where a volcano erupted on Wilshire Boulevard and spit flaming balls of lava in the path of geologist Anne Heche. It had been years since he'd driven, but still—there was no need for that kind of dramatics.

"How you doing back there?"

Patrick glanced in the rearview mirror. Maisie was sitting behind the passenger seat with Grant's head in her lap. He was awake now, but groggy. She met her uncle's eyes in the mirror. "Is the car even on?" Maisie asked, concerned.

"Yes, it's on. We're moving, aren't we?"

"It's so quiet!" She still yelled like she was trying to be heard over a revving engine.

"It's supposed to be quiet. It's electric." Patrick stepped on the gas to prove they weren't in neutral.

"I'm hot."

"Okay, sit tight." Patrick reached for the touch screen that housed the Tesla's controls. His eyes focused on the road, he activated one of the car's ridiculous Easter eggs, producing a video of a roaring fire on the enormous center console.

Maisie screamed. "The car's on fire!"

"Oh, god. No it's not. That's romance mode. This is exactly why I Uber!" He pushed a few more buttons. The fire stopped, but he couldn't figure out how to turn up the AC and stay focused on driving, so he cracked the windows instead. "Grant, what's your name?" He hollered it over the howling wind, wondering if either of them would appreciate that he gave away the answer in the question.

"Maisie," he muttered, and Patrick thought, *Close enough.*

The Eisenhower Medical Center lay ahead in Rancho Mirage. Patrick had been there exactly once, when a persistent flu masqueraded as pneumonia. You couldn't miss the names associated with the hospital. Bob and Dolores Hope. Frank and Barbara Sinatra. George Burns. Lucille Ball. On buildings. On signs. In hospital literature. While all these people were like a thousand years old, Patrick reasoned they wouldn't have donated to a hospital that didn't have a pediatric wing. And there was another name on his mind: *Greg.* The main campus was not far from his brother's rehab facility, should they need to enlist him for Grant's treatment.

Patrick was relieved to see lights as they pulled into the hospital drive. Whether they had power or were relying on generators he wasn't sure and didn't care. He pulled the Tesla into a parking spot near the emergency entrance just as the first hint of pink appeared in the eastern sky; it was the first time in years he'd been awake to see the sunrise. This morning, it was a welcome sight. "We're here."

Inside the emergency room, orderlies produced a gurney for Grant and wheeled him into an examining bay. Patrick stumbled relaying their situation to the admitting nurse: Sara was gone, Greg was unavailable. The nurse tried to steer him toward the relevant facts as he mumbled and overexplained.

"Yes, I know the facility," the nurse said when Patrick finally got through to her about Greg. She looked tired, her mousy-brown hair stuck to one side of her forehead as if plastered there by a hand propping her awake. An earthquake, he gathered, was more than one bargained for on the tail end of an already brutal shift. "We can call over there and speak to the father."

Patrick looked at his phone to see if there was any word from Greg. There wasn't. But he knew his brother, if Greg felt the quake (he wasn't on pills—even sleeping ones, he presumed—so how could he *not* have), he was scaling the walls in an effort to escape. "The thing is, if you do that . . ." He glanced down at Maisie, who was snuggled up next to his side. "Maisie, would you mind getting us a seat over there?" He pointed to the waiting area. When she walked over, settled in a chair, and started staring blankly at a TV, Patrick turned back to the nurse and spoke in a hushed tone. "If you call there and tell him his son's been injured, he will bust out of rehab. I'm serious. He will break down the front door if he has to. Like in the cartoons. There would be a hole through the wall in the shape of my brother. And I would prefer he not do that. Not leave his treatment, unless that was absolutely, one hundred percent necessary."

The nurse looked up at him with a weary expression. Was he really putting her through this? She checked the watch on her wrist.

"I have his insurance card. I have a letter from him that he gave me. A power of . . . something or other. And I can pay any deductible, or sponsor a new wing, or whatever it takes." Patrick fished his wallet out of his pocket, as if that made any difference. He was still wearing gym shorts but had managed to throw on a tee. He looked a half step above homelessness at best, which was not helping his cause.

The nurse unwrapped a peppermint from the dish on the counter. "Are you on TV?" she asked skeptically as she popped the candy in her mouth.

"I was. I was on TV, yes." He smiled weakly. "If that helps."

"They play your show here every night." She pointed at the televisions in the waiting room. "The reruns."

"That's right. I think, what, they air back-to-back episodes between ten and eleven?"

"Eleven and twelve. That's when I know to take my break."

Patrick offered a weak smile.

"You got old."

Ouch. He ran his fingers through his hair in an attempt to make himself more presentable; he'd have to find a bathroom to wash the serums off his face. "Can we just wait and see what the doctor says? I'm sure the boy's going to be fine. I'm sure I'm here only in an abundance of caution. I'm new at this." Patrick pleaded with his eyes. "I'm thinking of two people's health here. Please."

The nurse studied his face as if deciding if he were famous enough to break protocol. "Take a seat, Rerun," she finally said with a sigh.

Patrick pressed his hands together like he was praying and mouthed, *Thank you.* He collapsed in the seat next to a sullen Maisie. He glanced in her direction, but she didn't say a word. "You okay?"

Maisie looked at her feet; she was wearing two different shoes. "I don't like hospitals."

"Your mom?"

Maisie nodded.

"They're not all bad, you know. Hospitals." Patrick sighed, scrambling for an example. His head hurt; there was a tiny person inside his brain kicking the back of his eyeball. If he were going to have an aneurysm, this was probably the worst time but best place. "You were born in one. That's . . . *good.* Right? It's where we met."

"You met me at the hospital?"

"Yeah. I wasn't going to. Fly all the way across the country. Babies don't really do anything, you know. I didn't see the rush. But your mom insisted and the show was on winter hiatus. She said I was Dad's brother. Her brother now, too. I was family. And that's what family does."

Maisie scrunched her features together in the center of her face. "What's 'hiatus'?"

"It's a break. Like, a vacation from regular life until things start up again." Patrick saw a connection. "You're kind of on a hiatus right now."

"And you met me and you were happy you did?"

"Oh, god no. It was a lot of pressure on me. A lot of people watching me, which—don't get me wrong. I normally like. But everyone was looking at me like you might somehow *change* me, and no offense, but we had just met."

"Change you how?"

"That's just it! I don't know. Get me to settle down with someone, maybe. Put me on a more secure path in the wake of . . ." *Joe*. "But babies are scary!"

"No they're not."

"They're *not*?"

"No."

Patrick considered this counterpoint, but didn't find the merit. "Well, I beg to differ. They're really small, for one. You have to support their necks. And they don't talk to you, they just scream. I never knew what you wanted. Which was, as it turns out, just fine with your mom. I don't think she really wanted to let you go." Maisie took his hand and held it. Patrick swallowed hard to clear his throat. "But everyone else. They just looked at me, holding you." Patrick glanced up at the television. It was tuned in to KMIR, a local station. They played the same shaky footage, mostly captured on cell phones, over and over on a loop. Traffic lights swaying. Jars and cans knocked off the shelf at Albertsons. That sort of thing. Occasionally they mixed in some footage of a needle going haywire on whatever the machine was at Caltech that measured seismic activity, and put up a graphic of a tweet from seismologist Dr. Lucy Jones.

"Why are there earthquakes, anyway?" Maisie sounded completely depleted, like she was struggling to remain interested in something that terrified her an hour ago.

"You don't like them?"

"No, I do not." She crossed her arms in protest.

"Well, the earth is made of different shifting plates and they sometimes rub together. This creates tension, and every so often that tension is released as energy. Like when I make you and Grant go run around the yard to calm you down. And when they do, that energy release is an earthquake." An older man in oversized glasses sat a few seats down in a row of chairs back-to-back with their own. Patrick grimaced. *Was that right?* Certainly it was sufficient enough for a child—even one as versed in science as Maisie. He hoped the man wasn't a geologist; Patrick's explanation might be lacking. But the man didn't look up from his newspaper.

"People cause earthquakes by running around?"

"No, no, no. It's the different-plate thing. I was saying it's *like* that. Never mind. Forget it. Guncle Rule number twelve: Every now and again it's good to relieve a bit of pressure."

Maisie nodded. "My shoes don't match."

Patrick looked down at his T-shirt. "My shirt is inside out."

The large swinging doors opened and they both strained their necks, hoping for news. Two doctors emerged, but they were deep in conversation and instead of approaching the waiting area, they walked away from it down a hall.

"How do you know about air pressure and not geology?"

"I think I was out that day," Maisie offered, as if natural disasters were all lumped together and taught in one afternoon, never to be spoken of again. "We missed a lot of school last year."

"Because of your mom?"

Maisie didn't reply. Through the sliding doors Patrick could make out the soft pink glow of the rising sun and it filled the waiting room with new hope. Then a loud *BEEP* rattled their nerves anew.

"You're right." Patrick gave her a little nudge with his shoulder.

"About what?"

"I don't like hospitals either."

◇◇◇◇◇

Well before the sun reached its full height in the sky, Grant had been moved to a room in the pediatric wing. They were lucky; Grant didn't require anything more than a large bandage and a few hours of observation to see if he had a concussion. No one called Greg, as there wasn't much treatment requiring authorization, and Patrick didn't have to further play the celebrity card. The three of them seemed to slip through the cracks of an unusually busy night in the ER. Grant wasn't even formally admitted, as far as Patrick could tell; doctors found him a bed simply because the emergency room was at capacity and it became difficult for the nurses to properly observe Grant in the midst of overwhelming stimulus.

A nurse arrived to take Grant's temperature, sticking a thermometer in the boy's mouth. "How's our patient doing?" Her scrubs were aggressively happy, pink with little cartoon bears that seemed to be giving Patrick the finger. They weren't, of course; on closer inspection the bears were holding balloons.

"Good. Good. Groggy, I think. Perhaps from being up half the night." After they were first moved, Grant struggled valiantly to keep his eyes open, but his eyelids were unusually heavy. When he relented and closed them, Patrick would make a grandiose pronouncement—dinosaurs probably had feathers, some cats like to eat soup, sometimes sandboxes were filled with quicksand—to garner his attention, wake him up so that he could remain under strict observation. Patrick assumed Grant's ears did most of the work to keep him conscious, listening for scraps of conversation, beeps from machines, announcements over the loudspeaker. Despite his weariness, he seemed desperate to be present for it all.

"Does he seem confused?" This woman seemed rested and alert, less spent than the staff last night. She was wearing fresh lipstick, something Patrick found at odds with the other weary faces they'd encountered. Perhaps she'd just started working, the day shift her normal rotation.

"He fell asleep in his bed and woke up in the hospital. That's pretty confusing."

The nurse smirked, perhaps masking a more frustrated expression. "Abnormally confused." She took the thermometer out of Grant's mouth and looked at the result.

"Grant, where are you?"

Grant turned his head away from Patrick. "Hothpital."

"Which hospital?"

"Connecticut."

Patrick shrugged. "Seems like the regular amount of confused to me."

"Temperature's normal. Any nausea? Vomiting?"

"No."

"Irritability?"

"Yes, but that's just my default disposition." Patrick winked, hoping she'd be amused. She wasn't. "Let me ask you something."

"Shoot."

"This pediatric wing. It's so quiet. Clean. More so than any other hospital I've ever been to."

"That's not a question, but thank you."

Patrick scratched several day's growth under his chin. "No, I was just curious. Is there an age cutoff to be a patient here? Like, would thirty-five be too old?"

The nurse shot Patrick a look as she tucked the thermometer in the pocket of her scrubs. *Thirty-five?*

Patrick cleared his throat, then whispered. "Forty-three?"

"Sir. The boy needs to stay until I can get a doctor in here for the all-clear. You, however, do not."

Patrick smiled to ease the tension. "Can we get lollipops?"

Maisie perked up. They hadn't had breakfast. Patrick had suggested they could sneak down to the cafeteria while Grant was dozing, but she wouldn't hear of leaving his side.

"Behave yourselves and we'll talk."

There was a low rumbling, like a truck passing by, and the floor began to shake. Maisie's face glazed with panic and Patrick took her hand. "It's okay. Just an aftershock."

The nurse grabbed the rails on the side of Grant's bed. "Oh, we're going to get a few of those." She turned to Maisie. "They make you nervous, sweetheart?"

Maisie nodded. The rumbling slowed its roll and then dissipated like a wave hitting the shore.

"What's your name?"

"Maisie," she replied. Patrick was surprised by how frail she sounded; in his mind she had hardened as the summer progressed.

"Maisie, I'm Imani. Have you had breakfast? I think we have some muffins lying around here. And maybe some orange juice. Would you like to come with me and see what we can find?"

She nodded again, and Patrick offered a grateful *Thank you* over Maisie's head.

After they were gone, Patrick sat with Grant. "Close your eyes, bud. It's okay. I'm not going anywhere." He took the boy's hand, and when Grant closed his eyes, and he thought it was safe, Patrick started to weep. It was next to a bed like this where he last held Joe's hand. He didn't remember everything, not even then, and certainly not now, time robbing him of a number of intimate and precious details. He didn't ever have a memory of being pulled from the car wreckage, and he'd long ago given up hope of recovering it. Nor did he remember much about his first few hours in the hospital, when he was the one in Grant's shoes, the one in the bed. Only his physical pain was seared into memory; even if it wasn't, he had a lovely scar as tormentor.

Joe lived for four days after the crash. One hundred two hours and thirty-four minutes. *Lived* wasn't the proper word. *Survived* wasn't, either. His heart pumped and his lungs drew breath, at least one of those with the help of machines; he never regained consciousness. He was Joe one second and then he was not. His face bruised and swollen beyond recognition, as almost to prove that point. *I'm unrecognizable. Don't try to save me. I am not myself.* Patrick was still Patrick, it would take months for him to change; they were no longer Joe and Patrick once Joe's family swooped in—they instantly took charge of all decisions. It was a male nurse, *Seth*, Patrick thought, although his name, too, was in danger of fading (*Could it have been Scott? Or Sam?*), who quietly ushered him in to sit with his love, to give them a last moment alone, while Joe's family retreated to the cafeteria—without him—to *decide*.

He'd held Joe's hand, he remembered that. It was warm; he was shocked. It fit in his, like it always did, even though the rest of him was misshapen. He traced Joe's cuticles and then knuckles, tried to make contact with every last cell of skin. There was a scrape on the web between his thumb and forefinger. It had to have been from the crash, but the way it was scabbed over, already on the way to healing, maybe it was from before. He wanted so desperately to recall. If Joe was healing, then he had to still be *there*. His skin would mend and then his bones. His organs would follow, and maybe his brain would be last, but it, too, would heal. It would remember its work, controlling his vital systems. It would tell his heart to beat, to pump blood away and then pull it back. It would tell his lungs to expand, drawing in oxygen, and then tell them to contract, forcing out carbon dioxide. He held Joe's hand until Seth or Scott or Sam returned, placed his own hand on top of his, on top of Joe's, and slowly pried their fingers apart.

When he walked out of that room, he never saw Joe again.

Patrick wiped his eyes with the back of his hands and found Maisie standing in front of him clutching three containers of orange juice with foil tops.

"You okay, GUP?"

Patrick inhaled deeply and said he was, but he couldn't hide his tears. *I want to be.*

But he couldn't do this again.

TWENTY

Patrick pulled the Tesla into his garage around five and, feeling no need to take it out again anytime soon, secured the car under the dustcover. Grant wasn't in the mood for lupper; Patrick forced him to eat half a peanut butter sandwich anyway so that he could take the mild painkiller that had been prescribed, changed the sheets on the kid's bed, and then tucked him in tight. After he was out, Maisie helped clean up the debris from the quake, holding a bag open as her uncle swept the remnants of some possessions with a broom and dustpan. The Jonathan Adler knick-knacks from atop the piano. A vase from Takashimaya that lived on the coffee table. A few shattered picture frames, photos of him on various sets, mostly, with other recognizable faces. They straightened ornaments on tinsel branches and marveled how so many had refused to be shaken from the tree. Maisie, for her part, seemed equally reluctant to shake her uncle's side.

"These don't really need glass, anyway," Maisie offered helpfully, assessing the picture frames.

"You're right," Patrick agreed. The photos themselves were undamaged.

They swept the tile floors and vacuumed the rugs, unsure where little shards and remnants could be hiding. He would tell the kids not to walk barefoot for a few days, and would put Marlene in her booties, the ones they used to protect her paws from the heat. And tomorrow when she was here, he and Rosa would sweep the floors again.

"You have a big house," Maisie observed, as if it had occurred to her for the first time. "Don't you get lonely when it's just you?"

"Sometimes," Patrick responded. "I think that's part of being an adult."

"I'm not going to be lonely. When I'm an adult."

"No?" He wondered how she could be so sure in the face of a loss like the one she was enduring.

"No. I'm going to have a smaller house. With three Siberian huskies."

"That seems wise." Patrick surveyed his spacious living room. It *was* too big for one person. "Will there be anyone else in this house? Any people?"

"How do you mean?"

Patrick shrugged. "I don't know. A husband—or maybe a wife?"

Maisie lifted another photo frame, the one Patrick had gifted her with a photo of her mom. A Christmas miracle—the glass remained intact.

"A husband maybe. I don't have to decide right now." She traced her mom's face with her finger.

Since either answer would be fine with Patrick, he agreed. "There's plenty of time to decide. The huskies, however, are an excellent start."

When they began on the shelves, Maisie cradled his Golden Globe—the globe part dented and bent—and quietly broke down in tears. "Hey, it's okay," Patrick said to comfort her. "It's the Hollywood Foreign Press. They give them out to anyone. Twiggy, for god's sake, has two." Patrick stroked her hair, mimicking the way Clara had carefully brushed it; he remembered how calming it had been for Maisie. This wasn't about some cherished possession. This was something else. Her growing fear that attaching herself to anything will only cause those things to break, wither, fall away—that maybe she would be lonely after all. "Things can be replaced," Patrick whispered, pulling her in for a hug. "Things can always be replaced."

Eventually Maisie retired to bed, choosing to stay the night with Grant—at least to start. Alone at last, Patrick surveyed their efforts. The house seemed more modest, elegant. It was like the earthquake unleashed Coco Chanel, dictating to the living room her old adage: *Look in the mirror and take one thing off.* Patrick kind of liked the new look, the simplicity. It was spare.

He set to work on his bedroom, wanting to thin it out to match his new aesthetic. The TV was busted, but he didn't mind; he had little use for it at night other than as background noise when he felt most alone. The books were easy to restack, but he pulled a few titles to donate, anyhow. Books should be an experience, he thought, not a trophy for having read them. The Slim Aarons photo on the wall outside his en suite was askew, but he easily slid it back on its hook, and everything, for a moment, felt level again.

Patrick found the letter in his bedside table, folded in thirds, beneath an old stack of *People* magazines in which he'd appeared. He'd stashed it there who knows when, years earlier, with a bottle of pills—enough to end things if they ever got that bad. He remembered taping the nightstand drawer closed for the movers when he left LA for Palm Springs; he didn't want to empty the drawer of its contents, be faced with any of it—the prescription bottle, its long expired expiration date, the letter. Patrick swore he'd never read it again, but also he never threw it away knowing that impossible promises made to oneself in youth are always going to be broken.

He climbed into his bed and pressed the letter to his heart. When he could bear it, he glanced at the first few lines.

I was a ghost for four days and then I wasn't. That's how I think of it now.

He was struck by how little his handwriting had changed in the intervening years. How could he be a fundamentally different person, but something as basic as penmanship, the way he formed words, remain the same? His scar, the other lines on his face. The salt in his beard. His arms were thicker after years of working out, lifting things in a vain effort to transform himself into someone strong enough never to hurt. Even his worldview had changed, the things he had to say. So how could his writing not reflect that? How could it possibly remain unchanged?

It was a long time before he could read on.

Joe.

I was a ghost for four days and then I wasn't. That's how I think of it now. How I prefer to think of it, for it means that for those four days we were together, neither of us present, neither of us gone. In the bardo, as you might say, never having shut up about East Asia. Maybe you're there now. Wouldn't that be something. Maybe at the end of those four days someone asked, "Where to next?" and you said, "Well, I read a lot of books about Bhutan, I rather think I'd like it there," and, poof, you're in some hut, or yurt, or whatever the fuck, hanging colorful prayer flags on the wall.

Of course you're not in Bhutan, just as I'm not at the Plaza Athénée or anywhere I would want to be. Were you even bathed in white light in your purgatory? I was drenched in hospital fluorescents in mine. I still can't open my eyes wide to this new reality, the world seems too ugly now, phosphorous, awash in a rotting, greenish hue. I keep them closed a lot. My eyes. Not wanting to sleep, exactly. But not wanting to be awake. (Sleep comes with the screeching of tires and that deafening crunch of collision. Remember how I would flinch in that last moment before falling asleep and kick you? The sensation of falling? Jimmy legs, you said. Now it's not falling, but crashing. And you're not there to make me laugh.)

I hope you never heard that hideous sound.

I was discharged from the hospital after just one day. The bulk of my injuries were not wounds that would appear on an X-ray, were not treatable by a doctor (unless you count the quack who assigned me this letter to write). They stitched up my forehead, I guess where it hit the dash. Wouldn't you know it, the passenger airbag was off. It's almost as if the seat didn't register me, thinking, "My, aren't you a dainty thing." I've decided to join a gym. To bulk up. Though I might not. The books say exercise is good, but also not to make any sudden changes. Once again, I'm torn between two worlds.

I came straight to see you, but your family had already descended. And you know more than anyone that they never acknowledged my existence. I know, I can hear you now. It's not personal—they wouldn't like anyone you were with unless they had a uterus and a nonethnic name like Beth from Payroll and knew how to do things like make a pot roast. (But let's be honest: mostly the uterus thing.) I was not allowed into your room—family only! I was not included in your vigil. Me. The one who loved you the hardest. The one who knew you best.

I think this is what kills me the most. (Horrific word choice, given that you're the one who is dead, but you'll never read this and I'm not supposed to cross anything out or edit myself in any way.) Your last breaths were taken surrounded by those who didn't know you. Only memories of you, like I have now. They didn't know all the best parts. The things that make you laugh. The things you believe. Your passions, your art, your politics, your pop cultural references. The way you taste. The way you bite my lip playfully when we kiss. The way your dick curves just to the left when you're at your most excited.

Remember that one time I signed your Christmas card "Yours in Christ" and we laughed and laughed as nonbelievers and at the ridiculous formality of it all? (We might have been high. I think more than anything you were stunned I sent you a card.) And the next thing you signed for me, you did the same but crossed out "Christ" and wrote "science"? It became a love language for us, a secret way to say I love you when our surroundings seemed unsafe. Yours in science. Or how every time I answered the phone you said, "That's a corncob!" because that's what Dustin Hoffman says to Jessica Lange in the movie "Tootsie." Or how I could say for dinner I wanted that thing we had at that place that one time and you always knew which thing, remembered what time and the exact place. And you wanted it, too. Or maybe you were just kind enough to once again let me have my way.

I wandered the halls. Your family could keep me out of a room, but they couldn't evict me from a building. Eventually they would relent, this family of yours who didn't know you. Sooner or later they would crack. Someone would say, "Get that boy in here, the one wandering the halls." They wouldn't like it, but they would recognize that we had you in common. After a few awkward hours your mother would reach out and hold my hand in fellowship. No? At the very least someone would need me. At some point you would require clothes, you would need to be dressed. To come home, or—as it turns out—to not. They had the key to your room, but I had the key to your things. That never happened. I think they bought you a suit for the service at—god help you—the Beverly Center. That's the thing about putting a hospital across the street from a mall. Haunt them, would you? Like, rattle some fucking chains. I want them never to sleep again. I imagine this is what it was like at the height of AIDS. This awfulness. Hateful families swooping in and erasing loving partnerships. You'd think we'd left all that in the last century, but no.

It's this anger that's taken over. I used to be scared of anger, and that's because I bottled it up inside. Not anymore! It's like vomiting after drinking too much. Sure, it's unpleasant in the moment, but then you feel so much better! Anger is beautiful if you express it just right. Let it out. You should see the face of the woman who ran over my shoe with her cart at the grocery store. She won't do that again! (That's an extreme example; I probably owe her an apology.) Anyhow, I only mention this because they'll probably tell you in Bhutan that finding a way around anger is a form of enlightenment, and I'm telling you that that's a load of horseshit. Anger, when justified, is glorious.

Do you know what it's like to be so close to you when you needed me most and not be able to cross a ten-yard divide? There was a minefield between us, filled with explosives made from years of brainwashing and religion and intolerance and spite. I could have made a run for it, like a soldier storming Normandy in a war film with things detonating all around me—I could have broken through. But I was so afraid. I was afraid I wouldn't make it, that I would step on the land mine that is your mother, who would have me removed from the hospital altogether, in pieces if necessary, and if that happened I knew I would regret it for the rest of my life.

Instead I regret this.

There was a kind man who took pity on me. His name was Seth, a nurse. He brought me in to see you when your family stepped out. I held your hand and we said goodbye. As best as I was able.

Your organs have been donated. At least that's my understanding. I looked up the form and the questions they ask. Sexual history. Do you think your parents knew how to accurately answer? I don't. I think they lied. Isn't that the way? They won't take our blood, but they'll take our organs! This fucking world. I've about had it with straight people. Although I suppose they'd take our blood if we lied on those forms, too.

I am less me. I left part of myself with you. I don't know what it was, but I felt it leave my body the last time I held your hand. It was incinerated with you, with that cheap suit from Macy's and, I assume, scattered with you. Wherever that may be.

I will continue. I'm told repeatedly I have to. Greg threatened me not to do anything stupid. (Although, what recourse he would have if I did, I don't know.) Sara is flying here to be with me. She's arriving tomorrow. I was supposed to pick her up, but I told her that cars were traumatic and she said, "Of course, I'll take a cab." If I play this hand correctly I may never have to drive again. Certainly not to LAX. I will grow old and you won't ever have to. You will always be perfectly Joe. With your skin and your hair and your teeth and your ability to do three sit-ups and somehow see results.

My life will be different. For a bright, shining moment I was part of a team. I thought we would see the future together and be—oh god, writing it like this sounds so maudlin—A FAMILY. Now I don't know. I don't even know what family means. I'm adrift in black space like an untethered astronaut, each star I float past a shining memory reminding me that I don't live that life anymore.

Yours in science,
Patrick

PS This is dumb. I'm not going back to this therapist.

TWENTY-ONE

The visitors' lounge at the Coachella Sober Living Facility smelled familiar—eerily recognizable; Patrick couldn't quite place it and it was driving him mad. The walls were painted concrete brick, like an elementary school classroom, the furniture equally unimpressive. Not in a donated way: there was no sagging, puffy sofa one might find in an old church basement, batting spilling out of a tear in the arm. But certainly nothing high-end or evocative of the clientele this place seemed so desperate (according to their literature and pricing structure) to attract. Patrick took a seat on a chair that was as uncomfortable as its spare design suggested and inventoried the other furnishings. The lines were clean, the design Swedish, Danish perhaps, but everything looked disagreeable and had an air of mass production. Restless, he stood and paced the room in a hyped-up panic, like a dog whose owner promised to be right back.

The door to the hall was closed and Patrick was alone, trapped. The whole place was unsettling and still, there was an eerie quietude—like a reading room, in a nunnery, on a mountaintop, on Mars. Patrick's mind raced. He imagined residents tiptoeing around in paper slippers while adhering to vows of silence. The temperature was cool, but air didn't seem to be circulating from the vent. He had been offered a cup of coffee by someone with crooked teeth named Kevin, which he regretfully accepted; the coffee was weak, stale, bland—much like the first impression Kevin himself put forth. Patrick clung to the cardboard cup tightly, both as something to do with his hands and because there was nowhere to throw it away. The corner offered a lone plant; he considered dumping the coffee in the wicker basket that housed it, but the plant was fake and the basket contained craft foam, not soil, and he didn't want the coffee running through the loosely-woven reeds and across the tile floor, pooling like evidence in a grisly crime.

That fucking letter. Rereading his letter to Joe had kept him from sleep for the second night in a row. If he didn't take this next step quickly, sleep might never come again.

Sara arrived in a taxi that night. She used the key Patrick hid on top of the light fixture outside his apartment door; he heard her fumble with it in the lock. She came in and sat next to him, pulling him into her chest, kissing the top of his head. There were wooden blinds covering the windows, blocking out most of the light; the thin slats of sun that made it through fell across Patrick's face like prison bars.

Joe had been dead for less than a week.

"I got here as fast as I could."

Patrick nodded, his chin hitting the top of her breast. "They wouldn't let me see him."

"I know."

Patrick gulped for air. "He must have been so scared."

"They're monsters."

That's all it took—*acknowledgment*—and Patrick broke down in ugly heaving sobs. She held him until he was empty of tears.

"Let's get drunk."

Patrick laughed, not a lot but a little, and nuzzled his face in the scoop of her T-shirt. Her chest was soft, welcome. Is this why straight men obsessed over breasts? It seemed wrong to sexualize something this comforting. Grotesque, even. He squeezed her tightly. They would get drunk. Was it possible relief was that easy? What was it Evelyn Waugh had written in *Brideshead Revisited*? "Ought we to be drunk every night?" It was Sebastian. *Yes. Yes, I think so.* In college, it was his and Sara's solution to everything. Difficult test, bad grade, hard day, awful date: get drunk. And off they went to Richard's, a neighborhood bar with bottomless pitchers and a popcorn machine. And it actually, usually, momentarily helped. Patrick just wasn't sure what witchcraft alcohol could conjure to settle something this dark. "I don't . . . know what we have."

He said *we*, but he was now an *I*.

Sara pulled a bottle of tequila out of her bag and set it on the table with a thud. "Shots."

And it did. *Help.* After the fourth shot. Temporarily, at least, to ease the grip of the fist that was closed tightly around Patrick's heart. They started with a souvenir shot glass from the Sands that Patrick had acquired on a trip to Las Vegas with Joe; after the third shot Patrick knocked it over, and it rolled under the couch. The Sands itself was long gone, imploded to make room for a newer casino. There was perhaps some symbolism there, but Patrick couldn't imagine building anything new on his own ground; he wanted to exist as rubble, a fallen monument whose lights once shone bright. "Fuck it," Patrick said when Sara tried and failed to retrieve the glass; they each took a swig straight from the bottle.

They shared memories of Joe, but they could only speak a few key words out loud. *Wretched, putrid and sub-par* conjured a telephone call Joe had made to a hotel in San Diego to complain after a disastrous stay. *Clams casino*, a weekend with food poisoning that was only funny now. *Jim jinlet*, the way he would try to pronounce gin gimlet after consuming two or three. Full stories were painful and unnecessary. The memories were fresh, the history recent. They played out like little movies on a screen inside their brains. Fleshed-out memories would come later, when the edges started to soften in the fog of memory, when the details needed to be spoken to be recalled.

"You lied to me," Patrick said when they were sufficiently drunk. The laughter had subsided and things, once again, looked starless.

"I've never lied to you," Sara protested.

Patrick stared into some middle distance. The lie was a long time ago. "You told me life would be easy."

Sara thought about this. "It still might." The way she said it, offhandedly, completely dismissive of the pain they were both currently in, was exactly what Patrick needed to hear. Not because it was true—they both knew it wasn't. But because they were still them. And it was something at least for him to hold on to. A reason, on that day at least, for him to continue.

When the visitors' lounge door creaked, Patrick spun, his heart in his throat. Greg appeared in the doorway, his hand gripping the knob as if it were the only thing holding him up, looking calm and rested and . . . *pale*. Did they not let patients outside? Wasn't the restorative nature of sunlight one of the key selling points of detoxing in the desert? Patrick locked eyes with his brother, much as they had in the Hartford airport right before this misadventure began. Neither of them said a word. Greg's eyes nervously darted, in search of the kids, Patrick supposed. They took each other in warily before moving in for a tight hug. Patrick grabbed a fistful of his brother's shirt, lifting it halfway up his back, and pushed his head into the meaty part of Greg's shoulder; the facility obviously had a gym and Greg had been making full use of it. Their chests pressed together, Patrick could feel his brother's heart beat.

"The kids okay?" Greg grabbed Patrick's arms and pushed him back so he could see the answer on his brother's face.

"Yes. Good. Good. They're fine."

Greg stared as this sank in. "I was crawling out of my skin after the earthquake. First Clara, and now this? It took the whole facility to calm me down, everyone advocating for me to stay focused on my recovery here. They promised me if you lived in Southern California, you had experience riding them out and you would call if anything was seriously wrong. Eventually I passed out, from exhaustion or from worry."

"Yeah, we . . ." Patrick made a gesture with his hand like a boat sailing smooth waters. "Rode it out."

"And the Clara thing? You're putting me through the wringer."

Patrick wanted to point out that neither an earthquake nor his sister's actions was his doing, but he simply let it go. "I took care of it."

He nodded and Greg nodded again, until his nodding dissolved into an inquisitive smirk. *Then why are you here?* There were twenty-four days left of his treatment, both had the exact number down. Greg thought it had been pretty clear they wouldn't see each other until then. The facility was family-friendly, visitations were allowed. But Greg was adamant; he did not want his children seeing him here. It would hurt, the separation, them and him, but then it would pass—the ripping off of a Band-Aid. Their time apart would soon be forgotten as the kids forged a new sense of normal, free of knowing, until they got older, that their father was an addict.

"So, they just let you walk around in here? Unescorted?" Patrick asked.

"Yeah. What did you think?"

Patrick wasn't sure, but had pictured Greg being frog-marched into the lounge wearing leg irons. "I thought I would be on the other side of some partition. And we would speak over telephones and hold our hands meaningfully up to the glass."

"This isn't prison, Patrick. I'm here voluntarily."

Patrick looked around the room, taking a second catalog of everything, his gaze landing on his coffee. The powdered creamer had congealed into several disturbing islands dotting a caramel sea. If internment here was voluntary, he didn't see the appeal.

"Where are the kids?"

"With JED."

"Who's Jed, your friend? Is he responsible? Up to watching both kids? They walk all over new sitters, you know. It can take more than two hands to keep them in check."

Patrick stifled a laugh. "JED's got it covered."

"Then why are you here?"

"It's good to see you, too."

Greg looked up and to the left, away from his brother. *You think it's not good to see you?* It exuded from every pore in his face.

Patrick took a deep breath and began. "Clara was right. She was right all along. I'm going to ask her to take the kids for the last three weeks. *Yes.*" Patrick agreed with his own words, as if this were perfectly settled. "Clara can take them back-to-school shopping and do those types of chores. You know. Get them ready. It's for the best."

Greg stumbled backward until his legs hit a chair and he sat down. "Ready for what? I was counting on *you*."

"I know and I'm sorry. It's just. They're all you have left. They're all you have, and seeing Grant the other night in the hospital, and sitting by his bedside, in that moment, I was right back with Joe and I promised myself then that I wouldn't put myself in this position—"

"Whoa, whoa, whoa. You said Grant was fine."

"He *is* fine."

"Then why was he in the hospital?"

Oh. "There's a sculpture over his bed I didn't have properly secured. It fell during the quake and hit him in the head. You know they were suspicious of that thing all along? Anyhow, he'll be bruised. Slight concussion. Small cut."

"Oh my god."

Patrick paused, as if the details were just beyond his grasp. "I told him his scar would match mine."

"Scar?!"

"Or maybe not. He's young. He'll probably heal much nicer. If not, I'll find a guy."

"To do what?"

"Get rid of it. Maybe he can work on your marionette lines. A twofer."

Greg stood and raised his voice. "You think this is funny?"

"No, I don't think it's funny! You have no idea what I'm dealing with! Maisie wants a husband, Clara wants a wife. I can't do this anymore. The earth is literally shaking underneath us. If that's not as clear a sign as anything that I'm messing everything up—"

"WHAT ARE YOU TALKING ABOUT?"

"I can't be the only one standing between you and having nothing left at all."

Greg grabbed his temples and rubbed them so hard Patrick thought his fingers might crack his skull. "I need a drink."

"Can . . . Can you do that? I mean, if your thing was pills?"

"My thing *is* pills, and no I can't do that, you dim-witted twat." Greg gnawed at his cuticle like he was working on a particularly irksome hangnail while he took a beat to calm down. "They have these smoothies here. Pear. Spinach. Ginger. Avocado, probably. Isn't avocado mandatory in California? That's all I drink anymore."

"That sounds pretty good." Patrick could even imagine it with vodka.

"Not *sixty-six* days in a row!"

Patrick agreed, bringing his hand to his mouth before realizing he was just copying Greg. It was uncomfortable. He'd never made his brother angry. Greg had never yelled at him so nakedly. "I took Mom to this restaurant once in LA after a taping of the show. This was years ago when she would actually fly. Upscale place. I thought it would be a treat. She took one look at the menu, slid it across the table at me, and complained that it was in another language."

"Was it?"

"No! I told her, 'That word is *avocado*—you know that!'"

Greg smiled weakly. Making fun of their mother was always safe terrain.

"It might have also said *crudo*," he conceded. "That's Italian, I guess. So maybe she was right.

"Patrick," Greg started and stopped. "Do you know *why* I asked you take the kids?"

"My ebullient personality?" He offered a weak smile.

"Christ. I *know* you're not over Joe. You float through life determined not to get attached to anyone or anything." Greg crossed over to the window and watched a family visit in the courtyard. "This is as much for you as it is for them, Patrick. As it is for me."

Patrick was appalled. "You gifted me your kids? To what, to *fix* me?"

"No. I knew they would be best off with you. But it was . . . What did you just call it?" Greg traced the lines that ran from each side of his nose to the corners of his mouth. "A twofer."

Patrick scoffed.

"You think you're so complicated. That you exist on a higher plane above everyone and everything else, thinking we can't understand you. But you don't and we do. You promised yourself you would never get that close to anyone again? And now all these years later you have allowed yourself. Or maybe not even *allow*—kids don't give you much of a choice. But you feel something, and you're scared and you're trying to run from it and, goddammit, I won't let you."

"You're going to stop me, locked up in here?"

Greg turned around and pressed his finger to Patrick's sternum, hard. "Fuck you."

"FUCK YOU!" Patrick took a seat on one of the sharply-angled chairs and waited for his anger to pass. "The stairwells in our college dorm. That's what this place smells like. I've been racking my brain since I walked in here."

"The stairwells?"

"Musty, mixed with old paint. Sara would get it." Patrick scratched his head. "I don't know how that's possible, how it smells wet. The average rainfall here is nothing. It's like Sara's following me." Patrick started to cry. "I should have come to see her." The words hurt when he said them out loud. "I reasoned every moment I spent with her I was taking away from you and the kids."

"She knew that. She understood."

"She wasn't mine anymore."

There was a long silence before Greg spoke. "She knew that, too."

Patrick turned and slapped the concrete wall with his open hand and it stung, reverberating through his wrist and arm. There was so much he had never processed. "I don't know where that comes from. My anger. There's a well, deep inside me. Most of the time I'm not even aware that it's there. But then it comes bubbling up . . ."

"Remember the house in New Hampshire?" Greg asked.

"Our house? That new construction? Barely. We only lived there, what, a year?"

"Do you remember why?"

"Dad got transferred back to Connecticut."

"No. It was the well. They dug and they dug and they dug and could never find enough water. Every night we shared an inch of bathwater, the three of us. I don't know what Mom and Dad did. Spritz themselves in the sink. We had like the second deepest well in New Hampshire. There was a cabin I think on Mount Washington that had one deeper, but only because they were digging into a mountain." Greg cracked his knuckles, a habit that drove Patrick mad. "Eventually Dad and some others in the development took them to court and the builder was forced to buy the homes back."

Patrick looked out into the shady courtyard. Too many trees. It was preventing the residents from getting sun.

"How am I the only one to remember this? I was the baby." Greg stood behind Patrick and put his hands on his brother's shoulders. "Your well is in a mountain," he said.

Patrick broke, his eyes filled with tears. Already Greg understood grief better than he did. *This fucking place.* What were they teaching? Maybe he should call Clara for real and then check himself in here, too.

He ran his fingers through his hair, messing it and smoothing it to one side again. "Dad probably made that up. Like the Siamese twins who were drafted."

"Only one twin was drafted and that was real."

"HOW DOES EVERYONE KNOW THIS BUT ME?" Patrick felt his mouth twitch and the corners of his lips spread into the widest smile. It was like his face was putty and someone was pulling his skin out and then up, stretching it against his will until it was so wide it might snap. Greg smiled, too, which set Patrick off further. "Stop."

"What?" Greg was honestly bewildered.

"Just don't." Patrick put both hands to his face and pushed it back into a neutral expression.

"Oh, good lord. Are you worried about the lines on *your* face? Just smile once in a while and enjoy it. Earthquakes happen, Patrick. It's not your fault. You should probably bolt your shit to the wall, but it's not your fault. What's more, I don't buy that you think it is. I think this is all because you're in spitting distance of sending them home. Of my taking them back to Connecticut. And you don't know what your life is going to look like after they leave."

Patrick stacked a few magazines before fanning them across the table in a perfect display of healthy living.

"So, come back with them. With us."

Patrick put his finger over a headline that read "Take Down the Flu, Naturally." "To Connecticut? Oh, hell no."

"Why not?"

"It's cold. You call yourself nutmeggers. You want me to go on?"

"I'm going to need a sober companion."

"Pass."

"Don't you even want to hear what it entails?"

"Does it entail being sober?"

"Well, yeah."

"Pass."

Greg turned away. He knew they were joking, but the sting of rejection was real. "Do you think this is fun for me? Locked up here alone with my thoughts? Awake at night because they won't give me anything to sleep? Do you know how dark it is? I've never seen more stars and been so lost. It's awful. I'm confronted with my every failure. I was taking her pills, Patrick. At the end. *Her* pills. That's how bad it was. That's how small I am."

Patrick was always surprised how quickly rage traveled through his body. After the accident that took Joe, he was given morphine. He remembered how it flushed cold through his veins, from limbs to fingertips, into each miniscule capillary, not an inch of him left unrewarded. One instant, pain; the next, blessed relief. This was that but in reverse. Molten anger all the way into his toenails. He started to sweat and his hands clenched into fists.

"It wasn't at her expense, I swear. Refills were easy to come by. There was always more than enough in the house. She never went without."

Patrick crossed over to the window and leaned on the sill. The mountains rose in the distance. *His well was in a mountain.* He let himself breathe, but it was the first time their looming presence around the valley's edge felt invasive, and not like protection. They were encroaching, holding him in, threatening to suffocate him instead of keeping danger out. "Celestial navigation. It's a sucker's game," he said, recalling Greg's comment about being lost.

So many nights Patrick had looked up at the desert night sky trying to find meaning, trying to locate himself. He would always come back to the same thing: stargazing was time traveling. He'd looked it all up, read every book in the library. We see the sun as it was 8.3 minutes ago. Alpha Centauri—the next closest star—was 4.3 light-years away. When he looked at Alpha Centauri, he saw light that was generated when Joe was still alive. He even remembered the time, 4.3 years and a day after that fateful night, when he looked up at the sky to see the first light generated after Joe had died; he wept like a child. The North Star? Three hundred and twenty light-years. Its light was generated long before either he or Joe existed. *It was a sucker's game*, he repeated, this time to himself. How can you tell where you're going when you're always looking up at the past?

"Go home, Patrick. Be with the kids. Show them your grief. Talk to them. Show them your grief and help them navigate theirs."

Patrick had a thousand questions; chiefly, what if he said the wrong thing? "And then what?"

Greg smiled. "I'll see you in twenty-four days."

Patrick looked back down at the magazines; there was no headline screaming "10 Former TV Stars That Will Help You Live a Healthier Life." The very thought of it, ridiculous.

Greg pulled his brother in for a hug. "Maisie wants a husband?"

"That's what you got from all this?" Patrick rested his chin on Greg's shoulder.

"I'm just surprised, is all."

Patrick squeezed. "Don't you dare hold her to it."

"All I will ever want is for her to be happy."

They stood there and held each other. As little kids, they would hug every night before bed. Patrick wondered when that stopped, when intimacy between boys became something to be mocked and not celebrated.

"The dog takes a pill for allergies. Is that going to be difficult for you to be around?"

"The *what*?"

"The dog. She takes a pill for her skin. I'm just trying to be sensitive. I don't want you popping them when you get back to Connecticut."

Greg stood dumbfounded; he could only fight one battle at a time.

Patrick couldn't read his reaction, so he shrugged—they could figure it out later. He took one last sip of his coffee before spitting it back in the cup.

TWENTY-TWO

Maisie and Grant had taken to wearing their bicycle helmets to breakfast. All day, really, except sometimes while swimming, as they worried about drowning. Despite Grant's injury, they acquiesced at night and slept without them because wearing a helmet to bed was impractical. But come daylight? The helmets were strapped tightly under their little chins like they were inspectors on a construction site, there to assess the structural viability of his house. All they were missing were coffee thermoses and a tube of blueprints. The previous day, Patrick had filmed a video of them clanking their helmets together like battering rams, a test, of sorts, of their own emergency system. He'd even handed his phone to Maisie afterward and left the room, tacit permission to post the video to YouTube. There were now several such videos on Patrick's channel. The first two; a video of the kids running an obstacle course he'd made around the pool that mimicked the one television show they seemed familiar with—some sort of ninja warrior challenge—along with his ongoing critical commentary; one where Patrick had hooked bungee cords around their arms and pretended to control them like marionettes; and one in the hospital they'd filmed in the style of a talk show, except they each held their tongues down with depressors. Patrick got a perverse kick out of the online response, although he didn't altogether understand it.

Likes and subscribers and comments came rolling in. First on YouTube and then on his old photos on Instagram. It was like people were remembering he was alive, discovering him all over again, blood flowing in the circuitry connecting him to the outside world.

But as the kids emerged from their rooms wearing their helmets for the fifth morning in a row, all Patrick could manage was "*Why?*"

"Aftershocks," Maisie said with a dismissive nonchalance. "Things could hit us on the head."

"The sky is not falling, Henny."

Grant produced a granola bar he was hoping to eat. "My helmet's on too tight for me to chew." Marlene began sniffing around his shoes, hoping he'd drop a bite of his snack.

"Well, the good news is, you look ridiculous." Patrick ushered Grant over and loosened his strap so the kid could eat his breakfast. "Finish up. We might as well go for a bike ride so you blend in."

Early-morning bike rides had become a staple, a way for them to burn off some of their energy before they were driven inside from the heat. This morning, however, they got a later start; riding in the midmorning sun was like pedaling into a wet cement wall that was slowly hardening around you. Five blocks from home, they dismounted their bikes to walk.

Patrick's heart was racing and his palms were sweating, he assumed incorrectly, from exertion. It wasn't until after they'd walked a block and his elevated heart rate refused to recede that he realized how apprehensive he was. It was long past time to tell the kids about Joe, and now he really didn't know how to begin. A small lizard scurried across the sidewalk, which was hot like a griddle, until it disappeared in some tall desert grass growing on a vacant lot. Patrick didn't call attention to it, for fear of losing his focus.

It didn't matter; he chickened out anyhow.

By afternoon every inch of his swimming pool was covered in enormous pool floats. The unicorn, the flamingo, the donut, the pizza slice, they'd all been drafted into service—even the lobster that Sara had given him to remind him of his New England roots. Patrick could hardly see signs of water peeking through the flotilla. Grant rode a silver winged stallion filled with glitter through this inflatable forest; Maisie kneeled on a pineapple, clutching its yellow sides. Both of them in their bicycle helmets still.

"What on earth?" Patrick asked as he emerged from the house to join them.

"GUP, look! I'm riding a Pegathus!"

Patrick focused his attention on Grant, who was pleased as punch, perched safely above the water. His forehead was covered with a flesh-colored bandage that shined in the sun. Patrick set a tray of smoothies he'd made on the patio table. "You're riding a pterippus. Pegasus was white. You know what? *Pteriffic*. Don't get your bandage wet."

"I'm floating on a pineapple!"

"I can see that!" Patrick cupped his hands above his eyes to block out the sun. "Where's my pool?" He took two steps forward and tripped over the cord to the pump that they undoubtedly used to inflate his stash.

"GUP, get your thwimthoot."

"Already wearing it, bud."

As Patrick entered the pool, John popped his head over the wall, holding a gardening trowel.

"Howdy, neighbors." John waved. "Just doing some planting, when I heard the kids playing. Thought I'd check on them."

It takes a gay village. "How's your house, John? Any damage from the quake?" Patrick could all but see JED's collection of tumescent sculptures shattered in ruins on the floor; it was a mystery how they ever stood upright to begin with.

"A few broken glasses in the kitchen. We have a cabinet door that likes to swing open by itself. Some knickknacks. No heirlooms. A mirror fell off the wall and shattered. That'll be seven years of bad luck."

Some knickknacks? "Sorry to hear."

"Don't be. They're just things. We're fine. Dog's fine. Cleaned up in a jiff. Grant, you're riding a Pegasus!"

"That's right!" Grant exclaimed. Finally, someone who got it.

"Pegasus is the symbol of wisdom and fame. Just like your uncle. Wise and famous."

"He's not *that* famous," Maisie scoffed.

"Pegasus was also a fountain of inspiration for poets," John added, leaning farther over the wall. "Some people called him the horse of muses."

Patrick took full opportunity of John's distraction to rub more sunscreen on Grant.

"You know, we wrote a limerick about you when you first bought the house," John offered.

"Oh, really."

"'There once was a man named Patrick; who moved in just over the brick. We looked over the wall; he was standing quite tall, with quite an impressive—'"

Patrick covered Grant's ears. "Okay."

John laughed. "I was going to say *picnic*."

Sure you were.

"A friend gave us one of those floats for our pool, too. Pegasus was the son of Poseidon, the god of the sea. According to legend, wherever Pegasus would strike his hoof on the ground a spring would appear from the earth." John had Maisie's and Grant's rapt attention. "Palm Springs is known for its springs, as well as its many swimming pools, so a Pegasus seemed like a symbolic gift. At least according to my friend."

"Wow, cool." Grant turned and splashed and looked at his uncle through his green lizard goggles. Patrick massaged the last of the lotion into Grant's skin and gave him a little push.

"Did you hear me before? Don't get your bandage wet."

John looked on, impressed. "You know, Patrick. You've become quite adept at that."

"What?"

John glanced at the sunscreen. "When we babysat the other day, I had an awful time with the stuff."

What was once the bane of Patrick's existence, making sure every inch of the kids' skin was coated with hellish lotion, now had become de rigueur.

"Huh," Patrick said.

Maybe he was more capable than he thought.

After John returned to his gardening, Patrick took up residence on the pizza slice and he tethered the three of them together by placing a foot on each of their floats. They lazily sipped their smoothies, dazed in the midday sun. Greg had entrusted him for a reason. It was time to share his experience.

"Hey," he began, but had to clear a frog from his throat. "Do you guys know why your dad wanted you to stay with me?"

Grant looked up at him blankly; Maisie focused on the sky.

"Because you have a pool?" To Grant, that was reason enough.

"Because Daddy is close by." Maisie, in character, was giving this more considered thought.

"Because you were friendth with Mommy," Grant added, as if unwilling to concede rational discourse to his sister.

"Well, all that is part of it. I *do* have a pool. And your father definitely didn't want to be far away from you, and your mom was very special to me. But it's more than that." *Deep breath.* "You had an uncle Joe, once. Or, I had a Joe. He *would* have been your uncle, too, had he lived."

"He died?" Maisie was immediately hooked. Patrick had observed her all summer in a quiet search for meaning; she was adrift without her anchor. The pictures she drew, the questions she asked, the stories she requested be told. One shiny lure and she bit hard.

"He did." Patrick swallowed the rock he felt in his throat. It was hot, as it had been lying all summer in the sun. "I loved him and he died."

"Was he your brother?" Grant asked.

"Was he Dad's brother?" Maisie added.

"No, what? Gross. *Why?*" With all due respect to Greg, this was already a mistake. "Oh. Not your uncle by blood. He was my . . ." Patrick suddenly struggled with the word, although he wasn't sure why. They knew exactly what the *G* in GUP stood for, what *guncle* meant. He wanted to convey everything that Joe was in a way that they would both understand. *Partner* seemed confusing, like they ran an investment firm. *Lover* seemed antiquated, although they had no context to understand why. "Boyfriend." Out loud it seemed not enough.

"How did he die?" Grant's preoccupation with death was different than his sister's. At six, his search wasn't so much for meaning as it was for grisly detail. It had taken Patrick weeks to understand it was to calm his own fears about dying. The more bizarre the circumstances were, the less likely they would happen to him. At bedtime each night he liked to list elaborate ways to bite it. Last night's death involved falling down a mountain while skiing, being mauled by a panther, hitting a half-dozen trees, catching on fire, and then tumbling into some sort of wood chipper.

"He was driving." Patrick led with that to ease Grant's anxieties; it was no being launched out of a cannon into a cheese grater before having your bits filtered through a pod of baleen whales, but Grant was still a good ten years from climbing behind the wheel of a car. "And he was killed by a drunk driver."

Grant sucked through his straw, slurping his drink and making an awful racket. *Jesus, kid,* Patrick thought. *I'm ripping my heart out here.*

"Were you in the car with him?"

Patrick nodded.

"Is that why you have your thcar?" Grant set his cup in the floating drink holder they'd bought their uncle for Christmas.

Patrick touched his forehead between his eyebrows gently, as if after all these years it might hurt. "Sadly, as much as I'd like it to be otherwise, I'm just not a boy wizard."

"When was this?" Maisie asked.

Patrick had to do some quick math in his head. "Before you were born." He reached out and intertwined his fingers with hers, further anchoring them together. "So, I've been at this grief thing a while."

Maisie fiddled with her helmet, sweeping her hair back underneath so it wouldn't stick to her brow. "When does it get easy?"

He thought about lying, but what was the point? Greg didn't send his children to Palm Springs to be lied to, and even if he had they deserved better. Instead, he squeezed her hand and said, "Any day now." And then he smiled to show them that grief wasn't the end of the world.

Maisie let one leg fall into the pool, defeated.

"But it does get *easier*. I want you to remember that. Because you're going to go home in a few weeks, back to your house and your belongings. And normal things, your toys for instance, might seem drained of their pleasure, of their ability to bring you joy. Games you played with your mom, maybe. And that's okay. You're both so big now." He reached for Grant's hand, too. "Maybe you've outgrown them. Maybe they will regain their powers over time. Either way, it's fine." Patrick sat up, careful to keep his balance. He leaned forward to unbuckle Grant's bicycle helmet, and then likewise loosen Maisie's. "Take these off. The sky is not going to fall. That's what I'm telling you. The pain you feel, the disaster you think is imminent. Those feelings fade. And some days you even miss it. Some days you miss the pain, because you're afraid. Afraid that as the pain softens so do memories of the one you lost." Patrick thought how best to explain this in a way they would understand. "Do you guys have chalkboards at school?"

"We have whiteboards," Maisie said. Patrick lifted the helmet off her head.

"But we have a chalkboard eathel at home."

"Weasel?"

"He means easel."

"Oh, so then—you know. It feels sometimes like Joe, whom I loved very much, is being erased. He's just a smudge now on a chalkboard, smeared in an effort to get rid of him to make way for something new. And I hate that. So there are times I wished it hurt *more*, because it would mean the details of him would still be sharp. And then there are other days out here in the desert—especially if you go way out, to Joshua Tree or beyond—when you can see the Milky Way. A whole smudge of stars across the sky. And you think, there's still so much in that smudge. So many gleaming, beautiful things that you could never erase them all."

"Do you have a picture of him?" Maisie asked after taking this new information in.

"Of Joe? Many. I put them away. I don't often look at them anymore." Patrick eased back onto his float. "I have a letter."

"That he wrote to you?"

"That I wrote to him. After he died."

"Why did you write to him after he died?"

The question hit Patrick hard. Was it merely an assignment from a therapist whose credentials he questioned at the time? "It helped me. And I think it might help you. When we go inside, I think we should all write letters to your mom."

They looked confused.

"We can't send them, you understand. But really, they're for ourselves. Years from now we can read them. You'll see where you were. And you'll see how much you've grown. And that will make your mother happy. Knowing, eventually, that you'll be okay." Patrick pushed Grant's drink back in his nephew's direction. "Finish your smoothies, kids."

"Why?" Maisie asked.

"Why?" Patrick reached for his own beverage. "Guncle Rule number thirteen: Fun drinks make everything more interesting."

They wrote their letters that afternoon.

◇◇◇◇◇

"Cassie Everest's office." The voice was androgynous, bordering on bored. So much so, Patrick almost forgot to speak.

"*Cassie?*" Had she finagled an assistant out of this promotion? Or was she lowering her voice an octave to fake one? Either way, he was impressed.

"May I tell her who's calling?"

"Patrick."

"Patrick . . . ?"

"Her *client*." Patrick was immediately jealous. He liked to have people's undivided attention. "Does she have other accounts?"

"Oh, *Patrick*!" There was a glimmer of light in the voice. This wasn't Cassie after all; she wouldn't take the charade this far. So who was this new being?

"Please. Let's not stand on ceremony. Call me Mr. O'Hara."

There was an awkward pause as this new addition to the team tried to assess if he was joking. "One moment, Mr. O'Hara."

Patrick emptied the dregs of the coffeepot into his mug, took a sip, and spat it in the sink. Maisie insisted on making the coffee each morning, and while it was drinkable freshly brewed, it did not stand up to the morning. He peered into the living room; it was empty. The kids were reading quietly in their rooms. It was a rare moment of privacy, and he was taking full advantage.

"This is Cassie." Her voice rang through the phone, serious, assured.

"Amy Adirondacks? Is that really you?"

"The one and only."

"Neal really did right by you." Patrick hoped to god this was true.

"Office. Assistant. Company credit card. And I have you to thank. He really listens to you."

"Everyone listens to me." The TV came on in the other room. Patrick screamed over the volume. "I said no television!" He could hear Cassie's smile through the phone.

"I think he's jealous of you, frankly."

"Neal?" Gossip was the way to Patrick's heart.

"He became an agent, but all things considered he would have rather been famous himself."

"You tell that prick the only way he's going to see his name in lights is if he changes his name to EXIT." It was an old line, but Cassie was young and didn't know all the old lines, and he punctuated it with a new panache, hoping she would later repeat it in the office lunchroom, allowing Neal to overhear. Sure enough, she laughed.

"What can I do for you, Patrick?"

All business, Cassie 2.0. "My Golden Globe is dented."

"It's dented?"

"It has a dent in it."

"A dent," Cassie repeated. The word was in danger of losing all meaning.

"A dent, a dimple, a depression. It fell. During the earthquake."

"Oh. Okay. We'll call over to the Hollywood Foreign Press and see about getting it replaced." Silence. "Are the kids all right? Do you mind me asking?"

"They are and I don't mind. Listen. I want you to look into something for me. Without saying you're looking into it."

"I'm not sure I understand, but okay."

Am I going to have to do all the work? "I want you to gauge interest."

"In?" Cassie asked.

"Employment opportunities." Patrick swallowed hard, as if trying to force the words from escaping. But it was too late. "In New York."

"Wow. New York."

"All right, well, don't blab it all over town." Although, wasn't that exactly what he was asking her to do?

"Any particular kind of employment?"

"I'm not sure I qualify to work at the UN."

"Television, movies, theater?"

Patrick remembered his protest the first time Cassie came to see him in this very kitchen. He was an unbroken stallion then, a tamed pony now. "Are you going to make me say it? I'm *flexible*."

"Okay. So I'm going to look into work opportunities in New York without saying I'm looking into it."

"Exactly. You're gauging interest."

"Any suggestions on how I do that?"

Patrick sighed. "'I hear Patrick O'Hara's looking to return to work and might make a run of it in New York.' That sort of thing. Start with gossip."

"And if there *is* interest?"

Patrick was hopeful there would be. "Quietly make note and move on."

"I can't do more than make note?"

For Patrick, returning to work was not merely a financial necessity, it was to be the final step of his own recovery. He had to remember how to *feel* things. And if he had to accomplish that in part by becoming someone else, some new role, then so be it. It was probably safer that way. But that didn't erase his hesitancy entirely. "Not yet, no."

"And why is that?"

"Because I'm still gauging mine."

TWENTY-THREE

The fight had been brewing for days. It seemed the closer they were to Greg's release the more they all succumbed to their frazzled ideas about what the future might hold. Maisie in particular was sullen, withdrawn—immune, suddenly, to her uncle's innumerable charms. On Tuesday she refused to do the dishes and told Patrick it was his job to do them as the grown-up. On Wednesday she said she didn't want to eat lupper, even though Rosa had cooked all day. It wasn't the menu she objected to, rather she wanted to eat *dinner* like a normal family.

"Normal is a terrible thing to aspire to," Patrick had said. "Aim higher."

"What do you even mean?" Maisie was exasperated.

"Want more for yourself."

"Talk like a regular person!"

Patrick sighed. "Normal families are boring." It was a slip on Patrick's part, a terrible thing to say to a girl who had lost her mother; her moodiness had brought out his own. He opened his mouth to apologize, but Maisie scuttled his launch before it got off the ground.

"*You're* boring!"

"You take that back."

"I will not!"

"I am a lot of things, many of them unflattering, but *boring* is not one."

Grant put up a withering defense of his uncle before Patrick put his hand on his arm, letting the boy know he could fight his own battle. Maisie glared at her uncle before storming off and slamming the door to her room.

"Why is she so pissy?"

Grant shrugged.

On Thursday they went for brunch at Cheeky's. Maisie didn't say a word to their Lyft driver, a woman named Mona who had her hair tied up in a scarf like she'd answered their call from a salon halfway through her appointment. Maisie didn't even offer a response when Mona asked her a direct question about Maisie's level of excitement about going back to school—something Patrick knew she was looking forward to, if only as a metric to measure a return to some sort of stability.

"Our driver asked you a question, Maisie."

Maisie just stared out the window.

"Aren't you excited to see your friends? What about Amy Beckwith?"

"AUDRA BRACKETT!"

"She's excited," Patrick translated to Mona.

"I'm going to be in firtht grade," Grant offered, cheerfully. Patrick nudged him in the shoulder, grateful for his willing cooperation.

"So grown up," Mona said, flashing them a smile in the rearview mirror.

At the restaurant the kids had their usual, fresh-corn pancakes with a side of hot tots, which is what Cheeky's called their potatoes. Patrick ordered the Paleo granola and a mimosa. The place was unusually hopping for the ungodly hour—it was one of the problems with Palm Springs. The blazing sun was a virus that turned everyone into morning people. Patrick thought he should break the mood with a joke. "Guncle Rule eleventy-five, special brunch edition: Bottomless mimosas are not the same thing as pantsless mimosas. Very different, in fact. Learned that the hard way."

"You didn't wear panth?" Grant asked.

"Grantelope, you have no idea how many restaurants I've been kicked out of for not wearing pants." Patrick bopped Grant on the head with a menu.

Grant mumbled some loophole about his shorts not being pants, when Maisie interjected.

"There are too many *rules*!" The word *rules* dripped with so much disgust, Patrick was taken aback.

"I'm sorry. Do you want to try that again and watch your tone?" Patrick traced his fingers on the hair over his upper lip; he'd shaved that morning, displeased with the gray on his chin, but left behind a pleasantly dark mustache.

"I'm tired of living here! It's a million degrees and your rules aren't funny and I want to go home!"

"Talk about hot tots," Patrick said under his breath, perhaps to Grant, who had become somewhat of a confidant over the last few days of his sister's souring mood. Grant, however, was trying to untangle silverware from his napkin and didn't pick up on the comment.

"What did you say?" Maisie narrowed her eyes; her anger was almost comical, but Patrick didn't laugh—it was coming from someplace very real.

"I said, talk about a HOT TOT. Satisfied?"

"I'm not a tot!" This was abundantly clear; it was like she'd morphed into a teenager overnight.

"Yes, I know. You're sixteen and you don't need a governess."

Grant gave his napkin a yank like a magician pulling a tablecloth. His silverware careened across the table, rescued from sailing off the edge at the last possible second by the jam caddy.

"Okay, can we all just take it down a notch? You're both at like an eight, and I need you at a four."

"What do those numbers even mean? A four of what?"

"Use the context, Maisie. I'm not that difficult to understand."

Patrick placed his napkin in his lap before sliding Grant's fork back across the table in front of him. A waiter appeared over his shoulder with Patrick's mimosa balanced on a tray with a rich-looking Bloody Mary. "I'm sorry, I hate to be a pest," Patrick started.

"Don't listen to him," Maisie interjected. "He *loves* to be a pest."

Patrick kicked Maisie under the table, but he also couldn't help but be impressed. If he sent these kids back to Connecticut with enough snappy comebacks to populate a screwball comedy, the summer would not be a waste. "Ignore her. She went to bed a sweet girl and woke up a surly teenager. I've changed my mind. Could I actually have one of those?" He pointed to the Bloody Mary on the waiter's tray. He back-pocketed his line about waving a tomato over the glass and having it be too much tomato juice, as he actually liked tomato juice.

"No problem. In fact, you can have this one." And then in a hushed tone he added, "Looks like you need it." The waiter placed the drink in front of Patrick and whisked the mimosa away.

"What is that?" Grant asked.

Patrick removed the olive and used the leafy celery stalk to muddle some horseradish at the bottom of his glass. "It's a salad. Want one?"

"Gross."

"That's not a salad."

"Sure it is. Celery. Olives. The tomatoes are a little runny."

"Then let's see you eat it with a fork." Maisie crossed her arms defiantly while Grant helpfully offered his.

Patrick took a long sip of his drink and inventoried each ingredient as it slid down his throat—pepper, Tabasco, lemon juice, Worcestershire—easing into the burn. "You think this summer has been a nonstop thrill ride for me? That there haven't been days when I had to sit on my hands so I wouldn't grab your suitcases, stuff you in them, and put you on the next flight east? Well, guess again."

"Then send us to live with Grandma and Grandpa!"

"I'll send you to your room without any lupper."

"I'm serious!"

"You don't want to live with Grandma and Grandpa."

"Why not?"

"Because they think Fox is news and raisins are food." Patrick looked down at Grant, who was rearranging the sugar packets. "Do *you* want to live with Grandma and Grandpa?"

"Do they have a pool?"

"No. But they're talking about getting one of those tubs for old people with a door you can walk through so you don't slip and fall getting out."

"Are they putting it outside?"

"No. In their bathroom."

"Oh." Grant was more than ready to move on. "Can I have a thinnamon roll?"

"They don't have those here, you're thinking of Koffi."

"A donut, then."

"No."

"Can we thee the big dinosaurs?"

"We've seen them three times this summer."

"I want to know if they're okay."

"They're not okay, they're extinct!" Patrick threw his arms up, exasperated. "You guys exhaust me, you know that? *Can I have this. Can we do that.* It's not good for my skin."

Maisie picked up a promotional card for a new breakfast sandwich with a braised short rib, while Grant put the finishing touches on the sugars. Patrick picked at the mesquite salt on the rim of his glass, wishing already that the sun was down so he could tick off one more day until Greg was free.

And then Maisie's reedy voice broke the silence. "*I hate you.*"

Patrick froze. Maisie's words were stark and unsettling, meek but with startling conviction; they sucked the air out of the restaurant. Patrick glanced around, wondering how others could breathe. He slid his feet back and forth under the table, trying desperately to get his footing, but the floors were a highly polished concrete and his feet comically flailed beneath him in Keatonesque fashion. Maisie's outburst was the aftershock he'd been afraid of. He reached up and touched his head, seeing the sudden wisdom in wearing a bicycle helmet for protection. He silently counted to ten to avoid saying something he would later regret; now more than ever, he had to be the adult. "No one hates me. Except the *New York Times*, but they hate everyone from LA." Back during the run of the show, they did five hundred eviscerating words on him that, to this day, still stung.

"*I* hate you." Maisie repeated the charge.

"I'm not so fond of *you* right now, if we're being honest."

"I want to go home."

"All right." Patrick pushed his drink away from him and started to rise. As much as he wanted that Bloody Mary, there was no way he was going to enjoy it under duress.

"To Connecticut."

He sat back down. "Just for that, we're going to sit here and take our time."

"No."

"And I'm going to tell them that it's your birthday so they'll come bang on some pots and pans."

"You can't make me stay here!"

"Oh, do you have any ride-share apps on *your* phone?" Patrick waved his phone at her tauntingly. Maisie lunged for it, but he pulled back just in time. She folded her arms in a pout.

"I'll walk."

"You can't walk, you'll get heatstroke and collapse from thirst."

Maisie picked up her glass of water and defiantly headed for the door.

"All right. That's it. NO MORE MR. NICE GAY!" Patrick threw his napkin on the table in disgust. "Sit. Down."

"Or what?"

The truth was, there weren't a lot of threats he could make and follow through on. But that didn't mean he was willing to be pushed around. "You can't spell *nemesis* without *me, sis*. And you do not want to make me your enemy." He stood up, placed his hands on her shoulders, and guided her back to the table; surprisingly, she didn't fight him. "Let's all just take a breath and wait for our food."

"Did you know a flamingo's knees are actually it'th ankles?"

"Is that true?" Patrick turned to Grant.

"Yeah," he said with a surprising authority.

Patrick thought for a moment. "Did you know a duel between three people is called a truel?" It was something he'd learned in a Shakespeare class in college, or thought he had. Memory was a tricky thing. He hoped it was true, as it was surprisingly relevant now. "You kids have it made. You know that? I have all the spoils of success and no natural heirs. All you have to do is be a little bit nice to me and I'll make sure you're set for life. That's all you have to do. And change my diapers when I'm old."

Grant laughed. "Gross!"

Patrick kissed Grant on top of the head and squeezed him into his side like an emotional support animal. He wasn't going to tell either one of them, but he had no plans to stick around that long. He never wanted to be the first to leave a party, but, unlike his friend Emory, he didn't want to be the last to hang around, either. He certainly wouldn't endure the indignity of diapers. "Yeah, you're right. We'll hire someone to do that."

The waiter arrived with precision timing. He placed the corn pancakes in front of the kids before handing Patrick his granola. "Everyone happy?"

"Happiness is overrated; we're all just fine enough. Thank you. Cheers." He lifted his Bloody Mary in a celebratory gesture to thank the waiter again for giving it to him.

"Can I have thyrup, GUP?"

Patrick pushed the syrup toward Grant. He poured the granola over his yogurt and topped it with fresh berries, remembering all the times he'd tortured his mother with smart-ass remarks. To this day he wasn't clear why. He grew four inches overnight and his bones hurt. Testosterone coursed wildly through his body, wreaking havoc on his skin, which was maddeningly both oily and dry. The acne medication he begged to be on required regular blood tests at the doctor's office he abhorred and made his lips chap. He loved a boy and didn't understand yet why, and the boy caught him staring and told the whole school, causing Patrick to feel more isolated than he already had and so desperately, totally alone. He told his mother she was a bad mother. He told her she had no life. When she asked him to clean his room one time he muttered, "Menopause must be hell." He thought he had whispered under his breath, but it was loud enough for her to hear. He cursed her silently at the dinner table, angry that she could not understand things that he would never allow her to see. But the whole time, he *had* a mother to curse, to hate, to forgive. He had a mother to stand there and listen, to take these tirades and to forgive him right back.

"I'm sorry, Maisie." Patrick reached out and put his hand on hers, which was gripping her fork in a tight fist. "For anything I said that upset you. I'm the grown-up and I should know better."

Maisie didn't say anything, or even really look up. But he thought he saw her head bob, and you could feel the slightest bit of air escape from this overinflated balloon.

Patrick continued. "Did you notice our waiter's name? Gale. It was on his name tag. Now, that's something I like. Men who can pull off women's names. Give me a male Hillary, or a Bertie. Sandy, even. Give me an Evelyn Waugh. I met an Ashley once on a plane and I almost married him. It might have been a latent *Gone with the Wind* thing."

"Boyth can have girl'th names?"

"Why not? Girls can have boy's names. Plenty of girls are named Alex or Frankie or Sam. A girl named Charlie?" Patrick put his fingers to his lips and gestured a chef's kiss. "It's the Wild West we're living in."

Patrick discreetly glanced at Maisie, careful not to make a production out of it. She wasn't amused, but she also didn't seem angry anymore. And she was eating. He had been worried a hunger strike might be coming next, so that in itself was a small triumph.

"Is that why you like Emily?"

"I don't like Emily." Patrick reached for his phone in his pocket. "Who's Emily?"

"Emily. From the party. You made us watch him on YouTube."

"*EMORY?!*" Patrick was appalled.

"Oh," Grant said. "I thought his name was Emily."

Patrick checked his phone for the time. And there it was. Right on his lock screen like an emotional hate crime. An annual calendar reminder from another life.

Everything was suddenly clear.

Patrick dismissed the reminder before tucking his phone in his pocket; one thing at a time. For now, he wanted to put this tension behind them once and for all. "Maisie? You look like your mom this morning."

She froze midbite and looked up from her plate.

"You do. You really do. I think it's the way the sun hits you just right." Patrick smiled and brushed the hair from her face, the way he used to with Sara. "More and more every day."

The table next to him, a couple in their sixties who reminded him of his parents, got up to leave. The woman, wearing those three-quarter-length pants that flatter exactly no one, handed him a folded napkin with a smile. Her husband, silk golf shirt, palm frond pattern, waved politely. Grant waved back.

Patrick held the napkin, unsure what to do with it. He was terrified it was another stark notification like the one on the phone. Something that should be clear, if he weren't so distracted and self-absorbed. He held the napkin below the table, away from Grant, and slowly opened it. Inside was a note.

Every parent has these days. You're very good with them. Your breakfast is on us.

"What does it say?" Maisie asked. She never missed a trick.

Patrick folded the napkin and slipped it in his pocket. *You're very good with them.* It was all he could do not to cry. He looked over his shoulder to thank the couple, but they were already passing the windows outside. He watched, hoping to catch their attention, until they were out of sight. Alas, they never turned back.

"It says we should go see the dinosaurs. So eat up."

Grant dropped his fork on his plate and threw his hands in the air in triumph. "*YETH!*"

"They may be extinct now, but you never know."

Sometimes things come back to life.

TWENTY-FOUR

The rain started midafternoon in torrential sheets and caught Patrick and the kids off guard; three hundred and fifty days of sun a year—why bother to ever check the weather? Each drop landed with a deafening thwack against his flat roof, the symphony outside a perfect score to the mood within. Patrick glanced out the front window. The gravel in his yard was already disappearing under a thin lake, the ground underneath too dry, too hard to absorb such a downpour quickly. Earlier in the day, he ordered a cake to be delivered. Now he wondered if it would show up at all.

Grant twirled into the room, his own cyclone. "Do you think I should write a letter to the toof fairy?" He had to yell to be heard above the rain.

"No."

"But I want to!" Grant climbed on his uncle's leather chair to look out the window, too.

"What are you, pen pals? You don't need to write her."

"Why not?" Grant implored.

"Because you don't have any loose teef."

Grant placed his hands on his hips defiantly. "Yeah, but I'm gonna. I'm worried she might forget me."

Patrick stifled a laugh. "She won't."

"She will!"

"Won't happen."

"How do you know?"

Patrick pried his eyes away from the front walk to focus squarely on Grant. "You're unforgettable, that's why."

Grant beamed, then stuffed his fingers in his ears. "THE RAIN ITH LOUD!"

Patrick agreed that it was, then added, "Feet off my chair," even though Grant couldn't hear.

The cake finally arrived while Maisie was in her room with the door closed and Grant was in the backyard. Marlene erupted like Vesuvius at the knock at the door, her hot, angry barking blanketing the entire house with panic. Patrick picked her up in order to answer the door; she wriggled the entire time to get free. Where was the silent-film star he brought home from the kennel? Everyone, it seemed, was changing.

"Cake for Jack Curtis."

"Whoa," Patrick exclaimed. Behind the deliveryman arched an enormous rainbow in the sky.

"Neat, huh?"

Patrick tipped the guy a twenty and balanced the pink pastry box in one hand. He marveled at the rainbow as the delivery guy returned to his van. *Sara, is that you?* he thought, but felt instantly foolish. What was a rainbow after all, refracted light? Gay people, Christians always fighting over the symbolism when rainbows rightfully belonged to the leprechauns.

He kicked the door closed and set Marlene on the ground, careful to balance the cake. The truce he'd established with Maisie since brunch was fragile; a ruined surprise could reignite their war.

As promised, Patrick had taken them to the Cabazon dinosaurs roadside attraction. At the base of the life-size brontosaurus, Maisie nestled into her uncle. It might have been to shield herself from the wind that came whipping through the exhibit, kicking up sand from the parking lot; it might have been to commiserate over having to go to the dinosaurs for Grant *yet again*. Patrick had put his arm around her anyhow; he was willing to take what he could get and she didn't openly rebel. They even dug for dinosaur eggs in the sandpit together, crouching low to avoid the wind.

"Can we do a video?" Grant asked. It was the one thing that never failed to bring them together.

"Sure. We'll film one in slow motion. You both run from the T. rex and look back over your shoulder like it's chasing you." Patrick fished his camera out of his pocket. "And scream. Make sure you scream big."

"I don't feel like screaming," Maisie protested.

"You're being chased by a dinosaur. Screaming is the most important part!" And then, without really thinking, Patrick screamed a long, hoarse yawp to prove his point. A weekday morning, the crowds were thin, but his carrying-on still turned a few heads. He scanned the startled gawkers and then pointed up at the T. rex's open mouth towering above them as explanation.

And then the kids screamed, too. And Patrick screamed again. And together they'd released these primal, mournful wails that were swallowed by the howling wind.

"What's in the box?" Grant asked, appearing through the sliding glass door. It seemed aggravatingly nosy at first, intrusive, the way he would materialize at the sound of the doorbell, until Patrick remembered how, for years after Joe died, the way his heart would lift whenever someone opened a door; he knew intellectually Joe wouldn't walk through, but in those fractions of seconds he remembered what hope felt like.

Patrick gently nudged Marlene out of the way with his foot to clear a path to the kitchen. "A surprise. Want to help me? I need to find matches."

Grant vibrated enthusiastically. He was conspiratorial by nature, and if lighting something on fire was a part of this, he was one hundred percent on board.

Together they tapped on Maisie's bedroom door. Patrick held the cake with three lit candles, their gentle flames dancing in the current from the air-conditioning vent. It had lavender icing and elaborate sugar flowers that crawled up the sides of the cake like vines. The design wasn't to Patrick's taste, but that was hardly the point. It wasn't for him. Grant held his ear to the door and snickered.

"Go away."

Patrick knocked again.

"I'm asleep."

"Then how are you talking?" Grant implored. He apparently found this hysterical, but worked hard to stifle his giggles.

After a pause Maisie replied, "I'm reading."

Patrick opened the door slowly, and when he saw Maisie's eyes connect with the cake he pushed his way in. The room was darkening, drained of its color the way things can look in the last of a gloomy day's light; the candles introduced a sunny, yellowish hue. Maisie was lying on the floor with a book and, betraying her inner determination, she looked up at her uncle with wonder.

"What's that for?"

"You tell me."

Maisie closed her book and sat up. She clasped her hands together and placed them under her chin. "It's Mom's birthday today."

"Yes it is." *Sara's birthday. Send flowers.* The message that appeared on his lock screen that morning.

"She's not here, though. To celebrate." Her voice dripped with defeat.

Patrick knelt in front of his niece and ushered Grant around. He held the cake between them. Maisie's eyes grew wet and a single candle flame danced in each of her dark pupils. For a flickering moment, he saw Sara in Maisie, plain as day. And then the light shifted and he saw himself, even though he knew it wasn't him, but rather his brother, Greg.

"Sure she is. Don't you think? And either way, we're here to celebrate for her. So it's up to us to make her a wish."

"What kind of wish?" Grant asked, joining them on his knees.

"Whatever kind you want. Let's all make one."

Maisie considered the cake, her demeanor softening as she took in each perfect detail, the color, the flowers, the buttercream swirls. Patrick could tell she was already wondering if the cake was vanilla, her mother's favorite; he couldn't wait to show her that it was. "I'll go." Maisie propped herself up on one knee and clutched her T-shirt at the neckline. "I wish that you're not alone, because it can be scary alone and I don't want you to be scared."

"That's a beautiful wish." Maisie glowed in his validation. "Now blow out one candle to make that wish come true."

Maisie blew gently, skillfully; all three candles flickered, but only one went out. Smoke trailed upward before dissipating in the air, like the wish had transformed into a secret only the three of them knew.

"Grant?"

Grant squished his face as he thought.

"Don't make that face, you'll need Botox when you're nine."

Grant shook his head. "I know! I got one!"

"Let's hear it."

"I wish I could hear you laugh."

Maisie objected. "That's a wish for you! Not for her."

"Easy, easy, easy." Patrick scrambled to intervene. "How about, I wish you much laughter where you are?"

Grant signaled his approval, very happy with this edit. Patrick shielded the candle closest to himself with his hand, and had Grant blow out the other one.

"Your turn, GUP."

A shiver ran though Patrick's body and his eyes began to sting; this was but an exercise for the children that he was overseeing, another activity like the letter writing, and the videos. How was this so difficult for him? "I wish you total freedom from pain. Freedom from the body that failed you. I hope that you're full of light, unconstrained, and that you can dance. Because I know how you loved to dance."

He looked at the candle, the last one lit on top of the cake. He struggled to summon a breath, as if the last of the light that was Sara could be fully extinguished with one forceful expulsion of air.

"I like that wish, GUP." Maisie rested her hand on Patrick's knee, giving him the permission he needed.

"Me too." Grant bounced up and down on his knees.

"Let's blow out the last candle, the three of us," Patrick said. "And that wish can be from us all. On the count of three?"

They agreed.

Patrick nodded, once, twice. And they blew.

The room went dark. They sat together quietly, listening for any hint that Sara had heard them.

"Can we eat thum cake?" There was sugar at the end of this endeavor, and Grant didn't want to further delay that reward.

"Come," Patrick motioned.

The kids followed their uncle into the kitchen, where Patrick set the cake on the counter. But instead of pulling out a knife, he produced a box of matches. He pulled a single candle out of the cake, struck a match, and relit the remaining two.

"Why are we blowing out candles again?" Maisie asked.

Patrick pointed at the stools and snapped his fingers; they hopped up to the counter like obedient dogs. Marlene, less disciplined, nipped at his heels. "I have two more wishes, one for each of you."

The kids looked up at him with twisted expressions, confusion mixed with whatever was just shy of delight.

"Grant. You are my funny boy. My wish for you is that your sense of humor remains intact. Life is not always funny, in fact it's not always fun. A lot of the time it downright sucks. But your humor will guide you, it will protect you, and it will heal you. So laugh hard, laugh loud, and make others do the same."

"Knock knock," Grant said, accepting the mantle of this charge.

"Jesus Christ. Not *now*."

"Okay."

"Okay, who?" Maisie added with a giggle.

Patrick dropped his head to the counter with a thud. "Just blow out a candle."

Grant leaned in and did just that.

"Maisie." Patrick stood up straight; there was a red mark on his forehead. "You are sensitive and kind and brave, just like your mother. My wish for you is that you carry the best of her inside you and build on that with all the special ingredients that make you, distinctly, beautifully *you*."

Maisie swallowed, tasked with this solemn responsibility. Patrick wondered if he should ease her burden, tell her how naturally he thought this would come. Instead he watched as she leaned forward and gently extinguished her candle as if with a delicate kiss.

"Now can we have cake?" Grant asked.

"One more thing."

Grant's shoulders drooped.

"For your mom." Patrick turned on the Bose speakers that sat on the kitchen counter and waited for the Bluetooth to connect with his phone. He opened iTunes and selected a playlist called DANCE. "She and I would always dance on our birthdays. Just go crazy to some really good music. In celebration. And I think we should do that for her." Patrick scrolled through the playlist until he found just the song. "Ah, here we go. America's third-favorite Wang Chung song, 'Let's Go!' It's actually the best Wang Chung song. People prefer 'Everybody Have Fun Tonight' or 'Dance Hall Days,' but people are generally wrong in this regard. Do you know it?"

They both shook their heads.

"It was a cut on their 1986 album, *Mosaic*, but wasn't released as a single until January 1987. You guys remember the eighties?"

They shook their heads again, as if it had been a serious inquiry.

"Jack Hues sings lead vocals, while Nick Feldman sings the bridge. Both sing the chorus. Wang Chung? Jack Hues? A play on the French,

J'accuse? No?" The kids were growing impatient. This lecture was delaying their cake. It was time to wrap this up. He hit play and the opening synth chords filled the room in full eighties splendor. "Play it in the morning and I defy you not to have at least a decent day. On some days it's the only thing that makes the day decent. You should know this. More people should know this. Everyone should know this. Guncle Rule number fifteen: *Let's go, baby, let's go, baby, c'mon*."

Patrick closed his eyes, letting the music take root inside him. His shoulders were inspired first, they shrugged in tune to the song. His wrists curled in, then up, then his arms opened wide and his fingers fluttered, ushering the kids off their barstools. He sang the opening words. "*Meet me in a restaurant*." He waved again, until they joined him. "Dance with me. Then we'll stuff our faces with cake."

Patrick grasped their hands, they formed a circle and began to sway until the crescendo building to the first chorus. He pulled his hands in close to his body and started jumping excitedly. And then his body exploded as he leapt in perfectly with the refrain. "*Let's go, baby, let's go, baby, c'mon!*" He danced as hard as he'd ever let anyone watch. Grant, inspired, waved his hands over his head and shook them like a Muppet; he had surprising rhythm, as if the music was emanating from inside him, and he swung his hips with an easy, admirable confidence. Maisie moved more timidly, decidedly off the beat, but her smile was all you could really see.

"Get your feet in motion!" Patrick crunched his abdominals and ran tightly in place. Maisie and Grant imitated their uncle and they moved in close until their noses touched, Patrick singing the words, the kids doing their best but not quite nailing it, before they all ran back to their starting places, bursting in joyous motion.

For one fleeting moment this was it, they were the music and the music was them, Wang Chung itself (or, more precisely, *huang chung*, Chinese for *yellow bell*), and all of their sadness rang out of their fingertips in radiant sunshine that warmed the darkening sky.

TWENTY-FIVE

Incredibly, Marlene slept through the knock at the door. Patrick wasn't certain if he was relieved or annoyed she would so easily shirk her responsibilities as guard dog just because she had put in a stint dancing. By the third song on Patrick's playlist (some *Ray of Light*–era Madonna), Marlene was a full participant, jumping on her hind legs like a Pentecostal brimming with the Holy Spirit about to burst into tongues. Eventually Patrick and the kids ate cake with their hands; plates, knives, and forks were instruments of other, more solemn people that stood in the way of their joy. They swayed to the music and Grant let Marlene lick frosting off his fingers. The sugar crash that followed hit hard. Patrick was the last man (child, dog) standing, and even he was splayed out on the couch watching *Desert Flippers* on HGTV, fighting to keep his eyes open. His first thought was that he might have imagined the knocking, that maybe he had drifted off and was dreaming or that it was coming from the TV—the hosts assessing the viability of a rotting home's framework. He sat upright before realizing the knock was real, and when he finally answered the door he was confronted with a familiar face waiting expectantly on the other side of his peephole.

Emory.

Patrick opened the door slowly to avoid the squeaking thing it did.

"So, I was in the neighborhood." Emory flashed this full-tooth smile/eye roll combo that looked not unlike that GIF of young Marlon Brando that everyone sends around. When Patrick said nothing in return, he leaned his head in the doorway and pouted with his lower lip.

Goddammit.

"No one's ever *in* this neighborhood, which is precisely why I live here." Patrick leaned on his door and it swung him flirtatiously closer to his guest. "Want to try that again?"

"It's Coachella," Emory offered.

"The music festival? That's in April."

"Modernism Week?"

"February, I think."

"Palm Springs Pride."

"November."

"The White Party?"

"I forget what that is, but I'm certain it's not going on now."

"Dinah Shore?"

"That's for lesbians."

"I could be a lesbian." His glasses were not unlike Rachel Maddow's.

"Sure."

There was nothing left for Emory to do but come clean. "Some friends of mine were renting a house in Palm Desert, so I crashed for a few days. Thought I'd stop by my friend Patrick's and see if he wanted to go for a swim."

Patrick considered the situation carefully, weighing the odds of waking anyone against his desire for company, and then stepped out of the way to usher Emory inside. "Kids are asleep."

"They still here?"

Patrick made a face—*Of course*—but they had never discussed his custodial arrangement, so Patrick had no reason to hold him at fault. "Drink?"

"Sure, I'm not driving."

"Then how are you getting back to LA?"

Emory gave it some thought, but not much. "I always find a way."

It was the thing Patrick missed most about youth, the assumption that everything would just work itself out. That and his back not hurting. He shook his head as Emory stepped inside and then motioned for Emory to follow him to the kitchen.

"Whoa," Emory said when he saw what was left of Sara's celebration on the counter. "You guys murdered that cake."

"Yeah, we did a number." He put some ice in two glasses; it landed with a nice clink that whet Patrick's thirst. "You know Wang Chung?"

"Gay Chinese place? Over on Indian Canyon?"

"Not even close."

"Then, no."

Patrick glared at his guest skeptically. "When'd you graduate high school?"

Emory attempted a quick calculation in his head. "I don't know. I took a test." He scratched his chin. "When was Obama president?"

"Oh, god," Patrick muttered while pouring two glasses of vodka; it was worse than he thought. He tipped himself a little extra before handing a glass to Emory. "Cheers."

They tapped glasses without breaking eye contact and then Patrick led him back to the living room.

"Still Christmas, I see." Emory glanced at the artificial tree. Patrick looked up, surprised, startled to see so much pink tinsel. It had sort of faded into the general décor; he hardly noticed it as out of place anymore. The tree had become a strange heart to the home, the white lights nestled deep in its branches pumping a flattering Pepto Bismol glow to their evenings. It was a salve when things felt unsettled.

"It's sort of a tie-a-yellow-ribbon thing. Their dad gets back next week. I told them they could leave it up."

"*Yellow* ribbon? It's pink."

Patrick sipped his vodka, letting it warm his throat. "Iran hostages? Yellow ribbons around old oak trees? Tony Orlando and Dawn?!"

Emory shrugged.

"Wang Chung is a band, by the way."

"Are you sure? Because it sounds made-up."

"It was the eighties. Everything sounded made-up." Patrick rattled off a list of bands in his head: T'Pau, Kajagoogoo . . . *Bananarama*. "People did a lot of coke."

Emory stared at him blankly.

Patrick cleared his throat. "Not that I'm old enough to remember."

His guest kicked off a pair of tennis shoes so white that Patrick wondered if he didn't clean them with Windex. Emory tucked a bare foot underneath him on the couch, leaning into the corner of the sectional. "So, are you like a dad now?"

It was a loaded question, and Patrick was at a loss for a smart comeback. He allowed himself to get lost in Emory's face. He didn't have the facial architecture that normally sent people scrambling; his nose was crooked in that sexy broken way, and his eyes were almost too far apart. It was inviting. It worked on him with an effortless ease, as if he'd practiced for years making his features work in concert, then committing it to memory so he could forget it all and project a certain nonchalance. The way he smiled out of one corner of his mouth was a perfect example. He probably learned all this in an acting class, or worse—a class on auditioning.

Is that what he was doing here? *Auditioning*?

"No, they have a father. I told you. He's coming home next week."

"I was talking about your mustache."

Patrick felt his cheeks redden.

"It looks good. I'll bet it tickles." Emory stretched out his leg to give Patrick a gentle kick, then left his foot resting against his shin. He was wearing pants that were part sweat, part yoga with a drop crotch that hid everything and highlighted nothing, and yet were deeply provocative. Perhaps it was the ease with which they could be removed. "Don't you go stir-crazy out here?" he asked. "What do you miss about LA?"

"Nothing."

"C'mon."

Patrick searched for an answer that was both benign and honest. "Everyone seems genuinely happy here. I'm baseline distrustful of it."

"So, unease is what you miss."

"Anxiety. Unease. You live in LA long enough, it becomes part of who you are."

Emory leaned forward to set his drink on a wooden cutout of Cher's face that people mistook for a coaster. "You're a mess."

It wasn't even that accusatory, the charge. There was even some tacit acknowledgment in the delivery that everyone was a mess to varying degrees, and that much was hard to argue. But in this moment Patrick felt more together than he had in a long time and so he was unnerved by Emory's words.

"Don't worry," Emory said, picking up on the look on Patrick's face. "I like a good mess. They can be fun to clean up."

Patrick studied the way Emory sat in front of him, face plastered with a goofy smile. It wasn't like the diagnosis came from Clara, or someone else whose words would be charged. Still, something about it flustered him. "How are things on *The Cracker Barrel*?"

"Tillamook?"

"Sure."

They stared at each other for a long time, until Emory looked down to pick something off his shirt. "Dumb. They're doing this supernatural story line, which means it's probably the last season. We start shooting next week. This time next year I'll be old and washed-up. Just like you."

Patrick narrowed his eyes. "You're really good at this."

"At what?"

"Being a dick, but like in a really attractive way."

"Does that mean I can stay?"

He raised his hands like paws to beg. Patrick found it impossible to put his finger on Emory's appeal. He was a chimera constructed of so many gay archetypes—twink, jock, otter, nerd—inhabiting none of them with anything resembling exclusivity. He even gave off some faint dad vibes himself in the way that twenty-seven-year-olds seem to relish growing a whisper of facial hair and anointing themselves with that crown as if three chin hairs transformed them into a Tom of Finland drawing. Emory embraced conformity while eschewing it, all while seemingly floating *above* it. Patrick didn't know whether to love him, hate him, admire him, embrace him, fuck him, or kick him to the nearest curb.

"Listen," Patrick began before glancing back over his shoulder to the kids' bedrooms. "I would like that. But now's not the right time."

"You're so sad."

"Pathetic?"

"No. Downcast. It's different. That's all."

Patrick was taken aback. "What does that mean?"

"I don't know. You tell me." But Emory didn't wait for Patrick to do so. "It's just. Gay people have a sad history, but most of us, we overcome it. We're kicked out of our small-town families, then embrace cities and make new families and build brilliant lives. We were beaten, and so we became strong, and now our bodies are envied. A generation wiped out by a virus, but our lives are still a celebration—we made frosé a thing, for god's sake. We're discriminated against, we become a political power. That sort of thing. We thrive, all of us. But you have this sadness. I see it."

It was a lot for Patrick to absorb. "You *see* it."

"I see you," Emory said.

"You're confusing me." Or was it the vodka? He felt warm in the face and dizzy.

"No I'm not."

"Yes you are, I'm confused."

"You're not confused, you're lazy." Emory leaned in until his forehead was touching Patrick's, and he rested it there until sweat started to form between them, cementing them together. Patrick grazed Emory's lips with his own, not kissing him quite, but the difference was negligible and would not stand up to scrutiny.

"Where are you from, Emory?"

"Boise." He could have easily said, *Dropped from the sky.*

"Were you kicked out by your family?" Patrick's question was barely a whisper.

"Once." Emory wove his fingers between Patrick's. "But they quickly welcomed me back."

They kissed, much like they had the night of the party under the moonlight, when Patrick had pinned him against the stairs of his pool. He reached out and grabbed Emory's face with both hands, eventually, reluctantly, pulling them apart.

"C'mon. Where's your bedroom?" Emory asked. "I'll do all the work. You can just lie there."

Patrick studied Emory. "Do something with me."

Emory crunched on an ice cube until it was gone. "I'm trying!"

For Patrick, these were uncharted waters. Did Mary Poppins have a bedroom that we ever saw? Did she ever invite a dirty chimney sweep to spend the night and . . . sweep her chimney clean? Maria the governess had private quarters we were allowed a peek inside. It had lousy curtains and she made them into play clothes. But when she was faced with sexual attraction she ran as fast as she could back to the abbey. Mame took a lover, and sent her nephew off to boarding school to make room for him. Should he hold out a few more days until he had the house to himself? Did any of this matter? These weren't real people. He was.

"Okay. Come to my bedroom. I need your help with something."

"I'm not helping you flip your mattress."

"Not that. *Although . . .*" There was a sudden appeal to having someone else around. "No. Not that. Just come. You'll see."

◇◇◇◇◇

Patrick and Emory lay perfectly still in the bed, feigning sleep but keeping a watchful eye on the bedroom door, Patrick aware the whole time of Emory's warmth and quiet breathing; it was comforting. As if on cue, just after midnight it opened—slowly at first—just enough to let a small crack of moonlight shine through. His eyes partway shut, Patrick could just make out Maisie poking her head through the open door to see if it was safe, a pillow tucked under one arm. Convinced their uncle was asleep, she motioned for Grant and they both crept inside, dragging blankets, one of them carefully closing the door behind them. He listened to the rustling of bedding as they settled themselves. Emory reached his arm over Patrick and squeezed his hand tightly under the covers; it was easy to envision Emory stifling history's most irresistible smile. Patrick counted to ten, then reached for his bedside lamp and turned it on with a click.

"A-HA!"

The kids screamed; even Marlene barked from her perch at the foot of the bed.

Patrick and Emory threw back the covers and sat upright, causing the duvet to flip sideways. "Caught you red-handed."

"What are you doing?" Maisie asked, annoyed to be awoken fully, as if Patrick were trespassing in her room and not the other way around.

Grant yawned, wiping sleep from his eyes. "Is that Emily?"

"*Emily?*" Emory exclaimed.

"What is he doing here?" Grant continued.

Maisie looked at the two of them in bed. "Is he here *every* night?" she asked, the color draining from her face. It was dawning on her that their nighttime visits might have been more of an interruption than she imagined.

"We knew he wath your boyfriend."

"Emory, not Emily. And he's not my boyfriend. We've gone over this."

"I am not your boyfriend?" Emory huffed playfully, delighted in making Patrick squirm.

"Not now," Patrick said to Emory, who reached for his glasses on the end table. "Also, Maisie. *Every* night? Are you kidding me?"

"No," Maisie insisted.

"Wouldn't you know if he were?" Patrick asked.

Maisie scooped her bedding into a little nest around her, too ashamed to admit in front of company that she slept in her uncle's room more nights than not. Patrick focused on his niece until he had her attention. She looked at him sheepishly. Patrick held her gaze until her look grew inquisitive, hoping to get his message across without embarrassing her further: *You don't ever have to sneak in here. I'm here for you, always.* The silence grew awkward as the message took root, then Masise nodded, as if she understood.

Grant interrupted the moment. "What ith he doing here *tonight*, then?"

Patrick turned to his nephew. "Didn't you get my invitation?"

"No." Grant furrowed his thin, worrisome brow. "What invitation?"

"For the slumber party. Emory, did you get your invitation?" Patrick turned to Emory, who was more than eager to play along.

"I did. Mine was embossed! A real work of art. I particularly liked the card stock. And the stamp!" Emory stuck his tongue out playfully. "Ten o'clock, the invitation said?"

"That's right," Patrick agreed. "You guys are late."

"We didn't get our invitations!" Maisie protested.

"Emory got his, Marlene got hers!" Patrick threw his arms in the air. "Well, I guess we'll have to talk to the mailman. Did you at least bring popcorn?"

"Popcorn for what?"

"FOR THE MIDNIGHT MOVIE! Oh, my god. There is a whole schedule of events."

Emory leaned his head on Patrick's shoulder, as if the kids would never get it. Patrick reached over and playfully mussed his hair. All summer he thought it would be awkward to show affection with another man in front of Maisie and Grant, but it was surprisingly a nonevent. More so, for years he thought it would feel unnatural to himself, and was shocked to learn that was not at all the case, either.

Emory plumped his pillow and tossed the rest of the twisted duvet to the side. "Well, get up here on the bed with your uncle. You want the middle? I'll go make the popcorn." He looked to Patrick for permission—did he even *have* popcorn? How far were they taking this ruse?

Patrick nodded to Emory, whispering, "*Thank you.*"

The depths of Patrick's gratitude seemed to catch Emory by surprise. Patrick worried this would send Emory scrambling, or diminish his enthusiasm for the very unconventional date they were on. But Emory did not startle easily and generally seemed unfazed. Instead, he leapt off the bed with surprising athleticism, landing an impressive dismount that got perfect tens from all three judges.

TWENTY-SIX

By mid-August it had been so hot for so long it seemed like it would never be cool again. Relief wouldn't come until it was time to set back the clocks; there was almost as much of the endless summer ahead as there was behind them. Eventually the temperatures would break. There would come a time when Patrick would reach for a sweater and heat the pool if he felt like swimming. The warm tub would become a hot tub again. It would rain, this time for longer. There would be new stars in the sky. The air would get downright cold, and in the higher elevations, snow would fall, capping the mountains with elite white powder wigs, transforming them into distinguished elders. Each year he looked forward to it, but now it seemed looming, encroaching—a time when he would be alone again.

Patrick and the kids had taken to long afternoon naps, waking for lupper, then finding relief in the night. Tonight the darkness offered not just comfort, but entertainment—a meteor shower best viewed in the predawn. The three of them dozed wearily on pool floats in the middle of the backyard lawn under a blanket of shimmering stars. As was custom, Grant claimed the Pegasus. Maisie selected the pineapple for her outdoor bed, while Patrick reclined on the lobster. Marlene curled up on a blanket, her claws too pronounced to trust her on something inflatable. It was two hours past midnight, and the kids were fighting to stay awake.

"Don't close your eyes, Grant," Maisie implored.

"I'm not," Grant protested.

"They go by so fast."

The meteor shower was best viewed farther north, near Joshua Tree perhaps, but away from Los Angeles and the never-dimming lights of Hollywood, and under the cover of the desert's darkness, they had a decent chance of witnessing *something.* So far, Maisie had counted three streaks of light across the sky. Patrick had only seen two; there was a chance Maisie was inflating her count, on the other hand it was a blink-and-miss-it affair.

A blink-and-miss-it affair. If that didn't aptly summarize their summer, Patrick didn't know what else could. "Are you looking forward to going home?" he asked, and the sound of his own voice in the darkness startled him.

The kids didn't reply, although Grant might have punctuated his silence with a perfunctory *Uh-huh* that could also easily have been a snore.

Maisie adjusted herself on her float; on the grass it was like trying to find firm support on a dreadful waterbed. "I keep thinking Mom's going to be there." And then she added, "It's silly, I know," as if her thoughts were girlish and unserious.

"I don't think that's silly at all." Patrick pointed to a quadrant in the sky for her to monitor, a demonstration of his belief in her and how much he understood. In some ways it had been like they were away at some posh summer camp, the dramatic change of scenery itself a serum to keep the worst of life out of reach, at least for small stretches of time—fleeting as they may be.

"You don't?" Maisie asked.

"Not at all. And here's the thing: she *will* be there." Patrick rolled his head to see if they were listening. "In the kitchen where she cooked for you, in your rooms where she kissed you good night. Some days you'll hate it. It will feel torturous. You'll be reminded of the bad things. She'll be both so close and so far. But other days you'll like it. She'll be a shadow on the wall, or a reflection of the light, and she'll look healthy and you'll be so happy to see her. And it will feel like a great big hug."

"How do you know this thtuff?" Grant muttered. Patrick was happy for confirmation he was awake.

"Because I do." *Because of Joe.*

"Will you come visit so you can see her, too?"

Patrick fluttered his feet, as if miming timid steps into an uncertain future. "We'll see." He was acutely concerned with the kids' ghostly presence in his own house after they returned to Connecticut. The warmth of a snuggle at bedtime. The faint echo of a laugh from the pool. He refocused his attention on the sky and tried hard to nudge such thoughts from his mind. "You know who *will* be there? Your dad." *Nice pivot*, he thought.

Maisie interrupted him. "Grant, you look this way, and I'll look that way."

"I don't want to."

"GUP!" Maisie bellowed. She didn't want to miss a single flash in the sky.

"Let him do as he will, upside-down cake." All summer he had failed to find the right nickname for Maisie; her preference for the pineapple float provided the only inspiration.

"I don't like it when you call me that."

"Really?" The name was growing on Patrick, but he was also happy to let it go. "Is there anything you want to do for your dad when he comes home?"

Grant rocked back and forth on the Pegasus. "We could draw him pictures. Or make a thign."

"A what? A *sign*?" Patrick scratched his chin. His skin felt tight, dry from too much time in the pool. In the heat it reminded him of how he felt as a child after a day in the ocean, the salt tightening his skin just enough to imagine he was trapped inside someone else's body. "'Welcome Home'? That sort of thing? That's not a bad idea." A few bars of Ace of Base ran through his brain. *I thaw the thign.*

"We still have the Christmas tree up. Maybe we could have Christmas again!"

Patrick smiled; Christmas was in danger of becoming a year-round event. "Welcome-home presents are fun, Maisie. We could put them under the tree without having it be a full-blown holiday."

"But then *we* don't get presents!" Grant was not falling for this.

"You just got presents! You both got presents all summer. Bikes, swim attire, pool floats, wisdom, time with me. A DOG. You must be so sick of presents by now."

"MORE PRESENTS!" Grant hollered, and Marlene looked up from her nap and yipped, as if she understood the suggestion that she was herself not enough.

"If you get any more gifts you won't be able to take them all home with you," Patrick argued, hoping reason would win out. "You'll have to leave them here with me, and then they'll be mine."

Grant took his hand. "No, *mine*. For when we come visit you." The accompanying look he gave his uncle was so sincere, Patrick felt his heart swell three sizes, smashing some invisible Grinch-like box that had kept him stunted until now.

"We could get a cake," Maisie suggested. "And make a wish for Dad."

"Jeez, you kids like all the greatest hits." Yet, cake *was* a celebration food—it set a positive tone. And it was a whole lot easier than another round of presents. Sometimes the greatest hits are great for a reason. "Okay. But your father likes pie."

Maisie's face soured. Even with her unorthodox taste in desserts, pie seemed like a bridge too far. "Pie is hot. Too hot for summer."

"Not key lime."

"Chocolate!" Grant yelled.

"Okay, good grief. One of every cold pie we can find and then everyone will have a choice. Satisfied?"

"Thnowman pie."

"Snowman pie? What's that?"

Grant shrugged, it just sounded good.

"Here's what I was thinking," Patrick offered. "We could do a number."

"What number?" Grant asked. *"Eleven?"*

"An eleven o'clock number, bravo!"

"I don't underthtand."

"A musical number. You know, a song that we choreograph. And sing. Something up-tempo to perform for your dad."

"Like *what?*" Maisie asked, with the slight disgust she usually reserved for girl's clothing.

Patrick thought about bribing them with an offer to film it and put it on YouTube, but this was the end of his reign. Their father was coming home, and it would no longer be up to him. He shouldn't insert himself so heavily in their reunion; now was time for him to step back. As much as he delighted in the image of the kids belting, "I'm Still Here" from *Follies*, wearing oversized oxfords like Elaine Stritch, it probably wasn't in the cards. "Remember you asked me once, when is the last day you're a child?"

"No," Grant said, unconcerned. The kid asked so many questions Patrick wondered if he even tracked them as they came out of his mouth.

"You asked me the first week you were here. I was just curious if you thought you were still kids. After this summer." Patrick swept his hair back from his forehead.

"Oh, yeth," Grant replied without so much as thinking. "I'm only in firtht grade and I like to sleep with a night-light."

"Some *adults* like to sleep with night-lights."

"They do?"

"Sure," Patrick offered.

"But they're not in firtht grade."

"No. I'll give you that. Maisie? What about you?"

"What about me what?"

"Do you think you're still a kid?"

Maisie stared at the sky as if the answer would pour out of the Big Dipper. "I think so," she said. "But not a little one."

"I couldn't agree with that more." Even he had noticed a marked change in her over the past couple of weeks, a fearlessness. The way she spoke out. How she jumped in the pool. It was hard to pinpoint, but she had faced the very worst and Patrick saw in her a glimmer of recognition: she was a survivor.

"What about you?" Maisie asked.

"Am I still a kid?"

"You don't look like a kid," Grant offered.

"Gee, thanks." He didn't know how to answer Maisie's question exactly. *Kid* as a word is open to interpretation; there were, for example, kids at heart. "I'm not a kid. But I'm not like most grown-ups, am I?"

Maisie took her uncle's hand, the two of them now connected as if they were in danger of floating apart. "What are you going to do after we leave?" she asked.

Grant gazed up at his uncle as if he were the sky full of stars.

"Oh. Well. Go back to doing whatever it was I used to do before you showed up."

"What wath that?" Grant asked. "What did you do before we got here?"

"You know, in this moment I'm not really sure."

"I'm scared," Maisie said.

Patrick was taken aback. "To go home?"

"A little."

"Me too," Grant added, floundering on his float. "Do you have any rules? Guncle Rules. We haven't had any of those in a while."

"Yeah," Maisie agreed. "How come?"

Patrick shrugged. "I don't know. I guess I've taught you the important ones. At a certain point you have to make up the rules on your own."

And just then they saw it—a ball of fire light up the sky. This was no mere shooting star, this was something trying to penetrate the atmosphere. To get to earth. To get to them. Even Patrick scrambled to a seated position, pulling himself up by inflatable claws. Maisie screamed in startled delight, but it was gone before they could do much more.

Patrick's heart pounded in his chest. "Did you see that, Grant?"

Grant yawned as he nodded, and the way he leaned against the Pegasus's neck, its head bobbed up and down, too. "That was Mommy."

Maisie sat up on her float. "Do you think?"

Grant expressed certitude, even though to Patrick he seemed half-asleep. "It was."

"GUP?" Maisie was desperate for confirmation.

Patrick was still stunned by what he'd seen. "I think it was. I think it was her saying hello."

Maisie's excitement melted into skepticism. "How?"

Patrick rolled onto his side, propping himself up on a claw; the lobster float was more like an armchair, the tail curled under him like it had already been cooked. "Trying to say how much your mom loved you is like trying to describe the size of the universe. It can't be quantified. Can't be done. I'll bet she finds a million ways to say hello. Your eyes just have to be open to seeing them."

For a fleeting moment, Sara had punched a hole in the sky. Or perhaps it was Sara and Joe both—maybe it took two spirits, and that's why it was so bright.

The night fell quiet again, until Grant started to snore. Maisie chuckled. She reached an arm out for her uncle again, and he reached back. They clasped hands, neither willing to tear their eyes from the heavens. With a hiss and a click that startled them both, water rained down on them like tears.

"What the . . ." Patrick began, but it was simply the lawn sprinklers set to go off late at night, when the sun wouldn't evaporate the water before it could seep into the ground. "*RUN!*" They charged across the slippery grass, the sprinklers finding new ways to twist and spit. Grant pulled a croquet wicket out with his foot from a game they had played the day before as Marlene shot through his legs.

"It'th like the toilet!" Grant squealed with unyielding delight.

"*IT'S A WASHLET!*" Patrick protested.

He grabbed the day's pool towels hanging over the outdoor furniture to dry. He wrapped both kids in a single giant towel and pulled them close. They quivered, but more from profound excitement than being cold.

"You know you are loved here, too. Right? Your dad loves you and he'll be back soon. Your grandparents love you. Marlene loves you. Aunt Clara loves you."

"And you love uth," Grant said.

Bundled like this in an enormous towel, they looked like fragile, conjoined twins. "Yeah, I love you, too."

The children shivered and smiled.

"But don't tell anyone," Patrick instructed. "It'll be our secret."

TWENTY-SEVEN

Maisie and Grant crouched beneath the window, sparks of energy, each igniting reactions in the other while stifling nervous screams. They crawled to the door to avoid detection as Greg exited his cab and made his way up the walk, then shrieked as they opened it, Grant stumbling backward, forgetting to let go of the knob. "WELCOME HOME!"

Patrick scooped up Marlene as the kids threw their arms and legs around their father, squirming tentacles searching for a place to attach and never again let go. Patrick hung back, already displaced, a substitute without a classroom now that the teacher had returned. Guncles may rule, but fathers know best, as evidenced by the deep, heaving sobs the three of them shared, Greg burying his face into their tight huddle. Patrick held back his own tears. He thought perhaps things were better, that he had done some good this summer, but their pain was raw, visceral, and had this whole time been lurking, a mantle just under the crust. Perhaps he hadn't accomplished much at all.

When Greg looked up from their hug, his eyes were drawn to the center of the room. "You have a Christmas tree!" he exclaimed, wiping tears from his eyes as they darted from the tree to his brother and back to the tree again. "And it's *pink*."

"We left it up for you!" Grant explained, raising just as many questions as it answered.

"Thank you?" Greg turned to Patrick for further explanation, but his brother simply shrugged as he set the dog on the floor. Marlene cartoonishly charged in place until her legs gained traction, and then plowed forward to be part of the hug, jumping three times on her hind legs for permission to enter the scrum. "Who's this?"

"That's Marlene!" Maisie said excitedly. "Her name was something else, but GUP changed it."

"I see." Greg patted the dog on her head, with a formality that struck Patrick as amusing. His brother had always carried a slight fear of dogs, even smaller ones like Marlene. "Did he change your names, too?"

"I'm Grantelope," Grant said, and he growled. What he was imitating was anyone's guess, although who's to say what noise an antelope (or cantaloupe) makes when no one's around?

"It's nice to meet you, Marlene."

Maisie hugged Marlene tight and said, "This is our dad." Marlene squirmed and wiggled until she was free, but instead of running for safety, stayed right in the thick of their embrace.

"Did you get us any presents?" Grant hung on to his father's arm as he tried to stand.

"It wasn't the kind of place where I could really shop. But I'll tell you what . . . We'll get presents when we get home."

Maisie jumped in. "We have presents for you!"

"And cake!" Grant added.

"Pie, silly," Maisie corrected.

"Oh, yeah. PIE!"

"You do? Boy, am I lucky. Were you kids always this nice?"

"YETH!" Grant hollered.

"It was our idea! And GUP's," Maisie declared, running over to Patrick. "His idea, too."

Greg gave his brother a gentle wave. Patrick waved back, cupping his hand slightly, like the queen.

"Dad, the toilets here have remote controls."

"Washlets," Maisie remembered.

"They do?" Greg asked.

"Yeah! They thpit at your butt."

At least he'd be remembered for something.

Maisie grabbed her father by one arm while Grant grabbed the other, and they dragged Greg slowly toward the kitchen for pie.

The kids fell asleep before they were even in bed, secure in having their father back under the same roof; it was like they'd been holding their breath for three months and were finally able to exhale. Greg carried Grant to his room while Patrick carried Maisie to hers. It made him queasy, the idea that neither Maisie nor Grant had slept well the entire time they were in his care. Maisie in particular, with one eye on protecting her brother. But then Maisie started snoring shallow, gentle breaths, like a kitten might, and Patrick's worry dissipated. He'd made it through. He had delivered these kids alive. Over dinner, as the kids had recounted the summer for their father, Patrick even softened his own harsh self-criticism. Perhaps he'd accomplished something after all. With them. Alongside them. For them. For him, even. And now his job was through and *he* could sleep, too, really sleep, perhaps for the first time in years.

Patrick and Greg collapsed on the sectional, splayed across the couch like two stoned teenagers overwhelmed by the size of the world. "How was your time in the paddy wagon?"

Greg groaned. He looked at the plates on the coffee table with the remains of pie-a-palooza; the sugar crash would come, but now he was riding the only high left available to him.

"What does that mean?" Patrick asked. He pushed a plate with crust and whipped crème to the center of the coffee table with his toe to keep it from tempting Marlene. "You've got to give me something more than a groan."

Greg propped himself up on his elbows. "Do you want the real answer? Or the bullshit one?"

Patrick gave this actual thought. Did he want to know if this was indeed behind his brother? Was it going to require a second stint to take? Would the kids be his again next summer, and perhaps the one after that? He fixated on the ceiling, as if the answer might reveal itself there. Instead he only saw a recessed bulb that needed replacing. "Real answer."

"It was hell. At least at first. I know in reality, it was a long time coming. Sara had been sick for years. But inside it felt like one day I had a happy family—a wife and two kids—and then the next day I had nothing."

"Not *nothing.*"

"They gave me slippers," Greg offered. "But otherwise, it felt like nothing. It was like a reverse *Wizard of Oz*. I was living a full Technicolor life, and then woke up trapped in a nightmare that was devoid of all color, with a cyclone bearing down." He smirked. "You have a lot of time to think. It's easy to get maudlin."

Patrick placed both palms against his eyes and pressed hard. "That's because everything in there was beige."

"It was so confusing. I was there against my will, even though it was my will that I was there. I don't know how to make that make sense. It had this smell."

"I was there. I smelled it."

"I'm not sure that you did. It creeps inside you, slowly, over time, until you feel like you can't take it. Your nose is burning, and your lungs are on fire, and you're screaming, but no one can hear you because it's all on the inside."

Greg reached behind his head to fluff a pillow. Patrick was grateful he'd tossed the sequined *pill*-ow at Christmas so that Greg wasn't confronted with its tackiness. "And then?"

"I don't know. Around day nineteen it clicked. It was like for eighteen days everyone was speaking a foreign language. I was determined to keep my head down and just power through, convinced I could go back to my old habits afterward and just handle it better this time."

"That's addiction talking." Patrick writhed to reach an itch between his shoulder blades. "So what happened?"

"On day nineteen I woke up fluent. Everything people said just started making sense. I didn't understand every word, not at first. But certainly enough to get by. To have it mean something. I started to listen. And I recognized myself in everything they confessed. The lying, the hiding, the excuses. The shame."

"That's good, right?"

"Everyone there was an addict of some kind, and I mean everyone. The receptionist, the cooks, the janitors. There wasn't a single person on the inside I didn't have everything in common with. They all had crazy stories. I mean some things that would make your eyes pop. But I listened to them all. And if I hadn't done it, or experienced it, I would have done it. I would have gotten there the way things were going. There was no question in my mind."

Patrick listened, but didn't have anything to add that didn't take something away. He could point out something about Joe, about Sara, and how he was fluent in the language of grief. But why do what he'd always done—pull focus from somebody else?

"How am I going to explain this to others? Like, how will Clara ever understand?"

Clara. "Well, I helped your cause there. At the moment she's angrier with me."

"Aren't you angry with her?"

"Aren't *you*?" Patrick imagined what it must have been like to receive court documents in rehab and not be able to do much about it.

"You said you'd handle it, and I guess you did. I still don't really know what happened."

"That makes two of us." It would be easy to assign Clara the blame, but he didn't. He relented. "I went too far. I pushed her buttons."

"You always push her buttons."

"Yeah, but something was different this time. I think she was coming to me for help."

Greg's head flopped to one side like a rag doll's. "What do you mean?"

"She's going through some stuff."

Greg kicked a leg in Patrick's direction, but the couch was so vast he didn't come close to making contact. "We're all going through stuff."

Patrick tilted his head back over the side of the sofa until he was looking at the Christmas tree upside down. It started with a point and broadened out from there, an upside-down pink triangle, glimmering with soft light.

"Can you make it right?" Greg asked. "I'm sort of in an all-hands-on-deck situation here."

Marlene glanced up from her perch behind Patrick's knees. She seemed concerned about this new arrival, unsure what Greg was about. She struggled to keep alert until she had a better sense of his agenda. Patrick stroked her behind the ears.

He wanted to make things right, but in the moment he didn't know how. He tore his attention from the tree, pulled himself back up on the couch, and shook the dizziness from his head. Greg looked healthier than he did at the funeral, less gaunt. He'd gained weight, in a good way; the result, he guessed, of having regular, healthy meals prepared for him and people ensuring he ate them. "She feels betrayed, but she'll get over it. She doesn't love Darren."

"What? That's crazy." Greg lazily tossed a throw pillow at Patrick, who tucked it into his chest and hugged his arms around it. "How would you know?"

"I have a hunch."

"You have a hunch she doesn't love her husband."

Patrick and Greg had once shot Clara with a BB gun when they were kids. Not Clara, exactly—a rock at her feet. But the BB ricocheted and stung her ankle like a yellow jacket. It was an accident; they were boys being stupid. But the vitriol that came at them, the historical grievances that they had to bear—paying the price for violence perpetrated against *all* women from seemingly the dawn of time—made it believable that there was no way she would ever be able to forgive mankind enough to forgive even one man. "I'll help her through this," Patrick said, suddenly eager for a new Sisyphean task. "I failed Sara. I can do better for Clara." Tomorrow, though. Right now, he wasn't getting off his couch.

"Wait, wait, wait," Greg protested. "Hold on. How did you fail Sara?"

"She would have expected more out of me. From this summer. With the kids."

"The kids love you, Patrick," he declared. "It's so obvious from the way they look at you."

"Oh, god, I hope not."

Greg leaned forward and punched his brother just below the knee. "What is wrong with you?"

"Ow!"

"*Seriously.*"

"That was my shin." Patrick massaged his leg for sympathy.

"I'll punch you in the other shin." Greg made a fist before abandoning it, and then let his hand drop to his side. "Your whole life is about being loved. By strangers, by everyone. Why not my kids?"

Patrick felt his throat closing from an allergic reaction to . . . attachment. He swallowed three times for air. "I walked away from all that. Adoration."

"And none of us understood why."

In the moment, Patrick wasn't quite sure he understood, either. He never wanted other people to see the sadness. He was so afraid people wouldn't laugh if everyone knew how twisted he looked on the inside. And then the show ended and he didn't feel like making people laugh anymore. To play other roles—serious roles—he would have to access parts of *himself*, and . . . he didn't want to do that, either. "Turns out it's painful to be loved. Intolerable even, at times."

Greg nodded, still in the throes of his own intolerable mess. "This was all Sara's idea, you know."

"What was?"

Greg made a gesture to encompass the room. "All of this. I came clean to her a few weeks before the end. About my addiction, the pills. Everything. Typical Sara. Sprang into crisis mode. By the end of the afternoon, she had cooked up this plan."

"For me to take the kids?" Patrick propped himself up on his elbows in disbelief. "She didn't think I'd screw it up?"

"I think she most definitely thought you'd screw it up." Greg smiled before adding, "But kids are resilient."

It felt like a betrayal of sorts, the benefaction of her kids. How dare she see him so clearly in need. They weren't friends like that. Not anymore. Not at the end. And yet, her last act was a gift? None of it made any sense.

Greg snapped to get Patrick's attention. "Was she right? Sara? Did she do the right thing?"

Patrick stood up, his head spinning. "All of you and your endless questions. All the time. 'What would happen if we didn't have any elbows—how would people eat soup?' And it's like, the fuck do I know? Do you eat soup with your elbows now?"

Greg laughed.

"It's not funny!"

"We do eat soup with our elbows," he declared. "Kind of."

"WHAT IS *WRONG* WITH YOUR FAMILY?"

"If you don't have any elbows, how the hell are you going to bring a spoon to your mouth?" Greg locked his arms straight like a zombie in an attempt to prove his point.

Patrick scrambled from the couch, Greg in pursuit, slowly, grunting like the undead. He followed his brother to the bookshelves, where something caught his eye.

"Your Golden Globe is dented."

"Yeah."

"My kids do that?"

"I'll put it on your tab."

Greg grimaced. He had no idea what a Golden Globe statue cost, but it couldn't be cheap.

"It fell in the earthquake," Patrick said, letting his brother off the hook. "And I was just kidding about your rotten kids. Of course I love them, too."

Greg pulled his brother into a tight hug; Patrick extricated himself before things grew any squishier. "You got affectionate in rehab."

"Is it too gay?" Greg winked at his brother. Patrick made a playful fist.

He led the way to the kitchen and retrieved a few of the pies from the fridge. Together, they eased back the plastic wrap and picked at a few bites. Chocolate, banana crème, coconut, lemon, key lime. They stood there in comfortable silence; only with family can total silence be this agreeable.

"Save some of the lemon for Rosa. She'll like that. She's always asking for lemons from my yard."

"Okay." Greg scraped his fork through some of the banana filling before letting it sit on his tongue. "How am I going to do it?"

Patrick reached for a bite of coconut, bent his elbow (newly aware of its importance), and brought the pie to his mouth. He let it melt, buttery and soft, until it reminded him of yellowtail sushi. "Grief orbits the heart. Some days the circle is greater. Those are the good days. You have room to move and dance and breathe. Some days the circle is tighter. Those are the hard ones."

Greg stabbed aimlessly at the banana pie. "They're all hard ones."

"Right now they are. The easier ones are ahead. They come with time."

"What do I do until then?"

Patrick smushed what was left of the filling against the back of his teeth and then carefully licked it off. "Endure." He felt sleep encroaching.

"Come home with us," Greg said.

"No."

"The kids—"

"—Greg."

"What?"

Patrick put his fork in the sink. For the first time in weeks he couldn't wait to walk through his front door and be completely, totally alone. He imagined lying still, luxuriating in the silence—the only annoyance the sound of the desert wind, and even that would be blowing his cares away.

He stretched the plastic back over the pies and returned them to the fridge over Greg's objections. "I wasn't done with that."

Marlene scratched her ears, her collar jingling a clarion ring.

"That's enough for tonight."

TWENTY-EIGHT

Patrick observed the kids run ahead, down the carpeted hallway and past the ticketing desks toward the entrance to the airport's second terminal that housed the arrival and departure gates. "Stay where I can see you!" It was almost laughable, his avuncular overprotection in the company of their father; he was the laborer who stayed after his shift to comment on everyone else's work. The airport itself was small (you could see clear from one end of the hall to the other) and largely empty; September was still the off-season. He dragged the kids' carry-ons as they wiggled like salamanders, forging ahead undeterred.

Greg offered, "It's not too late, you know."

"Too late for what?"

"For you to come with us."

Patrick stopped in front of the departures board; he wasn't having this conversation again. "You all need some time alone. As a family." He wiped the sweat from his brow with the back of his hand. The airport's cooling system was fighting a losing battle.

"We are family."

Sister Sledge ran through Patrick's head like they'd been transported to a 1980s gay bar. "I'm sure the kids have had enough of me." One of the wheels on Grant's suitcase caught on a snag in the carpet.

"I haven't had *my* time with you."

Patrick placed his hand on his brother's shoulder. Greg needed his own room to grieve. He shouldn't carry Sara inside him like Patrick had carried Joe these past dozen years; he didn't have the luxury of drifting through life unhealed—not with children to raise.

A young straight couple passed them; the woman, in hiking gear with a backpack and Nalgene bottle, focused her eyes on Patrick. Greg was invisible to them, but he stared back nonetheless.

"How do you do it?" Greg asked when the couple was out of earshot.

"What?"

"Those people who just walked by. Staring."

"What people?"

Greg pointed beyond Patrick's shoulder. He turned just in time to see the couple lean into each other and giggle. "I couldn't be watched like that. Just the thought of eyes on me all the time."

Patrick didn't even notice it anymore. "Get used to it. You're going to have eyes on you at all times. Mom, Dad. The kids as they get older. Clara will be on you like a hawk."

Patrick could see on his brother's face how much he wanted to just have everyone's trust without earning it.

"You can do this, you know. I have faith in you."

Greg looked everywhere but at his brother.

"Did you remember to put your phone charger in your carry-on? The kids will want to watch YouTube. Do you want granola bars for the plane?"

"Listen to you." Patrick was Sara in that moment, mothering him and the kids. Greg fished in his pocket for the boarding passes they had printed back at the house.

Patrick watched Maisie chase Grant in a tight circle. They were laughing in the way that you can when the rest of the world drops away. "I'm going to miss them, you know." The promise of a quiet house swiftly seemed less appealing. He wished like hell it was Wednesday just so

Rosa would be puttering around or he could smell her enchilada sauce simmering in the kitchen.

"Settle down, Patrick."

Patrick's hackles were instantly raised. "Am I making a scene?"

"No, *settle* down. Find someone."

Patrick chuckled. "I'm good."

"You could have kids of your own. You're so good with them. I watched you with Grant yesterday. Teaching him to put his face in the water. I was actually jealous of your time with them this summer. That should have been me."

"I wasn't teaching him to put his face in the water, I was trying to drown him." Patrick shoved his hands in his pockets.

Greg shook his head. "I hate thinking of you all alone."

Patrick removed his cap to muss his hair before crouching into a squat. He hid his face in his hat until he regained his composure. Greg fanned himself with the boarding passes. Maisie and Grant plopped in two chairs by the floor-to-ceiling windows to catch their breath. Patrick scrutinized Grant as the boy swung his feet, so carefree. Next summer his legs would properly reach the floor; another token of childhood gone forever.

Greg placed his hand on his brother's shoulder. "I worry about you."

Patrick stood, dragging his foot across the ragged carpet. He studied the sole of his shoe as if he had stepped in something unpleasant. "Don't."

The lump in Patrick's throat doubled in size. Coupled with the pounding in his chest, compounded by the precipitous drop in his stomach—it was time to rip off the Band-Aid. He pushed Greg forward until they reached the atrium, the dingy airport suddenly awash in sunlight. "I'm the normal one in the family. Remember that. I'm the most normal."

"You say it like it's a competition."

"Everything's a competition."

Patrick's phone dinged. He pulled it out of his pocket and studied the screen.

"What is it?" Greg asked.

"Package delivered from the Hollywood Foreign Press. I think it's my new Golden Globe."

Greg laughed. "Yeah. You're definitely the most normal." He looked up at the glass above them. There was a small brown bird, confused by all the windows, flying back and forth from one side of the glass enclosure to the other, looking for a way out. Greg waved at the bird. "That's us," he said. "Trapped," as if the atrium was their grief.

Patrick didn't want to be included in this diagnosis. "Maybe he's comfortable in here."

Greg offered a dismissive shrug. "Trapped, nonetheless."

And it was true. The bird didn't belong inside. There might have been comforts—air-conditioning, a Starbucks where people bought muffins that crumbled and left behind delicious, bird-sized treats—but it was ultimately out of place. An airport was not where a bird belonged; even the man-made birds needed to pull back from their gates to pick up speed and fly. The only way out was the sliding door. The bird, high above them, would have to sink lower in order to make its escape.

Patrick heard thundering footsteps with no sign of slowing. Maisie hit her uncle's legs with such force, Patrick took three steps backward to avoid toppling over. She wrapped her arms around him. "Bye, GUP." She didn't let go.

Grant arrived with a second, less forceful, thump, adding to their hug by gripping his sister, his little hands just reaching Patrick's leg. "Bye," he said, and added something in Grant-speak, something like *Thee you thoon*.

Maisie wore one of her rash guard shirts, as if the airplane might have a pool. Patrick smiled. He crouched to roll the sleeves up her forearms. "This is the best costume for today," he started.

Greg looked puzzled.

Maisie lifted her uncle's chin and replied, "And I can always take off the skirt and use it as a cape."

"Maisie, you're not wearing a skirt. You hate skirts." Greg scratched his chin. "What are you talking about?"

"We're doing a bit," Patrick replied.

"It's from *Grey Gardens*," Maisie added.

"What's *Grey Gardens*?" Greg was totally confused.

Maisie sighed. "It's a 1975 documentary by the Maysles brothers. We watched it while you were gone."

"I gave these kids an education," Patrick said. It sounded like edu-*gay-tion*.

Greg smiled. No doubt he'd be hearing about it for weeks.

Patrick's eyes burned; he stood, pinching the bridge of his nose in a futile effort to get it to stop. As angry as he had been with Greg for leaving his kids with him, he was now twice as angry at his brother for taking them away. He hugged them tight to his leg. "I need you to remember something. We'll call it Guncle Rule sweet sixteen: I want you to really live. To live is the rarest of things. Most people merely exist." It was another lesson cribbed from Oscar Wilde, but often what kept families apart was the unbearable thought that other people shared our own faults—and Patrick did not want to be responsible for the children sharing his.

Greg pulled Patrick in close; in all his life, Patrick could not remember being hugged this tight.

"Come home," Greg whispered.

Patrick flinched. He kicked his leg slightly to free himself from Maisie, taking a step backward until it was only Greg's fingertips on him, and then another step until he was just out of reach. "You're going to miss boarding."

Maisie frowned, then started to cry. Greg put his hands on his daughter's shoulders. This was just their uncle's way.

"You'll take care of Marlene?" Maisie sobbed.

It had been Greg's idea that Marlene stay in Palm Springs. He told a reluctant Maisie to think about her uncle. How he would be all alone once they were gone. How Marlene would be good for him, and how they would all be back to visit. "I will," Patrick agreed, but he wasn't certain he'd said the words aloud.

"She will take care of your uncle until we see him again. We love you, GUP," Greg said.

"We'll make you a video," Maisie managed through her tears.

"Yeah," Grant agreed. "We'll make you a video for YouTube!" Both kids broke free and rushed their uncle one last time. Patrick grabbed a stanchion to steady himself.

"See you on YouTube." Patrick swallowed hard. With the lump in his throat, those were the only final words he could say.

He gave each of the kids one last pat on the head, which culminated in a gentle push, then watched as they slipped through the automatic sliding doors leading to security, and beyond that the gates; he returned their wave when they spun around one last time. He continued to follow them as they were bathed in sunlight in the open-air pavilion between the two terminals, watching as their shadows grew taller and taller until they were swallowed by the second terminal and disappeared out of sight.

TWENTY-NINE

Marlene lapped the yard, frantically sniffing the perimeters as if she were leading a search party in the wake of a disturbing disappearance; she'd even corralled JED's dog, Lorna, into helping, the two of them weaving under and around the tall ficus that lined the west side of Patrick's property.

"Hey! Get out of there!" Patrick yelled when they disappeared below the hedges for too long.

"Leave 'em be," John protested.

"It's just . . ." Patrick began. "Who knows what's under there." He imagined a few desert rats might have taken up shelter. But the truth of it was, he just wanted them to knock it off, even though what they were doing was not at all off-kilter. No one was combing a field looking for clues or specific proof of life, there were no milk cartons, or bulletins hastily stapled to neighborhood telephone poles, but there were indeed two missing children. Marlene, apparently, found the quiet as disconcerting as Patrick did.

Sure enough, when he returned from the airport, a box from the Hollywood Foreign Press was waiting for him on his doorstep. Cassie did not fuck around. *Although, require a signature next time*, Patrick thought. Inside was a shiny new Golden Globe engraved with his name, wrapped in a kind of new age packing material that both frightened and intrigued him; he squished it in his hands until it left his fingers powdery and with an unusual smell. "Get a load of this," he said out loud, but there was no one there to hear him. The box included instructions on how to return his old statue, although now he wished he'd had the foresight to send it home with Grant, who always admired it most. A gift, although not from the tooth fairy. Patrick washed his hands and positioned the new Globe on his shelf before settling down for a nap.

When he woke, he slowly took down the tree while playing Dolly Parton's "Hard Candy Christmas" on repeat, chiming in with a half-hearted effort to sing. He dropped an ornament and it shattered, making him wish he had access to the same packing material as the Hollywood Foreign Press.

Dolly warbled, *"I'll be fiiiiine and dandy,"* her voice plaintive yet hopeful. It matched his mood closely enough. After the eighth time on repeat, he got up and called JED—enough was enough. He set the tree, still upright in its stand, in the garage. Actual Christmas would be here soon enough.

"Chicken's burning," John said, motioning toward the grill. When the throuple agreed to join him for dinner, Patrick took a Lyft to the grocery store. At checkout he discovered a box of fruit gummy snack packs, the kind Grant liked, which he added to his cart out of habit. He purchased them anyway and ate three of the packs on the ride home before throwing the rest away.

"Oh," Patrick said, snapping to attention and turning the drumsticks with tongs. He was thankful for the employment to keep his mind occupied, to keep himself from joining Marlene's careful search of the yard. The smell of chicken for his guests, the slight burn of the sweet marinade, made him both hungry and nauseous.

"It's ninety-eight degrees outside, you sure you want to stand so close to the grill?" John sat at the far end of the outdoor table, shooing a fly away from the guacamole. He was dressed reasonably tonight, in shorts and a tank top that said DAY DRINKING.

"I like the heat," Patrick replied. What was it he'd told Clara? *It was cleansing.*

"Suit yourself, crazy man."

Patrick wiped the sweat from his forehead and moved the corn to the upper rack away from the flames. "Corn's almost done. Chicken won't be much longer. Where'd the boys disappear to?"

"Dwayne went back to get the watermelon salad, and if I know Eduardo he followed to get his weed. Sit down, Patrick."

Patrick pointed to the chicken in protest, but John pointed with both hands to the chair beside him and his two hands seemed to overrule Patrick's one. Patrick walked in a daze over to John and did as his neighbor instructed. He pulled back a chair and fell into the seat cushion. He crossed his legs, letting his Greek sandal dangle off one foot. John squeezed a small amount of sunscreen on the tip of his middle finger and stood behind Patrick. "Close your eyes."

"Oh, no." Patrick was not falling for whatever trick John had up his sleeve.

"Patrick. Close your goddamn eyes."

Patrick relented because it was easier than arguing; whatever was going to happen would be over soon enough. He felt John's hands on his face, massaging lotion into his skin, starting on his forehead and working their way down. John massaged his temples and Patrick relaxed his head back. John's hands worked their way from the sides of Patrick's nose, sweeping outward; it felt like someone wiping away tears that had years ago run dry. Patrick couldn't believe how intimate it was, how his whole body went limp, or how Marlene's barking melted into the plaintive cries of the mourning doves that took residence on the power lines in the late afternoon.

Coo-OO-oo. Coo-OO-oo.

"You did a good thing this summer."

Patrick wanted to get lost in the sensation of lotion being massaged into his skin, but thought it impolite to tell John to stop talking. He made a sound, *Mmmmm*; his lips tickled. He snapped the grill tongs together a few times and they made a satisfying clack.

"I don't even want to think where those kids would be without you."

Clack, clack clack.

"Thank you," Patrick said. "But that's not the issue so much as . . . *now what*?"

"I'm of the belief that the answer will reveal itself in due time."

Patrick dropped the tongs on the table and they made their most satisfying sound yet. "You won't mind, I hope, if I think that's bullshit."

John smiled. "Nope. I won't mind at all." He worked his hands through Patrick's scalp until Patrick tensed reflexively. "You've trapped him in here."

"Who?" Patrick asked.

"The one you lost."

Joe.

John continued. "That's not fair to him, that's not fair to you. You can't hold on so tight."

Patrick lowered his shoulders, then the rest of his head, chin to chest, as John moved to the back of his neck.

"Pain doesn't lift until you feel it." And as if to prove a point, John found a knot in Patrick's shoulder and squeezed until a burning heat shot up and down his side. He did that two or three more times, and just as Patrick was about to tell him to stop, he suddenly felt free of something he didn't even know he was carrying. "See?" John rested his hands on Patrick's shoulders as Patrick slowly opened his eyes. "I'm also a licensed massage therapist."

"Minister. Grief counselor. Masseur. Is there anything you're not good it?" Patrick asked as he stood to turn the chicken. Patrick's sliding glass door opened and Eduardo and Dwayne reappeared.

"Monogamy," John answered with a laugh.

Patrick bellowed across the lawn. "MARLENE!"

John jumped, startled. Marlene looked up from the ficus.

"They're not in there. They went home." Patrick shook his head. How was he going to explain to a dog when he could barely explain to himself—he'd spent half the afternoon alone in a house wondering how walls could be so quiet. Patrick pulled a bottle of rosé out of the ice bucket and poured himself a glass. He placed his hand on the base of the stem and turned the glass three times. "Is this what life was like before?"

"Nice, isn't it?" Dwayne observed.

Boring, Patrick thought. How had he done this for four years?

"You'll get used to it right quick." John placed his hand on his friend's. "Like riding a bike."

They sat quietly, the only sound the evening wind, which, for Patrick, carried the echo of Grant's probing questions: *How did cavemen make tools if they didn't have any tools? How do you kill a ghost? Why do I need a mirror to see my eyes?*

Patrick leaned in to his wineglass. He could barely make out his reflection; the wine gave him a youthful, pinkish hue. "You're going to have to change into your night-drinking shirt soon."

John looked puzzled. Patrick pointed to his DAY DRINKING shirt.

Eduardo finished packing a bowl and held it up to the others. "Any takers?" He slid his lighter toward Patrick.

"I'm good," Patrick said, even though he wasn't sure that was true.

Patrick lay on his couch with his legs splayed, creating his custom nook for Marlene. She'd tired of her search for Maisie and Grant and slept soundly in this nest; sleep wasn't coming so easily for Patrick. He was exhausted for sure, but too unsettled to fully relax. The house seemed wrong. The only toys on the floor were the dog's. The Christmas tree was gone. That corner of the room had come to feel celebratory, now it looked dark, like depression, and he couldn't muster the energy to move a lamp to shine light in its place. Perhaps he should have done a few hits with Eduardo before JED went home. Just to make him sleepy.

He thought about the hot tub, but instead opened his phone to his YouTube channel. Another slew of new subscribers. He hoped they knew what they were signing up for; at the moment he didn't see his appeal. Now that the kids were gone, he wasn't sure what to generate for content. Clips of Marlene, perhaps, snoring as she was now. In the throes of a dream, her legs moving as if she were running, tearing through the grass in the gentle shade of evening. That was good for one video, maybe two—people seemed to post a lot about their dogs. Should he post one of himself? Did anyone really care to see him? He replayed the first video he posted with Maisie and Grant, at Lulu's with the cotton candy. It had four hundred and eighty-eight thousand views. Four hundred eighty-eight thousand people, he thought, who should find better things to do with their lives. He turned up the volume just to hear their laughter fill the house. Marlene lifted her head, alert, as if she'd been bamboozled. The kids were indeed here, hiding, and it might be up to her to find them. How could she have so easily given up the game? And yet, a quick survey of the living room made it pretty clear it was still just the two of them. No need to get down from a perfectly good perch on the couch. Patrick grinned a stupid grin, as wide as it was involuntary. Perhaps he was judging his new followers too harshly. Maybe they knew exactly what they were doing. Maybe this was the very best thing to do with free time. He watched the video of them from the party, from atop the mountain, and the others that he had posted. He scrolled back to a video he had shared of the final curtain call of *The People Upstairs*. Sixteen posts ago. Then a four-year gap where he was invisible. What had he done with his life in that time? Without documentation, how could he remember?

His phone rang, interrupting his dark thoughts. The word AGENT flashed on his caller ID. He stared at his phone, not quite sure he had the strength to answer. "Martha Mountain-Range?" he asked when he did, imagining it a hyphenated, married name. He'd exhausted his topographical knowledge, so he'd have to find a new shtick. "Do I *have* to send the dented one back? They would make iconic bookends."

"There's interest," Cassie blurted.

It took a moment for those two words to register.

"*Strong* interest. It's TV. Network. A family sitcom. It was going to be a single-father sort of thing—a modern take on *Father Knows Best*—but they saw your YouTube videos with the kids and they are freaking out. They would change the role to an uncle. Totally open. You meet. You dazzle them."

"*Gay* uncle."

"What?"

"Guncle. Can the uncle be gay?"

"They want *you*, Patrick. If all goes well, they would rewrite the whole thing for you."

Patrick said nothing. He just held the phone up to his ear and listened to the sound of her frustrated breathing. It was like a meditation app that carefully slowed his pounding heart.

"PATRICK. *In New York*."

Patrick's eyes grew red and he tickled Marlene under the chin.

"This is it. This is what you wanted. Don't you have anything to say?"

Patrick took one deep, sharp breath. "That ain't it, kid. That ain't it."

"THE FUCK IT'S NOT!"

Patrick sat bolt upright. It had only been a few short weeks, but calling him late at night without apologizing? Bringing him offers? Swearing at him through the phone? Cassie was going to make one hell of an agent. He liked her in this moment more than ever.

Not that Cassie could see, but he conjured a wry smile. "I just hope I'm not a Dance: 10; Looks: 3."

Cassie let fly with an infuriated wail that sang through the phone, as if wondering why she ever wanted this promotion at all. "What are you talking about?"

Patrick forced himself not to laugh; why was it so much fun to exasperate her? "I'm doing *A Chorus Line*, Cassie. I'm quoting your show."

The frustrated clacking of a keyboard as Cassie continued undeterred. "I'll see you in Los Angeles. Do I need to come get you? Escort you into the meeting? They want to see you on Monday. Can I trust you to be there?"

"*Los Angeles*," Patrick uttered, confused. "You said New York."

"The meeting's in Los Angeles. The show's in New York."

Patrick paused. He supposed that made sense. All the development people were in LA. "What are you doing? What's all that typing?"

"I'm emailing my assistant to get me a copy of that damn musical."

Patrick promised his agent he would dazzle; the last thing he did before he fell asleep on the couch was book a flight to LA.

On Saturday Patrick walked his bicycle around the block to JED's house. As he approached the front door Lorna started to bark. There were no cars in the driveway. Just as well. He'd decided to stay in LA for a time, and had more than his fill of goodbyes. He placed the bike across their front door, popped the kickstand down, and fished a note out of his pocket. Gifting his neighbor a bicycle had been on his mind since John had confessed at the start of the summer that the theft of his own bike had marked the end of his childhood. (If only the kids' bikes would suit Eduardo and Dwayne, he could have left a gift for all three.) Patrick didn't see much use for it anymore; in fact, depending on how things went in LA, he could see himself calling JED in a few week's time, offering them first dibs on more of his belongings. But one thing at a time. It was dangerous to put the basket before the bicycle.

Patrick tucked his note in the tire's front spokes. It read: *For John. A childhood should never be over.*

It surprised Patrick, their friendship, the deep affection he felt for John. For all three of them, really. He smiled, happy that life could still surprise. Maybe there were still a few good ones out there for him yet. He placed his palm on their front door as a gentle adieu, then walked to the corner to call a Lyft to the bank to withdraw money for Rosa. Advance her some salary to keep an eye on the place. He'd write her a note, too. Invite her family to use the pool whenever they liked.

Everything was happening so fast.

Marlene stuck her head out of the camel-colored leather pet carrier just as the plane picked up speed down the runway, lifting one eyebrow and then the other as if to say, *What the actual f*@k?* Patrick leaned down to comfort her; they were both in a slight diazepam haze. He'd read a magazine article once, soon after he booked his first show and it became clear that air travel would be part of his new life, about the best ways to combat a fear of flying. His wasn't so much a fear of flying as a general anxiety about crashing, but still he remembered the article's tips as if he'd read them yesterday. Not all of them were available to Marlene. Check the turbulence forecast. Familiarize yourself with airplane sounds. Talk to the flight attendants about any specific concerns. But one jumped out at him: hold a photograph of your destination. He reached for his phone in his pocket and opened his camera roll to a photo of Maisie and Grant wrapped in bright towels by his pool. He showed it to Marlene.

"We're on our way," he said. It was a roundabout journey, west before east, but this was the start of their new life. He took a good look at the kids himself before tucking his phone back in his pocket as the plane left the ground and rose upward into the sky.

THIRTY

"Patrick." The man introduced himself as Scott LaBerge, and then went around the conference room saying words that may or may not have been names. *Brant. Abner. Dottie. Basil. Sable. Kelsi. Quill.* Patrick greeted each face, determined to forget these unfortunate names as quickly as he was assaulted with them. Were there assigned seats? There was a bottle of water in front of each chair, but no name cards; he waited to be told what to do.

It was downright cool in Los Angeles (at least in comparison to Palm Springs). Cassie had met him at LAX, dressed in an upgraded wardrobe that suited her new title, and spent the ride filling Patrick's head with encouraging nonsense. They arrived at the studio lot early. She begged to accompany him to the meeting, but he assured her he worked best on his own; she said she'd eagerly wait for his call and left him with time to explore. He strolled past bungalows and soundstages and backlot sets, that one town square that's stood in for many a whistle-stop, the alley with its urban flexibility, the White House portico (an unexpected sprout, even in a very fertile garden), and the enormous tank you could flood for water scenes. Several faces looked familiar, a few people waved. A foursome on an electric golf cart pointed as they quietly whizzed by. It felt both familiar and strange, home and foreign. Patrick kept his hands in his pockets and made his best attempt to enjoy it; it was like trying on an old sweater to see if it still fit.

"I'm so glad you could join us on such short notice," Scott continued.

"It's an easy flight from Palm Springs," Patrick offered as they continued to stand awkwardly around the table.

"There's a flight from Palm Springs?" one of the staffers asked, insinuating the obvious—it was probably an easier drive. Patrick found there was a uniform banality to network staffers—certainly this bunch—like they all got their hair cut at the same place, or held similar opinions on something unknowable, like the future of broadcast TV.

"There is." Patrick was lucky to get the direct, otherwise you connected through Phoenix. "I don't drive," he offered as explanation, not sure if it made him seem less eccentric to a potential employer, or more.

"Take a seat," Scott gestured. His face was boyish, betrayed only by some premature graying over the ears. Instead of adding gravitas, it made him look like he had powdered his temples to play a part. Patrick took an open chair at the table's midpoint; Scott assumed a seat at the head. Patrick faced the room's window, looking out on a bubbling fountain. He thought momentarily of Maisie and Grant on their pool floats before focusing instead on the room. Several execs produced pens, but none of them had anything to write on.

Everyone breathed in unison and exhaled.

"We loved you in *The People Upstairs*. Big fans," cooed the one that may or may not have been Kelsi. She wore oversized glasses and had some kind of topical lapel pin; political but not controversial. In fact, it might have just said WOMEN.

"That's nice to hear. It's been a hot minute. You worry people forget."

The table murmured some version of "Never."

Patrick continued. "People don't even watch TV anymore. Do you know there's something called TikTok?"

The table laughed. They knew. But also, they were there to defend.

"How much tik could a TikTok tok if a TikTok could tok tik?"

The table laughed again, harder this time. Someone declared, "That's too much!"

Scott signaled everyone to be quiet. "Well, we watch TV here. This table loves TV."

"And people watch our network. You should see our live+3. And our streaming service? We're changing the metrics of how you measure success." Someone (Abner?) flung a spiral-bound report in his direction; it came to a stop three inches from the edge of the table with the network's logo facing him perfectly.

"And you know who else watches TV?" asked the one in a bow tie. "*Families*."

Again the table murmured in agreement. Bow Tie grinned, proud of his contribution. And then he winked, as if to broadcast his queerness, too, and define this as a safe space for Patrick.

"That's right," Scott confirmed. "Which is why we are always looking for a new take on the family comedy."

The sun passed behind a cloud, momentarily darkening the courtyard. Patrick hoped this wasn't an ominous sign, but no one else seemed particularly bothered.

"We all loved the videos you posted with your kids."

"My niblings."

"Excuse me?"

"My niblings," Patrick whispered, as if leveraging them was a betrayal. But this was supposed to be *for* them, so he attempted confidence in his voice. "My niece and nephew."

"What's that?"

Patrick cleared his throat. "They're my brother's kids."

"Right."

"Their mother passed away last spring and they came to live with me for the summer."

"Our condolences."

Murmur.

"That's good, we can use that."

Patrick started to object, but Scott raised a hand to apologize, agreeing it was crass.

"You have a real chemistry. With children. The way you talk to them! Like little adults. It's edgy, but . . . *safe*. That's the tone we're looking for. New. But familiar. Tone is everything. The rest we can figure out, the circumstances and whatnot. Plot. With your input, of course."

Patrick nodded; as a response it was better, but shy of great. "Thank you. To lose one parent may be regarded as a misfortune. To lose both looks like carelessness." The room erupted with glee. Patrick didn't even bother to attribute the quote, he'd already moved on to other concerns. (If they were going to model the show on him, they would learn soon enough about his love of Wilde.) Did he have chemistry with the kids? Is that what it boiled down to? Not connection, but chemistry? Not love, but *science*? "I do have a certain rapport with those kids, I suppose. It developed over time. They don't drink martinis, so we had to find something else to bond over."

Stop! You're right! That's rich.

It had been a long while since Patrick had been "in a room." But it was all coming back—including how much he despised it. It was a first date, a job interview, a talk show appearance all rolled in one. The room was an audience to entertain. And with minimal effort, he could have them eating out of his hand. But did he want to? Not really. But it wasn't just that he owed this to Cassie. He owed it to Greg, Maisie, and Grant. He owed this to Sara. She could only rest if her family was taken care of. And he owed it to Joe, who would want him not just to survive—but to thrive.

"After the events of this summer I've got a tight ten on child-rearing. I could drop in to a Giggles in Dayton or Comedy Hut in Tulsa and kill." Patrick looked around the room as the table leaned in, desperate for more. *Wait, wasn't one of them named Tulsa?*

Patrick closed his eyes and pictured Maisie and Grant. And when he had a crisp, firm image of them, he began.

"For instance, why is it kids lose their baby teeth? Why not their baby nose, or baby ears? Why doesn't a chubby little arm fall off when it's time for their adult arm to come in?" Patrick mimed his arm falling out of its socket for effect, but it was wholly unnecessary. They were already devouring this. "My nephew calls pockets snack holes, and honestly it's changed my whole outlook on fashion. And food." He mimed reaching into his pocket. "Anyone want a pistachio Oreo Thin? Please ignore the lint."

The room got very loud. Some scrambled to take notes, before discovering the dearth of paper. Others turned their own pockets inside out as if looking for snacks, and commenting how brilliant that was. Others still, made plans: *You know who we should get to write this? You know who could play the brother? The love interest? The kids?*

The excitement around the table melted something deep inside him. He was picking up steam, hitting a stride. He was the Tin Man with freshly oiled joints after a long time rusting in the rain. A lion finding the courage to go on a journey. A scarecrow confessing he wasn't all that scary. After a few minutes of his routine, Patrick was standing in front of the open arms of Scott LaBerge, the wizard, asking for a brand-new heart.

"Well, we should wrap this up. I took the kids bowling last month, and my nephew's ball should be reaching the pins any minute now." He looked at an invisible watch on his wrist. "I should be there to cheer him on."

"This is the show," Scott LaBerge declared, tapping the table excitedly with his pen. "You are the show, Patrick. You're the head of the modern family. A *Father Knows Best* for the era."

"*Uncle Knows Best!*" said Basil, or Abner or Quill.

"Guncle *Knows Best*," said Bow Tie, and the room went wild. The sun emerged from behind a cloud and all seemed right with the world again. Or did it?

Scott LaBerge pounded on the table, calling the meeting back to order. Everyone grabbed ahold of themselves and renewed their rigorous posture. "Clearly, we're excited. I hope you're excited. We'll get down to work here and I hope you're looking forward to moving back to LA."

"Back to LA?" It spilled out of his mouth like *ELL LAY*.

"Well, yeah. The show will shoot in LA."

"I thought it was going to be in New York?"

"We thought it would take place in New York, there's a certain precociousness to city kids. But, no. We would film it here." Scott LaBerge looked confused, and even went so far as to let the tip of his tongue slide out one corner of his mouth. "Costs and such to consider. Is that a problem?"

The room began to spin, but Patrick said nothing. *He owed this to Sara.*

Cassie got the call with an offer an hour later.

Patrick, the city whispered.

After his meeting he strolled the back lot again, his thoughts reeling. This was supposed to be his way back to the kids, now he was, what—*farther away*? He chuckled when he got to the New York set, which seemed only to exist to taunt him. He took a seat on a stoop across from the facade of a bagel shop. It was eerie, New York, when empty of the people that make it such a pulsing, vibrating place. He looked down the street, past an NYPD car and several Yellow Cabs parked by the curb. Steam rose from a subway grate, which somehow added to the artifice. But the street was indeed vacant. He was hearing things, on top of everything else.

"Patrick!" His name rang again.

Another ghost, he thought, calling to him from a different time, from actual New York, when he would walk home on empty streets late at night from his gig at the Greek restaurant, plotting a better, more promising life that didn't involve setting people on fire. He stood up and continued down the block, charmed by the store windows with colorful mannequins in angular garb; they must be dressing the set to film.

Footsteps pounded behind him, and Patrick felt someone grab his bicep.

He spun around to see Emory.

"I thought that was you," Emory said. His glasses, oddly, were spotted with rain.

"What are you doing here?" Patrick shook his head, amused. Emory wore a beanie slouched to one side, making him look like an idiot.

"On a break from filming." Emory pulled the hat off his head, and Patrick was relieved it was part of a costume. "I sometimes come back here to think."

Patrick looked around. This could be his world again soon enough. "Your glasses are wet."

Emory crossed his eyes and focused on his lenses. "Oh. I ran past the Western town. They're filming something with rain."

What a bizarre occupation we share, Patrick thought.

"What about you? You're a long way from home. What are you doing here?"

"Me?" Patrick asked, as if Emory could be inquiring about anyone else. He looked around at the brick and stone buildings that lined this New York block. "I'm a little lost."

"No shit."

"I was meeting about a show," he said with a sour face. "If you can believe that."

"Of course I can believe that. You're a goddamn star."

A plane went by overhead and they both paused to look up at the sky.

"What about the desert?" Emory inquired. "Coming out of retirement?"

"I don't know." Patrick tried to balance himself on a fake cobblestone. "The desert will always be there. But it's time for me to rejoin the world."

Emory smiled. "I'll miss that pool."

"I'll loan you the house."

"I'd miss you in it." He smiled even broader. He had one chipped tooth Patrick hadn't noticed before. Another flaw that somehow made him ideal. "Where you headed?"

"Now?" It was a good question. Patrick was lost in his thoughts; he wished there were more of the city to walk through. Alas, it ended ahead, melting into more bungalows and a small park set with a gazebo. "Back to my hotel. I have to walk the dog."

Emory smirked. "Is that a euphemism?"

"No," Patrick chuckled, remembering his explaining euphemisms to the kids. "No, it's not." Marlene, who was not used to hotels or the sounds of people walking a hallway outside her door, was certainly antsy and waiting to go out. "What about you?"

Emory's eyes lit up from behind his spattered glasses. "I have one more scene to film, but then grabbing a drink with you."

Patrick removed Emory's glasses so he could see his eyes. "What are you looking for, Emory?"

"Nothing." He winked like he had the night that they first met. "Everything."

Patrick tried to call Joe's face to mind. It came, blurred. Smudged. The features weren't quite right. It'd been a lifetime since he'd seen it. Patrick did his best to dry Emory's glasses on his shirt. "Well, I'm looking for . . . *something*."

Emory nodded. "Any idea what that is?"

Patrick had never really seen Emory without his glasses. He looked older, more mature. "I think I'd rather like to do a play." The words took Patrick by surprise. But they were in his head, planted by Cassie in his kitchen the day of their very first meeting. Being in LA felt like repeating something; Patrick desperately wanted to start something new.

Emory took a step forward and they stood nose-to-nose. He gestured at the Manhattan streetscape around them. "You're in the right city, then."

Patrick smiled in spite of himself. "I guess I am."

"A play sounds like fun."

"Does it?" Patrick was already second-guessing. It would mean saying no to a network show and the paycheck he was chasing for his family.

"Have a drink with me," Emory encouraged. "We'll talk it all out."

They stood like this, on the sidewalk, at an impasse. Patrick blinked. Their eyelashes were almost touching. Emory wasn't right for him, the age difference was just the start. But he also wasn't wrong, and Patrick knew himself well enough to know when he was making excuses. Emory was full of life, a yes to his no. And the whole point of leaving the desert, coming out of isolation, was to stop. Making excuses. Saying no. "One drink," Patrick relented. "Four max."

Emory flagged a couple of extras wearing fringe vests and boots on their way to the Western town. "This is my friend Patrick," he said to one of them. "He's going to do a play."

Patrick blushed. It was so stupid, Emory's celebration of him.

"Beats doing a Western in the rain," the extra huffed before continuing down the New York block on their way, perhaps, to an old saloon.

Patrick handed Emory back his glasses. "We really do need to walk the dog first."

Emory scuffed the sidewalk with his shoe. "Okay," he said. "But we're making that a euphemism."

Patrick kissed Emory in the middle of the street until all of New York fell away.

THIRTY-ONE

"TEN MINUTES TO CURTAIN!"

The frantic banging on dressing room doors up and down the hall caused Patrick to smirk; it was just the jolt of electricity he needed before this performance. He poked his head out of his dressing room just as the stage manager, a rather humorless nonbinary person named Kacey for whom he'd developed a begrudging respect (even though they were immune to Patrick's innumerable charms), passed his dressing room. "The house seats I asked for. Did that all work out?"

"Work out how?"

"Are they *here*," Patrick implored.

Kacey rang for the box office on their headset. "House seats for Patrick O'Hara. How many. All five?" They covered their microphone. "All five."

"They've arrived?" Kacey nodded, yes. "Okay, that's good. *Good*. Thank you. Go." He gave them a nod to keep moving, not wanting to be responsible for holding the curtain.

"Fall down some stairs," Kacey said before screaming, "NINE MINUTES. NINE MINUTES, PEOPLE."

Patrick laughed. It wasn't exactly "Break a leg," but since the play was Michael Frayn's *Noises Off* and he was playing Garry Lejeune, the play-within-a-play's leading man, he would indeed be, as part of his blocking, falling down a flight of stairs after slipping on a sardine. A choreographer friend taught him to do it just so, but still after a tech and three dress rehearsals he was feeling sore, especially after the second dress when he twisted left instead of right and his shoulder took the brunt. He stepped back inside his dressing room and sat, then studied himself in the mirror. The mustache was still there. He thought he might shave it after the kids returned home, but he'd grown accustomed to it and it seemed to fit his character. The lighting was good; throughout rehearsals he'd taken goofy selfies and sent them to Greg for the kids. He looked older, but he liked it. He had lived a life and survived it.

On his table sat a program. *Westport Country Playhouse Presents NOISES OFF*. He had nearly given Cassie a small heart attack when he told her to turn down the pilot, but she managed to work it all out. Patrick told her he needed a year, and they compromised: it takes a year to get a show off the ground anyhow, and as long as he made himself available in March to shoot the pilot he could have most of that time for himself. She'd even found him a play in Connecticut, earning her commission and then some. It wasn't Broadway, but it held some prestige with the New York critics, so it wasn't such a bad deal; he could see the kids through their first year back home, meeting them most days after school. He was even introduced to Maisie's friend Audra Brackett, who was—as advertised—a delight. Once his new TV show began production, he'd be six months in LA and six months in New York. For the first time in his life he'd be bi.

Patrick glanced at his photo in the program and at those of his castmates. It made him happy, being part of a team. His solo show in the desert had gone on long after it should have closed. He was excited to show the kids what he did, firsthand. GUP. Their guncle. Onstage. YouTube didn't stand a chance against the magic of live theater.

Knock, knock, knock.

Taylor, one of the stagehands, stood behind him, reflected in the mirror, looking nervous. "Visitor," he said. "I told her there was no time, but she insisted." He stepped back to reveal Clara standing in the doorway, holding a bouquet of roses.

Patrick chuckled. "It's okay, Taylor. Thank you." It wasn't his fault. Someone in his position of low authority would never win an argument with his sister.

"For you," Clara said, handing him the flowers. She took in her surroundings, seemingly unimpressed.

"It's not *The Tonight Show*, Clara. The dressing rooms are small."

"I've never been backstage at a theater," she said. "It's kind of exciting."

Patrick hugged the bouquet. "Thank you for these." He slipped open the card. Inside was a note. *Welcome back*, it said, and it was signed, *Your biggest fans*. "From everyone?" Patrick asked, and Clara indicated that they were. He placed the flowers on his dressing table, stood, and kissed her cheek. It was awkward, but forgiving, and Clara seemed to smile. When he stood back, he adjusted his gaudy powder blue suit, his costume. Clara smoothed the wide lapels. "Oh, hey listen. I'm supposed to do press tomorrow. Do you think you could meet the kids after school?"

"I'm happy to," Clara said, and she was.

They stepped out in the hall and Patrick led his sister down the stairs and then a second set of stairs that led backstage. *Break a leg. Break a leg, Patrick. Good show. Break legs.* An enthusiastic high five from everyone. "This is your stop," he said, pointing his sister toward the auditorium door.

"Break a leg, Patrick. We can't wait to see you onstage." She smiled before disappearing through the auditorium door.

Alone, he found the quiet spot backstage he liked. When he stood just so he could peek through the set window. Usually it was to watch the rehearsal before he made his entrance; tonight he could see the audience. Greg, Maisie, Grant, Emory, already seated, and then Clara taking her place alongside them, fifth row center. They chatted excitedly with each other, the theater alive with hummed conversation. Maisie wore a bow tie and Patrick melted. *His influence.*

For a moment he felt out of place. Like he was the audience and not the other way around. An alien on a mission to observe how people live. An advanced being, in some ways, with his own wisdom to share, pioneering cures for what ailed primitive humans. And in turn, they had magical elements, raw materials that were healing to him, too.

The houselights dimmed and the faces in the crowd disappeared. Instead he saw Joe's smiling down on him. And then, for a fleeting moment, Sara's.

Their friendship began in darkness. In the pitch-black of a stairwell that led to a roof. And now so did his relationship with her kids, although their darkness was very different. But they, too, had become his light.

"Thank you," he whispered to Sara, for orchestrating this past summer.

Patrick retreated from his vantage point, taking his place backstage left. Kacey nodded, confirming his arrival; Patrick nodded back. *Let's do this.* Chatter on the headset.

"Places."

Final Guncle Rule. There are two tragedies in life: one is not getting what you want, the other is getting it.

Patrick had lived both; the second was preferable.

A hush fell over the house. The final unwrapping of a candy. The rustling of a coat. The crinkle of a program folded open.

Patrick was exactly where he belonged. An ephemeral thought as the stage light came on, spilling warm light across his face. He loathed it then; he loved it now.

And that's how you do it.

Acknowledgments

I often say that novel writing is a very solitary occupation, but that's more of an emotional truth than a factual one. While it can feel very lonely at times, the reality is I have access to incredible lifelines—for support, for company, for motivation.

At the top of that list is my editor, Sally Kim. I previously wrote an entire book celebrating editors and if you knew Sally you'd understand why. Thank you for recognizing the inspiration for my next novel right under my nose. You bring so much magic to the process it's hard not to think of you as *my* Auntie Mame. I can all but hear you encouraging me in true Mame fashion to write on a light breakfast—*black coffee and a sidecar.* (*Live!* That's the message.)

In these unusual times when we've all felt isolated, my agent, Rob Weisbach, has been a tether to the outside world and I rely on him more than I should. Rob is an extraordinary and generous talent and I'm so lucky to benefit from his immense experience. If there's a punchline in this book that falls flat, I guarantee he pushed me to find a better one and I was being stubborn.

This book has many friends and they include Michael Peters, Kate Howe, Kathleen Caldwell, Wende Crowley, Harlan Gulko, Trent Vernon, Ryan Quinn, Zac Hug, Nicholas Brown, Chris Neuhaus, Roswell Encina,

Julia Claiborne Johnson, and the tireless team at G. P. Putnam's Sons who never missed a beat in these challenging times: Alexis Welby, Katie McKee, Ashley McClay, Emily Mlynek, Nishtha Patel, and Gabriella Mongelli. They are true professionals and their energy and creativity is infectious.

Stephanie Chernak Maurer, I miss you every day. I think back to the sixth floor and wonder how it could all have gone by in a blink.

Thank you to my parents, Barbara Sonia and Norman Rowley, for being examples of unconditional love.

I am the guncle of five of the most amazing kids, to whom this book is dedicated. I love them for many reasons and as the remarkable individuals they are, but also because they are extensions of my siblings Laura Rowley, Sam Rowley, and Sue Wiernusz. You were my first—and remain my *best*—friends and it is rewarding to watch you parent.

To the guncles out there and the many LGBTQ+ people raising beautiful kids, I say cheers. You're inspiring a generation of children to love without prejudice and to celebrate their authentic selves. I'm in awe of what you do.

Finally, to Byron Lane: a thousand times YES. (In the acknowledgments for his novel *A Star Is Bored*, Byron proposed. In case anyone had read his book—*you should*—and then was waiting for *my* next book to see what my answer was, NOW YOU KNOW. At the very least, I wanted my acceptance documented in the Library of Congress alongside the contents of Abe Lincoln's pockets and a lock of Walt Whitman's hair.) I'm so damn lucky to spend my life with you.

the GUNCLE

STEVEN ROWLEY

Discussion Guide

Excerpt from The Celebrants *by Steven Rowley*

PUTNAM
— EST. 1838 —

Discussion Guide

1. Patrick and his sister, Clara, each have different viewpoints on what would be best for Maisie and Grant after their mother's death. Which approach did you agree most with? Did that change by the novel's end?

2. Patrick is meant to take care of his niece and nephew for the summer, but Maisie and Grant prove to be just as impactful on Patrick. What do the children teach their uncle? Discuss the ways in which they learn from one another.

3. *The Guncle* asks the question: At what point does one stop being a kid? How is this explored in Maisie and Grant's life? What about Patrick's?

4. Did you have a favorite Guncle Rule? If so, which one? How would you implement it in your own life? If you had to create a new Guncle Rule, what would it be?

5. JED are an unconventional—and hilarious—set of neighbors. How does the throuple play a role in this novel? What were some of your favorite moments with them?

6. Grief is a major theme throughout *The Guncle*. Discuss the different ways in which Patrick, Grant, and Maisie each learn to cope with their grief. How do Patrick's memories of Sarah come to impact all of them? Does the endless sunshine of Palm Springs help or hurt them in these darker moments?

7. Why do you think Emory is the first person Patrick considers opening his heart up to since Joe's death? How is Patrick now ready to explore a relationship?

8. By the novel's end, Patrick has decided to revive his acting career. Were you surprised by his choice of project? What type of performance would you love to see Patrick do?

9. Patrick is always his authentic self, something he draws on as a guncle. In what ways does he encourage the kids to celebrate their own unique qualities? Have you had a guncle or Auntie Mame–type figure in your own life? If so, what have you learned from them?

10. What do you think happens next for Patrick? For Grant and Maisie?

Keep reading for an exciting excerpt from *The Celebrants* by Steven Rowley

He was an astronaut, he imagined, like in one of those movies; his mission took him to a distant planet on the far reaches of the solar system, Saturn, perhaps, or Neptune. He was gone a nominal amount of time—three years, maybe five, significant but not interminable—but somehow everyone Jordan Vargas knew on Earth had aged a lifetime while he was in space. Naomi with her readers, struggling to figure out the television's remote as if the technology had eluded her, her irritated face twisted in frustration. Craig in the kitchen employing the flashlight on his phone to read take-out menus, muttering the whole time about the Big Sur retreat's soft ambient light while confusing yellow curry with green. What was the difference? *The color, yes, obviously.* But one had more turmeric. *What the hell color is turmeric?* Marielle educating them in great detail about the kittens she'd brought for the weekend. They were born without eyes, *a condition called microphthalmia*, she explained, caused by a genetic mutation that can sometimes result in smaller-than-usual tongues. And Jordan Tosic, loyal Jordy, his husband and other half, the man who made them the Jordans to so many. (Should we invite *the Jordans*? You don't know *the Jordans*?! We love *the Jordans*!) Jordy's metamorphosis, like Jordan's own, was less shocking as they'd been together since college and had witnessed each other aging slowly, each having had ample time to adjust to the other's weathering like the wearing of a beloved chair's upholstery over time.

Of course Jordan Vargas wasn't an astronaut, or anything close to it. He was a public relations executive, bound to Earth by gravity, a mortgage, a business he owned with his husband, and aging immigrant parents who moved the family from Bogotá when Jordan was eight to give him and his brother a better life. He was someone who vibrated not from sitting above liquid-fuel cryogenic rocket engines aboard a shuttle ready to launch, but with the genuine thrill of securing his clients ample media coverage. Or at least he used to, until slowly over the years he came to resent both the clickbait-ification of journalism and troublesome clients whom he saw more as crises than people. And it wasn't space travel that kept him away from these friends, a dangerous mission (as poetic as it might be to imagine), so much as his own busy life and the sad fact that friends—even best friends of thirty years—drift apart.

Jordan was growing impatient with Craig's inability to read a simple take-out menu. They were only in Big Sur for the long weekend; their time together, as always, was limited. He rolled up one of Mr. Ito's old *National Geographic* magazines from a rack next to him and, from the recliner where he sat, swatted the coffee table. "Jesus, Craig. How old *are* you?"

Craig sighed his displeasure.

Naomi peered over her glasses. "Don't do that to my father's magazines."

Cowed, Jordan rolled the magazine the opposite way to flatten it. "Will someone help Nana with the menu? I'm famished."

"I just need to turn on some lights." Craig ran his hand against the dated backsplash in search of a light switch, managing only to trigger the garbage disposal instead.

"I told you. All the lights are already on." Naomi strained to open the remote, but the plastic latch was stuck. Her mother would use a dime to open battery compartments, but no one carried coins anymore.

"I'll help," Marielle offered. "My eyes are still *young*." She was also the youngest by a year, having skipped a grade somewhere, the only one of them yet to turn fifty. Her hair was untamed, an ashen blond with streaks of gray, and only a delicate whisper now of its former red. Of the five of them, she had updated her style the least, and she looked much like the lone female member of a once-popular folk trio—all she was missing was a tambourine.

"There's nothing wrong with my eyes. It's the light," Craig groused.

"It's not the light," Naomi insisted.

Jordy chuckled. "Unlike the cats."

"There's nothing *wrong* with their eyes," Marielle admonished, fussing over the laundry basket at her feet she'd requisitioned to make the kittens a nest. "It's just they don't have any."

Jordan looked up at Craig. "Toss me your phone."

"I only have one bar." The cell reception at the house was almost non-existent.

"I didn't ask you how many bars you had, I said toss me your damn phone!"

Marielle, in a sincere yet comical overreaction, jumped in front of the kittens to act as a human shield and everyone laughed.

Naomi Ito, Craig Scheffler, Marielle Holland, Jordy Tosic, Jordan Vargas. They were nineteen the night they met; it seemed like just moments ago. They, along with Alec Swigert, were transfer students to Berkeley who shared a dormitory floor, graduating with the Class of 1995 (except for Alec, who didn't live long enough to collect his degree).

Jordan tapped the back of his husband's hand and pointed to his own phone on the charger, thinking he had a better chance of placing a takeout order online, even with one bar of service, than Craig ever did of deciphering a printed menu. Jordy reached for the phone and Jordan could still see in his six-foot-four frame the young athlete he fell for in school. They jumped at the sound of three rapid raps, Naomi banging the remote on an end table; the table lamp's shade went askew. Naomi looked up to everyone's scorn. "What! Craig's eyes are weak, not his heart."

"We have dog with a weak heart at the rescue, stage five murmur, a Basset," Marielle offered as she sat in the recliner, placing the kittens on her lap. She tucked her legs underneath her so that they disappeared entirely under her dress. "He made friends with a deaf Malinois. They're so cute, the two of them, so we're trying to place them together." Several years back Marielle had left her life in D.C. to open an animal rescue in Boring, Oregon. ("That's not a commentary on Oregon," she had repeated several times as if obligated to do so by the Beaver State's Chamber of Commerce. "That's literally the name of the town.")

Craig peered up from the menu, raising his phone in the process and blinding Jordy with his flashlight. "Do you guys even *want* Thai? We could also just order pizza."

Naomi finally had the remote open. "These batteries are corroded. I think my mother kept replacements upstairs." She had maintained the Big Sur house as a shrine to her parents years after they died.

"What about sushi?" Jordy suggested, still rubbing the light from his eyes.

"Surprise, surprise. The Jordans want sushi."

"I'm Switzerland," Jordan insisted.

"I stand corrected. Tosic wants sushi, Vargas wants . . . fondue."

"No sushi. I'm vegetarian," Marielle reminded them.

In unison, they shouted, *"WE KNOW."*

Naomi headed for the stairs and Marielle followed as if she'd been dying to get her alone.

As much as they had all aged, the house in Big Sur seemed revived, its retro style that felt so dated twenty-eight years ago when they assembled here the night Alec was buried was once again in architectural vogue. The house sat high above the water, built over a cliff between a grove of trees and craggy rocks overlooking the ocean. It was all wood paneling and glass to make the most of the breathtaking views, the whole place a paean to the American midcentury and its minimalist aesthetic. While much of the house was a single story on stilts that jutted out over the water, there was a small second story built over the back end of the house by the driveway. There were clean lines throughout; in fact the stairwell to the small upper bedrooms didn't even have a banister. In an unfortunate pun, the house was named Sur la Vie.

When the guys were alone Craig pointed to Jordy's tee. "You haven't bought a new shirt in thirty years?"

Jordy glanced down to see *BERKELEY* written in blue. "Jordan got me this for my fiftieth when I started swimming again." Jordy's doctor had told him running was taking a toll on his knees, and his Chelsea Piers health club had a pool. "I set a goal of doing the 20 Bridges Swim around Manhattan."

Craig recoiled. "You would swim in the East River?"

"It's actually the cleanest it's been in years."

"Mount Saint Helens is the most dormant it's been in years. I wouldn't lower myself in the crater."

Jordan studied a painting that hung just shy of level on the living room wall. He remembered the seascape from their first visit to Big Sur after Alec died; he hated it then, it was a shade too bright and too cheery for both their mood and the sea, but he had a certain fondness for it now that he saw the world as a darker place and welcomed a smattering of light. "You know, I think this is an actual Rembrandt."

"Funny," Craig said, obviously not amused.

"No, I'm serious, Nana. Maybe you can confirm." Nana was a nickname Craig earned in college by wearing nightshirts and falling asleep before nine.

A commotion drew their eyes up to the landing; Marielle and Naomi reappeared at the top of the stairs.

"It's true!" Marielle said, in the midst of a tense conversation. "For the last year or so at least I've been feeling like my own worst enemy." She turned to look at Naomi, expecting perhaps the sympathetic nod of female companionship.

"Is that so." Naomi clutched a package of likely expired AAAs.

Marielle nodded.

"Because I'm literally going to push you down these stairs if you don't move any faster." With her glasses and the gray in her hair, Naomi looked not unlike her late mother, and she had an inscrutable demeanor to match.

"OH MY GOD!" Marielle shrieked, grabbing Naomi's hand. "Is that a *ring*?" She studied the double gold band with an oval green stone.

Naomi snatched her hand back and headed down the stairs, Marielle in hot pursuit. "Let's not make a big deal of it."

"Does this mean you and . . . ?"

"I said, let's not make a big deal!"

"But it's jade." Where romance was concerned, Marielle was one for tradition.

"It's an inside joke." Naomi wanted off the subject as quickly as possible.

"I don't get it."

"That's because you're not on the inside." She knew her friends. There was no weaseling out of an explanation with such intense focus on her. "Jade is supposed to cure . . . I don't know, kidney ailments or something. Gary says I'm a pain in his side, but he wants to marry me anyway."

"Romantic," Jordy offered.

Naomi wasn't about to take relationship advice from the Jordans, who never had to endure modern dating. To her it was the perfect proposal.

Marielle's face lit up. "We have to celebrate!"

Jordy interjected, "We are celebrating. We're celebrating Jordan."

Naomi buried her face in her hands. "You know, I was with Fleetwood Mac when you called."

"*The* Fleetwood Mac?" Marielle asked.

"No, Fleetwood Mac and Cheese, a lounge act in Reno. Yes, *the* Fleetwood Mac." Naomi, an executive for the band's music label, had been sent out to check on their tour.

Craig emerged from the kitchen. "So, Jordan. Are you going to tell us why you assembled us here?"

Jordan pretended to be immersed in his phone as Naomi slipped the new batteries into the remote. "Don't you think we're getting a little old for the pact?"

Marielle chastised Naomi. "You only say that because you had *your* funeral already."

"As did you, if I recall," Naomi said. "As have we all."

"Actually, I haven't," Jordy said, and all eyes turned toward him. *"I haven't!"* he stressed.

"Oh, sweet Jordy." Naomi dropped her head to feign sorrow. "Always a pallbearer, never a corpse."

Craig gathered the stack of menus. "I'm taking these outdoors where I can read them under the floodlights you use to scare the raccoons. No one follow me."

"No one is," Jordan clarified, but Craig was already gone.

"Should we tell him the floodlights are there to scare away mountain lions and not raccoons?" The batteries now secure, Naomi turned the television on to a rerun of *The People Upstairs*, keeping the volume on mute. The warm glow of the TV helped everything feel so familiar.

"I used to love this show," Jordy said.

Craig burst back inside.

Jordan looked up. "Mountain lion?"

Craig recoiled. *Mountain lion?* "No. There's a putrid smell out there."

"Those are trees. It's called nature," Naomi clarified.

Craig, who still lived on the Lower East Side of Manhattan near the gallery where he once worked, replied, "That's not it. It smells like *mulch*."

"WHAT DO YOU THINK MULCH IS?" Naomi made exasperated gestures with both of her arms to emphasize all the bark and wood that surrounded them.

Marielle checked on the kittens, then flopped on the couch, kicking one leg over the armrest. She turned to the Jordans. "You two should adopt my dogs. The Basset and the Malinois."

Jordy shot his husband a panicked look. They had just arrived at the cabin, hadn't even ordered food. Were they going to get into their news before a second bottle of wine? "It's not a good time."

"It's never a *good* time. That's just an excuse. You just do it because there are so many in need." To Marielle it was like having children. If she had waited for the right time, she never would have had Mia, and she loved her daughter (despite her complicated feelings for Mia's father).

Jordy scrambled for an excuse. "We live in the city. In an apartment. There's no room for a large dog."

"Oooooh," Marielle cooed, not ceding an inch. "I know four bonded maltipoos." She said it in a boastful way, the way one might announce they knew Michelle Obama.

"FOUR!" Craig exclaimed.

"I'm not talking to you! I'm talking to the Jordans."

"Look at their faces! Tosic is apoplectic!"

Marielle sat up, put her hands on her hips, and said, "Aren't you supposed to be in prison?"

Craig frowned. He had been granted early release but wasn't quite ready for jokes.

If Jordan squinted he could still see them as they were when they were twenty-two, the night they first came to Sur la Vie. They listened to music that night, Sarah McLachlan and Sophie B. Hawkins and Shawn Colvin, and the Carpenters for some reason too; he vividly remembered that, as Naomi had made such a fuss. They stood around with a sort of stunned bemusement, the finality of Alec's death yet to sink in. Alec would burst through the door at any moment—they were *convinced* of it—high on his signature trail mix, a blend of ecstasy, ketamine, and god knows what else (none of them were privy to his recipe—he was like Colonel Sanders that way) and make a grandiose proclamation like no two people have ever met, or that they only existed inside him. The invincibility of youth had been pierced that night, but the air had yet to fully escape. Before that, like most young people, they had all thought they would live forever.

"Someone put on music," Naomi instructed. "It's like a wake in here."

Jordan said very plainly, "Ha."

"I will!" Marielle volunteered.

"Someone other than Marielle."

Marielle protested, but they all knew exactly why Naomi objected. Marielle liked the highlights, the songs they played on the radio. Naomi detested singles, had spent a life at war with popular music, professing only to like deeper cuts. It was that way now that she worked in the industry, and it was that way in college when they were randomly assigned as roommates, as far back as history took them. Naomi arrived with a milk crate of albums, Marielle with a shoebox of cassingles.

When Naomi looked away, Jordan slipped his phone to Marielle and encouraged her to choose. She beamed. Seconds later piano chords unspooled through the speaker; Marielle reached for Jordan's hand and together they started to dance as Karen Carpenter's rich voice, thick as cabernet, filled the room.

When I was young, I'd listen to the radio . . .

He'd teed Marielle up and she'd knocked it out of the park.

"NO! VETO!" Naomi came running to grab Jordan's phone.

"OVERRIDE!" Jordan laughed.

Naomi exhaled her displeasure. "It's your funeral," she mumbled, giving up. It had been twenty-eight years, more than half their lives, since they made their pact and that joke was never not a source of amusement.

Jordan hooked his arms around Marielle's waist as if they were at a seventh-grade dance, and she placed hers on his shoulders, leaving just enough room between them not to alarm adult chaperones. She rubbed her hands over his sweater and a look of concern crept across her face.

So thin, her eyes said.

Don't worry about it, his said back.

"What about the place we went for Alec?" Jordy asked, still focused on dinner.

"Nepenthe?" It was a Big Sur institution, but Naomi hadn't been able to go back since.

"Right. It was Greek, or Middle Eastern."

"Mediterranean."

Jordan and Marielle held each other tight as they swayed to and sang along with every sha-la-la-la, every whoa-o-o-oh.

"Do they do takeout?"

Naomi grabbed her hair in fists. "I CAN'T THINK WITH THIS GODDAMN MUSIC!"

Marielle whispered to Jordan. "She called it *music*."

Jordan whispered back. "That's an improvement!"

"Craig, call them and see. They had fish, I think. And shawarma. Chickpea salad for Marielle. Just order whatever. Order everything. Baba ghanoush."

"Gesundheit," Craig said.

Jordy smirked as he reached for his wallet. "Dinner tonight is on me."

Marielle whispered, "You need to eat."

Jordan had hoped the sweater he'd chosen, in part because he was always cold thanks to both the treatment he was undergoing and his significant weight loss, but also because it was bulky, disguised just how much he was no longer himself. "I will."

It was indeed his funeral they had congregated to celebrate. Just as they had in years past gathered to celebrate Marielle's, then Naomi's, then Craig's in their individual hours of crisis and need, the result of the decades-old pact they had made in their grief over Alec to throw their funerals while they were still living so that none of them could ever question exactly what they meant to the others. *Leave nothing left unsaid* had been Marielle's motto when the idea was first hatched. If nothing else, it would be clear that they were loved. But this funeral was unlike any of their prior affairs. They were not here for Marielle in the wake of her divorce, or Naomi after her parents' private plane went down, or Craig when he pleaded guilty to art fraud. This was not their little game as usual, "funeral" as *pick-me-up*, designed to give them a chance at a new life when they felt most at wit's end with their old. This funeral was a real goodbye. Only none of them knew that yet. Not Craig as he phoned in an order for hummus plates, not Naomi as she tried to pair her own phone with the speakers to rid her ears of seventies AM gold, not Marielle as she danced to Karen Carpenter with a partner who was likewise dangerously thin.

Because Jordan had yet to tell his friends that the cancer that started several years back in his prostate had returned with a vengeance and was now in his lungs, liver, and bones. Instead of saying that out loud just yet, Jordan Vargas imagined himself an astronaut readying for another mission, this time with no discernible end; it was easier than telling the best friends he'd ever had that he was dying.

THE JORDANS

The waiting room inside Memorial Sloan Kettering on York and 68th was blindingly white; whoever had chosen this paint color had grossly misfired. There were hundreds of shades to choose from, Jordan thought—Polar Bear, Whisper, Frost, Pure, Swiss, Dove, Cloud, Icicle, Mist, Paper, Lace—and this was what the decorator went with? Something that reflects life's stark impermanency back in your face in the gravest moment of one's existence? Jordy reached over and gripped Jordan's thigh tightly with his right hand while flipping through his phone with the left, as if there were a person he could call to fix this if he could just think of exactly whom. The appointment had gone as Jordan feared, not as they both had hoped. But Jordan knew. It wasn't any one symptom, although he had several (including a mass he could feel in his abdomen on the right side, something tangled in his lymph nodes), but rather a deep foreboding in the way you just know when something is not at all right. His entire body felt like he'd slept on it wrong for a month and there wasn't enough caffeine in Starbucks' largest bucket-sized iced coffee to shake his recent malaise.

"What did they tell you when you finished your treatment last time, five years?" Jordy asked.

"Five years," Jordan confirmed. That was what his doctors had said after his first diagnosis and successful course of chemo. Make it five years without a recurrence and he'd go from in remission to cancer free.

"And how long has it been?"

Jordan shifted in his seat; the backs of his legs were sweating. "Four years, ten months, and three days."

"Then this has to be some sort of cruel mistake."

Two months. Sixty days. Fourteen hundred hours. The finish line so tantalizingly close he could almost graze it with his fingertips. Alas, it wasn't a cruel mistake so much as just cruel.

Jordy gave up on his phone. They were well connected, but they knew no one with the authority or expertise to fix this. "So we reset the clock. We did it once and we'll do it again."

We. Jordan bristled. Also, it wasn't like he'd fallen off the wagon and had to restart sobriety. Hand in a coin and work to earn it back. If anything there was a very different stopwatch that had just started, ticking off the time that he had left, and they were wasting precious minutes sitting in this glaring white.

Jordy tried a different tack. "What about dinner tonight at the Carlyle?"

Jordan turned to his husband, who was almost as white as the walls, with an expression just as blank. "To celebrate?"

"No. To . . ." Jordy didn't know how to finish that sentence, at least not out loud. He was already making a mental list of favorite things he wanted to do with Jordan again before his husband was too sick to do them. "To take our mind off this."

It would have been almost sweet that Jordy thought a good martini and lobster bisque could make one forget a death sentence if it weren't also so misguided. Jordan closed his eyes to imagine permanent darkness, but there was too much light from the windows and ambient noise to lose himself in the idea of nothingness. "Why do you think Alec occupies such a large space in our lives?"

Jordy looked surprised. "What does Alec have to do with anything?"

Isn't it obvious? Jordan thought.

"Are you invoking the pact?"

"I'm not invoking anything. I'm asking you a question."

Jordy gazed out the window at the East River and Roosevelt Island as he gave that real thought. The afternoon clouds formed a low ceiling on the concrete city that made him want to shrink into his chair. After a spell he said, "He's the embodiment of our younger selves."

Jordan clasped his hands tightly, grateful not to have had his question evaded. And Jordy's answer made a certain sense to him. Alec was the version of themselves that was forever young. In dying, he had somehow become immortal.

Jordy held up his own arm and pinched some skin at the elbow. "I mean, what is this?" he asked as the skin all but refused to snap back. He meant it to demonstrate that they were no longer young themselves, but all his gesture did was draw attention to his enviable arms; they were as muscular as they had ever been.

Jordan pushed his arm away. "That doesn't mean you're old. It means you're dehydrated." And indeed there had been a fair amount of tears in the doctor's office.

In the distance a bell rang, the same bell Jordan rang five years—no, sorry, four years and ten months—ago that marked the end of his chemotherapy. Someone else had just successfully finished their treatment. "They should have a gong for people like me." *Gallows humor,* he thought, but he did have the urge to strike something.

"You'll ring the bell again," Jordy said, but it wasn't what Jordan wanted to hear. They were going to have to accept his fate, and fast if they wanted to make the most of the time he had left.

"Lobster bisque, huh?" Jordan's mind drifted to the supposed healing power of soup. Maybe going out made some sense. They had come directly from the office for this appointment, which meant they were already dressed for dinner, and going home seemed too sad.

"I was thinking the octopus carpaccio," Jordy said, as if the real decision were in what to order. "Can you stand?"

Jordan's legs were Jell-O. "Not yet." They sat there perfectly still studying others in the waiting room who looked equally grim. "I don't believe in an afterlife."

"Neither do I," Jordy said, but in the moment he was open to changing his beliefs.

"And yet I keep picturing Alec and me together, wandering around in some sort of heaven."

"Would that be heaven?" Jordy asked; Alec one-on-one could be *a lot*.

"Alec is twenty-two and I'm *fifty*, and people keep asking if I'm his dad."

"So you're in hell, then."

Jordan came close to smiling, but he wasn't fully able. "Yeah."

"You'll be older than fifty," Jordy said optimistically; he massaged the back of Jordan's neck how he liked. "Much older."

Jordan crossed his fingers on both hands. "C'mon fifty-one." It had never been more clear to him that aging was a gift. But no matter how much more time he had, Alec would still be twenty-two. "I don't want to go," he whispered, his voice cracking on *go*.

"To the Carlyle, you mean?"

That wasn't what he meant, but if he had to make himself understood he might start crying again and not stop. Instead he said, "Do you think I should?"

"Should what?" Jordy asked as he continued the neck massage.

Jordan fished for his phone and scrolled back until he found the group text chain with Naomi and Marielle and Craig. It had been named *NANA'S HUNGRY LITTLE PIE EATERS*. He held it up for Jordy to see.

"The pact," Jordy said, now understanding.

Jordan pointed to *PIE EATERS*. He couldn't in this moment remember the joke.

"Remember? Craig brought that pie."

Jordan didn't.

"To Marielle's."

It rang a faint bell.

Bell.

"I thought you believed in the pact even less than an afterlife."

Jordan stared at his phone. Not believing in something and not needing something were two different things. He didn't know how to explain it yet, and frankly maybe he never would, but everything from here until the end would be different. All bets were off. That was just the way it was. "Do you remember how it started?"

"The pact?"

And this time Jordan couldn't help himself, because he always smiled when his husband said *I do.*

Photograph of the author © Bryon Lane

STEVEN ROWLEY is the bestselling author of four novels, including *Lily and the Octopus*, a *Washington Post* Notable Book of 2016; *The Editor*, an NPR Best Book of 2019; *The Guncle*, a finalist for the Thurber Prize for American Humor and Goodreads Choice Awards finalist for Novel of the Year; and *The Celebrants*. His fiction has been translated into twenty languages. He resides in Palm Springs, California.

VISIT STEVEN ROWLEY ONLINE

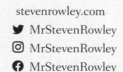

stevenrowley.com
MrStevenRowley
MrStevenRowley
MrStevenRowley